"The Inside Story"

• A little-known British scientist, working in total secrecy, stumbled on a brilliant armor design that provides almost complete protection against antitank weapons. An American general incorporated the new armor into the M-1 at the eleventh hour.

• Fierce competition erupted between international armed forces and manufacturers...resulting in costly delays, compromises, and cheating during test trials.

• The M-1's revolutionary turbine engine has made the tank so fast and quiet it's earned the nickname "Whispering Death."

• Bidding between Chrysler and GM resulted in a series of reforms in the Pentagon procurement process.

• As a result of the M-1's dramatic combat capacities, the U.S. Army has developed a brand-new aggressive battle plan for fighting future wars.

KING OF THE KILLING ZONE

ORR KELLY

BERKLEY BOOKS, NEW YORK

This Berkley book contains the complete
text of the original hardcover edition.

KING OF THE KILLING ZONE

A Berkley Book / published by arrangement with
W. W. Norton & Company, Inc.

PRINTING HISTORY
W. W. Norton & Company edition published 1989
Published simultaneously in Canada by Penguin Books Canada Ltd.
Berkley edition / October 1990

ISBN: 0-425-12304-9

A BERKLEY BOOK ® TM 757,375
Berkley Books are published by The Berkley Publishing Group,
200 Madison Avenue, New York, New York 10016.
The name "BERKLEY" and the "B" logo
are trademarks belonging to Berkley Publishing Corporation.

PRINTED IN THE UNITED STATES OF AMERICA

10 9 8 7 6 5 4 3 2 1

For Mary, Charles, and Barbara,
who make everything worthwhile

Contents

Introduction

King of the Killing Zone is the product of a reporter's curiosity.

During most of the years between 1967 and 1986 I was the Pentagon correspondent for the *Washington Star* and, later, for *U.S. News & World Report* magazine. It was a turbulent two decades, with the war in Vietnam, the growth of the Soviet nuclear arsenal, the decline of the American military during the 1970s, and then the largest peacetime buildup in U.S. history, beginning in the Carter years and intensified even more during the Reagan presidency. Through all this period, even when money was relatively short, the great weapons programs went ponderously along: fighters and bombers for the Air Force; planes and ships for the Navy; and guns, helicopters, and tanks for the Army.

Like all Pentagon reporters, I covered these weapons programs with more or less intensity. Typically we focused our attention on a particular weapon when something "newsworthy" happened—a budget decision, the rollout of the first model, or a lively congressional hearing—or when something went wrong—a crash, a critical report from the General Accounting Office, or a budget overrun. But from the beginning of the development of a weapon to the time it is deployed is, at best, many years—longer than the tenure of defense secretaries, members of the Joint Chiefs, program managers, and most Pentagon reporters. Few, if any, of us saw one of these big programs whole and reported on it consistently and in detail.

I wondered what it is really like behind the scenes as one of these huge weapons programs moves slowly from drawing board to potential battlefield. How much do we reporters and, through us, the American public really know what is going on, beyond our facile reports on overpriced toilet seats and hundred-dollar hammers?

The sale of *U.S. News & World Report* by its owner-employees, of which I was one, in the mid-eighties presented me with the opportunity to retire earlier than I normally would have and to embark on a new career as a book writer. It also gave me the opportunity to look behind the scenes, to see one important part of the Pentagon from the inside.

Mike Hamilburg, who became my agent, was the one who first suggested a book on the Army's long effort to equip itself with a new tank, and it proved to be a fascinating and challenging task.

Much of my research was done at the Pentagon. Mabel Thomas helped me get the most from the Pentagon Library's impressive resources. I also spent many hours in the offices of the *Current News*, whose staff clip articles from a wide range of publications and distribute them throughout the Pentagon in several editions each day. Harry Zubkoff, the longtime head of the office, who has since retired, and his staff were especially helpful.

My friends in the *U.S. News & World Report* library, especially Kathleen L. Trimble, Rose Marie Atkinson, and Kate V. Forsyth, were a frequent source of friendly assistance.

I also relied heavily on Army public affairs officers, both here and abroad. Special thanks go to Lieutenant Colonel Craig C. MacNab and Major Phil Soucy at the Pentagon, Patricia Kukoski at Fort Knox, Kentucky, Arthur E. Volpe of the Tank-Automotive Command headquarters in Warren, Michigan, Don McClow of the Army Materiel Command, Major George C. Creech, press officer for the Third Corps at Fort Hood, Texas, and Colonel Charles W. ("Bill") McLain, Jr., at headquarters, U.S. Army Europe, in Heidelberg.

For help in obtaining pictures, I owe special thanks to Laurie Viggiano of the public affairs office and the staffs of *Armor* magazine and the Patton Museum, all at Fort Knox, and to John Yaquiant, Ann Silirie, and Athena Petry of the Test and Evaluation Command public affairs office and Tim Tidwell of the Ordnance Museum at Aberdeen Proving Ground.

Both the editors with whom I worked at W. W. Norton—first Starling Lawrence and, for much of the book, Hilary Hinzmann—helped immeasurably in bringing my research together into a book.

To the extent to which I have succeeded in making a highly technical subject understandable to the nontechnical reader, I have Hinzmann to thank. He suggested the chapter on the history of armored warfare and its predecessors, and he also suggested the organizational plan, bringing each of the technical subjects—armor, engine, and main gun—together in separate sections. He also forced me, at many points, to make my explanations of these technical matters as simple, direct, and nontechnical as possible.

I owe special thanks to Brigadier General Philip Bolté (U.S. Army Ret.), who read a late draft of the manuscript for technical accuracy and saved me from several embarrassing mistakes.

Many of the others who were helpful to me are mentioned in A Note on Sources at the end of the book.

While at work on this book, I happened to read a book on the media's coverage of politics by a former colleague, David Broder, the *Washington Post* political writer. In his *Behind the Front Page*, published by Simon and Schuster in 1987, he says: "What journalism can produce for a society always falls short of the society's needs, and even further short of historical or philosophical truth. The way we cover the news is to dig for facts, in hopes that they will yield an approximation of truth. They rarely do."

In *King of the Killing Zone*, with time to dig more deeply than the daily or weekly journalist ever can, I hope I have come close to the truth about the Army's long struggle to design and build a new tank and put it in the hands of the troops. And although each development program is different in many ways, I hope to have provided some insight into how the system works.

1

In the Footsteps of the Dinosaur

"THE DEATH OF THE TANK." Army tankers spluttered in indignation when they read the title of the lead article in the January–February 1972 issue of *Armor*. Their own magazine! And not even a question mark after the title!

With the prominent display given to such heresy, even the United States Armor Association, publisher of the magazine, seemed to be siding with the aviators and high-ranking Pentagon civilians who were ready to write off the tank as obsolete.

Lieutenant Colonel Warren W. Lennon, an Australian who had served as an exchange officer with the American Twenty-fifth Division in Vietnam, pulled no punches in his article. Reflecting the thinking of many who had fought in the jungles of Vietnam's highlands and the tangled waterways of its delta, he dismissed the tank, calling it "as anachronistic as medieval body armor." He went on: "Though it has many obvious advantages, it has evolved to the stage of imminent extinction because it has become increasingly inefficient in an age which demands more of machines than ever before."

The article appeared within days after congressional action killing the only American main battle tank then under development. Even the most dedicated tankers had good reason to fear that as far as the American Army was concerned, the tank really might be following the dinosaur into extinction, not that they agreed for a moment that the tank had outlived its usefulness, especially on the European battlefield.

Certainly the Russians didn't agree. Marshal Ivan I. Yakubovsky, then commander in chief of Warsaw Pact forces, spelled out his army's unwavering commitment to tanks in an article in *Red Star*, the Soviet Army newspaper, in 1967: "The striking power of the ground forces is primarily insured by the vast extent to which they are saturated with tanks." To back up the doctrine, the giant factories built during World War II continued to turn out tanks by the thousands.

In 1972 the Warsaw Pact's tanks already outnumbered those of the North Atlantic Treaty Organization (NATO) by more than two to one: 19,000 in the East, 8,000 in the West. The American Seventh Army in Germany had six and one-third divisions—two armored divisions, two mechanized infantry divisions, two armored cavalry regiments, and one mechanized infantry brigade—a total of 190,000 men and fewer than 3,000 tanks. Soviet divisions are somewhat smaller, but there were thirty-one along the East-West border, including ten tank divisions in East Germany and two tank divisions each in Poland, Hungary, and Czechoslovakia. In the Soviet Union west of the Urals were another sixty divisions.

Though many of the Soviet tanks were older models, there was a constant attempt to improve those coming off the production lines. One American officer, who had the same model tank each time his career took him to the East German or Czech border during the sixties and seventies, calculated unhappily that the Red Army fielded a new tank every time he was promoted.

To make the situation even worse, the American Army in Europe was a hollow shell, bled by a constant turnover of manpower, plagued by racial enmity and drug use. With money drained off to buy bullets and bombs for Vietnam, the Army's equipment was old and deteriorating. Its slim chance of beating back an attack—short of a quick use of nuclear weapons—depended on weeks of warning, time to prepare to fight.

No wonder soldiers assigned along the border lived in constant fear of a bolt-from-the-blue attack that would deny them time to prepare a defense. Among themselves they agreed that their resistance would be futile and brief.

Of the five or six invasion routes that the Soviets might choose for an attack on Western Europe, one—the Fulda Gap—is the most critical. To the west lies the heavily forested mass of the Vogelsberg. To the north is the rugged Knüllgebirge. To the south is the equally formidable Hohe Rhon. But the "gap" itself is a broad, eminently "tankable" north–south bowl that leads into a succession of valleys aimed west toward the European heart of American military power, clustered about Frankfurt, only sixty-two miles from the border with East Germany, one day's hard fighting by the Red Army's ambitious standards.

At least once a century for four hundred years or more, armies have traveled this natural invasion route. Belgian cavalry, heading east to fight the Turks and Hungarians, came through in 1595. Two years later there was the arrival of Spanish troops engaged in the Franco-Dutch War. King Gustavus Adolphus of Sweden fled through the pass in 1628, pursued by imperial Catholic troops. Prussian Black Hussars occupied the area in 1759 until they were driven out by Württemberg soldiers backed by French cavalry. Napoleon marched east on the way to his debacle in the snows of Russia in 1812. Most recently General George S. Patton, Jr., led his Third Army through the gap in 1945 in pursuit of Hitler's shattered Wehrmacht.

The nightmare that made the Americans' sleep uneasy and troubled their minds during the day centered on an attack through the Fulda Gap.

The first warning is the rumble of diesel engines and the clatter of tracks. As the predawn mist lifts, Soviet tanks by the hundreds and then the thousands emerge, each with its distinctive rounded turret looking like nothing so much as an inverted frying pan, with a cannon in place of the handle. Overhead, waves of bombers and fighter-bombers roar westward, hugging the ground to avoid radar coverage.

The Americans on guard at Observation Post Alpha, halfway between the former twin villages of Rasdorf, in West Germany, and Geisa, in East Germany, barely have time to sound a shrill alarm before their tower is blown away by a high-explosive shell. The first crew to move its M-60 tank toward the enemy is hit by a heavy projectile fired at a speed of a mile a second from a big Soviet tank gun. The shell cracks through the four and a half inches of the American's frontal armor, decapitates the loader, fills the turret with fragments of metal, and passes out through the rear. As the tank commander and gunner scramble to escape from their damaged tank, ruptured tubes spray them with burning "cherry juice," the red oil used in the hydraulic system. Only the driver, riding deep in the hull of the tank, escapes serious injury.

A second M-60 pops up into view, catches an approaching tank in its sights, and fires its 105 mm gun, but the hit is a glancing blow. The shell bounces off the superbly shaped turret of the advancing Russian. The tank shudders, hesitates, and then resumes its course, swinging its gun around for the kill.

Quickly the American tanks and armored vehicles, all obviously pinpointed for attack before the battle began, are picked off—some by rockets, others by the heavy shells from the big Russian tank guns.

Other American crews, riding in unarmored jeeps, form a hasty defense and begin firing their TOW missiles. The TOW (the acronym for "tube-launched, optically tracked, wire-guided") is new to the battlefield, having just been tested in action by the United States for the first time at Kontum in South Vietnam. Ironically, the target destroyed in that first wartime firing was a captured Korean War–era American Bulldog tank. With the TOW, the operator fires the antitank rocket and then sends guidance messages through a wire that trails out behind the projectile, tracking the target as it tries to dodge out of the way. He must remain exposed to enemy fire for about sixteen seconds, until the missile reaches the target. Most of the crews have never fired their new weapon in practice because of the expense. A few of them have never even seen one fired.

Still, some of the TOWs find their targets. First one of the attacking tanks and then another burst into flames. In their tiny, claustrophobic turrets, the little Russians (only men between five feet and five feet four inches tall are assigned as tankers) are surrounded by ammunition and fuel. When a Russian tank is hit, there is fire, explosion, and death. But the Americans face what is euphemistically known as a target-rich environment. There are far more tanks than there are missiles to destroy them. Many of the Americans are killed by machine-gun bullets. Others fight on until they are squashed by the enemy tanks.

The nightmare ends with the Soviets beyond the Rhine, in firm control of the heartland of Europe. The factories and laboratories of West Germany, the Netherlands, and Denmark are theirs, barely damaged in the brief war.

If such a superblitzkrieg seemed farfetched, the worried soldiers had only to look back four years. In 1968 Soviet and Warsaw Pact forces were engaged in their annual fall maneuvers. Then, during the night of August 19–20, they imposed radio silence to deceive Western intelligence and crossed the Czech border. By the time the NATO allies realized what had happened, the Soviet tanks were in Prague.

The Americans on the border would have been even more worried if they had known as much about the Soviet tank force as is now known. They would easily have recognized the old T-54 and T-55 series tanks with their 100 mm gun and the newer T-62. When the T-62 first made its appearance in the early 1960s, it caused a stir in the West. Most of its features were familiar. But it had a new 115 mm smoothbore gun, different from and more powerful than anything in the West, a frightening hint of things to come.

By 1972 there was another and much more worrisome weapon in the Soviet arsenal: the T-64. Developed during the early 1960s, it went into serial production later in that decade, but Western intelligence didn't know that until much later. It would have come as almost a total surprise, truly a secret weapon. This is a tank worth a careful look.

For the first time a Soviet design bureau had broken sharply with conservative tradition, in which each new tank had shown only small evolutionary changes from its predecessor. This tradition had been followed religiously and usually with success for decades. Two years after the first Five-Year Plan began in 1928, the Soviets acquired the chassis of two experimental tanks built by an American, J. Walter Christie. He sold the machines to Amtorg, the Soviet trading company, only after being rebuffed by the U.S. Army and coming close to bankruptcy. The Soviets adopted the unique Christie suspension for a mass-produced cross-country armored car and continued to use it for their World War II T-34 and as late as the T-62 in the 1960s.

Similarly, a rugged diesel engine of about five hundred horsepower was developed at the Kharkov engine plant in the 1930s and was still powering Soviet tanks half a century later. Like most other tank-producing nations, the Soviets had settled during the 1950s on the four-man crew: tank commander, loader, gunner, and driver.

When the designers were finished with the T-64, much of this had been left by the wayside. Many of the changes are of interest primarily to other tank designers and tank junkies: a new torsion bar system to replace the familiar Christie suspension; a flat five-cylinder engine with horizontally opposed pistons in place of the old V-12 Kharkov engine.

But it doesn't take a tank expert to appreciate one change. Anyone who has driven an old truck that had to be double-clutched can understand the importance of the hydraulic synchromesh transmission in the T-64. In the older tanks, Soviet drivers not only had to double-clutch but often used a small sledgehammer to coax the shift lever from one gear to another.

Despite all the improvements, the T-64 was no supertank. Like every tank, each component involved at least some compromise. Soviet designers have always been willing to accept the penalties that come with relatively small size and a low silhouette—attributes that make more sense in the flat, open steppes of the Ukraine than they do in the forested hills of Germany.

As it approaches across the battlefield, the T-64 is a small target. It weighs about 42 tons—some 20 tons less than the latest American tanks—and hugs the ground, with a height just under eight feet and ground clearance of only a foot and a half. With its gun facing forward, its overall length is 30 feet, but the track actually touching the ground covers only a little more than 13 feet. Its top cross-country speed is rated at 31 miles an hour, and it has a range of about 280 miles provided by a fuel load of 260 gallons, roughly a mile to a gallon. Like many other military vehicles, it can burn a variety of fuels, from gasoline to kerosene and diesel oil. To protect the crew from nuclear radiation and chemical and biological weapons, air entering the crew compartment is filtered. Then the air pressure inside the turret is kept slightly higher than the outside pressure to prevent unfiltered air from leaking in.

Alongside the main gun is a 7.62 mm machine gun with 3,000 rounds, and mounted at the tank commander's station is a 12.7 mm antiaircraft gun with 500 rounds of ammunition. The designers of the T-64 found room for only 40 rounds of ammunition for the main gun and little space for the crew members. The inside of the tank is cramped, inefficient, and dangerous. Soviet crews are likely to arrive on the battlefield tired, uncomfortable, and at least a little sluggish in their reactions.

Because the turret is so small, the gun is limited in elevation, a defect shared with other Soviet tanks. The cannon can be depressed only five degrees, so the crew must expose itself to the view of the enemy to get into firing position. Since the muzzle can be raised only eighteen degrees, the crew is helpless if the enemy is shooting down from above.

This limitation is not just of academic interest, as was brutally demonstrated on October 13–14, 1973. On that weekend Egyptian tankers in Soviet T-54/55 and T-62 tanks assaulted Israeli forces holding the Sinai passes with American and British tanks. As the Israelis picked off their targets from above, the Egyptians milled helplessly in the killing zone, unable to elevate their guns enough to shoot back.

Even though the T-64 had a new engine, it still seemed to Western experts to be underpowered. And the T-64, like its predecessors, will almost certainly burn if hit. Part of the fuel is stored inside the tank, surrounding both the crew and the ammunition. The rest is carried in external tanks, vulnerable to small-arms fire.

All the deficiencies of the T-64 seemed almost insignificant when Western tank experts turned their attention to the big improvements in the business end—the gun and fire control system. For the first time in a production tank the T-64 carried an automatic loader. This meant the crew could be cut from four men to three. Rumors spread in the West that the autoloader tended to load shoulders and arms as well as ammunition, but those problems apparently occurred only in the early prototypes.

By eliminating the loader, the T-64 was able to carry a bigger gun than the T-62 while remaining at about the same 42-ton weight and less than 8 feet high—actually a few inches lower than the T-62. The first T-64s carried the 115 mm gun, but it was quickly upgraded to 125 mm, bigger than the NATO standard 105 mm cannon and even bigger than the 120 mm gun on the British Chieftain. With a muzzle velocity of 5,330 feet per second, the new gun was powerful enough to blast through the frontal armor of any Western tank. Accuracy was improved by a new range finder to measure the distance to the target and by a stabilization system that permitted the gunner to aim on the move.

At the time this new tank was being issued to the Red Army, the U.S. Army had not had a truly new tank since World War II. The M-60, which came on the scene in 1959, had been hastily cobbled together from parts of two earlier tanks. With a cupola for the tank commander, it had a higher silhouette than any other tank. Even before it entered service, the Army's research chief complained the new tank "doesn't suit me." But with some improvements added along the way, it was to remain the Army's main battle tank into the 1980s.

The military is often accused of exaggerating the quality of Soviet equipment, especially at budget time. But there is a powerful force in the other direction as well. If a potential enemy has better equipment, officers hesitate to give their soldiers a candid appraisal for fear they will be reluctant to fight. This was very much a factor in comparing the M-60 with the newer—and far more numerous—Soviet tanks.

Even though intelligence reports were giving an ominous, if often confusing and always incomplete, account of these new Soviet tanks, the U.S. Army pretended, at least publicly, that its own tank was as good or better. The fact was that the Soviets had, as one general later put it, "turned inside us." They had managed to field a tank that, despite its shortcomings, was ahead of anything in the West. American tankers were right in thinking that if war came, they would almost certainly lose—and lose quickly. While armor officers and senior noncoms were becoming almost frantic in their desire for a new tank, it was not until 1972 that a just retired senior armor officer said bluntly in public what they had been discussing among themselves.

When General James H. Polk commanded the U.S. Army in Europe in the late 1960s, he praised the Army's fighting ability. But once in civilian clothes, he wrote an angry article describing the Army's main battle tank as "the tired, old, second-rate M-60 series." Even after a modernization program, then under way, Polk wrote, the reworked tank "will not be the best tank on the European battlefield by any stretch of the imagination." The article appeared in June 1972, only five months after the editors of *Armor* had featured "The Death of the Tank." It ran first in *Army*, the magazine of the Association of the U.S.

Army and outlet for semiofficial Army policy, and was reprinted the following month in *Armor*.

Expressing the long-held frustration of many tankers, Polk complained that American tanks had been outgunned during World War II by the German Panther and Tiger tanks and beaten again by the old Russian T-34s they met in Korea in the early 1950s.

Polk was one of the young World War II tankers who fought under Patton and experienced firsthand what it means to go to war in an inferior machine. In his diary entry for July 22, 1944, Patton notes: "Put Jim Polk in command of the 3rd Cavalry Group. He is 32 years old and seems awfully young, but I was a colonel at 31 in command of a much larger force."

At one point Polk's tank was hit point-blank by the powerful 88 mm gun of a German. He still recalls the incident vividly: "My tank got hit in the front plate. It went right through the middle of my driver. I think it went between my legs. It went through the fire wall in the back and hit the engine and set it on fire. I thought I was dead. I was covered with the driver's gore. It just sounds like you're inside an anvil or something. Terrific ringing sound. It didn't knock me out, kind of stunned me. The gunner kept yelling, 'Get the hell out of here!' He couldn't get out till I got out."

Like other American tankers who survived the war, Polk had a horror of being outgunned. Clearly, from what the intelligence people were able to learn, the new Soviet tanks had problems of their own. But those big Russian guns were a matter of deep concern.

One of those with ample reason to be concerned was General Welborn G. Dolvin, who had been picked in 1963 to manage the U.S. effort in what turned out to be the first round in the Army's long struggle to equip itself with a new tank—in this case an ambitious American-German effort to use the most advanced Western technology to produce a true supertank.

Dolvin (his friends all called him Tom, not Welborn) had also been outgunned, in an experience much like Polk's. In the bruising battle for Monte Cassino, Italy, in 1944 he commanded a battalion and an attached company totaling about thirty-five tanks. Dolvin, then a major, was standing in the turret of his Sherman when they came upon a German tank force. The Americans fired first and saw their shells bounce off the enemy armor.

The green tracer marking the path of the first shot by the high-velocity 76 mm gun on the German tank seemed to be aimed directly at Dolvin. But it passed just over his head. He watched helplessly as the German corrected his aim. The next shot went right through the tank and into the transmission, causing a dreaded "flameup" of hot oil. All five crew members were injured and burned, but they all got out alive. Somehow the gunner, a good-size man, went right past Dolvin and out the tank commander's hatch. When Dolvin later accused him of abandoning the tank without orders, the sergeant replied: "I know that, Major. I wasn't right sure you knew that tank was on fire, but it was burning me!" Dolvin dropped the subject.

Recalling that baptism of fire years later, Dolvin said: "The main thing that really fried your ass, believe me, is you get in battle and you get the first hit and you see it ricochet off. And you know the big bastard is going to turn the turret around and the next one is going to go right through you. And that's discouraging. You need a gun. The fellow riding in that tank deserves to win if he gets the first hit. That's all there is to it."

If Dolvin, Polk, and the other World War II tankers had had their way, the Army would have hurried, in the early sixties, to produce a new tank with a big gun capable of outshooting the Russians. But two powerful forces combined to send the Army off on a long, expensive detour.

The first was a study done in 1958 by a blue-ribbon panel of civilian experts. They concluded that the tank killer of the future would be the long-range missile rather than the kinetic energy round fired by the tank gun. The two systems work on different physical principles. The missile, with a range much greater than that of the gun, flies relatively slowly and uses an explosive to create a stream of metal that cuts its way through the armor. But only a gun has the power to propel a projectile so fast that it needs no explosive. Its mass and speed are enough to penetrate armor. When the shell strikes the tank, its high-speed motion is abruptly changed into concentrated energy that enables it to cut through the armor. It is a sophisticated version of the old brute-force cannonball: The heavier it is and the faster it travels, the more damage it does.

Advances in missilery were so promising, the panel reported, that the Army should push this new technology—even if it meant underfunding or even giving up efforts to improve tank guns and kinetic energy ammunition. The old soldiers did not readily abandon their prejudice in favor of a big gun. But what they really wanted was the best weapon for killing tanks. If what the experts said was true, it was hard to argue against the missile. The Army, although not without some misgivings, went all out for missiles.

The second force that came to bear on the Army's tank program was even more important. It was Robert S. McNamara, the former head of the Ford Motor Company, who became secretary of defense when John F. Kennedy entered the White House in 1961. McNamara was the epitome of the mid-twentieth-century American industrial manager, with an almost unbounded faith that any problem was subject to the rational processes of the human mind. At the time American management techniques were regarded with much the same kind of respect later accorded to the Japanese. McNamara, who had received his master's degree at the Harvard Graduate School of Business Administration and later taught there, set about applying the wisdom of the business schools to management of the U.S. military establishment, one of the world's largest enterprises, larger than any industry, larger than most governments.

McNamara and the too often arrogant young analysts he brought with him to the Pentagon—the so-called whiz kids—were thought of as a kind of human extension of the new computer technology. In reality, they used computers as a tool for a new way of thinking, known generally as systems analysis and first used in an embryonic form in World War II. McNamara was one of a number of young industrial managers fresh out of the management schools who were attracted to the most technological of the services, the Army Air Forces. There these experts on production turned their skills around to achieve the maximum in destruction.

When McNamara moved into his office on the third floor of the Pentagon and settled himself behind the huge desk that had once belonged to General John J. ("Blackjack") Pershing, the World War I American commander, Germany was no longer an enemy but instead an increasingly important member of the North Atlantic Treaty Organization. To McNamara's rational mind, it was illogical for the United States not to work more closely with Germany and with its other allies in the design and production of military equipment.

Only 5 percent of the weapons used by the allies were jointly produced. The United States, Britain, and France each produced their own tanks. The Germans used the American M-48 but fully intended to replace it with a tank of their own design as soon as possible. If forced to fight, the allies would go to war with a hodgepodge of equipment. They would need separate supply lines for different types of ammunition, spare parts, replacement vehicles, and even fuel.

McNamara decided that a good start toward changing this situation would be a joint effort by the United States and Germany to build a new main battle tank. He hoped other NATO nations would join in the effort so the alliance would have a tank that was jointly produced and shared by all the armies.

He was convinced that by sharing ideas and costs, the allies could produce weapons that not only were better and cheaper but would be easier and less expensive to maintain than if each nation continued to go its own way.

What McNamara wanted and what the Army wanted were quite different. The Army wanted a new tank. McNamara wanted a new process for providing weapons for the alliance. The tank was to be the means for creating this process.

To an Army already feeling a desperate need for a new tank, the joint program was not good news. But the message it heard from McNamara was clear: If you want a new tank, it will be the joint American-German tank.

This new tank would not be ready for seven years, at best, and probably not for a decade or more. In the meantime, the Army would have to make do with its older M-48 tanks, try to improve the newer M-60, and hurry work on a new light tank known as the Sheridan. The fifty-ton M-60 would fill the role of the main battle tank while the sixteen-ton Sheridan—light enough to be parachuted into combat—would be a light reconnaissance vehicle. Both the improved M-60 and the Sheridan would carry the Shillelagh weapon system—a gun capable of firing both a missile and a big 152 mm shell.

While work on these two systems continued, the major effort was focused on the German-American tank. In the U.S. Army the importance attached to a program can be measured by the amount of support it gets. Programs with support get good managers, continuing high-level attention, and money. Except for a period in the late sixties and early seventies, when the war in Vietnam absorbed most of the Army's attention and money, the tank program had strong support. Without exception, the officers assigned to manage the program were the best the Army could find for the job. One indication of the quality of the program managers is that most of them went on to important command assignments. Too often assignment to manage a procurement program is the end of an officer's career.

The first of the program managers was Dolvin, a native of Georgia, a West Pointer in the class of 1939, and, by 1963, a forty-seven-year-old brigadier general. Although the United States had worked with its allies on military equipment during both world wars, it had never been involved in a joint program on such a scale. When he was named project manager for the American side, Dolvin was not even sure what a project manager was or what he was supposed to do. About the only thing simple and straightforward about the program was the name. It was called the MBT-70 by the Americans, Kampanzer 70 by the Germans. That defined the ultimate goal: It was to be a main battle tank (MBT) and it was to be available about 1970. (The German word *Panzer* means "tank" and is derived from the word for "breastplate or armor," as worn by a medieval knight, and not from the word for "jungle cat," which is *Panther*.)

In choosing Dolvin to head the tank program at that early stage, the Army had the good sense to choose an officer who was both a tanker and an experienced research and development manager rather than an ordnance officer without experience as a tanker. After combat in both World War II and Korea, Dolvin had been involved in the development of all of the Army's tanks. He could talk with authority to both those who would build the tank and those who would use it.

Not only did Dolvin know his business, but he is one of those men with an infectious enthusiasm for whatever they are doing, whether it is fighting tanks, building tanks, or growing loblolly pines on the tree plantations he established in Virginia after his retirement. He also has what the Army calls command presence, an aura of authority that leaves no doubt about who is in charge. During his Army career he was notorious for his insistence on cutting through the bureaucratic underbrush in his desire to get things done. Once, after his retirement, he was asked by the chairman of the Joint Chiefs of Staff to undertake a sensitive and very secret international assignment. He turned down the job when the chairman refused to permit him to report directly to the President.

When he took over as project manager, Dolvin had three challenges: (1) to set up an office for managing the American side of the project and choose a contractor to do the development work; (2) to work out a cooperative arrangement with the Germans; and (3) to get agreement on the characteristics of the new tank.

The Army went through the motions of a competition to

choose the contractor on the American side. The contenders were Chrysler, General Motors (GM) and a joint venture of Ford and FMC. In reality, Dolvin called the shots, and he picked General Motors. He quickly rejected the Ford-FMC combination because it proposed to do the work at the FMC plant in San Jose, California. On the East Coast there was a three-hour overlap in business hours with Germany. On the West Coast there would be no overlap at all. Chrysler was an imposing contender because it had for years been the tank maker for the Army and had delivered a total of thirty-five thousand tanks, from the M-3 in 1941 to the newest M-60 in 1963. But Dolvin chose GM in July 1964 because he thought there was a better chance of getting new ideas and, even more important, because he wanted to be able to call upon the expertise of the world's largest industrial enterprise. If he got in trouble with the new technology McNamara wanted to push, Dolvin knew GM could bring in entire teams of experts from its divisions to help him solve any problem that might come along.

In Germany a different approach was used. A number of firms joined together in a new entity, the German Development Corporation, to work on the tank program.

Management experts strongly urged Dolvin to set up his own headquarters in Detroit. Instead, he put his main office in Washington with a branch in Detroit. He reasoned that technical decisions would be made in Detroit but that questions about money would be answered in Washington. He chose to be where the money was and never regretted that decision.

If Dolvin had had his way, he would have reported directly to the secretary to the general staff or the vice chief of staff of the Army, but he never was able to short-circuit several levels of the bureaucracy. At one point he almost quit when a mid-level functionary at the Pentagon took it upon himself to undercut a deal Dolvin had made with the Germans. Despite his failure to get the full authority within the Army that he desired, he had a powerful ally in McNamara.

Within a month after Dolvin had taken over the program,

McNamara ordered him to report directly to him once a week, either in person or in writing. McNamara also took Dolvin along on many of his European trips so they would have time to talk about the tank program. Although Dolvin had misgivings about his direct reports to McNamara, cutting out the whole chain of command, he found the weekly reporting requirement extremely valuable. Everyone in the Army knew that Dolvin reported to McNamara every Monday afternoon. No one wanted to be singled out as the one responsible for a delay or for failure to deal with a problem. The system was unorthodox, but it worked.

While Dolvin had an admirable mastery of American tanks and tank production and of the Army and Pentagon bureaucracy, he was venturing into almost totally uncharted territory when he sat down for the first time in October 1963 with his German counterpart, Dr. Fritz Engelmann, a civilian engine expert who had received his doctorate in engineering from the Munich Institute of Technology in 1934 and had previously worked for Messerschmitt, which had made some of the most formidable warplanes of World War II.

It was not entirely clear which country had more to gain from the transfer of technology involved in the joint project. Officers familiar with tank factories in both nations found the Germans far behind the Americans and were surprised to hear McNamara speak of the advantages to the United States of this access to German technology. They suspected that because of his studies of German industry during the war, he had an exaggerated notion of how much the United States could learn from the Germans. Still recovering from the war and the postwar ban on rearmament, the West Germans were producing only a few tanks by a tedious handmade process. If there were any technology transfer, it seemed to many in the Army, it would be from the west side of the Atlantic to the east, rather than vice versa. But McNamara's major reason for starting the joint program with the Germans rather than with the British, as many American armor officers would have preferred, was that with their rapidly expanding economy, the West Germans had the money to take part in such an ambitious program.

Certainly McNamara was not unaware of the complex problems in such an effort. While in charge of all auto manufacturing at Ford, he had pushed development of a small front-wheel-drive car with a sophisticated V-4 engine. A joint effort of engineers from Detroit and Taunus (the German branch of Ford), the car, known as the Cardinal, was designed to compete with the Volkswagen Beetle in the European and American markets. This was not a cooperative effort like the tank program. McNamara was the boss, and he could call the shots on both sides of the Atlantic. Still, the Cardinal never made it to the American market. Lee Iacocca, who took over at Ford when McNamara became defense secretary, derided the Cardinal as "that Cock Robin" and convinced the company's directors to write off the thirty-five million dollars McNamara had poured into the effort.

One of the most difficult practical problems the Americans would face became apparent at the very first meeting between Dolvin and Engelmann. While neither Dolvin nor most of the other Americans were comfortable speaking German, Engelmann and many of his associates spoke English fluently. The Germans also had a superb staff of professional translators, on whom the Americans came to rely. In effect, in some sessions the real negotiators on both sides of the table were Germans.

Never in the six years of the joint MBT-70 program did the Americans field a satisfactory team of translators. Just to get agreement on the meaning of words required the compilation of a thirty-thousand-word English-German dictionary of technical terms. When one language didn't have a word to match one in the other, a new word was created or one was borrowed from the other language. The Germans agreed, for example, to use the American word "trade-off" because their language didn't have a word with its precise meaning. Still, there were unending misunderstandings resulting from the language difference.

The Americans' difficulty with the language was compounded by the decision to do the development work in Augsburg, a provincial city in the south of Germany near Munich. A factory that had been producing garbage trucks and typewriters was available there. In this first phase the Americans traded location for control: They would be the bosses, and the Germans would be their subordinates. In the second phase, involving fabrication of prototypes, they all would move to Detroit, and the Germans would be the bosses. Dolvin and his Army colleagues, for whom frequent moves and service in foreign countries were a way of life, were astounded how reluctant the ninety-nine General Motors engineers—and especially their wives—were to move to Germany. The Army eventually took over an apartment building, furnished it with American-style kitchens and baths, and gave the GM people the simulated rank of captain so they could use U.S. military stores and other facilities.

On the technical side other differences, some of them seemingly trivial, caused unexpected problems. It was awkward for draftsmen from the two countries to work together because the Germans work sitting down, the Americans standing up or using tall stools. One difference was quickly solved: The Americans agreed to use the German scale of one-fifth, one-tenth, one-twentieth rather than the more familiar one-fourth, one-eighth, one-sixteenth. Another difference proved more difficult. German draftsmen use the first-angle method of projection; Americans use the third-angle method. This means that when an American draws a part, he shows the right side of the object to the right of the drawing of the front of the object. In the same position a German shows the left side of the object. Engineers and draftsmen can easily distinguish the difference. But in the factory a craftsman using unfamiliar drawings is likely to put holes in the wrong side of the metal.

Few things caused more contention than the system of measurement. The Germans—like most of the world—use the metric system. The Americans use inches. Neither Dolvin nor Engelmann had the authority to force a decision on which system to use. Eventually the issue went to the ministerial level—to McNamara and his German counterpart, Defense Minister Kai-Uwe von Hassel. Even there a clear-cut choice proved impossible. In a compromise the defense ministers outdid Solomon: They actually cut the baby in half. The Germans would use metric measurements in the parts of the tank they supplied; the Americans would use inches in theirs. At the points where the parts were to be fastened together, they would use metric—a major concession to the Germans.

At first it was proposed that all the plans contain both metric and inch measurements. But it was sensibly decided that this could open the door to all sorts of mistakes in the factories. The cumbersome solution was to maintain duplicate sets of all drawings, one set using metric, the other inches, one with the first-angle method of projection, the other with the third-angle method. As soon as a drawing was done or revised in one system, it was immediately translated into the other.

Other difficulties arose from the different ways the American and German governments deal with industry and from differences in the industrial process in the two countries. In the United States the government normally pays a contractor to do the research and development on a new weapon. This is expensive, but in the end the government owns the results of the research. It is free to invite competition for production of the weapon and, if it wishes, refuse to award the contract to the company that did the original research. In Germany the contractors fund most of the research, they own the results, they profit if their components are used, and they are reluctant to have anyone, even the government, see what they are doing. When it came time to decide what components would go into the joint tank, each of the German manufacturers pushed vigorously for use of its technology. The failure of some Americans to understand the importance of this basic difference was to cause serious problems for years to come.

Endless confusion also resulted from the different approaches the two countries take to quality control. Americans rigorously test the products coming off the production line; in fact, of the fifty-five days it now takes the Americans to produce a tank, thirty-six days are devoted to testing and fixing of defects after the tank is essentially complete. The Germans, on the other hand, do relatively little of this kind of testing at the end of the production process. Instead, they will close down a factory from time to time to examine and calibrate all the jigs and fixtures used in building the tank. Their reasoning is that if everything in the plant is perfect, a perfect product will roll off the end of the line.

It must be said to the credit of Dolvin and Engelmann that the tank that resulted from their efforts did not look as much like an animal designed by a committee as it might have. One reason is that they used what at the time was the most sophisticated computer analysis ever attempted in the design of a tank.

The Lockheed Missile and Space Company was chosen to do the study under a $377,000 contract. It took various possible components in use or under development by the two countries and loaded them into a big IBM 7094 computer. Then it added the characteristics of known Soviet arms and put them all together in two large-scale scenarios for a war in Central Europe. Up to that time it had been possible to analyze tank duels with one or at most two tanks on each side. But Lockheed, by straining the capacity of its computer, was able to conduct sixty company-size battles, each involving scores of tanks. The results, spelled out in a mountain of computer printouts and diagrams of the battles imposed on maps of Germany, provided more information than designers had ever had before.

For tankers whose idea of a good tank was one with a reliable engine, tough armor, tracks that stayed on, a gun big enough to blow a hole in the other fellow's armor, and a decent heater, the mass of detail was overwhelming. They were told the number and rate of actions completed successfully for each friendly tank killed and the number and rate of actions completed successfully for each million dollars of combat cost expended. For each battle they were told how much fuel the friendly forces used and where the shells fired by each side landed. There was even a chart showing how time spent on development affected the "military worth" of a tank over its expected lifetime.

How much the Lockheed study actually influenced the design is unclear. Most likely the study's major importance was to help justify decisions that would have emerged anyway. That agreement could be reached at all was rather surprising considering the differences in the war-fighting philosophies of the two countries. The Germans at the time favored a tank specifically designed for fighting in Central Europe: a relatively small, agile tank with moderate armor protection, a gun capable of fighting at relatively short distances, and with the best nuclear protection they could get. The Americans demanded a tank that could fight anywhere in the world. They favored a heavily armored and therefore heavier tank with a missile capable of killing other tanks at long distances and with little effort to provide special protection against nuclear radiation.

The designers were faced with awesome wish lists from the tankers in both armies. It was here that Dolvin's experience as a "user" came in handy. At one point the Armor Center at Fort Knox, Kentucky, demanded that the new tank be able to ford twenty feet of water. Six feet had simply been added to the capability of the existing M-60 on the assumption that if fourteen feet was good, twenty was better. Dolvin found a study proving that a tank that could ford fourteen feet of water could cross any stream in Europe, including the Rhine. He was able in this case to head off the kind of "gold-plating" that can add enormously to the cost of a weapon without adding to its usefulness on the battlefield.

It is still possible with some effort to find and examine one of the half dozen prototypes of the MBT-70 produced in this country. In a dusty warehouse at Fort Knox one of them is housed with a ghostly collection of old American, British, and German armor. Despite its long-neglected condition, it is easy to see why engineers who worked on the project think it is a shame their tank never went into production. In some ways its technology surpasses anything the United States has since put into the field.

The first impression is that the turret is big, both front and rear. The U.S.-designed 152 mm tube, part of the Shillelagh system, capable of firing both kinetic energy projectiles and missiles, looms out the front. It is almost two inches bigger in diameter than the gun on the M-60 tank. To the rear, in a monstrous bustle, the automatic loader contains both missiles and shells.

As the Germans demanded, the turret encloses a radiation-resistant capsule to protect the three-man crew. On the right side the tank commander has his station with a hatch and a 20 mm antiaircraft gun. The gunner is deep in the turret with his laser range finder and computer. The driver is not down in the hull, as in a conventional tank. His little compartment fits into the left side of the turret but revolves independently of the turret. This permits him to face forward even when the gunner turns the gun to the side or rear. His automatic windshield wiper carries operating instructions in both English and German. The one obvious disadvantage of the driver's position is that the large bustle obscures his view to the rear. The MBT-70 was not designed to run away.

The two major advances that permitted the MBT-70 to fire accurately while moving rapidly over rough country are not apparent as it sits inert in a warehouse. One is the hydropneumatic suspension that not only gives the tank a smooth cross-country ride but also permits the crew to raise or lower the profile of the tank by eighteen inches. With this "kneeling-squatting" feature, the tank can crouch out of view behind a slight rise in the earth or rise up to peer over.

Firing on the move would be impossible without some method of stabilizing the gun or the sight. The decision was to stabilize the sight, because it is lighter than the gun, and then permit the gun to fire only when it was aligned with the sight. The calculations involved were said to be as complex as those for a moon landing, and a workable stabilization system had been a long time coming.

Years before, as a young officer, Dolvin had been assigned to work with Westinghouse on a gun stabilization system for the Sherman tank, and he was the executive officer of the first battalion that took it into combat in World War II. He quickly became the first to turn the system off for the duration of the war. Air leaked into the mechanism and caused it to give faulty readings so the gunner was worse off than if he simply eyeballed the target. It was another quarter of a century before the Army had, in the MBT-70, a stabilization system that worked well. It was so good, in fact, that critics found it unbelievable. At Aberdeen Proving Ground in Maryland one day, an electric bulb was placed in the center of a downrange bull's-eye so a group of visiting congressmen could pick out the target. An MBT-70 shot out the bulb while traversing rough terrain at more than thirty miles an hour. A few of the congressmen accused the Army of blowing it out with a preset charge.

The MBT-70 prototype evolved less from true joint development than from a simple process of adding on. The dispute over nuclear protection was settled by adding on the German capsule. The gun versus missile dispute was settled by changing the American missile system to fire the kinetic energy round demanded by the Germans. Each country, to some extent, continued to go its own way. Both developed their own powerful diesel engines, and the Americans also worked on a turbine. The Germans refused to abandon work on a 120 mm cannon, and the Americans suspected—rightly, as it turned out—that it would be substituted for the 152 mm Shillelagh at the earliest opportunity.

All this cost money, and it was excessive cost—or, more important, the perception of excessive cost—that contributed more than anything to the ultimate failure of the MBT-70 program. There were technical problems, to be sure. The Germans couldn't make their automatic loader work right, but the Americans solved the problems. The American engine never did live up to expectations, but the German engine, though bulky and heavy, was a signal success. The Shillelagh gun-missile system, which was developed independently of the tank, was a disappointment and was eventually abandoned. The tank was criticized in Congress as too complex and too risky technologically, but its fatal flaw was that it seemed to cost too much. This question of cost was to have an extraordinary influence throughout the Army's effort to build a new tank, and it is worth taking a moment to see what happened in the case of the MBT-70.

The real problem came at the very beginning when McNamara, the American defense secretary, and Hassel, his German counterpart, set the development cost at $80 million, leaving open the possibility it might rise to $100 million. The two countries agreed to split the cost fifty-fifty. It is probably fair to characterize this as up-front money, the funds put up by the partners to start the enterprise, and the relatively low figures probably helped win initial support from the U.S. Congress and the West German parliament, the Bundestag. Certainly no one in the Army took those numbers, picked out of the air before there was even agreement on what the tank would look like, as valid estimates of the actual development cost. It was obvious to anyone who looked closely that the figures were too low for such an unprecedented joint project. But they were later to be treated as though they had been engraved in stone and carried down from the mountain by Moses.

By 1969 critics found it possible, by adding in such items as trainers and advanced production engineering that had not been included in the early estimate, to show that the cost of the MBT-70 had risen by more than 500 percent—from $80 million to more than half a billion. The truth was that the cost had risen, but nowhere near that amount. The real cost increase had been about 120 percent—from the $138 million estimate made by the Army after the design of the tank had been agreed upon in 1965 to the $303 million estimate as a production decision neared in 1968. While the increase in development costs raised a caution flag, it was estimates of production costs—as much as $1 million a tank—that later led many to conclude that the MBT-70 was simply not affordable.

Despite technical problems and the growing cost, the program seemed to be in pretty good shape when Dolvin left in October 1966 to assume command of an armored division. About that time General Creighton W. Abrams, then vice chief of staff, told Congress: "It is a personal conviction of mine, having attended several meetings with the Germans, as well as staying on the periphery of this program from the outset, that we will have a better design and a better tank than we would have if we had done it alone."

But Dolvin's successor, Major General Edwin H. Burba, quickly became disenchanted with the joint effort with the Germans. Burba has since died, but Brigadier General Bernard R. Luczak, who succeeded him in mid-1968, says that both he and Burba recommended trying to find a graceful way to end the transatlantic marriage because it was the source of most of their most serious problems. They were told the program was a "sacred cow." No one had the audacity to kill it.

It was not until 1969 that Luczak found a man audacious enough. David Packard, a big, blunt-spoken billionaire with roots in California's high tech electronics industry, had moved into the Pentagon as deputy to Melvin R. Laird, Richard M. Nixon's first defense secretary. One of Packard's assignments was to increase efficiency and save money. After a visit to Germany at Easter time, he returned convinced that Luczak was right: Trying to build a joint tank was not working out. It took months of negotiations, but in January 1970 the Americans and the Germans agreed to end the joint program and instead to cooperate closely as each country built its own tank.

The United States began a major overhaul of the tank design and even gave it a new name. It was called the XM-803, a deliberately meaningless designation that defined neither the type of vehicle to be built nor the date it would be available.

This drastic change in the program put Luczak in an awkward position. He had been picked for the job on the assumption that the MBT-70 was about ready to go into production. A graduate of Stanford rather than the Military Academy and an ordnance officer rather than a combat soldier, he was a stickler for efficiency, even down to switching off unneeded electric lights—an ideal man to handle the transition from research to production. But he was suddenly thrown back into the design phase, trimming the MBT-70 back to an austere, affordable version.

During the three and a half years he managed the program, Luczak felt himself buffeted on one side by tankers who couldn't make up their minds what they wanted and on the other by a sometimes arrogant, high-cost contractor.

The tankers began to question such basic decisions as whether the new tank should have an automatic loader, a three-man crew, and the gun-missile system. "The 'armor community' cannot seem to agree on what it wants in the way of a new main battle tank," Luczak complained in an unusually candid report written in 1972 and covering his four years managing the tank program. "There is . . . internal dissension within the armor community concerning the role of the tank—if any."

Luczak understood that the tankers, despite all their arguing, really did want a new tank. If they could only have made up their minds on what they wanted, Luczak concluded, the Army could have saved two years and $175 million.

His relationship with GM was equally stormy, although the situation improved after the joint program with the Germans was ended. "General Motors often repeated a statement that the government constitutes less than 4 percent of their business and more than 96 percent of their headaches, and that they would not change to accommodate the government," Luczak wrote. He also complained that GM was a high-priced contractor, sometimes adding on the same charges at the division and corporate levels. On one occasion the company charged the government for sending six people to a meeting in Washington when Luczak thought that one, or at the most two, would have been enough.

On several occasions, however, Dolvin's faith in GM's depth of expertise paid off during the time when Luczak was converting the MBT-70 into the XM-803. General Motors' Delco Division took three sights from the MBT-70 and combined them into one component in a remarkably short time, cutting the cost of the tank without cutting its performance.

The company's Detroit Diesel Allison Division was called in to perform a rescue operation on the automatic loader. The loader is a simple concept. In effect, it is like a giant soft-drink machine on which you push a button and get the flavor you want. But something happens in the process of adapting a machine designed to deliver a twelve-ounce can of soda pop into a machine that will deliver a forty-pound cannon shell. The Germans struggled with the problem and just couldn't get it right (satellite photos showing Soviet tanks with their autoloaders arrayed on the ground behind them indicate the Russians had similar problems). Allison's engineers took over where the Germans left off and quickly produced a workable model.

One of the austere XM-803 prototypes that emerged from this period of redesign can be seen displayed as a lawn ornament at Fort Knox. It still looks much like the MBT-70. Money was saved by using a less powerful engine, a simplified suspension system, and a type of armor that was easier to fabricate than that on the MBT-70. With its autoloader and three-man crew, it was similar to the new Russian T-64. The difference was that one was in use by troops and the other would never be. The XM-803 would still have been a very good tank, and it might have been produced in significant numbers if the time for decision had not come in 1971.

Disenchantment with the McNamara era at the Pentagon was at its peak. Congress had discovered a two-billion-dollar overrun in the cost of the Air Force's big C5-A transport plane. The F-111, which was to be an all-purpose fighter-bomber for the Air Force and Navy, had run into severe cost and technological problems. The Navy was becoming aware of a mess in its shipbuilding program that was to plague it for a decade. The Pentagon had been forced to scrap both the Army's Cheyenne helicopter and the expensive manned orbiting laboratory.

Failures of two other programs involving the gun-missile system—the Sheridan light tank and a version of the M-60—had focused congressional attention on the tank issue. Hundreds of the M-60s were warehoused because their gun-missile weapons didn't work, and the Sheridans proved a disaster when they were tested in Vietnam. The list of Sheridan defects seemed endless. The engine overheated (not a problem except in combat, a general explained), carbon monoxide sometimes filled the crew compartment, the caseless ammunition easily caught fire, and the vehicle was so noisy that enemy troops could hear it three miles away. A recently retired general finally gave Congress candid advice on what to do with the Sheridans: Line them all up and drive them into the Pacific.

Even the so-called experts in Congress didn't know much about tanks at that time—except that they cost too much. One congressman who had had innumerable briefings and should have known better complained in a floor speech that the MBT-70 could not shoot on the move but the latest Russian tank could, while the truth was just the opposite. Still, it was in this period that a few members of Congress and a small group of staffers began to learn about tanks, building a background of expertise that made Congress a powerful force in later decisions about what kind and how many tanks the Army would have.

In the atmosphere of 1971, with the American involvement in Vietnam declining and pressure growing to cut defense spending, the impact of Congress on the tank program was almost entirely negative. Critics were able—unfairly, the Army thought—to label the XM-803 a "million-dollar tank." Although some in the Army argued that it made no sense, and would actually cost more money, to cancel a tank ready for production and to start over again, that was what Congress ordered. On December 18, 1971, just a little more than eight years after the MBT-70 effort had begun, the XM-803 was killed. Three days later the Army canceled its contract with General Motors. There was some consolation in the fact that Congress had provided twenty million dollars for studies of a new tank, but there was no assurance the studies would ever reach the hardware stage.

In his report on his four years as program manager, Luczak summarized what had gone wrong. A major reason for the high cost, he concluded, was the time and money involved in running the joint program. He also blamed early estimates made with "rose-colored glasses," a high inflation rate, a contractor that charged more than others in the defense industry and technical problems with the German autoloader and American engine.

To this list should be added some measure of blame for the Army managers. They failed to recognize and control the rapid rise in cost, they failed to recognize the critical importance of cost control in the political atmosphere of the late sixties and early seventies, and they failed to demand, early on, an end to the joint program with the Germans. It is unlikely that other managers would have done better, or even as well. Perhaps answering the question of whether to continue such an international program is above the pay grade of any army officer. And perhaps there is something basically unworkable about joint tank development. Britain, Germany, and France made several such attempts, and they all ended in failure.

Congress's decision meant starting over, almost from the beginning, although much of the technology developed in the earlier program later proved useful.

It was a gloomy time for the Army. It meant being without a new tank until the early eighties, at best, and it meant living for nearly another decade with the nightmare of an attack by Russian tanks that were not only more numerous but technologically superior. Hardly anyone had the foresight then to guess that the abrupt death of the XM-803 was one of the most fortunate occurrences ever to befall the U.S. Army.

With the beginning of the new year of 1972, the Army set about the long, tedious, difficult, and often contentious process of deciding what kind of tank it wanted, designing it, building it, and teaching the soldiers to operate and maintain it. Although the technology was to be the latest product of the electronic age, many of the challenges the Army faced went back to the very beginning of armed conflict. The modern tanker may be protected by two feet of armor rather than a shield made of hide, and he may kill his enemies with a 120 mm gun rather than a short thrusting sword; but the problem is the same: how to protect a man so he can survive on the battlefield and arm him so he can prevail.

2

From Chariot to Land Ironclad

WHEN ALEXANDER THE GREAT rode out on the plain of Gaugamela on the afternoon of September 30, 331 B.C., he saw an army specially raised and trained by Darius III, king of the Persians, to destroy him and his army. Arrayed in ranks as far as the eye could see were Persians, Susians, Cadusians, Medes, Albanians, Scythians, Babylonians, and Bactrians, the sunlight flashing on their armor. Looming over the troops were the forms of fifteen war elephants, the first to go into battle outside their native India. While elephants have been used in warfare off and on over the centuries and Hannibal even went to the trouble of bringing his elephants over the Alps, they often proved more trouble than they were worth. Hannibal even equipped each of his mahouts with a mallet and a spike to be driven into the beast's brain if it turned and began trampling friendly forces.

Accounts of the numbers on the Persian side vary—from two hundred thousand to a million infantry and from forty-five to one hundred thousand cavalry. We shouldn't take the numbers too seriously. They were meant not to be precise but to indicate a vast multitude.

Alexander, who had conquered Egypt and then marched northeast in search of Darius, headed a much smaller force: forty thousand infantry and seven thousand horsemen. He had crossed the Euphrates River and then the Tigris near the ancient city of Nineveh (close to the present-day city of Mosul in northern Iraq) and was advancing on Arbela (now the Iraqi city of Irbil) when he came upon Darius's army, arrayed for battle, on the large plain of Gaugamela about thirty-five miles west of the city.

As the Macedonians scouted the battlefield, they were puzzled by strange scrapings on the ground. As Alexander, confused by shadows cast by the afternoon sun, viewed the marks from a distance, it appeared to him that the Persians had created an array of obstacles of some sort. It later became evident that Darius had gone to the opposite extreme in preparing the battlefield. He had ordered a huge area in front of his army cleared as smooth as a parade ground. On this level field he planned to use his equivalent of the main battle tank: two hundred chariots with sharp knives attached to their wheels. As the chariots slashed through the Macedonian infantry phalanx, heavy cavalry would follow closely behind to break up the formations.

The scythe-bearing chariots, culmination of more than a thousand years of technical development, were a horrifying sight. A Roman writer described their effect on the battlefield: "Reeking with indiscriminate slaughter, they lop off limbs so instantaneously that what has been cut away is seen to quiver on the ground before any pain is felt. One man perceives not that the wheels and devouring scythes have carried off among the horses' feet his left arm, shield and all; another while he presses forward sees not that his right arm has dropped from him; a third tries to get up after he has lost a leg, while the dying foot quivers with its toes on the ground close by."

As the trumpets sounded on the morning of October 1, the Greeks formed up in the phalanx, a military formation first seen about 2500 B.C. and brought near perfection by Alexander's father, Philip. Each soldier carried a twenty-one-foot pike, long enough for the spear of the man in the first rank and those of the men in the four ranks behind him all to protrude in front of the formation, creating a human porcupine. The soldiers were trained to attack on the run and maneuver in such a way that they could meet an assault from any direction. The phalanx was so densely massed that penetration from the outside was extremely difficult. By the same token, it was virtually impossible for individual soldiers to break ranks and run away. Outside the phalanx were smaller units of light and heavy infantry, plus the cavalry.

His bright armor singling him out among his mounted companions, Alexander took the position of honor on the right front of the advancing force. But instead of marching head-on to meet the Persians, he slanted off to the right in the military maneuver known as a right oblique. As the Macedonians approached, Darius suddenly became aware what was happening: The battle was quickly shifting from the parade ground he had so carefully prepared to rougher terrain off to his left. He sounded the order for his chariots to attack while they could still make their assault on a level field.

Then came the next surprise. Instead of slashing into the densely packed phalanx, the chariots encountered Alexander's light infantry, his "antitank" troops. They attacked the horses and charioteers with arrows and javelins. A few brave soldiers even dashed in close enough to cut the traces linking the horses to their chariots. The phalanx opened a gap to permit passage for the few chariots that survived, and they were quickly captured. Some of the chariots, their scythes still slashing wildly, were driven back upon the Persian infantry.

Darius, who entered the battle confident the outcome would solidify his control over his empire, looked out over the field of conflict and suddenly began to fear for his very life. Abruptly wheeling his horse about, he abandoned his army and galloped toward Arbela, where he had left his supplies and his harem. By the time the victorious Macedonians reached the city that night, Darius was gone, soon to die at the hand of an assassin. Alexander, hailed as a conqueror, took Babylon without a fight and then marched east through the present-day Iran and Afghanistan and down into India.

Had Darius's chariots—his armored force—been successful, world history would have been quite different and the chariot might have achieved new respect. But the failure of the chariot force at the Battle of Arbela, as it came to be known, marked the end of a remarkable era in which a single weapons system dominated the world's battlefields and shaped the culture of the then-known world for more than a thousand years. By the time Hannibal came over the Alps to invade what is now Italy little more than a century later, the chariot, as a fighting vehicle, was fading into history.

It is worth a look back at the great chariot empires of the Bronze and Early Iron ages and the seemingly simple vehicle—the predecessor of today's main battle tank—that contributed so much to their power. The chariot, which first appeared about 1800 B.C. in the steppes of south-central Asia, was made possible by two developments: the domestication of the horse and the invention of the technique for combining copper and tin to make bronze. Although most of the early horses were not strong enough in the back to carry an armed man, they were strong enough to pull a cart carrying several men. Archaeologists have recently found reports of mounted troops as early as the mid-seventeenth century B.C., but horses capable of carrying a lightly armed man did not become generally available until about 900 B.C.

The problems faced by chariot designers were surprisingly similar to those that confront today's tank designers. The logisticians and strategists who build and support today's tank forces and prepare to take them into battle face problems that would be familiar to their counterparts of the chariot era. Should the chariot carry one or two or three or four men? Should it be propelled by two or four horses? How much weight in treated-hide shields should it carry? As weight was added, there was a loss of speed and mobility. Doubling the number of horses to pull the additional weight meant compounding the logistics problem—doubling the task of acquiring, breeding, training, and feeding horses in a society where they were not widely used in agriculture.

As the designers made their trade-offs, chariots emerged in

a variety of models. The earliest were awkward four-wheeled carts drawn by two horses and carrying a crew of two. As the chariot builders' skill evolved, different models emerged: carrying a driver and an archer; a driver and two archers; a driver, a shield bearer, an archer, and a spearman. Temple carvings depict light chariots carrying only one man, but it is hard to imagine how he could handle two high-spirited horses while loading and firing his bow. One theory is that the warrior rode his chariot to the battleground and then dismounted to fight.

The bow, which was the main armament of the chariot crew, was a technological marvel. Called the composite bow because it was made of three different materials, it consisted of a core of flexible wood encased on the outside by stretchable sinew and on the inside by horn. The compressed horn and the stretched sinew both added their power to send the arrow on its way. The result was a weapon that could propel an arrow more than a quarter of a mile. It was so powerful that an archer standing in the end zone of a modern football field could penetrate the bronze armor of another man standing in the other end zone. Even the celebrated English longbow, which didn't come along for another three thousand years, was not as powerful as this ancient weapon.

In terms of the economies of those early chariot empires—the Hittites, the Assyrians, the Egyptians, the Mitanni, the Kassites, and the Hyskos—the chariot was inordinately expensive. It is almost possible to hear, echoing down through the centuries, the same complaint about chariots that is heard today about tanks: They cost too much! To make the bronze fittings for the chariots and the armor for the charioteers put a heavy burden on the limited number of skilled craftsmen. The ingredients necessary for the manufacture of brass were seldom immediately available and had to be bought—or looted. Creating a composite bow required a skilled craftsman and time—as much as a year for the animal glues to set properly. When the chariots and their crews had been outfitted, there was no metal left to make armor for the foot soldiers, and this led to the rise of an armored aristocracy, the charioteers. In effect, the nations that lived by the chariot found themselves living for the chariot.

The major military powers were able to put thousands of chariots into the field. Even tiny Israel, under King Solomon, had an "armored division" of twelve hundred chariots. One of the greatest and most feared of the chariot empires was Assyria, which dominated the Middle East from the twelfth to the eighth century B.C. Byron captured the power of the Assyrians in poetic language:

> The Assyrian came down like the wolf on the fold,
> And his cohorts were gleaming in purple and gold;
> And the sheen of their spears was like stars on the sea,
> When the blue wave rolls nightly on deep Galilee.

The period in which the Assyrians held sway was a transitional one. As the use of iron spread, foot soldiers received arms and armor that permitted them to exist on the battlefield with the chariots, giving new life to the infantry. And the availability, about 900 B.C., of a horse capable of carrying an armed man gave rise to the use of cavalry. But the Assyrians were so wedded to the chariot that they sent their first cavalrymen out in teams—one to hold the reins of both horses and the other to fire his bow.

In the end the demands of the chariot-based economy proved too great a burden for Assyria. As the army advanced, the countryside was laid waste to prevent any threat from the rear. Cities were destroyed as a lesson to those tempted to resist the conqueror's might. But a wasteland will not support an army. By the seventh century B.C. the empire was in serious decline.

While the chariot did not fade entirely from the scene, for the next thousand years the dominant force throughout Europe and much of Asia was the armed and armored infantryman—the Greek hoplite and especially the Roman legionnaire. The long pike similar to that used by the Greeks was still in evidence. But many legionnaires carried a different weapon, a seven-foot throwing javelin made of wood with a long iron point. At the opening of the battle the Romans threw their spears, expecting not to kill their opponents but to disable them. To fend off the spears, the enemy soldiers raised their shields. The soft metal tip of the spear bent and locked itself into the shield. Often a single javelin would go through the shields of several men, tying them together. Julius Caesar described the effect during a battle against the Gauls in 58 B.C.: "The Gauls were greatly encumbered for the fight because several of their shields would be pierced and fastened together by a single javelin-cast; as the iron became bent, they could not pluck it forth, nor fight properly with the left arm encumbered. Therefore many of them preferred, after continued shaking of the arm, to cast off the shield and so to fight bare-bodied. At length, worn out with wounds, they began to retreat."

Unlike the tightly massed formations employed by earlier armies, the Roman units entered battle with about six feet separating one soldier from another, room enough for the individual to exercise his own fighting skill. The legionnaire, advancing in disciplined ranks and protected by a metal helmet, upper-body armor, and a large shield, did his killing with a short double-edged sword, the gladius, that was used for both cutting and thrusting. Considering the centuries over which it was used, the gladius may well rank as the single most deadly weapon in history, but of course, there is no accurate "body count" to support that conjecture.

The Roman legions were dominant into the fourth century A.D., until they were overwhelmed by the cavalry of the Goths and other invaders from the east. But the cavalry remained a light fighting force, the riders gripping the horses' flanks with their knees while firing their arrows, much as the plains Indians were to do centuries later.

The great change on the battlefield came with the emergence of the heavily armored knight. He required a specially bred horse capable of carrying a total of up to three hundred pounds of man, armor, and weapons. What made the knight so formidable was the introduction, about the eighth century A.D., of an incredibly simple invention, the stirrup. With something to brace his feet against, the knight could swing his powerful battleax or sword against the hapless peasants below. And when confronted with others of his kind, the knight set his feet in the stirrups, couched his lance against his body, and trotted forth at ten to fifteen miles an hour (the best the horse could do with all that weight) to knock his rival from the saddle.

Without the analogy being stretched too far, it is possible to see how the knight played much the same role on the battlefield as the modern tank. Both weapons systems—the knight with his horse, his armor, and his sword and the tank with its engine and tracks, armor, and guns—protect the man and permit him to move about and use his weapons.

Like the charioteer, the knight made an enormous demand on the economy and the society. He provided protection for the community. In return, a large proportion of the community's wealth went to support him, creating a knightly aristocracy at the apex of a feudal system.

The knight's period of supremacy might not have been so long if the secret of the composite bow had been remembered. The bowman of the Middle Ages was armed with a cumbersome weapon known as the crossbow that was difficult to make, was awkward to operate, had a short range and poor penetrating power, and took an appreciable time between shots. It was not until the fourteenth century that a new weapon, developed by the Welsh, found its way to the Continental battlefield.

This new weapon, the longbow, was six feet long and made of a variety of woods, the best of which was yew imported from Spain or Italy. The longbow was relatively simple, very portable, accurate at ranges up to four hundred yards, and very powerful. A steel-tipped arrow, fired at short range from the longbow, could penetrate four inches of oak—impressive to anyone who has struggled to pound a nail into an oaken beam.

One account of a battle at Abergavenny in Wales in 1182 gives a graphic account of the power of the longbow. A knight was hit in one leg by an arrow. It went through his chain-mail armor, his thigh, the leather and wood of his saddle and into his horse. When he swerved around, another arrow pinned his other leg in the same manner.

A skilled bowman, the product of years of intensive training, could fire one of his three-foot-long arrows every six seconds. Typically, massed archers would fire their arrows into the air so that they would follow a high trajectory and then fall on the enemy in waves, thick as raindrops.

The importance of the longbow has probably been overstressed, largely because of the romantic image of the humble yeoman defeating the flower of knighthood at the battles of Crécy (1346), Poitiers (1356), and Agincourt (1415.) Actually the archers were a generally rough crew, many with criminal records. And gunpowder, introduced to Europe about the same time, would soon have made the knight obsolete in any event.

In the brief period of the longbow's ascendancy, armorers struggled to devise new armor that would withstand the arrows, and they did find a way to protect the knight himself. But they gave up after adding ninety pounds in a vain effort to make armor strong enough and still light enough to cover and protect the horse. The knight whose horse was pierced by an arrow was just as vulnerable as the tanker whose mobility has been lost to a shot in the track.

If we date the decline of the knight from the middle of the fourteenth century, then infantry, with support from cavalry and artillery, dominated the battlefield for the next five hundred years, through the wars of the Swedish king Gustavus Adolphus, Frederick the Great, Napoleon, and Wellington and down to the American Civil War in the nineteenth century. Fighting in disciplined rectangles, the infantry was capable of withering firepower. Cavalrymen feared to approach an infantry box, and gaps made by cannonballs were quickly closed up by the disciplined troops. Victory depended on the discipline and training of the soldiers and the skill of the generals. While penalties for breaking ranks were harsh, the men also realized that the safest place on the battlefield was close to their fellow soldiers in the infantry box.

But by the time of the American Civil War safety was no longer to be found in the togetherness of massed infantry. The changes that gave rise to the need for the tank can be seen in that conflict. New weapons made it increasingly difficult for the infantryman, the cavalryman, or the artilleryman, no matter how well trained and sternly disciplined, to move in close to the enemy and survive long enough to be effective. The individual muzzle-loading rifle of the Civil War was far less deadly than the machine gun, which came along later in the century. But it had a new rifled barrel, and that permitted the infantry, firing from behind trees and stone walls, to lay down a withering and accurate fire on enemy soldiers a quarter of a mile away. The combined effect was much like that later achieved by the machine gun. Toward the end of the war firepower on the battlefield was increased further by the introduction in the North of rapid-firing magazine carbines using a metal cartridge rather than a muzzle-loaded ball.

European military men carefully studied the battles of the Civil War, but few seem to have been able to look far enough ahead to understand the implications of what they had studied. The problem—and the solution—seemed obvious enough to a nonmilitary man, H. G. Wells, who published a short story called "The Land Ironclads" in 1903. In it he foresaw the coming of trench warfare and the way in which the tank would break the stalemate. His ironclads were bigger than the tanks we know—eighty to a hundred feet long—and they traveled on podlike feet rather than on tracks. But the concept was right on the mark.

Even earlier C. B. Brackenbury, a British colonel, wrote a remarkably farsighted article, "Ironclad Field Artillery," for the July 1878 issue of *The Nineteenth Century Review*, in which he stated: "As surely as ships of war can carry iron plates sufficient for defense against heavy guns, so surely can field artillery carry sufficient protection against the fire of infantry and shrapnel bullets. . . . If we add the use of defensive armor which can be carried by artillery and cannot be carried by cavalry and infantry, a power will be created which must seriously modify the tactics of the battlefield."

But when the First World War began in August 1914, thirty-six years after Brackenbury's prescient article, neither side had anything like a "land ironclad," the one weapon that the new realities of the battlefield demanded. The fighting quickly bogged down into the horror of trench warfare, dominated by two weapons: barriers of barbed wire, fifty yards or more in depth, and carefully positioned machine-gun nests. Whenever the infantrymen went over the top, the machine guns fired lengthwise down their ranks, killing them by the thousands; in the first day of the Battle of the Somme in 1916, nineteen thousand British soldiers died that way. The killing zone encompassed the entire battlefield. For the attackers there was no place to hide.

The solution seized upon by the generals was greater and greater use of artillery. At the beginning of one battle in 1915, the British fired 18,000 shells to cut the wire and knock out enemy weapons. Two years later the softening-up barrage before an attack consisted of 4.3 million shells.

But artillery didn't solve the problem. It gave unmistakable warning of an attack. And soldiers quickly learned to hide deep underground and then climb up to man their weapons as the enemy charged. Gas, first used by the Germans on April 22, 1915, added a new horror to warfare and gave the attackers an initial advantage, but this was quickly nullified by the issue of gas masks.

One of the earliest advocates of the tank and, as will become apparent later, one of the most influential theorists of tank warfare was a British officer named J. F. C. Fuller, then with the rank of lieutenant colonel. Sizing up the stalemate on the western front, he wrote:

> All these solutions were spurious because the problem was not clearly understood. It was not to remove trenches and entanglements, but to neutralize the bullet; the question was how to disarm the mass of the enemy's riflemen and machinegunners, not gradually but instantaneously. Obviously the answer was bulletproof armor and not an increase in projectiles—whether bullets, shells, bombs or even gas. . . . Though the soldier could not carry bulletproof armor, he could be carried, as the sailor was, in a bulletproof armored vehicle, and as this vehicle would have to travel across country it would have to move on caterpillar tracks instead of on wheels.

Almost as soon as the war began, the situation on the battlefield made it obvious to a few that a new weapon was needed. Lieutenant Colonel E. D. Swinton, later a major general, was struck with the need for a tanklike vehicle as early as October 1914 during a visit to the front. He urged production of "a power-driven, bulletproof, armed engine capable of destroying machineguns, of crossing country and trenches, of breaking through entanglements and of climbing earthworks."

Winston Churchill, then first lord of the admiralty, had read and remembered Wells's short story. He put both enthusiasm and money behind the tank idea even though the Colonel Blimps snorted in derision. Lord Kitchener, the secretary of state for war, dismissed the tank as "a pretty little toy." An admiral wrote: "Caterpillar landships are idiotic and useless. Nobody has asked for them and nobody wants them."

Churchill persisted, and prototypes were built. Swinton is credited with coining the name tank as a cover word for the secret project. He got the idea from the workmen assigned to build the experimental vehicles. For security reasons, they were told they were building water containers for use in the Middle East and took to calling them "that tanklike thing."

The first prototype was called Little Willie, and it was not much more than a rectangular metal box sitting on the chassis of a farm tractor. It was quickly followed by a model called Big Willie or Mother, and this was to set the pattern for most of the tanks turned out by the British during the war. Mother was shaped like the geometrical figure known as a rhomboid, with the top and bottom parallel to each other and with the ends, also parallel to each other, sharply angled so that it seemed to be leaning forward. Guns were set in turrets on either side, and the track ran along the bottom, up the ends, and over the top.

This was a big tank—eight feet high, thirty-one feet long, and more than thirteen feet wide, and it weighed thirty-four tons. By comparison with modern tanks, its interior seemed roomy—until its eight-man crew climbed in. There were a tank commander, a gearman and two brakemen to operate and steer the machine, two machine gunners and two cannon gunners. The tank was noisy, hot (up to a hundred degrees Fahrenheit), and often filled with noxious fumes. It was a rough rider, with no suspension, springs, or shock absorbers. Its boiler plate armor was only half an inch thick, and shell fragments often found their way through the cracks where the metal sheets were riveted together. In the early models the fuel tank was at the front of the hull. If it was punctured, flaming fuel ran down into the crew compartment. If the tank nosed down into a shell hole, the gravity flow system didn't work and the engine stopped.

With its 105 horsepower engine, Mother crept along at about four miles an hour. That seemed sufficient, the same speed as a marching infantryman. But then it was decided that something faster and more nimble was needed to cut off fleeing enemy forces. What resulted was the Whippet, a seventeen-ton tank with four machine guns and capable of moving at eight miles an hour.

It is tempting to be critical of the military men and politicians who failed to see the need for the tank sooner. If it had been available to restore mobility to the battlefield, the war almost certainly would have been shorter and millions of lives might have been saved. But considering that it now takes about a decade to design, test, build, and field a new tank, it is almost incredible how rapidly, once the need had been acknowledged, a farm vehicle was transformed into a military weapon, crews were trained, tactics were devised, and the new weapon became a formidable force on the battlefield.

The first tank moved on its own power on September 8, 1915. On February 11, 1916, the British War Office ordered the first hundred production models. By early fall forty-nine tanks had been delivered to British forces in France, and thirty-six of them took part in an attack at Flers in the Battle of the Somme on September 15—one year and one week from prototype to battlefield. A Royal Flying Service observer looked down and radioed: "A tank is walking up the high street of Flers with the British Army cheering behind it." Overall the performance of the tanks was less than spectacular: Only eleven of them even got through no-man's-land into the enemy positions. But the British commander was so impressed by the potential of the new weapon that, three days after the battle, he demanded the immediate production of a thousand tanks of an improved design.

While the British awaited the new machines, available tanks were used ineffectively in three battles in the spring and summer of 1917. The British would have been well advised to have kept their tanks hidden, trained their crews, and then used the new weapon as a surprise in a major, war-winning offensive. That is exactly what the French had begged them to do. Fortunately for the Allies, the Germans, despite the preview of this new weapon, failed to develop more than a few prototype tanks of their own.

Instead, the Germans turned their attention to antitank weapons. The first was a special round, known as the K bullet, made with a tungsten carbide core and capable of penetrating the boiler plate armor of the enemy tanks when fired from the standard Mauser rifle. When the Allies improved their armor, the Germans introduced the T rifle, a beefed-up version of the Mauser so heavy it had to be fired from a tripod, and it became the most effective infantry antitank weapon of the war. For years after the war this rifle, capable of dropping an elephant with a single shot, was a great favorite with big-game hunters.

The Germans also built special antitank forts with large field guns, mortars, and specially trained men.

None of these innovations was enough to stop a determined tank assault. It was thus possible for the British to achieve a major breakthrough when they first used tanks properly in a combined arms attack involving infantry, artillery, and cavalry at Cambrai on November 20, 1917. One key decision was to forgo the lengthy, massive artillery barrage that normally preceded an infantry attack. This gave the attackers the advantage of surprise, and it avoided pocking with shell holes the terrain over which the tanks would have to travel. In many places the battlefield had been so churned by artillery shells that frontline soldiers could be supplied only by use of pack animals. In attacks across such terrain, tanks threw tracks, tipped over, or simply became mired in the mud.

At Cambrai the tanks moved forward in groups of three. Fastened on top, they carried great bundles of brushwood, tightly bound by chains and weighing about a ton and a half. These bundles were called fascines, a word derived from the Latin for a bundle of sticks, the same Latin word later used by the Fascists to name their movement. Following a tactic devised by Fuller, the first tank crushed the wire, turned left, and raked the first enemy trench with machine-gun fire. The second tank dropped its fascine to bridge the twelve- to fifteen-foot trench, crossed, and turned left to fire on the troops in the support trench. The third tank deposited its fascine in the second trench and led the way toward the objective. The infantry ran forward through the holes in the wire to seize the trenches before the enemy could recover.

The attack at Cambrai was proposed by Fuller as a demonstration tank raid. But the brass turned it into a full-scale attack, and that was a mistake. When the initial assault ran out of steam, there was no reserve to keep things moving. Within a few days the Germans were able to bring up their reserves and retake most of the lost territory.

Tanks were used more intelligently as part of a combined arms force in the Battle of Amiens, which opened in the predawn mist at 4:20 A.M. on August 8, 1918. Moving forward behind a sudden rolling barrage by 2,000 guns, 324 heavy tanks and 96 Whippets rumbled toward the German lines. Once again, a lack of reserves limited the Allied gains. The 42 tanks held in reserve were barely sufficient to replace losses from enemy action and especially from mechanical breakdown. There were no extra tank battalions ready to exploit the spectacular early breakthrough, and by the end of the first day the offensive had petered out. Even so, the battle was a disaster for the Germans—the most decisive of the war. General Erich Ludendorff, the enemy commander, described August 8 as the "black day of the German Army." Negotiations to end the conflict were opened, and the armistice was declared three months later.

The French, drawing the same lessons from their experience of trench warfare as the British, developed two large tanks but then agreed to concentrate on a two-man tank—basically a wire cutter and moving machine-gun nest—while the British produced the bigger machines.

The Americans, who did not enter the war until April 1917, saw combat with three battalions of British and French tanks. The tank was still so new that when ten Renaults were acquired to begin training American crews in March 1918, only one of those present when the vehicles arrived at the training site had ever even seen a tank before. He was George Patton, who entered the war as a captain and quickly rose to the rank of colonel and command of a tank brigade. The tank force that emerged from this training suffered heavy casualties and played only a negligible part in the outcome of the war. But if the war had continued into 1919, the influx of American-built tanks would have been a significant factor.

Late in 1917 the French sent a Renault light tank and the metric drawings to the United States. But after the drawings had been translated into inches, they were found to be incomplete and inaccurate. So the Americans took the Renault apart, measured all the parts, and prepared new drawings. They also made a number of modifications, including use of a different engine. In short, they thoroughly Americanized the French design.

The French Renault and the American Six-Ton based on it were the first mass-produced turreted tanks—the first, in other words, to have the look of a modern tank. The tank was very small by modern standards, a little over thirteen feet long and with a crew of only two. The driver sat deep down in the hull while the tank commander sat in a web seat in a turret. Using his feet for leverage, he could swivel the turret manually in a full circle. He served as his own loader and gunner, firing either a 37 mm cannon or a .30 caliber machine gun. A thirty-nine-horsepower engine gave the tank a speed of six miles an hour, but it could go less than thirty miles before stopping to refuel—if it got that far before being forced to stop for repairs. Unlike the big British tank, the Six-Ton had a suspension system, and that made it somewhat comfortable for the crew.

Early in 1918 the U.S. Army placed an order for 4,440 Six-Ton tanks (which actually weighed eight tons) at a fixed price of $11,500 apiece from three contractors: the Van Dorn Iron Works, the Maxwell Motor Company, and the C. L. Best Tractor Company. In October the first tank was delivered. When the war ended in November, 64 tanks had been completed, and 10 had actually arrived in France, although none had been used in combat. By the end of December, 209 tanks had been finished and 289 more were being assembled. At that rate, the American tank force would have made a sizable contribution to the planned spring offensive of 1919.

The United States also built 100 British-designed tanks known as the Mark VIII or the Allied. They were very similar to the original British Mother, but bigger. They weighed 43.5 tons, carried a crew of eleven, and were distinguished by a small commander's cupola, an American innovation. Built by

The British called their first operational tank Big Willie or Mother. These early tanks scored impressive victories and helped bring an end to World War I. Mother was a thirty-four-ton monster carrying a crew of eight, with cannons on each side in turretlike protrusions. The large wheels at the rear helped the gearsman and two brakemen to steer the machine. (Icks Collection, Patton Museum)

The Americans built a hundred Mark VIII tanks for the 1919 campaign, but the war ended before they entered combat. Although patterned on the British tank, they were larger, weighing 43.5 tons and carrying a crew of eleven men. This well-preserved specimen is on display at the U.S. Army Ordnance Museum of Aberdeen Proving Ground, Maryland. (Photo by the author)

The American Six-Ton tank, shown here demolishing a sizable tree at Fort Meade, Maryland, in the early 1920s, was an Americanized version of a two-man mobile machine-gun nest fielded by the French in World War I. The American tanks did not arrive in time to enter combat. (U.S. Army photo courtesy of Patton Museum)

ON THE OPPOSITE PAGE, TOP TO BOTTOM:

J. Walter Christie's innovative designs were copied by the Soviet Union and Great Britain but neglected in the United States. Here Christie, standing, confers with his son in 1931 or 1932. (U.S. Army photo courtesy of *Armor* magazine)

With its tracks removed and stored on racks above the wheels, the Christie was capable of speeds up to seventy miles an hour. Here a Christie performs a demonstration at Aberdeen Proving Ground in 1931. (U.S. Ordanance Museum)

Moving cross-country on its tracks, the Christie was capable of traveling forty-two miles an hour. A later model was powered by an aircraft engine and could hit more than a hundred miles an hour. Christie proposed fitting it with wings to hopscotch across the battlefield. (U.S. Army photo courtesy of *Armor* magazine)

Desperately short of tanks and money during the 1920s and 1930s, the Army modified commercial trucks to serve as armored cars or scout cars and practiced armored tactics later used in World War II. (U.S. Army photo courtesy of *Armor* magazine)

Tanks of the Fourth Armored Division's Thirty-seventh Tank Battalion, led by Lieutenant Colonel Creighton W. Abrams, gather on a snowy hillside outside Bastogne on January 14, 1945, three weeks after the unit had freed American forces trapped in the Belgian village. (U.S. Army Signal Corps photo)

American soldiers inspect a German Panther V tank abandoned after a shell became jammed in the breech of the gun near Grandmenil, Belgium, in January 1945. The Panther, fielded in 1943, was the best tank to see service in the latter part of World War II. (U.S. Army photo)

U.S. GIs take a ride on a captured German Tiger tank after they had put it back in operating condition in December 1944. (U.S. Army Signal Corps photo)

The American Sherman tank, produced in enormous numbers, was easy to maintain and operate, but it was outgunned by the Germans. Here a row of Shermans burn after being knocked off by a German 88 mm gun during Operation Cobra in France. (U.S. Army photo courtesy of *Armor* magazine)

The Porsche Tiger, also known as the Elefant or Ferdinand, carried a formidable 88 mm gun when it was introduced by the Germans at the time of the Battle of Kursk in 1943. But it lacked a machine gun, and Russian soldiers soon learned how to isolate and destroy the new monsters. This captured tank is on display at the U.S. Army Ordnance Museum at Aberdeen Proving Ground. (Photo by the author)

The life of a tanker is an endless round of hard work. Here, during World War II, Red Army soldiers rearm their T-34, the best tank of the early years of World War II and an unpleasant surprise to the Germans. The T-34 design relied heavily on technology developed by J. Walter Christie, the American whose work was largely ignored in his own country. (Icks Collection, Patton Museum)

the Ordnance Department at the Rock Island Arsenal, they cost thirty-five thousand dollars apiece and were intended for the 1919 campaign.

The United States continued tank production through 1919, using up the components on hand. In all, 950 tanks were produced. They were to be the only tanks produced for the U.S. Army, except for a few experimental models, between 1919 and 1936.

Whatever lessons might have been derived from the experiences of the European battlefield about the uses for this new weapon were not only forgotten by the U.S. Army but deliberately and forcefully put out of mind in the period between the wars. Except for a few farsighted officers, both infantrymen and cavalrymen saw the tank as a threat to their budgets and their traditional military roles and treated it as such.

In 1920 the separate Tank Corps was abolished by act of Congress, and tanks were parceled out to infantry units scattered from the East Coast to Hawaii. The 1921 budget provided only seventy-nine thousand dollars for use by tank companies, not even enough to buy gasoline for proper training. This fitted right in with the thinking of much of the brass. When a proposal was made to experiment with a separate mechanized force, Major General Stephen O. Fuqua, the chief of infantry, denounced the plan as being "as unsound as was the attempt by the Air Corps to separate itself from the rest of the Army." Fuqua set out his position in uncompromising terms: "The tank is a weapon and as such it is an auxiliary to the infantryman, as is every other arm or weapon that exists."

The infantry, for the most part, thought all that was needed was a tank capable of slogging along at the walking pace of a rifleman. In one early demonstration an officer led the tank attack on foot with colored signal flags. The few officers who spoke out in favor of new, high-speed, forms of armored warfare put their careers at risk. Two young lieutenant colonels who found themselves in this position were Patton and Dwight D. Eisenhower, battalion commanders in the postwar Tank

Corps. When the separate tank force was abolished, they returned to their original services, Patton to the cavalry and Eisenhower to the infantry. Though Patton was to become the dominant American armor commander in World War II, he played little part in cavalry mechanization between the wars. When Eisenhower, still fascinated by the possibilities offered by armored warfare, wrote an article espousing what seemed to his superiors to be revolutionary ideas, he was told that his thoughts were both wrong and dangerous and that from then on he was "not to publish anything incompatible with sound infantry doctrine."

If the Army had been more receptive to new ideas, it could have developed a superior tank force. During the entire period between the wars the Army carried on a tortured courtship with J. Walter Christie, the irascible genius whose ideas in tank design were so far advanced that the stuffy Army bureaucracy simply couldn't keep up. An early-day race car driver who competed against Louis Chevrolet and Barney Oldfield, Christie developed and built his first tank on his own in 1919, but with the war just ended, no one was interested.

By 1927 he had converted his early model into a remarkably advanced fighting machine. It had a low-slung chassis, weighed ten tons and mounted a 57 mm cannon and a .30 caliber machine gun in a round pillbox-shaped turret. Most intriguing, it displayed for the first time the Christie suspension, a scheme which provided a separate suspension for each road wheel and permitted switching between tracked and wheeled operation. With the tracks it could hit better than 42 miles an hour cross-country. Running on a roadway with wheels, it could do 70 miles an hour. That same year George Souders had to average only 97.54 miles an hour in his Duesenberg to win the Indianapolis 500. A few years later Christie turned out a prototype that, he claimed, could do 120 miles an hour. He proposed fitting it with wings so it could hopscotch across the battlefield.

Christie sadly became a pawn in the maneuvering for position among the ordnance department, the infantry, and the cavalry. When the infantry favored a Christie design, ordnance found fault because it had been developed outside its system. When the cavalry showed interest, the infantry told it to stick to its horses. The other part of Christie's problem was Christie and his prickly disposition. He used the press, political connections, and spectacular demonstrations without restraint. In one instance he sealed his tank, added two propellers, and showed it off by having it swim the Hudson River and then climb the Palisades above the Jersey shore. But he was so full of his new ideas that he had little patience with such mundane matters as reliability, on-time delivery, and cost.

He told one interviewer: "All I want the Army authorities to do is say: 'Give him the money and let's see what sort of machine he can turn out.' I won't let them change a thing on it. If they try to, I'll walk out. I won't let them tinker with it."

The result of Christie's off-again, on-again romance with the Army was that although the United States had troops test experimental models, it never did put a Christie tank into production. But the Russians and the British bought prototypes and used them as the basis for highly successful combat vehicles. One theory about why the British and the Russians were able to turn Christie's designs into excellent fighting vehicles is that, unlike the Americans, they got the eccentric inventor's technology but didn't have to deal with the man himself. The British got their prototype in 1936, after Christie, in one of his defiant gestures, parked a tank the United States had rejected in the courtyard of the State, War, and Navy Building (now the Old Executive Office Building) next door to the White House. When the British showed interest, Christie reclaimed the tank, took it apart, and shipped it to England. To avoid export controls, he labeled the chassis "a farm tractor" and the accompanying containers "grapefruit."

With the infantry's death grip on the tank, the only American experimentation with high-speed mechanized warfare was carried out by cavalry units equipped with armored cars with wheels in front and tracks in the rear—half-tracks—plus a few experimental Christies. Small batches of armored cars were built during the 1920s and 1930s, either at the Rock Island Arsenal in Illinois or under its direction. Most were basically four- or six-wheeled commercial trucks protected by sheets of armor and each topped by a turret carrying a 37 mm cannon or a .50 caliber machine gun. Manufacturers included the White Motor Company, Marmon-Herrington, Joseph Cunningham Son & Company, Studebaker, Pontiac, International Harvester, and even LaSalle, a luxury car division of GM.

The guiding genius of the effort to mechanize a reluctant Army was General Adna R. Chaffee. Although a cavalry officer and a horse lover, he had been impressed with the potentialities of the tank ever since, as a major, he saw one demonstrated in 1927. Seven years later, in 1934, his small combat car unit took on the horse cavalry in maneuvers at Fort Riley, Kansas, and confounded the mounted troops with a sixty-mile-an-hour end run. Even after this spectacular demonstration Chaffee was unable to gain approval for the creation of a separate armored force, not because he had failed to impress the horsemen but because, in the tight budget days of the Depression, the cavalry would have to have given up some of its horse units to pay for armored units.

It was not until the German invasion of Poland in September 1939 and the first demonstration of the blitzkrieg, or lightning war, that the U.S. Army set about creating an armored division. Even then there was more squabbling than action as the infantry and cavalry fought over which branch would control the new division. Finally, in the spring of 1940, two events galvanized the Army and forced action.

One of these events was the German attack on the Low Countries and France on May 10. In little more than a month the German panzer divisions forced the surrender of France and the evacuation of the British Army from Dunkirk. The other event, now barely a footnote in the history books, may have had even more impact on the thinking of Army leaders. That was a major mock battle conducted, at the same time as the actual blitzkrieg, in the Sabine River district of Louisiana. The maneuvers became one of the great turning points in Army doctrine and equipment.

For purposes of the maneuvers Chaffee beefed up a brigade of combat cars with other units to represent a full armored division. The performance of this makeshift division was so impressive that on July 10 the U.S. Armored Force was created and plans were made to form at least two armored divisions. This was of only marginal legality because the law passed in 1920 still assigned all tanks to the infantry. To squeeze around this restriction without risking a request to Congress for a change in the law, the Army resorted to the fiction that the new armored force was being created for the purposes of a "service test."

Chaffee is remembered as the father of the U.S. Armored Force although he died in 1941, before he had the opportunity to lead his force in combat. Major General Robert W. Grow, who worked with him in the thirties and then commanded an armored division in Europe in World War II, rated Chaffee, "the finest tactician that I ever knew," with Patton second.

The armored force created in 1940 looked much more formidable on paper than in the field. The entire U.S. Army could muster only 464 tanks—roughly the number being destroyed daily on the battlefields of Europe. A week after the force was created, the Army contracted with Chrysler to build an arsenal in Detroit and turn out 10 tanks a day at a price of thirty thousand dollars. But almost immediately reports of the fighting in Poland and France convinced the Army it needed a tank with at least a 75 mm cannon rather than the 37 mm gun then in use. Within two weeks of the contract award, the Army was back with a rudimentary sketch showing how the tank should be modified by moving the turret to one side and sticking a bigger cannon on the side of the hull. Despite the changes, Chrysler completed the arsenal and, in April 1941, rolled out the first production M-3 tank, known as the General Lee by the Americans and, in slightly modified form, as the General Grant by the British. By the time production of that model ended in December 1942, 5,628 of the tanks had been produced.

While the United States dithered through two decades, other countries—especially the two big losers in World War I, the Germans and the Russians, moved ahead in both technology and war-fighting doctrine. Much of the theoretical work on the use of tanks in warfare was done by General Fuller and Captain Basil Liddell Hart in England, but the British didn't form their first armored division until 1938. It was the Russians and the Germans who converted theory into hardware and tactics. In Germany General Heinz Guderian insisted on the creation of special panzer units to concentrate the striking power of the tanks. He assumed command of the Second Panzer Division in 1935, and by 1939 the Nazis had six tank divisions. Many of the tanks were to prove too lightly armored and undergunned, and the Germans struggled throughout the war to improve their tank designs. The French actually had more tanks than the Germans, but most of them were scattered among infantry units rather than concentrated in hard-hitting tank divisions.

For a number of years Germany had evaded the restrictions of the World War I peace treaty by testing its equipment and tactics secretly in the Soviet Union in cooperation with the Russians. That cooperation with a potential enemy ended after Adolf Hitler, always suspicious of the Bolsheviks, took power. Up to the time of the Spanish Civil War, in the mid-1930s, when Germany and the Soviet Union took opposite sides and tested doctrine and equipment against each other, both countries were headed in the same direction, toward development of what came to be known as the blitzkrieg concept. Moscow's commitment to tank warfare was especially vigorous.

While the gestation time of a new tank is now considered about ten years, it took the Soviet engineers only five months to adapt the Christie design from the two prototypes they had received in 1930 and to begin production. These were the first of tens of thousands of Soviet tanks based on the Christie design. Delivery of new lightly armored fast tanks, capable of running on either tracks or their road wheels, began on May 23, 1931. The tank production program was part of the first Five-Year Plan, announced in 1928. At the time the Soviets had about a hundred tanks. By 1933 they had produced seven thousand—enough to permit both infantry and armor units to experiment in their use.

But the Russians made a grave mistake in the years immediately preceding World War II. The Red Army generals drew a faulty conclusion from the limited experience in Spain, where both infantry and armor encountered serious trouble when the tanks ran ahead of the foot soldiers. This caused the Soviets to abandon the work they had been doing on the development of high-speed armor units, a change that was rapidly but painfully reversed after the German attack in 1941. But the experience in Spain also caused the Russians to make a decision that may well have saved their country. They immediately set about designing a more heavily armed tank with tougher armor. The result was the T-34—not a perfect tank by any means but certainly the best in the early years of World War II.

The first T-34 was delivered in June 1940, and although the world was not to recognize the fact until much later, it clearly established the Soviet Union as the world's leader in tank development. The T-34 derived directly from the Christie design but also benefited from a number of Soviet innovations. While the U.S. and other armies did not abandon their dangerous, fuel-hungry gasoline engines until well after the war, the T-34 had a new 500 horsepower diesel power plant that gave it a top speed of 34 miles an hour and a range of 188 miles. Projectiles sped from the muzzle of its 76 mm long-barrel cannon at 2,200 feet a second—almost exactly double the muzzle velocity of the 75 mm cannon on the German Mark IV. The high-powered gun, together with a completely new turret design and new bulletproof armor, meant that in almost any battlefield situation the T-34 could pierce the armor of a German tank while shaking off the shells fired at it.

The Nazis, buoyed by the success of their blitzkrieg attacks on Poland and France, crossed the Soviet border in June 1941 with supreme confidence. In the first few weeks of the war that confidence seemed justified. But German intelligence was faulty on two counts. The Wehrmacht generals did not realize that the Soviet force numbered 21,000 to 24,000 tanks, compared with the 3,350 with which the Germans began their invasion. That failure at tank counting might not have been fatal because the Soviet tank force was made up of a hodgepodge of models, many of them poorly armed and poorly protected, but German intelligence also missed something more important: the technically superior T-34.

Soon the surprised Germans were speaking of the "tank terror" even though there were still relatively few T-34s. In the year before the invasion Soviet factories turned out only 1,225 of the T-34s, a hopelessly small number measured against wartime losses. Even that level of production was endangered as the Germans ran rampant over much of the industrialized western portion of the Soviet Union. Kharkov, at whose locomotive works the new diesel engines were developed, was taken. The tank plant at Leningrad, although still in Russian hands, came within artillery range. The entire Leningrad plant was dismantled and sent east of the Ural mountain range, along with much of the machinery from other plants. Two major tank facilities were formed. A complex known as Uralmashzavod was set up at Nizhniy Tagil and began to build T-34s. Work at Chelyabinsk, in a complex dubbed Tankograd, was devoted to production of KV tanks and engines. The KV, another surprise, was a fifty-ton heavy tank that shrugged off German projectiles and kept on coming.

Eventually forty-two factories concentrated on turning out just these two types of tank. They required some innovative production techniques such as electric welding, but they were, for the most part, simple to build and so easy to operate and maintain as to be virtually soldierproof. The peak rate of about thirty thousand tanks a year—more than eighty tanks a day—

was about the same level reached by American tank factories.

In their first winter in Russia the Germans began to realize how badly they had underestimated their foe. The Germans reached the very suburbs of Moscow before they ran out of steam. Then, on December 6, the counterattack came. The Nazis suddenly encountered more than a hundred divisions whose existence they had not suspected. Through a long, bitter winter they held positions deep inside the Soviet Union, but the hopes of a quick victory were gone.

With the coming of spring in 1942 the Germans were again on the offensive, cutting deep to the south, overrunning the Crimea, which juts out into the Black Sea, reaching the suburbs of Stalingrad on the mighty Volga River, and lunging for the oil of the Caucasus. Here again the Germans and their allies faced a devastating winter offensive when a million and a half of Stalin's troops, by then receiving twelve hundred new tanks a month, attacked at dawn on November 19, 1942—in a blizzard.

The Germans could have fought their way out of the trap at Stalingrad, but Hitler gave the insane order to fight to the last man and the last bullet. On February 2, 1943, the remnants of a 285,000-man army, having fired their last bullets, surrendered. There were only 91,000 Germans left to hobble off into captivity, and of that number, only 5,000 lived to return to the fatherland. Church bells tolled a dirge, and a four-day period of mourning was observed throughout the Third Reich when news of the end of the battle was received.

Defeat of the Nazi Army at Stalingrad came just on the heels of another staggering loss. For months the British and, later, the Americans on one side and the Germans and Italians on the other had been playing out a great back-and-forth drama. The vast reaches of the North African desert, like the broad surface of the ocean, provided the stage for a display of almost pure tank warfare. Instead of standing toe to toe and slugging it out, commanders borrowed tactics directly from war at sea. Time after time, armored units made wide, high-speed sweeps through the desert, seeking to take the enemy from the flank. But then, on October 23, 1942, the British launched an offensive at El Alamein in the Egyptian desert that culminated in the total defeat of Field Marshal Erwin Rommel's Afrika Corps. Hitler lost both his control of the southern shore of the Mediterranean and his chance to seize Egypt and the Suez Canal.

Together these two major defeats constituted one of the great turning points of the war. From the winter of 1942–43 onward the Germans, even when they seized the offensive in one theater or another, were clearly on the defensive. They still controlled the heart of Europe, from the Atlantic to deep inside the Soviet Union. The question no longer was whether they could expand their area of control but how much of the vast conquered territory they would be able to retain.

In the spring of 1943 the answer to that question was not nearly so apparent as it seems now in retrospect. The battlefield situation near the city of Kursk offered the opportunity for a test of which way the future would go. The battle fought there in the summer of 1943 is treated in a paragraph or two in most Western accounts of World War II. But it deserves more attention, especially in any consideration of the development of tank warfare. It ranks with Alexander's victory at Arbela and Napoleon's defeat at Waterloo as one of the world's few great pivotal conflicts, determining the outcome of the war and shaping the world's future. And it was history's greatest tank battle.

Kursk, which had a prewar population of 120,000, lies in an area of grainfields and orchards 300 miles south of Moscow, about halfway to the Black Sea resorts so popular with the Russians in peacetime. In the summer of 1943 Kursk was at the center of a semicircle that extended the Russian lines about 75 miles into German-held territory. Although the bulge was about 250 miles long, its base was less than 100 miles across. Political leaders and military commanders on both sides quickly recognized this bulge as a great danger and a great opportunity.

Both sides began making plans for the Battle of Kursk. This was not a battle like Gettysburg in the American Civil War where the two armies blundered into each other and fought. At Kursk both sides knew the location and, roughly, the time of the battle, almost like two heavyweight contenders who sign on for a championship fight at a specific time and place. We can see them moving almost in lockstep toward the fateful engagement.

The Germans prepared to attack; the Soviets prepared to defend themselves and then to go on the offensive. The German goal was to slash across the base of the semicircle from both north and south and join up in the vicinity of Kursk. If they could do this, they would capture or kill thousands of Russian soldiers and seize a huge arsenal of war matériel. While a victory at Kursk held the possibility for a new lunge at Moscow, a more realistic hope was that it would straighten out the front and checkmate a Soviet offensive, at least for the remainder of the year.

In Moscow, Joseph Stalin's war council, the Stavka, pondered the situation. An offensive was a possibility. But the Russian troops were tired and in need of supplies and reinforcements. The decision to accept the defensive role was the logical one. Stalin gave his approval on April 12, three days before Hitler issued his order for the battle. Soviet Marshal Georgi Zhukov later described the decision: "We deemed it feasible to counter the anticipated offensive with a powerful defense, to bleed the enemy white, and then to strike with a counteroffensive to destroy him completely. . . . Our defense plan was clearly not forced on us, but was deliberately decided upon." This strategy of preparing the battlefield for a strong defense as the preliminary to moving over to a powerful offense has become a hallmark of Soviet military thinking, emerging repeatedly in the Arab-Israeli wars, although with less satisfactory results for the Soviets' Arab clients.

While an attack in the spring, as soon as the ground firmed up after the thaw, might have succeeded, Hitler repeatedly postponed Operation Citadel, as the Germans named it. Significantly, the reason for the delay was the existence of the superior Russian tanks. Guderian, named by Hitler as inspector general of the armored forces that summer, was so concerned about the quality and numbers of the enemy's tanks that he actually recommended that Germany go on the defensive and sit out the year on the eastern front while its factories produced new tanks.

But such a respite wasn't politically feasible even if the Russians had been willing to give the enemy time to catch his breath. The Germans would always have had difficulty matching the Soviet tank force. Under Stalin's orders, Soviet factories were engaged in a single-minded effort to turn out T-34 and KV tanks. In contrast, the German tank effort was a shambles. While the tanks that had already been demonstrated to be inferior on the battlefield continued to be produced in small numbers, work was under way on competing versions of two new main battle tanks plus a light tank. Hitler's fleeting enthusiasms didn't help. One day he ordered emphasis on tank production. Then it was self-propelled guns. Then it was both at the same time. He used his designers' talents on hundred-ton tanks that never reached the battlefield and even had them working at one point on a thousand-ton "land monitor."

The start of the battle was delayed from week to week and then from day to day as the Wehrmacht waited for the new tanks, coming with painful slowness from the Krupp, Henschel, and MAN factories. When the battle began on July 5, 1943, there were three new tanks: the medium-weight Panther, the heavier Henschel Tiger, and the monstrous Porsche—really an 88 mm gun mounted on a tank chassis. Troops nicknamed it the Elephant or, in honor of Dr. Porsche, the Ferdinand.

While the Germans delayed, Zhukov served as overseer of a defensive effort that strains the imagination. To move supplies into the area, an entirely new rail line was laid. Then troops, aided by three hundred thousand civilians, were set to work digging. By the time of the battle they had dug more than six thousand miles of trenches and set up thousands of strongpoints with from three to twelve antitank guns backed up by mortars and machine guns.

The raw numbers of men and weapons involved underscore the scale of this conflict. The Germans moved toward the offensive with 900,000 men, 10,000 artillery pieces, 2,700 tanks and assault guns, and 2,500 airplanes. It was the largest offensive force ever concentrated on such a short front. The Soviets dug in with 1,337,000 men, 20,220 artillery pieces, 3,306 tanks and assault guns, and 2,650 planes. Each side committed many more men to this one battle than the manpower of today's entire U.S. Army.

The German preparations were accompanied by a massive propaganda campaign designed to stimulate the troops to a superhuman effort for victory. But if the soldiers could have eavesdropped on their leaders, they would have been dismayed. Even Hitler had second thoughts. At one meeting to discuss the offensive, he confessed: "Whenever I think of this attack, my stomach turns over."

The Russian soldiers watched in awe as the new German tanks moved forward. The armor on the Panthers and Tigers was a match for that on the Soviet tanks, and the 88 mm gun—designed as an antiaircraft weapon capable of hurling explosive shells five miles into the sky—was more powerful than the Red Army's. The monstrous Ferdinand was particularly fearsome as it blasted away tanks, strongpoints, anything that obstructed its progress. But then the word began to spread among the Russian soldiers: These new machines on which the Nazis had pinned their hopes for victory were vulnerable, each in its own way.

Unaccountably the brilliant Dr. Porsche—or at least someone with a say over the design—had sent the Ferdinand into battle without a machine gun. As soon as the monster outran its infantry support or became separated from friendly tanks, it was helpless against anyone it could not blast with its one big gun. The Russian soldiers would swarm over it like cavemen attacking a prehistoric beast, tossing grenades through the hatches or setting it afire with bottles of gasoline.

The other two new German tanks carried machine guns, but each also had vulnerabilities that were quickly identified and exploited. The Tiger could not move and turn its turret at the same time. And the medium-weight Panther, which eventually evolved into one of the best tanks of the era, went into battle at Kursk straight from the production line, without adequate testing. The result was that the new tanks were plagued by mechanical defects—and a breakdown on the battlefield means death.

The Battle of Kursk was notable not only for the size of the forces involved but for the ferocity of the combat. In many areas the fighting broke down into fierce hand-to-hand struggle. Battalions and companies melted away to tiny groups of survivors. Tank formations disintegrated, leaving the field littered with burning hulks. The remaining tanks milled about in the dust, gunsmoke, and haze from burning cornfields, ramming each other when all else failed.

Early on July 12—the eighth day—the Battle of Kursk came to a climax near the village of Prokhorovka. The Soviet commander watched from a hillside above the town as his force of about 850 T-34s and self-propelled guns moved forward for a counteroffensive. Suddenly from the opposite direction came a German force of almost 700 tanks, including 100 Tigers. They collided head-on in what is known in military terminology as a meeting engagement, with neither able to take up a more desirable defensive position. According to standard doctrine, the goal in a meeting engagement is to gain quick superiority with a hail of bullets. But the forces that day were so evenly matched that neither could gain the edge that might have led to quick victory.

What happened next is described in the *Soviet Official History:*

The battlefield seemed too small for the hundreds of armored machines. Groups of tanks moved over the steppe, taking cover behind the isolated groves and orchards. The detonations of the guns merged into a continuous menacing growl.

The tanks of the Fifth Guards Tank Army cut into the Nazi deployment at full speed. This attack was so fast that the enemy did not have time to prepare to meet it, and the leading ranks of the Soviet tanks passed right through the enemy's entire first echelon, destroying his ability to control his leading units and subunits. The Tigers, deprived in close combat of the advantages which their powerful gun and thick armor conferred, were successfully shot up by T-34s at close range. The immense number of tanks was mixed up all over the battlefield, and there was neither time nor space to disengage and reform [*sic*] the ranks. Shells fired at short range penetrated both the front and side armor of the tanks. While this was going on there were frequent explosions as ammunition blew up. Whole tank turrets, blown off by the explosions, were thrown dozens of yards away from the twisted machines.

At the same time fierce dogfights were going on in the air over the battlefield, with both the Nazi and Soviet air forces attempting to help the troops on the ground to win the battle. . . .

Soon the whole sky was overhung with heavy smoke from the fires. On the scorched black earth, smashed tanks were blazing like torches. It was hard to determine who was attacking and who defending.

The battle raged all day with each side losing more than three hundred tanks, and at the end it was the Russian commander who ordered a withdrawal, leaving the Germans in possession of the battlefield. But Prokhorovka was the last "victory" for the dreaded panzers.

German records captured by the Allies show that while Kursk did not present the drama of Stalingrad, with an entire army destroyed, Nazi losses in the battle that began at Kursk and in the following Soviet offensive were far greater: 907,000 men killed, missing, and severely wounded at Kursk, compared with 543,000 during the entire battle at Stalingrad. The Soviet Union has never revealed its casualties in the battle, but the intensity of the fighting makes it likely the losses were similar to those of the Germans. The number of tanks destroyed is hard to determine because tanks are routinely repaired and sent back into battle. Both sides probably lost one to two thousand tanks. For the Soviets, the losses were replaceable. For the Germans, they were not.

Although Hitler still dreamed of victory, his generals knew that the initiative had passed to the Soviets and that they would be fighting an increasingly desperate defensive war. At Kursk the Soviet Army ceased its defense of Moscow and began its inexorable march toward Berlin, a march that ended only with the capitulation of the Third Reich on May 7, 1945. In its impact on the map of Europe and the postwar world, the Battle of Kursk—whose outcome hinged on the capabilities of the opposing tank armies—ranks among the most important in history.

In the West in the summer of 1943 the Allies landed in Sicily and then moved up to confront the Germans in Italy. The buildup for the Normandy invasion was under way, but the attack across the Channel, on June 6, 1944, was still nearly a year in the future.

Once they had geared up, American factories turned out tanks by the thousands, reaching a peak of nearly thirty thousand in 1943. The M-4, or General Sherman, classified as a medium tank and carrying a crew of five, became the Allied workhorse of the war, with more than forty-eight thousand produced. There were almost as many variations on the basic Sherman as Heinz had pickles. Various models carried eleven different power plants. The basic gun was 75 mm, but Shermans were also seen with 105 mm howitzers and 76 mm and British 17-pounder guns. Many of the Shermans were adapted for special purposes. One example was the amphibious tank, a Sherman with a collapsible canvas screen that permitted it to float and "swim" ashore to deliver firepower to Normandy beaches early in the attack. There were also tanks with chains attached out front to flail the ground and explode mines, bulldozer tanks, bridging tanks, flamethrower tanks, and heavily armored assault tanks, all based on the same vehicle.

The Sherman was agile, remarkably reliable, and easy to maintain, and it was available in large numbers. But it was also notoriously underarmed and underarmored in comparison with the German tanks it faced.

The American—and British—obsession with numbers was based on faulty intelligence estimates that pegged the German tank force and production rate at twice what they were in fact. This was a grievous mistake, and it cost many lives. In hindsight, it is clear that the Western Allies would have been much better off to cut back on production long enough to improve the quality of their tanks.

Only seven days after the Normandy invasion the Allies received a deadly demonstration of the damage a superior tank, under the command of an experienced officer, can inflict. A British unit, spearhead of the Seventh Armored Division, moved rapidly through a small town south of Bayeux. In the woods nearby Obersturmführer Michael Wittmann watched from the turret of his Tiger. He made the daring decision to attack without waiting for help. His first shot knocked out the British tank at the head of the column. The second shell destroyed the last tank in line. Wittmann then raced down the road. His 88 mm cannon took out the tanks while his machine gunner cut up the more lightly armored half-tracks. Twice his tank was hit but not penetrated. In fewer than five minutes Wittmann had destroyed nineteen tanks, fourteen half-tracks, and fourteen Bren gun carriers and blunted the division's advance.

The American and British tankers soon learned to deal with the superior German tanks by outnumbering them, swarming around so that at least one of the attackers could shoot at the vulnerable sides or rear of the enemy. The Allies also benefited from total air superiority. Wittmann, who had knocked out 119 tanks on the eastern front and seemed invincible in tank-on-tank warfare, was killed by the largest carpet bombing of the

Normandy campaign about a month after his attack on the British column.

With control of the air and superior numbers on the ground, the Allies broke out of the Normandy beachhead, liberated Paris and much of France, and raced for the German border. Then, in late September, the supply system collapsed. For six weeks the tanks were halted for lack of fuel, giving the Germans time to prepare for one last thrust in the Battle of the Bulge. One officer recorded the frustration of Patton and Major General John S. Wood, commander of the Fourth Armored Division, which had led the American armored advance: "One evening just at dusk, I saw them standing alone, faced to the east, with tears in their eyes as they foresaw the awful waste of life—lives of our boys being sacrificed, unnecessarily so, by the lack of fuel for their armor."

One can only speculate what might have happened if Patton's forces had had a smaller number of superior tanks. There would have been fewer engines to be supplied with fuel and fewer guns to be provided with ammunition, but there would have been greater fighting power and he might have kept going. Would the war in Europe have ended in 1944 rather than in May 1945 and would the border between East and West—soon to become the iron curtain—have been drawn farther to the east, changing the course of postwar history?

When the war ended, the United States rapidly demobilized. That it would be involved in a major war in Korea within five years seemed unthinkable. When that war did start in 1950, one of the biggest shocks came as old Russian T-34 tanks rumbled down from the north and the Americans, with their closest tanks in Hawaii, had nothing to stop them. The T-34 should not have come as a surprise. In the short period of postwar euphoria, the Soviet Union had even given a couple of them to the United States, and they had been tested and analyzed at Aberdeen Proving Ground. But nothing was done to prepare the troops in the field to deal with this aging, though still formidable, weapon.

Although tanks were used in limited numbers in both Korea and Vietnam, neither war involved extensive use of armor in the way that it had been used in World War II. The attitude toward armor in Vietnam was epitomized by a battalion commander who clung to his small tank force because, without the tanks, he would have no way to tow disabled vehicles. The closest thing to a major armored operation by American forces in Southeast Asia was the attack on the North Vietnamese in Cambodia in the spring of 1970. During the fifties and sixties armored force soldiers found themselves in a kind of backwater while paratroopers and advocates of airborne warfare dominated Army thinking. Even a few armor officers conceded that perhaps the helicopter might replace the tank just as the tank had replaced the horse.

By 1972, with the Army's role in Vietnam virtually at an end, the scene was changing. Weary of the confusing conflict in the jungles against an enemy that broke all the rules, the Army turned with relief to its earlier focus on a more understandable and manageable kind of war in Europe—and that meant tanks.

3

"A Simple Tin Box"

BUILDING A NEW TANK was not just a high priority for the Army. It became the very highest priority. For that, the tankers have an infantryman to thank.

Work on the new tank should be seen as a central part of the Army's effort to rebuild itself after the long trauma of the Vietnam War. By 1972 it was virtually out of Southeast Asia. Its size—1.6 million in 1968—had been cut in half, and so had its budget. To complicate the situation, the Army had also been made the lead player in an unprecedented social experiment: maintaining a large peacetime military force made up entirely of volunteers.

Much of the Army's equipment was left behind in the war zone. What it did bring home was obsolescent, the result of the failure to keep up the pace of research and development during the war. A major effort to procure modern equipment was clearly needed, but the Army couldn't agree on what to buy.

All together there were proponents of at least nine major new weapons systems vying with one another for a big slice of a shrinking budget. It wasn't uncommon for bemused congressmen to hear that a tank was needed to kill a tank and then to hear another witness from the same Army testify that all the Soviet tanks could be knocked out by the latest expensive helicopter or a newfangled guided missile or some far-out technology still on the drawing boards. Top Army officers even acknowledged publicly that they were badly split, unable to speak with one voice.

Into this vacuum stepped an infantryman, Lieutenant General William E. DePuy, the assistant vice chief of staff. A brilliant, hard-driving officer who inspired fear as well as admiration, DePuy was for years one of the service's most influential behind-the-scenes operators.

Worried about dissension and the growing confusion on Capitol Hill, DePuy called together six generals representing the Army's main power bases: matériel command, combat development, research and development, logistics, operations, and aviation. For several days in early 1972 the generals quietly slipped away from the Pentagon and drove about a mile west on Route 50 to Arlington Hall Station, home of the Army Security Agency, a supersecret code-breaking outfit. There, in bugproof security that kept the discussions secret from foreign spies and, more important, from the rest of the Army, the generals bargained away nearly half the weapons that had been competing for top-priority dollars.

The result was a list of five weapons that everyone agreed to support. There were two helicopters, an infantry fighting vehicle, an air defense system, and a tank. Even though the panel was, if anything, weighted against armor, the highest priority went to the new tank. Despite all the talk of systems that could knock out Russian tanks, when pushed to a hard decision, the Army stuck with the tank as the best way to deal with other tanks.

The Big Five, as the Army dubbed its list of weapons, had the look of a public relations gimmick, and to some extent it was. But the agreement inspired by DePuy did force the Army to speak with one voice, and the weapons that evolved have had a lasting influence on its doctrine and battlefield tactics and strategy. In effect, the weapons decisions in the early 1970s have shaped the way the Army would fight in the 1980s or 1990s.

To head a task force to get started on the tank project, the Army chose Major General William R. Desobry, commander of Fort Knox and the Armor Center located there. He was alone in his office when the call came through from Washington one day in January 1972. It was a lonely feeling.

In his thirty-year career Desobry had never been involved in tank development. A tall, lean soldier who much preferred being out in the field with troops to sitting behind a desk, he had been an armor officer—a "user"—since the early days of World War II, when he went directly from an ROTC unit at Georgetown University to the Army. He was also one of the dwindling number of American officers who had been involved in the large-scale tank warfare of World War II. The Army is one of the nation's most youthful institutions. By 1972 most colonels and a growing number of generals were too young to have fought in the big war.

At the time of the Battle of the Bulge, the Germans' last great offensive in the winter of 1944–45, Desobry was a major commanding an almost surrounded tank unit at the Belgian town of Bastogne. He was wounded by a German shell and then captured when the American position was overrun.

The German siege of Bastogne was broken the day after Christmas 1944 by a tank battalion headed by a young lieutenant colonel named Creighton W. Abrams. Friends associated Desobry and Abrams with the famous battle at Bastogne and assumed they were friends. But Desobry was already a prisoner when Abrams arrived, and the two didn't meet for another twenty years. Abrams was still commander of U.S. forces in Vietnam when the task force was formed, but he was soon to become chief of staff of the Army and to play a key role in determining the kind of new tank the Army would build.

As Desobry set about work on his new assignment, his World War II experience weighed heavily on his mind. He was one of those who knew firsthand how badly outgunned the American tankers had been when they faced the Germans. He swore to himself that as far as he could influence the situation, the Army would not again make the mistake of sending its troops into combat with a deficient tank.

In addition to his battlefield experience, Desobry was a wily veteran of the bureaucratic wars. To the outsider the Army may look like a huge monolith. But to career officers it is a small community. They double-date as young lieutenants, remember the birthdays of their friends' children, and comfort one another after losses in combat. If two officers don't know each other personally, they almost certainly have mutual friends and know each other by reputation. Desobry used his knowledge of the Army bureaucracy and his network of friends to make sure he did not get tangled in red tape.

First, he asked for the assignment of Colonel Charles K. Heiden, whom he knew as an effective staff officer, as his executive. Heiden was stationed at Knox as representative of the Combat Development Command (CDC), whose job it was to develop new weapons for all branches of the Army, and he had already taken some of the preliminary steps needed to get started on a new tank.

The next move for Desobry was to have himself appointed deputy commanding general of the CDC for tank development. Under this arrangement he reported to Lieutenant General John ("Jack") Norton, one of his oldest and best friends. This cut through the bureaucratic underbrush and gave him direct access to the Pentagon.

Desobry and Heiden flew to Washington to begin staffing the task force. In the next few months they took that flight so often the Eastern Airlines manager in Louisville, grateful for the business, upgraded them to first class whenever there was room available.

One of the first names suggested as a member of the task force was Richard ("Dick") Lawrence, a lieutenant colonel and a West Pointer recently back from Vietnam, where he had commanded an armored unit attached to the Americal Division. One of the new breed of highly educated post–World War II officers, Lawrence held a doctorate from Ohio State in operations research. ("Operations research" is another term for "systems analysis," in which mathematical tools are used to solve problems involving large systems.)

Desobry did not know Lawrence. But it didn't take him long, through the grapevine, to learn that Lawrence would also be DePuy's unofficial representative on the team. The tank was shaping up as the Army's most important and most expensive weapon program, and DePuy wanted his own man in at the beginning. This could have set the stage for vicious infighting. Fortunately it didn't. Lawrence and Heiden earned Desobry's trust as his two key aides, with Heiden serving as executive officer and Lawrence in charge of integrating all the parts into a tank.

Clerical workers who already had security clearances were borrowed from Heiden's old office, and the team took over the third floor of one of the fort's stolid old red-brick buildings near where the base Burger King now stands.

Together Desobry and his two deputies knew everyone in the Army's relatively small and close-knit armor community. Within days the first of a stream of handpicked members of the task force arrived at Knox. If such a group had been assembled twenty years before, most of its members probably would have been tankers and nothing more. It is symptomatic of the changes in the Army and the American military generally during the years that Robert McNamara was defense secretary that of those who gathered at Knox in 1972, many of the tankers also had advanced degrees in such fields as systems analysis or computer science. They had quickly learned to play the whiz kids' own game. One complaint when they finished their work was that they could have used even more systems analysts.

Despite its importance, such a task force was not the sort to attract much attention to itself. With only thirty-three members, it was lost in the hugeness of the fort. Located near the Indiana border in north-central Kentucky about 30 miles south of Louisville, Fort Knox sprawls over more than 170 square miles, containing not only housing and training facilities for the soldiers but twenty-five tennis courts, two eighteen-hole golf courses, seven swimming pools, seven elementary schools, two junior highs, and a high school.

It is at Knox, named for Henry Knox, George Washington's chief of artillery, that young soldiers learn to be tankers and sergeants perfect their skills in advanced training. And it was to Knox that some of the first models of the M-1 were to be brought for testing.

The main body of the fort, with a daytime population of forty thousand, is built in the valley of the Ohio River. But off to the east the land rises quickly into steep, heavily forested hills, much like parts of Germany along the east-west border. Tanks and other armored vehicles clatter up and down the dirt and asphalt roads going to and from the gunnery ranges. The crack of high-velocity tank guns and the chatter of machine guns echo through the valleys as young soldiers prove themselves as tankers. There is little doubt that the rugged Kentucky terrain, which limits the ranges at which targets can be seen, exerted a subtle influence on the tank the United States eventually built.

Armor of sorts made its first appearance at Knox, established as a World War I artillery training center, in November 1931, when a caravan of 170 armored cars and transport vehicles, shepherded by seventeen motorcyclists, arrived after a four-day, 750-mile trek westward from Fort Eustis, Virginia, to take advantage of the larger training area in Kentucky. Four fifty-four-thousand-dollar Christie tanks made the trip by rail. Pictures taken at the time show a strong cavalry influence. The officers are dressed in olive drab shirts with black ties tucked in between the second and third buttons, khaki-colored riding breeches, knee-high boots, and broad-brimmed campaign hats. Armored car crewmen are seen in similar uniforms with helmets and goggles replacing the hats.

To soldiers, Fort Knox is synonymous with armor. It is more familiar to others as the site of the United States Bullion Depository, which houses most of the nation's hoard of pure gold bullion. Built in 1936 on a piece of land acquired from the Army by the Treasury Department, the fortresslike two-story depository squats just off Bullion Boulevard near one of the main entrances to the fort. Thousands pass it daily, but no visitors are permitted inside.

Beginning in 1940, as the United States created its first armored divisions and prepared to enter World War II, expansion of the fort was explosive. From 1940 to 1943 an average of 160 buildings a month were erected. Most of them were two-story barracks designed to hold a company of soldiers. The first of the three-story brick buildings that give the installation a look of permanence were also constructed at that time. As befits an armor center, old tanks adorn almost every lawn.

The task force formally came into being on January 20, 1972. But by the time its thirty-three members had arrived and settled down to work, it was already early February. They had a budget of $217,500 and just a little less than five months to decide what the Army needed in the way of a new main battle tank.

Desobry broke the group into three teams. The first, known as the matériel need team, focused on what future Soviet tanks might be like and the performance required to beat them any time in the next twenty years. The second, the components team, was responsible for compiling six catalogs of available technology covering fire control, secondary armament, engines and transmissions, primary armament, track and suspension, and add-on missile systems. The third, the systems integration team, had the responsibility for computer and cost studies and for bringing the task force's work together into a recommended Army tank program. This third team, headed by Lawrence, was heavy with systems analysts and computer specialists.

To guard the task force from the danger that its decisions would be made in an ivory tower environment, cut off from the muddy real-life world of Army tankers, Desobry took two precautions. First, he sent a three-page questionnaire throughout the armor force, asking every soldier, from private to general, for his opinion of the most important characteristics of a new tank.

He also took advantage of the Armor Center's depth of experience by setting up what the Army calls a murder board consisting of Brigadier General Homer S. ("Huck") Long, a veteran, no-nonsense tanker; three colonels; and a cadre of sergeants, none of them members of the task force. Desobry wanted this group—his devil's advocates—to help him by balancing the results of the computer studies and newfangled systems analysis with the hard-nosed judgments of experienced soldiers. Desobry found the advice of the murder board invaluable, especially in making subtle judgments about characteristics of the new tank. But the one major confrontation between Long's group and the armor whiz kids had a surprise ending, as we shall see.

The work of the task force was divided into three main categories. First, it would answer three basic questions about the tank. How much should it weigh? How large a crew was needed? What weapons should it carry?

Second, it would create the catalog of existing technology. After the experience with the MBT-70 and XM-803, Congress had made it very clear that whatever the Army recommended had to be relatively simple—no pushing into risky technological ventures. Nothing that was not already in successful use or had not been thoroughly proved in tests would be on the list (this rule was later violated).

Third, it would list the characteristics of the tank in order of priority. Was it more important, for example, for the tank to be able to hit an enemy target on the first shot or for the crew to survive an enemy hit?

The job of the task force was not to design a tank. Instead, it was to prepare the Army to tell the competing contractors what the tank would be expected to do. The component catalogs would give the contractors the widest possible range of choices in designing a tank and building prototypes. At one point the task force listed 128 feasible configurations, most of them involving various combinations of weapons. That was later trimmed down to 72 configurations—still giving the contractors plenty of freedom.

The message from Congress and the Pentagon was clear on one point: Each new tank should not cost more than about half a million dollars. The goal was not the best tank that could be built. The Army had tried that with the MBT-70, and it had never reached the field. Rather, the goal was to produce the best tank possible for a limited amount of money. It also had to be significantly better than the tanks already in service to justify the cost of a new machine.

It is easy to underestimate the difficulty of that challenge. Ever since the first tanks made their appearance on the battlefield in 1916, there has been a tendency on the part of the uninitiated to think of a tank as a relatively simple mechanism, a big tractor or bulldozer with some armor and some guns. Since it is simple, it should also be relatively cheap, especially when compared with a complex vehicle such as a helicopter or jet fighter. But a modern main battle tank represents a remarkably delicate series of compromises involving weight, degree of protection, types of guns, ammunition-carrying capacity, speed, range, agility, engine power, and survivability. Change one element, and you are likely to end up changing most of the others.

Major General John G. Willis, recently retired as director of vehicle procurement for the British Army, was often frustrated by the inability of his political masters to understand how very difficult it is to design and build a tank. He tells of his thoughts after one particularly trying session with the politicians: "The charge was leveled at us, the tank community . . . 'After all, the tank is a simple tin box.' I didn't respond because the charge came from high-level politicians but on reflection in my bath later that evening, I felt that what I should have said was:

" 'Yes, you're absolutely right that a tank is indeed a simple tin box. Unfortunately it is a simple tin box that must move across country. To move across country, it requires an engine of the highest possible power density you can get and is therefore putting out a lot of heat. What do you do if you wrap the engine in a box and therefore make your cooling problem even worse than it was before? You start putting thermal stresses on this engine that no engine should be subjected to.

" 'What is more, you then put a gearbox behind it. You ask of that gearbox that it not only give you a range of gears in forward and reverse but also act as a steering mechanism. Furthermore, you demand of that gearbox that the power you do not require for the outside track when you are turning is delivered to the inside track so you do not waste any power. You produce a gearbox the like of which has no civilian application whatsoever.

" 'You wish this vehicle to move across country at a reasonable speed and therefore have to supply it with a suspension and tracks which must be capable of withstanding the shocks of cross-country travel but not so heavy as to totally nullify the whole thing. This box also must carry fuel which is highly volatile. And so on and so forth. And you end up by putting in it human beings, without whose presence the vehicle would be a total nonevent, but who, of all of the elements within that weapons system, are probably the most vulnerable.

" 'So yes, the tank is a very simple tin box.'

"The trade-offs," Willis says, "are infinitely more difficult to achieve than in an aircraft. People say to me that perhaps weight doesn't mean very much in a tank. It is crucial . . . crucial!"

Weight was at the top of Desobry's list, and it was very much on the minds of the members of the task force. About three months before the group assembled, Heiden listed, on a sheet of yellow foolscap, the attributes he would like to see in a new tank. Number one was the problem of weight. He wanted the tank to be as light as possible, a goal he was to fight for even to the point of risking his career.

This did not mean a minitank. It would still be a sizable

monster, probably thirty-five to forty tons. But there was general agreement among American, German, Swedish, French, and, apparently, Russian tank designers that, with modern guns and missiles and with ammunition capable of cutting a hole through the hardest steel, no amount of the homogeneous rolled steel armor then in use would protect the tank and crew from a hit.

To most tank designers of the early seventies it appeared that armor plate had about reached its maximum usefulness. They were looking for something else to protect the tank and its crew: small size and low silhouette, high mobility, high acceleration, and a high horsepower-to-ton ratio, all contributing to make the tank a fleeting target. They assumed the crew members would use the terrain as their armor, dashing from one position to the next and exposing themselves as little as possible.

Thus they all were concentrating on making tanks so small as to be hard to find and nimble enough to avoid being hit, even if found. The fact that missiles fly relatively slowly—about the speed of a jet airliner—meant that an alert crew in a fast-moving tank could survive by dodging out of the way. At a missile's maximum range of a little more than two miles, the tank crew would have as much as eighteen seconds to move or kill the man guiding the projectile. The two exceptions to the small-is-better school were the British and the Israelis, who were willing to pay the penalty in reduced mobility to carry as much armor as possible.

The importance of holding down the weight was underlined in a letter Desobry received in April from five retired officers. It was signed by General Jacob L. Devers, who had taken over when General Chaffee died in 1941 and was largely responsible for fielding an American armored force in World War II; General Bruce C. Clarke, whose forces held off the Germans in the Battle of the Bulge until reinforcements could arrive; and three other veterans of World War II tank battles. "The overall weight of the tank should not exceed 45 tons," they agreed. They added: "Armor protection should be provided to the extent that it is practicable without exceeding the total weight limitations."

The letter distilled the wisdom of the only generation of American soldiers who had ever fought in major tank-against-tank battles. But how much weight should the task force give to their experiences? After all, World War II had ended twenty-seven years ago, before the introduction of battlefield nuclear weapons, helicopters, wire-guided missiles, artillery-scattered mines, modern ammunition, and smart bombs. The letter was a reminder that the task force was, in many ways, venturing off into the unknown.

Desobry agreed with Devers and the others on the need for a relatively small tank. But, whatever the weight, he insisted on a twenty-five-to-one horsepower-to-weight ratio: twenty-five horsepower for each ton of weight. This would guarantee that pickup and speed would not be sacrificed if the weight grew. The power favored by Desobry would give the vehicle almost twice the get-up-and-go of the M-60, then the Army's first-line tank, with its power-to-weight ratio of only thirteen-to-one. To Desobry, high speed and acceleration not only enabled the tank to move quickly from one hiding place to another but also permitted the commander of an armored unit to pull his forces together quickly and shock the enemy with concentrated firepower. In Desobry's mind, this was the way to win battles and save the lives of American soldiers.

In this emphasis on speed, he differed from Devers and his World War II colleagues. They said a top speed of thirty-five miles an hour would be satisfactory while sustained cross-country speed need not exceed fifteen miles an hour except for short spurts. The tank eventually built is much faster. It was not until years later, after the Abrams had been tested over and over in simulated combat, that the designers knew whether that extra speed would pay off on the battlefield.

To achieve the kind of speed and agility Desobry and his associates envisioned would require a first-class suspension and track, and there were several promising suspension and track systems. It would also require an increase in engine power to offset any increase in weight. But this did not seem to be a problem.

If the tank weighed about fifty tons, which then seemed on the high side, that would require a 1,250 horsepower engine. Work on the MBT-70 had left the Army with two engines, one diesel, the other a turbine, both theoretically capable of turning out that much horsepower or more. Although neither had been perfected, both were in an advanced stage of development. It was natural for the task force members, long used to operating diesel-powered tanks, to assume the new tank would have a diesel engine. It was also understandable, in view of all the work already done, that they assumed there would be little difficulty putting a new engine into the new tank. Both assumptions were to prove dead wrong.

The task force recommended a tank with a weight of forty-six to fifty-two tons. Only later would many members of the task force learn of the underlying reason for what seemed to them a distressing increase in weight. They then passed on to the next question: crew size.

There are good arguments in favor of a large crew. Operating a tank is hard, hard work. It is not unusual for a bone-weary tanker to fall asleep while standing in the turret of a moving tank, his muscles instinctively keeping him upright. With four or five men, rather than three or even two, there are more men to stand guard, load fuel and ammunition, service the tank, and replace casualties. World War II tankers still argue that the five-man crew of the Sherman is the optimum size.

Thought was given to having a separate maintenance crew for each tank, much as the Air Force has ground crews to keep its aircraft flying, or to assigning two crews to each tank—a Gold team and a Black team—similar to the Blue and Gold crews that alternate in manning submarines. But both those plans would have pushed Army manpower above the ceiling set by Congress.

When time came for a decision on crew size, the task force realized that the choice had really been preordained by the warning from Congress against "gold-plating." To many in Congress the automatic loader seemed the ultimate in such gadgetry. With the order from Congress, along with concerns about cost, it was natural for the task force to reject the automatic loader, even though the bugs had been worked out and there seemed little technological risk in using the device. The most important result of this decision was to require a human loader. This settled the question of crew size. There would be four: tank commander, driver, and gunner, plus loader.

Doing without the automatic loader is a good example of the thinking that controlled most choices from about 1972 on. During the 1960s the emphasis was on advanced technology and international cooperation. Beginning with the Desobry task force, the dominant concern, verging on obsession, was to hold down the initial cost—the "sticker price"—of the tank. To achieve this goal, the Army gave up performance and even accepted increases in total life cycle cost. Nothing would have done more to lower the total cost of building and operating the tank throughout its lifetime than to cut the crew from four men to three. That would have reduced by one-fourth the cost of recruiting, training, equipping, feeding, housing, and eventually providing pensions for the crew. But the automatic loader, which would have made possible a three-man crew, was rejected largely because of the up-front cost.

Another of the embellishments ruled out early in the game was the fancy hydropneumatic suspension that permitted the crew to raise and lower the profile of the MBT-70. Desobry was not a fan of the "kneeling-squatting" feature.

A great believer in keeping things simple and making them as soldierproof as possible, Desobry considered the complex suspension system gold-plating at its worst, something that probably wouldn't work and would give only a marginal advantage when it did work. He liked to quote one of Abrams's aphorisms to task force members: "Abe used to say you can take an Army soldier and give him an iron anvil, a big hunk of metal, take him in a truck, and dump him out in the desert. Leave him for two or three days with that anvil out there and nothing else. Come back to pick him up, and you'll find that anvil broken. You give the guy a squatting-kneeling tank, and it'll be broken in no time, I'll guarantee you."

Whether Desobry was right is still a matter of some debate in the Army. Proponents of the system note that the Japanese later adapted the technology and made it a highly successful feature of their new tank.

Tankers are a remarkably contentious lot, capable of intense disagreement over seemingly minute issues. They even argued over whether the new tank should have a coffeemaker or heating element. Heiden ended the argument when he snapped, "We're building a fighting machine, not a mobile snack bar."

If the tankers argued over little things like a coffeepot, they were capable of monumental disagreements over important things like the kinds of weapons the new tank should carry. Surprisingly the biggest disagreements did not involve the main gun so much as they did the other weapons. One reason was the disastrous experience with the combination gun-missile on the Sheridan and one model of the M-60. There was little support left for such a system although one faction contended unsuccessfully that the tank should carry missiles strapped to the outside.

The logical choice—and the one the task force arrived at—was to use the 105 mm tank gun already in service on the M-60 and on most tanks in the other NATO armies. Although this seemed a fairly straightforward decision at the time, the question of the main gun on the new tank later became the source of a major controversy within the Pentagon and between the United States and two of its major allies.

The decision to do without missiles and rely on a gun was a result, to some extent, of the task force location at Fort Knox. It was easy, looking at the Kentucky hills and imagining the situation in Germany, to conclude that the tankers, down in the smoke and haze of battle, would seldom be able to see far enough to use their missiles effectively. Doing without the missiles, obvious as it seemed under the circumstances, marked a fundamental change in thinking about the way the tank would fight. Until that time the goal was a tank that could go into combat pretty much on its own, using its missiles for long-range targets and its big gun for fighting at two miles or less. The tank that emerged from the task force's effort, with a single big gun as its main armament, is dependent on missile-carrying vehicles standing above the fog of battle, in overwatch positions on nearby hillsides, to protect it from distant foes. This makes planning for the successful use of what the Army calls combined arms—tanks, infantry, artillery, aircraft all working together—absolutely essential.

Even after the task force had decided on the 105 mm gun, a secondary argument broke out over what kind of ammunition should be carried. Soldiers with experience in Vietnam, which was largely an infantry war, argued vehemently for what is called a beehive round. That is an artillery shell packed with tiny darts. After it leaves the muzzle, it explodes, expelling a shower of darts capable of tearing men to bits. Other soldiers, with memories of World War II, argued just as strongly for a shell containing white phosphorus. In combat they had found the puff of white smoke from such a shell invaluable for marking a target and concentrating the fire of a group of tanks.

When the arguing was over, both the beehive and the smoke shell had been rejected in favor of loading the tank with the maximum number of shells capable of killing other tanks. The result was to leave the new tank more dependent on accompanying infantry to protect it from enemy foot soldiers, again reinforcing the need for combined arms discipline.

While some of these issues were bitterly fought, the arguments were mild in comparison with the violent disagreements that rent the task force over the question of what other complementary or secondary weapons would be on the tank. Should it carry machine guns? How many? What caliber? Should it have a mortar or grenade launcher? What kind of weapon should be mounted in the turret beside the main gun?

It was this weapon—called the coaxial gun because it is fixed in the turret and points wherever the main gun is aimed—that brought about a bitter Saturday morning confrontation between General Long's murder board and the systems analysts headed by Lawrence, who had just been promoted to colonel.

Long took a strong position: He wanted to mount two .50 caliber machine guns in the turret, one on each side of the main gun. For anyone who has ever fired a .50 caliber gun, it is easy to understand the fascination it held for the veteran soldiers. It is the ultimate macho weapon, just about the biggest gun a man can take hold of and fire with his two hands. He feels the heat on his face and smells the cordite while the hot shell casings shower down around his feet. Downrange, the bullet is big enough to rip a hole in a lightly armored vehicle or tear a man apart. Mounted in a stabilized turret, twin-fifties would be accurate out to more than a mile.

Lawrence, who had commanded an armored unit in Vietnam, understood the appeal of the big machine gun. But his computers said no.

As part of the effort to determine what weapons the tank should carry, the task force had taken every possible weapon that might be hung on a tank out into the Kentucky hills and had fired thousands of rounds of ammunition, trying to compare their "kill potential." Altogether some forty combinations of weapons were tried out. The results of the live firings were loaded into the computer and analyzed in elaborate studies similar to those pioneered by Lockheed in the mid-sixties in its work on the MBT-70. By 1972, with improvements in computers, many of the soldiers had dropped their skepticism and were willing to accept well-done computer studies as a valuable way to answer questions about how a weapon would perform in combat. Faith in these studies was bolstered when weapons such as the TOW worked just as well on the battlefield in

Vietnam as the computer said they would.

One crucial question to be answered about each weapon focused on what the Army calls stowed kills. In other words, how many of the bullets carried in a tank for use in a particular weapon will damage or destroy an enemy target? After all, it doesn't make much sense to carry a lot of ammunition if it is not going to kill enemy soldiers and tanks. All the studies showed that because the .50 caliber shell does not explode, the weapon causes relatively little damage compared with the amount of ammunition it fires. The computers concluded: The coaxial .50 caliber guns would kick up a lot of dust and cause a lot of fear, but they wouldn't do much damage.

Lawrence and many others on the task force strongly favored another weapon: a 40 mm rapid-firing grenade launcher already in use as an air-to-ground weapon in helicopters. With its explosive projectile, it could be counted on to do a lot of damage. But Lawrence had to admit that his computers said no to his favorite weapon, too. The grenade launcher was effective when fired from the air by a fast-moving helicopter, but its muzzle velocity was too low to be effective when it was fired from a tank.

A third candidate for the coaxial position was a rapid-fire 25 mm automatic cannon known as the Bushmaster that was also to be the main weapon of the Bradley fighting vehicle. Although it was still under development, the computers said it was worth serious consideration.

The Saturday morning argument over the coaxial weapons permanently strained some friendships, and it left Desobry in an unenviable position. He had to choose between the veterans, some of them lifetime friends, and the whiz kids. He mulled it over for several days and then announced his decision: There would be no coaxial twin-fifties on the new tank; if the Bushmaster worked out, it would be the choice. The old soldiers had lost, and the new breed, with their advanced degrees and computer printouts had won.

Desobry, who normally left the day-to-day running of the

task force to Heiden so he would be free to act as referee, weighed in personally on the issue of secondary armament. He insisted that unlike the M-60, the new tank should have a separate machine gun for use by the loader.

"The gun for the loader was strictly my idea," Desobry says. "My only reason for it was that I think the tank ought to carry as many guns as it can. Why put all the money and effort in the thing and have a guy standing up there with a forty-five caliber pistol? I said, 'Give him something to use.'"

Although World War II tanks had bristled with as many as eight machine guns, the M-60 carries only a tank commander's gun, in a little cupola atop the turret, in addition to the main gun and machine gun fixed in the turret. Desobry reasoned that with machine guns on both sides of the turret and with the tank on the move, the commander could cover the front and right with his gun while the loader covered the left and rear. Since the tank travels with a round in the main gun, the loader could remain at his machine gun until they encountered enemy tanks. Desobry admits that a soldier firing a machine gun from a moving tank is unlikely to hit what he aims at. But, he says, "that's all right; scare 'em to death."

A few of the most critical issues remained until the last minute. Some of the decisions made in the final effort to hold down cost and weight later seemed terribly shortsighted. One of these was the decision to eliminate the so-called hunter-killer feature. This is a separate sighting system that permits the gunner to shoot at one target while the tank commander is fixing the next target in his sights. As soon as the gun goes off, the gunner swings onto the new target, ready to fire in moments. Also regretted later was the decision to leave off an auxiliary power unit, which permits a tank to operate its radios and other equipment without using fuel to run its main engine.

After all the arguments the task force recommended a .50 caliber machine gun for the tank commander and Desobry's 7.62 mm machine gun for the loader. In the interests of simplicity and reduced cost, the tank commander's weapon was not stabilized. As a result, it is not accurate enough to serve as an antiaircraft gun even if it were heavy enough or fired fast enough for that purpose. This meant the tank not only would be dependent on other weapons systems and infantry to protect it from ground attack but would also require separate antiaircraft protection.

The argument over secondary armament on the tank goes on to this day. In training and mock combat the troops tend to give much more emphasis to skill in using the main gun than they do to using their machine guns effectively. In Germany soldiers say they consider the loader's weapon just a spare machine gun in case the tank commander's gun breaks down. At Ford Hood, Texas, troops on the firing range practice shooting their main gun, the tank commander's machine gun, and the coaxial gun mounted in the turret. But the loader is given little opportunity to practice firing his weapon. Apparently the value of some weapons becomes apparent to the soldier only when someone out there is trying to kill him.

This worries Desobry, long since retired to a home on the outskirts of San Antonio, Texas. He complains: "The American Army has lost the value of the machine guns on the tank because they're not precise weapons. If you read General Patton, you'll see he was shouting for more machine guns. I say we've got to have more machine guns. All the tank guys are gone. People today are completely taken in by tank-on-tank. They are mesmerized by the tank main gun."

His view was reinforced when he visited Fort Knox after the new tank had been issued to the troops. A lieutenant proudly took him around a simulated combat course in the M-1, banging away with the big gun. The ride took about half an hour. "You do that, and you wouldn't go two hundred yards before you'd be dead," the old general exclaimed.

Cursing at the effort required to do what had been so easy when he was young, Desobry climbed back up into the tank and told the lieutenant to go around the course again. He tried to impart the sense of fear and caution that rides with the tanker in combat. "When you are the lead tank, you are scared to death by the stillness and quiet," Desobry told him. "It is the most frightening thing in the world."

At the first corner he ordered the lieutenant to stop, climb out, peer around the corner, and describe everything he saw. What about that abandoned farmhouse? Does it hide an anti-tank gun? Are there soldiers with missiles crouching behind that haystack? When they started up, Desobry ordered him to move fast and rake with his machine guns everything that might conceal an enemy soldier. At each corner the same procedure was followed. The circuit of the course took two hours rather than half an hour.

As the task force members struggled with the problem of weight, horsepower, agility, crew size, and weaponry and began to try to put together their list of priorities, a subtle change took place in their thinking about the tank's most important characteristic.

As a result of the World War II experience, tankers traditionally listed the chances of hitting an enemy with the first shot as their highest priority. That put the main emphasis on being able to find the enemy and then to aim and fire quickly and accurately.

Firing tests in the Kentucky hills confirmed the instinctive judgment that the crew that hit first would win. But computer studies by the systems analysts added an intriguing new twist. They found that the tank crew that saw the enemy and fired first was most likely to win—even if the first shot missed.

The more they thought about this bit of information, the clearer it became that victory on the battlefield depended not on just one element, such as first-round-hit capability, but on a combination of a number of elements, all contributing to what they decided to call crew survivability. This meant not just hitting on the first shot. It also meant agility to avoid a return shot and the ability to fire quickly a second time. It meant good armor, and it meant storing fuel and ammunition so even a direct hit would not kill the crew.

This new line of thought recognized that with the proliferation of antitank weapons, tanks were likely to be hit no matter how good they were at killing other tanks. Analyses of tank battles also showed that armies tend to run out of crews more quickly than they run out of tanks, which can be repaired and sent back into battle. Survival of tank crews permits an army to reconstitute its forces and keep fighting.

This central concept of crew survivability came to dominate the thinking of task force members. Later, as Army leaders realized that in any future war they were likely to be outnumbered, this emphasis on survival of tank crews became a major ingredient in a new war-fighting doctrine for the U.S. Army.

The task force didn't abandon such goals as the probability of hitting on the first shot. But when choices had to be made to hold down weight or cost, slightly more emphasis went to factors like agility, armor protection, and, especially, storage of fuel and ammunition in such a way that even if the tank were hit, the crew would live.

Eventually, when all the priorities had been sorted out, the contractors were given guidance on weight and cost plus a list of nineteen characteristics in which they were expected to exceed the performance of the existing M-60 tank. The items on the list and the order in which they were listed were heavily influenced by the responses to the questionnaire distributed throughout the tank force. The characteristics were listed in this order of importance:

1. Crew survivability
2. Surveillance and target acquisition performance
3. First- and subsequent-round hit probability
4. Time to acquire and hit
5. Cross-country mobility
6. Complementary armament integration
7. Equipment survivability
8. Environmental impact
9. Silhouette

10. Acceleration and deceleration
11. Ammunition stowage
12. Human factors
13. Producibility
14. Range
15. Speed
16. Diagnostic aids
17. Growth potential
18. Support equipment
19. Transportability

It became clear both within the Army and to the contractors that there was really one overriding goal: crew survivability. Everything else was important in relation to its contribution to that goal.

The task force finished its work at Knox in early August. Looking at the recommendations was like watching a sculptor in the early stages of his work. You could see the rough outlines of a tank, but it was impossible to get a very good idea of what the finished product would look like. The new tank would be between forty-six and fifty-two tons and would carry a crew of four. It would have either a diesel or turbine engine, probably a diesel, capable of providing both agility and cross-country speed of about forty-five miles an hour. It would carry a 105 mm main gun and a .50 caliber machine gun for the tank commander. If possible, it would carry the Bushmaster as the coaxial gun. The loader would have a 7.62 mm machine gun, although there was still the possibility he would be armed with the 40 mm grenade launcher. And most important, every effort would be made to provide for crew survivability.

The task force recommended that the Army build 3,312 of the new tanks, a number that was pretty much pulled out of the air. Later, when Congress insisted on a more careful look at how many tanks really were needed, the figure was nearly doubled, to 7,058, and the number eventually built will probably exceed that.

The new tank would be a very impressive fighting machine. Yet would it be good enough? The satisfaction of having worked night and day on the Army's highest priority project was diluted for many members of the task force by a vague sense of unease. Would the tank on which they had worked so hard be that much better than the existing M-60? Would it be good enough to hold its own on the battlefield of the future?

These doubts were mostly unspoken. But they made themselves apparent in two ways.

One of the questions the task force considered was what name the tank should bear. The decision was that it should be named for General George Catlett Marshall, the World War II Army chief of staff and later secretary of state. Papers produced at the time refer to the tank as the XM-GCM. But few were told what those initials meant. The task force intended that the choice of a name should remain secret, to be revealed only when, and if, the tank was an acknowledged success. They didn't want Marshall's name attached to a lemon.

Another indication of doubt was reflected in the choice of a background for the group picture. They assembled in front of a T-20, a tank developed just at the end of World War II. It was not a success and didn't see service except as a lawn ornament. Task force members told each other, only half in jest, that the picture shows them grouped around a "monument to failure."

What worried many members of the task force was that they had permitted the weight to get out of hand but had failed to meet their chief goal of insuring survival of the crew. The doubters would have been much more cheerful if they had been let in on a secret known only to Desobry, Heiden, Lawrence, and a few others with a strict need to know: The tank was to be built of a revolutionary new armor, the most important development in tank warfare in a quarter century or more.

4

What Price Armor?

THE ARMY BRASS gave Bill Desobry everything he asked for: money, authority, and expert help. But they told him to forget about "Burlington." And that little detail almost sent the Army's latest—and probably last—effort to obtain a new tank sliding off into yet another disaster.

It was not until the spring of 1972, when the task force was well into its work on the new tank, that Desobry received an eye-opening introduction to Burlington, the code name the British had given their highly secret and spectacularly effective new armor. That he learned of it at all was a fluke.

General Norton, head of the Combat Development Command and Desobry's boss and old friend, received a briefing on a new tank gun under development by the British. Excited by what he had heard, he called Desobry and suggested he fly to England to see the new gun. Norton is a paratrooper, and Desobry didn't think he knew much about tank guns. It was only after Norton gave him a direct order that Desobry, grumbling about being sent off on a wild-goose chase, broke away from his busy schedule at Fort Knox and flew to London the next day.

From London, Desobry and his British hosts drove southwest into the gentle Surrey countryside to what was then known as the Fighting Vehicles Research and Development Establishment, since changed to Royal Armament Research and Development Establishment. It is more commonly known by the name of the nearest village, Chobham. The visitor needed only a few pointed questions to satisfy himself that the British gun was not a serious candidate for use in the new American tank. By the time the group sat down to lunch the American general was, as he says, "browned off" by the futile trip and apparently showing it.

Sensing his frustration, a scientist at the table asked if he had been briefed on the newest British armor. Desobry, vaguely recalling a meeting where he had been told to ignore reports of a breakthrough in armor technology, snapped: "I got all the stuff from our guys in Washington."

"No, your people have dropped it," the scientist said. "We've continued it. If you want, after lunch I will personally brief you on it."

Exactly what Desobry was told in that briefing is still highly classified, even after all these years. But it is possible to describe how the new armor technology was discovered and, in general terms, how it works.

In those early days the armor was referred to as Harvey's armor, for its inventor, Dr. Gilbert Harvey. It later became better known as Chobham armor, for the lab where it was developed, although those in the know referred to it simply by its code name, Burlington.

Harvey, who has since died, was one of those faceless scientists who spend their lives in government research, laboring on projects so secret that no matter how successful they are, their work will never result in fame or fortune and seldom even in public recognition. Harvey's name is virtually unknown to the public, and even tank experts familiar with his work can't recall, or never knew, that his first name was Gilbert.

The problem Harvey was wrestling with was one that had plagued armorers since World War II. In this age of high technology there is normally a fairly rapid cycle back and forth between defensive and offensive weaponry. First one surges ahead; then the other gets out in front. But the problem confronting the armorers had persisted for two decades and seemed likely to become even more troublesome in the future. The challenge was how to defeat a form of antitank ammunition known as the shaped charge. The development of this type of projectile by both sides during the war had created a grave new threat to the tank.

The nose of the shaped charge projectile contains a hollow copper cone. When the shell hits a tank, it sets off an explosion that turns the cone into a stream of tiny bits of copper capable of cutting a hole to a depth as much as five and a half times the warhead diameter. This meant that even a relatively small weapon, light enough to be carried by an individual soldier, could penetrate the conventional homogeneous steel armor of most tanks. Suddenly, with the emergence of the hand-held antitank weapon, each soldier was a potential tank killer.

The British fielded an antitank weapon known as the PIAT (projector, infantry, antitank). The Americans called their weapon the bazooka, after the strange musical instrument played by Bob Burns, a then-popular comedian and musician from the Ozarks. It fired a 2.36-inch rocket-propelled shell. Because of its small diameter, its penetrating power was limited, as American soldiers learned when the weapon proved ineffective against Soviet-made T-34 tanks in Korea. The Germans, who first used the shaped charge in an antitank gun in 1942, produced a soldier-size weapon called the *Panzerfaust*, literally "tank fist," but, more loosely, "tank killer." It consisted of a recoilless weapon that fired a 6-inch-diameter grenade. Its large size made it capable of penetrating eight inches of armor.

The new weapons are not by themselves enough to stop a determined attack by massed armor. Soldiers will drop their weapons and run away rather than face certain death in standing up to such an assault. Even as well trained and disciplined as the German soldiers were, they were reluctant to fire a *Panzerfaust* and expose themselves to the likelihood of being squashed under the tracks of a tank. When World War II ended, Germany's stockpile of the vaunted new weapons was big enough to kill every Allied tank ten times over, but they were not fired. Even so, the very existence of such a weapon increases the tank's vulnerability and makes the commander more cautious.

Shaped charge weapons are most dangerous when fired in volleys from well-hidden positions, especially against the sides or rear of a tank that has already been damaged or separated from the rest of the tank force.

By the mid-sixties it was clear to the armorers that they had to be concerned not only about shaped charge projectiles fired from guns and shoulder launchers but also from a variety of rocket launchers, then under development, capable of deadly accuracy over distances of several miles. The search for a way to deal with this new threat took the scientists to the archives of naval architecture, back several hundred years before the invention of the tank.

The first naval guns fired simple solid iron cannonballs. By the late 1700s it was noticed that a lighter, hollow cannonball could be fired at a greater velocity and had a better chance of penetrating the sides of a wooden ship. In the early 1800s it occurred to gunnery experts that the hollow ball could be filled with an explosive that would cause severe damage once it got inside the ship.

The ship designers responded first by putting metal plating over wooden hulls and then by building ships with iron hulls. About the time of the American Civil War came the development of the Palliser shell, named for Sir William Palliser, a British cavalry officer and inventor who was knighted in recognition of his contributions to the empire. This shell consisted of a hardened steel nose, to penetrate the hull, and an explosive charge to cause damage after penetration.

At this point the naval architects came up with the kind of sophisticated response that later provided clues to how to deal with the shaped charge. Their contribution was compound armor. This consisted of a sheet of very hard steel applied over softer iron plate. When the brittle nose of the Palliser shell hit the hard steel, it shattered, while the softer iron underneath the steel absorbed the impact. It did not take long for the offense to come back with a less brittle nose that would not shatter. But compound armor of various kinds continues to this day to be the basis for every effort to defeat armor-piercing shells.

One of the most effective forms of compound armor consists of two or more layers of armor separated by spaces. It is called spaced armor. The outer armor is intended to slow the projectile, strip off its explosive fuze, and cause it to disintegrate. If the shell penetrates the outer armor, the hope is that it will explode in the space between the layers of armor, with the inner wall protecting the crew and equipment inside the ship. In some cases the space between the layers is so large it is used for storage of fuel.

The contest involving designers of warships, guns, and projectiles culminated in the monstrous battleships built in the first half of this century. Layers of compound armor protected the ship while guns ranging up to eighteen inches in diameter and capable of firing a projectile weighing as much as a small automobile were designed to penetrate enemy armor.

To Harvey and his associates it seemed obvious that the answer to the shaped charge—if, indeed, there was an answer—would be some form of compound armor that would cause the shell to malfunction, break up, or burn out before it reached the interior of the tank. But a tank is not a battleship. Adding enough conventional steel armor to have any hope of defeating the shaped charge would result in a behemoth weighing as much as ninety tons. It was the same problem faced by medieval armorers. If they loaded on enough iron to protect a horse, the poor beast wouldn't be able to move.

Until that time armorers had focused their attention on trying to find some magic material that would break up the shaped charge or absorb its energy. They experimented with various alloys of metals and with ceramics. They even tried the plastic known as polypropylene, that white, popcornlike stuff used as a packing material. Strangely enough, it gives more protection than an equivalent weight of steel but, used alone, is too bulky to be practical. They also worked with a variety of ways to create spaces between layers of armor. One of their most effective tricks was to slope the armor. When a projectile strikes sloped armor, it penetrates at an angle and thus has a longer path to follow to get inside the tank. But none of this was good enough.

The breakthrough came when Harvey was experimenting with a system for storing fuel in such a way that it would not explode if hit by a shell. To his surprise, the honeycomblike fuel storage system seemed to deflect the jet of metal particles created by the shaped charge and absorb its energy. It is fair to say that Harvey stumbled on the solution to the shaped charge problem, but it is also true that he was well prepared to recognize what he had stumbled onto and to follow up on his discovery.

Harvey's contribution was to understand that much greater protection can be achieved by arranging the layers of armor at odd angles, in a series of baffles, rather than by lining the layers up parallel to each other. The result is to deflect the jet of hot metal, much as light passing through successive sheets of glass set at different angles is deflected first one way and then another.

The breakthrough came about 1964. A dozen years later the British government briefly raised the veil of secrecy shrouding the new armor before quickly pulling the curtain down more firmly than ever. The occasion was the announcement on June 17, 1976, that London had secretly agreed to sell twelve hundred new tanks to the shah of Iran, a big boost for the troubled British economy.

Roy Mason, the British defense minister, boasted that the tanks, to be called the Lion of Iran, or *Shir Iran* in Farsi, would be equipped with a new type of armor which "represents the most significant achievement in tank design and protection since the Second World War. . . . Weight for weight it gives significantly better protection than all existing armors against attack by all forms of anti-tank weapons."

David Cardwell, the Royal Army's chief scientist, added that it provides "adequate protection against all types of round that can be foreseen."

The British even released official drawings comparing the

performance of the new armor with conventional steel armor. The drawings, without revealing the composition of the new armor, show four different types of antitank projectile penetrating the steel armor but being stopped by the new armor. The drawings represented the results of tests in which thousands of rounds of ammunition were fired at targets made of the special armor.

The first experiments involved arrays of conventional armor materials. But scientists rapidly expanded the types of materials to include not only various alloys of metal but also ceramics, epoxies, and plastics. One of the great advantages of the new armor is that the baffles are enclosed in a steel box. The box can be opened up, and the armor "recipe" changed, to incorporate the latest armor protection into older tanks at a tiny fraction of the cost of buying new tanks.

The recipe is necessarily a compromise designed to protect against two quite different threats: the large-diameter shaped charge and the very small-diameter kinetic energy shell. At least in its early versions, the new armor provided almost total protection against shaped charges but, despite Cardwell's boast, was only marginally better than steel in fending off kinetic energy rounds. Much of the research and experimentation done in recent years have focused on finding a formula for the arrays of armor that will defeat both kinds of ammunition.

When the British scientist had finished his briefing, the usually voluble Desobry sat for a few moments in stunned silence. If what he had been told were true, this armor would revolutionize the design of future tanks. In the few months before his report was due, he had a lot of work to do.

As he flew back to Knox, he had three big questions in mind: (1) Was this stuff as good as the British said it was? (2) Could it be fabricated and applied to production-line tanks? (3) Could it be fabricated in large quantities at a price comparable to steel armor—in the range of two to four dollars a pound? Since armor accounts for half the weight of a tank and Desobry was under strict instructions to hold down the cost, the last question was perhaps the most crucial.

As soon as Desobry returned to Knox, he sent Heiden hurrying to the Army's Ballistic Research Laboratories (BRL) at Aberdeen Proving Ground in Maryland to see what the scientists there knew about the new armor.

Heiden came back excited. The scientists knew of the British work and not only felt that it held promise but were already working on improvements. Dick Lawrence was let in on the secret, and he went to Aberdeen for a demonstration.

What he saw stunned him. He watched a target made of the new armor shrug off shells fired at point-blank range. It was beyond the wildest dreams of a veteran tanker. The task force had set crew survivability as its highest priority without knowing how to reach that goal. Here, suddenly, was the answer.

Desobry had enough money to fund a crash effort on the new armor by the Ballistic Research Laboratories. Heiden also contracted with both General Motors and Chrysler to determine if the new armor could be fabricated and incorporated into production-line tanks and if this could be done at a reasonable price.

Encouraging word came from the laboratories and the manufacturers: The armor not only worked and was being improved but could be fabricated at an affordable price. The reports were so positive, in fact, that the task force violated its rule against recommending new or experimental technology. The results promised by this invention were so great that it was worth the risk.

The excitement Desobry, Heiden, and Lawrence felt was tempered by a bitter, lasting anger that vital information about this revolutionary new technology had been withheld from them after they had been entrusted with responsibility for the Army's top-priority weapons program.

Lawrence, who went on to become a three-star general, says: "I'll tell you I was put out that we had been involved in such a crucial issue and we had to get this through the back door and that people were not forthcoming until we found out about it. I was put out that there was such a lack of communication and such a reluctance on the part of the various parties to talk to each other. Whatever the reason, it was very unfortunate that we had to languish along for a period of a couple of months when everybody knew that survivability was our number one priority before we found out about this in an indirect way."

To Desobry the apparent withholding of information about the new armor was even more perplexing. Early in his task force assignment he had been called to Washington and specifically told that regardless of what he heard about breakthroughs in armor technology, he should not count on it for the new tank. He had been told to put it out of his mind, and he had—until his chance visit to Chobham.

The three task force leaders were left with the impression that someone who knew how good the British armor was had made a deliberate decision to keep the news from those working on the new tank. That isn't what happened. What really happened is more complex, an object lesson in the perils of excessive secrecy, bureaucratic inertia, and the dangers of NIH—the not invented here syndrome.

The story begins in 1965, shortly after Harvey's discovery, when the British invited the Americans to send someone over for a briefing on a new kind of armor. Major Donald Creuzinger, an armor officer stationed at Fort Knox, was ordered to Washington and told to go to England and listen to what the British had to say. An Army scientist was assigned to accompany him. The modest rank of the two men accurately reflected the degree of American interest. Before they left, someone realized that the British would be miffed when such a low-level delegation arrived to be briefed on their precious secret. At the last minute an assistant secretary of the army was added to the group.

In London the Americans met the British master general of ordnance and were asked to sign a secrecy agreement. Then they were taken to Chobham for a briefing. The British scientists said they still weren't sure why, but the new armor worked almost miraculously, especially against the dreaded shaped charge projectiles.

When the Americans returned to London, they talked over what they had been told. Creuzinger wrote out and signed their report. As part of the secrecy agreement, only a single handwritten copy was prepared. It concluded that, although the British research was very, very interesting, it did not have any potential for practical use at its present stage of development. The armor would have to be two feet thick, and that was too much to put on a combat vehicle.

With hindsight, it seems obvious that the negative assessment expressed in Creuzinger's handwritten report was too extreme. True, what the delegation saw and heard represented very early results of laboratory experiments, nothing resembling tests involving actual military hardware, and Creuzinger contends that later development work overcame the deficiencies noted by the group. But there also seems to have been a failure of vision. The Americans were familiar with the M-60, with its four inches of armor. They had never seen a tank with armor two feet thick and simply were not prepared to accept such a thought. As it turned out, the armor on the M-1 is two feet thick.

On the basis of the negative report written in 1965 Desobry had been told by officials at the Pentagon, in 1972, to forget about a breakthrough in armor technology. By 1972 a small number of Americans, particularly at Aberdeen, knew how good the new armor was and that the British had installed it successfully on a test vehicle. But the word didn't make it the seventy miles from Aberdeen to the right offices in Washington.

Part of the blame for that failure of communication belongs with the scientists or bureaucrats at the laboratory. At least that is the opinion of British officers who were both puzzled and frustrated by the reluctance of the Americans to pay attention to their Chobham armor.

Almost from the beginning, the British tried to interest

scientists at BRL. In the late sixties the British master general of ordnance gave an unusual assignment to Major General Jonathan Dent, who had been program manager for the Chieftain tank. He was ordered to "sell" the new armor to the skeptical Americans. Since the British were still producing the Chieftain and would not be able to afford a new tank for a number of years, they wanted their American allies to have the best armor in their new tank.

At first the reaction from BRL scientists, reluctant to accept an invention from across the seas, was, "Look, it's no bloody good; it doesn't work." To Dent it seemed that the American armor experts "didn't like swallowing this pill." He felt that "NIH was rampant." Finally, in 1969, he prevailed on the scientists at Aberdeen to do the tests properly, and they saw that the material really did work.

When the Americans began to show genuine interest, the British were in an awkward position. The armor was of obvious importance on the battlefield, but it was also of great potential value in commercial arms sales. It fell to Dent to draw up a memorandum of understanding that would protect secrecy by restricting the number of Americans who had access to the technology and would protect the British commercial interest in sale of tanks containing the new armor. The two sides signed the memo, and by 1972, as Dent says, the Americans "had the whole beans." But the agreement turned out to be a flawed document in several respects.

Scientists at Aberdeen quickly "Americanized" the armor. The Americans were later to insist that the armor in their tank was really not Chobham but their own development. At first they used the British term, Burlington. But then they even gave it a new code name: Starflower. This did not amuse the British. The American turn for anger came when Great Britain decided to sell tanks containing Chobham armor to Iran. This seemed in Washington to be a blatant violation of security. As it turned out, the shah was deposed before the tanks were delivered.

Arguments over security and foreign sales caused a very frosty period of about a year and a half between the British and American armies. But as far as the United States was concerned, the most important impact of the memo of understanding was the restriction it placed on distribution of information about the new armor. The blame for this should not all be borne by the British. The Pentagon was perfectly capable of its own excesses of secrecy.

The supersecrecy imposed on the subject certainly contributed to the failure to pass along to the task force details about this vital new technology. And after Desobry's visit to England, it was to plague his dealings with high officials in Washington whose names were not on the tiny list of those in the know.

As information about the new armor was fed into calculations about the tank, the weight began to grow inexorably. It was clear that the weight would be far greater than the original goal of thirty-five to forty tons. The excessive secrecy about the very existence of the new armor led to angry confrontations as Army brass in the Pentagon became more and more critical of the growing weight.

One day Desobry blew up after taking a blasting from what he describes as "some idiotic major general who didn't know what he was doing." Desobry pushed back from the table, stood up, glared around the room, and snapped: "Gentlemen, until you get yourselves cleared for this work we're doing, I'm not going to brief you. I'm going back to Knox, and I'm going back right now.

"Pack up. We're going home," he told his team. As they left the room, he shouted back over his shoulder: "When you're cleared, I'll come back." About a week later they were called back to the Pentagon to brief a small group of officials who had been told enough of the secret to understand what they were hearing.

While the frustration of dealing with those who didn't know about the new armor is understandable, it soon became apparent that even the task force members who knew about it had failed to grasp the full implications of this new technology. Still heavily influenced by their early commitment to a light, very agile tank, they deluded themselves that the Army could build a tank that was both heavily protected with the new armor and still relatively light in weight.

When he took the results of the task force study to the Pentagon, Desobry had a hardball strategy in mind that he and Heiden were prepared to follow even at the risk of their careers. The task force recommended a tank of forty-six to fifty-two tons, and Desobry and Heiden, through their widespread connections, had rounded up strong support from other tankers for a goal of no more than fifty-two tons. They even had the commander of Army forces in Europe in their corner. By hanging tough, they hoped to force the Army Materiel Command—the people responsible for building the tank—to produce a machine that was both heavily armored and still light enough to be fast and agile. They were also acutely aware that weight cost money. An eight-ton increase, from fifty to fifty-eight tons, would add more than twenty-two thousand dollars to the cost of a tank.

From past experience Desobry suspected that the ordnance officers would hedge their bets by setting a goal they knew they could achieve. He wanted to force them to outdo themselves by setting a difficult, seemingly impossible goal.

But Desobry and Heiden soon found they had an adversary even more formidable than the folks in the matériel command in the person of General DePuy, the powerful assistant vice chief of staff.

The first hint of real trouble came on September 22, 1972, in a dry run at the Pentagon for a meeting scheduled the following week at which the Army would make its decisions on the new tank. A civilian scientist stepped to the podium. He had gone over the task force's figures and had worked out a series of curves showing the relationship between weight and armor protection. In many Army briefings the display of Vu-graphs in a darkened room is time for a little shut-eye. But these charts quickly commanded rapt attention. They showed that the special armor would make the new tank much better than the ones then in service. But they also showed that the maximum effectiveness of the new armor would not be achieved until enough had been added to bring the weight to about fifty-eight tons.

The task force members had a gut feeling that agility—the ability to avoid being hit rather than to survive a hit—was worth a good deal. But that is something much more difficult to measure than the amount of protection provided by a certain number of inches of armor. They couldn't match these formidable charts.

DePuy, chairman of the meeting, let it be known he was impressed by the argument in favor of a bigger tank. It reinforced what he was already hearing from his own staff. He was one of the few with the vision to recognize that a heavy tank would be required to take full advantage of the new armor, and he became the leading advocate of the fifty-eight-ton tank.

When Heiden first heard DePuy espousing such heresy, he was appalled at this sudden turn of events. Normally a mild-mannered man, he shot back with the kind of accusation that a colonel with any concern for his future does not normally level at a three-star, especially one as formidable as DePuy: The whole armor community had signed off on a tank weighing fifty-two tons or less, and here was an infantry officer advocating "a big, nonmovable tank . . . forgetting the purpose of armor on the battlefield." Others in the room were astounded by Heiden's remarks.

It is not difficult to imagine the feelings of Desobry and Heiden in what was becoming an increasingly bleak fall. They had been totally immersed in the challenge of outlining the characteristics of the Army's most important weapon. And now it looked as though all their work were in danger of being upset. If the weight went up, that demanded a more powerful engine, a bigger transmission, and a heavier track. All these things would mean more cost—and Congress had already made clear it was not about to buy "a million-dollar tank."

There were about thirty people present for the September 27 meeting in room 2E-635, the army secretary's conference room, at the Pentagon. This was the meeting where the future of the new tank would be settled. The stars on the generals' shoulders presented a dazzling display, more than most of those present had ever seen in one place before. The atmosphere in the room was electric. For the Army, the tank was as important as the hottest fighter and the newest bomber to the Air Force or the fastest destroyer and the biggest carrier to the Navy.

As the brass, both civilian and military, settled into place, a seat at the head of the table remained vacant. Then, to the surprise of many, Abrams, who had not yet been sworn in as chief of staff, entered the room, took the vacant seat, and unwrapped one of his ever-present cigars. Longtime Abrams watchers had noticed that when he was in a placid mood, he smoked; when he was angry, he chewed. The tension eased just a shade when he lit up.

The chief of staff-to-be had just passed his fifty-eighth birthday. A short, chunky man who had been barely big enough to win his letter as a guard on the West Point football team, Abrams had a square-jawed, rugged-looking face with skin the texture of old leather, from years spent with troops in the field. He was probably a little uncomfortable with this big, formal meeting. Perhaps because he had spent long tours of duty in the Pentagon, including a stint as vice chief of staff, he had little patience with the Pentagon bureaucracy or with Washington generally. He complained that the Army had "hundreds of midgets checking little things," and he once likened the Pentagon to "an asylum run by the inmates." In his blunt way, he noted that, in Washington, "the system around town is cluttered up with a lot of crap."

He was known for his attempts to cut through the crap, whenever possible. Once, when a congressional committee asked him his opinion of the .45 caliber pistol, which had an almost hallowed status as the Army's standard-issue sidearm, he responded that it was "a splendid weapon for defending oneself in a crowded elevator."

To Desobry, who represented the task force at the meeting, the presence of Abrams, even though he was not yet officially the chief of staff, was a good sign. Little more than a month before, Abrams had spent a day at Fort Knox, and the visit had been highly encouraging to the task force members.

Heiden and Lawrence briefed him for about three hours on the work of the task force. Even for two relatively senior officers it was a daunting experience. Both were in awe of Abrams, who seemed to them the epitome of the professional armor officer. They felt that when he talked, it was like receiving word on the mountain.

Abrams was not an easy man to brief. He could listen for many minutes without comment or change of expression until something displeased him. Those who knew Abrams well marveled at his ability to express displeasure by the silent treatment, chewing on his cigar and staring into space. And everyone who had to deal with him feared his anger, whether feigned or real. After a long period of silence, while his neck turned red and his face took on a bluish tinge, he would erupt in a scathing, marvelously profane dressing down of the unfortunate who had earned his displeasure.

Having heard such stories of the formidable General Abe, Heiden and Lawrence ended their briefing with a warm feeling of accomplishment, a feeling that he blessed what they were doing. If they could have looked a few weeks into the future, they would not have felt nearly as euphoric. But for the time their feeling of well-being was reinforced even more by what happened that evening.

Desobry, who occupied the stately brick commandant's quarters at Knox, invited the members of the task force and a number of other officers to his home for a stag barbecue. All through the night Abrams held court, telling stories of his days as a young lieutenant in the horse cavalry at Fort Bliss, Texas. Desobry served as a kind of traffic cop, making sure that everyone had a chance to get up close to Abrams's chair.

There were a couple of guitar players there, and the tankers sang some songs. Abrams, who could carry a tune pretty well, sang several himself.

The talk turned to World War II. It had been the thirty-year-old Abrams, more than any of the other young officers in Patton's army, who epitomized the aggressive, hell-for-leather dash across Western Europe by the American tankers. Abrams nicknamed all his tanks Thunderbolt and wore out six of them.

Abrams told of his old mentor, Major General John Shirley Wood—known to all the tankers as P, for "professor," a nickname he picked up at West Point when he helped other cadets with their lessons. Abrams was one of the officers who helped Wood organize and train the Fourth Armored Division, which led the sweep across France. Wood, who burned out after four months in combat and was relieved, was described by a British military critic as the "Rommel of the American armored forces." And Patton said: "The accomplishments of this division have never been equalled . . . in the history of warfare."

"General Abe talked of him almost like a saint," Lawrence recalls. This strong bond between generations is one of the striking characteristics of the small community of tankers. Here was an officer who had started out in the horse cavalry and had as his model a man born in the previous century, decades before the invention of the tank. To those working on a machine that would be equipped with a laser range finder, a thermal sight, a turbine engine, and a digital computer and would be in service into the next century, Abrams was a visible link between past and future.

The party went on until the early hours of the morning, when Abrams finally had to leave to fly back to Washington. The task force members felt that the Army's preeminent tanker left Knox a strong supporter of what they were doing.

As the Pentagon meeting opened, the group saw the charts and heard the argument in favor of a tank of about fifty-eight tons.

Desobry listened in growing anger and frustration. Then he rose and did his best to turn the tide against the heavy tank. Summoning all the moral artillery at his command, he pleaded "as commander of the Armor Center and on behalf of the armor community," for a tank of no more than fifty-two tons.

Pounding the table, he shouted, "The last thing we need is a fifty-eight-ton tank!" An embarrassed silence followed Desobry's outburst. Afterward there was speculation that he had just destroyed his chances for promotion. As it turned out, lively dissent was not punished and may even have been rewarded. A short time later Desobry received another star and command of a corps in Europe.

All eyes turned to Abrams. Both sides had been heard, and now the decision was up to him. For a moment at least he seemed to be leaning toward Desobry's side. "The Germans in World War II were slowed down, although they were less vulnerable than we were, by heavy tanks," he said. He told how the Americans, with their inferior Shermans, ganged up to defeat the better German tanks. But then he focused on the advantages gained from the new armor.

Abrams had not come into the meeting cold. He had seen a demonstration of the new armor and, like other tankers, had been astounded. After examining the target and confirming for himself that the armor stopped a shaped charge cold, he had exclaimed: "The tank lives again!" Before the meeting Abrams had also been briefed on the impact of the new armor on the weight of the tank, although there is no reason to believe he had made up his mind before hearing the issue debated in the conference.

Without the full use of the new armor, he mused, the new tank would be not much better than the old M-60—"warmed-over potatoes from last year and the year before." Abruptly he announced his decision: "Let's set the weight at fifty-eight tons."

Desobry had lost. And he felt he had lost to Bill DePuy, who had beaten him with his own information. The curves showed that the new armor didn't provide a real advantage until the tank reached about fifty-eight tons. Despite his bitter disappointment at the time, Desobry later admitted that DePuy had been right and he had been wrong.

Probably no one realized, as the Pentagon meeting broke up, the full implications of the decision that had just been made. But when it later came time to sketch out what the tank would look like and how it would be built, it was obvious that the new armor would dominate the design, weight, and cost of the tank and even require a new method of manufacture.

The turrets of the M-60 and its predecessors were made by pouring molten metal into a casting. The cast turret had a rounded shape, carefully engineered to cause projectiles to glance off or explode harmlessly outside the tank. But it would be extremely difficult to make a cast turret that also included the intricate arrays of materials that give the new armor its magic. The Army was thus forced to switch from cast to welded turrets for the M-1.

The change had a pronounced impact on the looks of the tank. While the M-60 and most other tanks have a rounded, almost streamlined look, the M-1 is distinguished by its angular appearance, created by the rectangular sheets of steel welded together to enclose the baffles of the special armor. The extraordinary size of the two-foot-thick armor also gives the M-1 a noticeably boxy look.

Although the tanks are built in two separate factories—the Detroit Army Tank Plant and the Lima (Ohio) Army Tank Plant—all the special armor was, until recently, created in one building, set off from the rest of the plant, at Lima. The boxes that will contain the special armor are welded together on the production line. Then they are taken off to the armor building, where workers with special security clearances install the arrays of armor inside the boxes. They are then tack-welded shut, so workers without the special clearance cannot see inside.

This method of production has permitted the Army to upgrade the armor on new tanks at least three times. The prototypes and first production tanks were made with materials much like the original Chobham armor obtained from the British. These early tanks—the "Plain Janes"—were withdrawn from service in Europe as soon as tanks with improved armor came along. An even better—and slightly thicker—armor was installed on the next model, known as the M-1A1.

But the Army was still not satisfied. While the special armor shrugged off attack by shaped charge projectiles, its resistance to kinetic energy shells left something to be desired even after several rounds of improvements. For four years, in a secretly funded, "black," program, scientists scrambled to find a way to protect against both kinds of attack. They had already found out how to "tune" the armor to match the kind of ammunition a tank was most likely to face. But that was not the same as an armor that could defeat anything fired at it.

The breakthrough came in the latter part of 1987, when tests confirmed that armor containing an alloy of depleted uranium would stand up to any antitank ammunition the Warsaw Pact might put into the field well into the 1990s.

The improvement in the armor was a major technological development, a significant addition to the survivability of the Abrams and its crew. But the Army did not trumpet the achievement. If the scientists had had their choice, it would not have been revealed at all. But depleted uranium is mildly radioactive, so the brass felt compelled to announce that it would be used in the tank in an effort to reassure workers, crew members, and the public that the material, as it is being used, is not a danger to health.

This is the way DU, as it is called, is used in the improved armor: Depleted uranium is a green salt that is a by-product of the enrichment of uranium for use as fuel to make electricity. It is mixed with other materials to create an alloy and then installed, at a secret location, along with the metals, epoxies, and plastics that make up the baffles inside the big steel armor boxes that cover the front of the tank. DU is extremely dense, having two and a half times the density of steel. But since a relatively small amount is used, it adds less than a ton to the weight of the tank—not enough for the crew to notice a change in speed or handling.

Even this breakthrough in armor technology does not, unfortunately for the tankers, mean that the Army's newest tanks are invulnerable to enemy action. The problem faced by the tank designers is that it would cost too much in added weight and money to provide equal protection against attack from all directions. So they try to provide the most protection where the danger seems greatest.

The decision on where to concentrate the armor in the M-1 was based on a study done in 1951 by the Ballistic Research Laboratories and reinforced by later studies, especially those focused on what happened during the Yom Kippur War of 1973. In the 1951 study the scientists used information from 544 tank casualties during World War II to determine where tanks were hit most often. When the hits were plotted on the silhouette of a tank, the result was a mathematical curve, known as a cardioid distribution because it is heart-shaped. The cardioid curve showed that 40 percent of the hits on the turret were in front and only 10 percent in the rear while 37 percent of the hits on the hull were in the front and only 4 percent in the rear.

The result, in the case of the M-1, is a tank with its heaviest armor concentrated in a sixty-degree frontal arc. Protection provided on the back, sides, top, and bottom, while at least as great as that on the M-60 tank, is less than up front. It is safest for a tanker to have his tank and his gun pointing toward the enemy. And if he has to move away, he backs up until safely hidden by the terrain. This distribution of armor has the advantage, for a commander, of keeping his tanks pointed in the right direction.

The direction the turret is pointing does little, however, to protect the tank from top attack, and this is a matter of growing concern. Since the M-1 was originally designed in the 1970s, there has been dramatic progress in development of new weapons designed to hit the top of the tank, where it is weakest. In one system an unmanned drone aircraft flies over a tank formation and drops scores of bomblets. Each little bomb contains a sensor that guides it to the top of a tank. In another system a hidden soldier sends a missile over the battlefield and then looks through a fiber optic filament that connects him to the missile. When he sees a tank, he sends the missile crashing into its top.

The M-1, like all tanks, is also vulnerable to mines, striking from below, and new methods of planting mines—by artillery and aircraft—assure that battlefields of the future will be liberally sown with these deadly devices.

In the fall of 1972, of course, concerns about attack from top and bottom and decisions on the shape of the tank, the method of manufacture, and many other issues were well in the future. For Desobry, the Pentagon meeting was the end of his responsibility for the tank program. Task force members were already returning to their regular jobs or taking up new assignments. Years later the three leaders of the task force were involved, each in his own way, with the new tank. Desobry was called in as a troubleshooter when problems developed with the early models, Lawrence commanded one of the first divisions equipped with the M-1, and Heiden was involved vicariously when his son, an armor captain, was assigned to an M-1 unit at Fort Hood, Texas. But now a new team was taking control of the tank program.

On July 18, 1972, Brigadier General Robert J. Baer, a forty-seven-year-old armor officer, had been named project manager for the new tank. He received a seven-page charter giving him a direct channel of communication to the chief of staff and secretary of the army. After signing the document, the civilian secretary penned this note at the bottom: "Gen. Baer: You have a very tough and vitally important assignment. I'm counting on you to do a bang-up job. Let me know if I can help."

Baer, who had returned to a Pentagon desk job in 1969 after two tours of duty in Vietnam, is one of a whole generation of armor officers who have little or no experience in tank combat. He entered West Point during World War II, and during the early fifties he served in the tank-intensive Army of Occupation in Germany, not in combat in Korea. In Vietnam, where his radio code word was Stingray, he saw enough fighting as a brigade commander to win the Silver Star, one of the Army's top awards for bravery. But he also won the Air Medal with eleven oak leaf clusters because the unit he commanded was equipped with helicopters, not tanks. By the time Baer took over the tank assignment, he had also had three years of intensive experience as a manager of the Army's tank and other vehicle programs in the Pentagon.

Unlike Tom Dolvin, manager of the MBT-70 program, who remained in Washington to be where decisions on money were made, Baer established his headquarters in a rented building in a shopping center at Dequindre and 12 Mile roads about three miles from the big Detroit Army Tank Plant in Warren, Michigan, and moved his family into a comfortable old brick house at nearby Selfridge Air National Guard Base. He compensated for the distance from the capital by frequent trips and by setting up a strong Washington office, staffed by a succession of trusted armor officers who looked after his interests in the Pentagon and cultivated powerful allies on Capitol Hill. They all shared, with an almost religious fervor, the determination to put a new tank into the hands of the troops as quickly as possible.

Shortly after Baer had received his new assignment, Major General Donn A. Starry was named to command the Armor Center at Knox. Abrams, who did almost all his business in person rather than in writing or by telephone, called the two men to his office separately. Both had served under him and were known as Abrams protégés. He told them he was holding them personally responsible—Baer as the builder and Starry as representative of the users—for the success of the tank program.

"Don't let them add bells and whistles," he ordered Baer. "We have got to keep it simple; we can't afford the best of everything." Abrams stressed simplicity and what he liked to call fightability—the design features that would assist the crew to do its job well in combat. "Fightability" is synonymous with "ergonomics," the science that seeks to adapt working conditions to suit the worker. "Fightability" may be a less elegant term than "ergonomics," but it seems more appropriate when applied to a fighting machine.

Starry met with Abrams on May 22, 1973, just before going to his new command at Knox. The younger officer, who keeps a meticulous diary, noted his orders from Abrams: "You've got to keep Desobry informed. You've got to keep Europe informed of what we're doing to make sure their input is reflected in the tank. I hold you responsible for coordinating all that, to include coordination with the developer. Keep it simple."

Baer and Starry had known each other since they entered the accelerated three-year class at West Point in 1944. When the war ended, the class was split. Baer finished in three years. Starry remained to graduate with the four-year class of 1948.

Baer is a soft-spoken, mild-mannered, seemingly unflappable officer. He does have a temper that comes on with all the sudden ferocity of a summer thunderstorm, but it quickly passes, leaving the air refreshed. Starry is more flamboyant, a visionary, and he is sometimes hard to get along with. He has many admirers, but he also has his share of detractors. They complain that he tends to surround himself with a small group of close associates and to exclude others, especially if they are not tankers.

An officer who was two years behind Starry at West Point recalls the day the upperclassman was assigned to coach the plebe swimming team. Starry didn't stand at poolside, as most coaches would. Instead, he mounted the high board and punctuated his instructions with the crack of a large bullwhip.

When Baer and Starry went to Europe to look at allied tank designs in the mid-seventies, they made a strong enough impression that one of their British hosts recalls the visit clearly: "They struck us as a very balanced team in the sense that Starry was very much an extrovert and a talker, and I don't mean that unkindly, whereas Baer was a much more in-depth person who I think regarded himself as being, in a way, the watchdog to see that Starry didn't go too far into the realms of fantasy."

Despite the marked differences in style and temperament, Starry and Baer established a personal and working relationship that served them and the Army remarkably well. They worked so closely, in fact, that they often held joint briefings, which quickly became known as the Donn and Bob Show. They swore at the beginning that they were not going to let anyone drive a wedge between them, and they didn't.

As soon as Baer became program manager, he faced two immediate problems. One was to establish cost goals. The other was to set in motion the process that would lead to the choice of two contractors to develop and build prototypes of a new tank.

The decision at the September 27 meeting to load on the new armor and build a heavier tank than contemplated by Desobry's group pushed the issue of cost to the forefront. On orders from Abrams, Baer set up a cost committee and began marathon meetings in a basement office at the Pentagon.

Congress had left no doubt that the tank could not "cost too much," but what did the word "cost" mean? One faction argued that the tank would be in trouble if the figure for the total program rose too high. Concern about total cost contributed to the decision of Desobry's group to recommend building a relatively small number of tanks. Others insisted that the cost of the individual tank was the critical factor. After all, they noted, the sudden demise of the XM-803 came when critics were able to label it a "million-dollar tank." The whole discussion took place in a kind of never-never land. Committee members didn't know what the tank would look like, how many would eventually be built, where they would be built, or who would build them. They were talking about the cost of a tank that would not begin coming off the production lines for another six or seven years and would be in production more than a decade later.

The unreal atmosphere is captured in an exchange between two of the officers as they sought to estimate how much would be saved through competition.

"How can you compare the alternatives without keying a cost [savings] to the advantages of the competition?" one asked.

"We can't do it" came the reply. "We have no experience. I don't know—maybe you could say five percent."

"Why five percent?"

"I don't know. If you have a better number, let's use it."

No one had a better number, so five percent was adopted as the amount to be saved through competition.

The argument over how to measure the "cost" of the tank was settled by an agreement to use the amount the government would pay for an individual tank—what is known in Pentagon jargon as the design to unit hardware cost or, simply, hardware cost. The figure was arrived at by making an estimate—admittedly rough—of the cost of each component of the tank, such as engine and fire control, and then adding the column of numbers. The hardware cost was an artfully contrived number that covered building an individual tank and even included the cost of tools. But it did not include funds needed for research and development or for production facilities. This magic number was set at $507,790, to be measured in 1972 dollars.

The Army would have to live with that number for years into the future, and it was a very demanding goal—smaller than estimates, made several years earlier, of the cost of the XM-803 and about the same as the amount Desobry's people had contemplated for a tank at least six tons lighter.

The figure the Army picked is probably the lowest meaningful number it could honestly use—as far below the lethal million-dollar tab as possible. It has the advantage of being loosely comparable to what most people want to know—the sticker price. Those who oppose a weapon, on the other hand, like to use a much larger figure, expressed in inflated dollars and including all the costs of research, development, and production. By that measure, the M-1 was already pressing at the million-dollar mark before contractors had even been asked to bid.

As the M-1 program demonstrates, neither of these figures tells the true costs of a major weapons system. The only figure that tells the whole story is the life cycle cost, which covers not only developing and manufacturing a new weapon but also operating it as long as it stays in service.

Much of the saving came by cutting the number of prototypes and reducing the amount of money available for testing. On orders from a top Pentagon civilian, Baer slashed an additional $40.5 million from the budget. When alarmed Army officials got permission to restore that cut, they couldn't find a way to do it without making it appear that the cost of the tank was already getting out of control. So they did without the money.

The limits on the number of prototypes and on testing imposed by the tight budget later caused the Army some very difficult days. But the strict budget did have the advantage of imposing an iron discipline on Baer and his successors as managers of the program. From experience, he knew that as long as he stayed on schedule and within the cost ceiling, he would be left alone. But as soon as his cost or schedule began to slip, he would have more help than he could use.

He also knew the cost figure chosen by the Army was the number by which Congress would measure his performance. How seriously he took that measure was emphasized once when the House Armed Services Committee asked about costs. He assured them he was still under the ceiling and added: "As far as I am concerned, if we break that, we bring our resignation along with it and terminate the tank program at the same time."

As Baer set about his other urgent task—lining up competitors for the Army's biggest weapons purchase of the final quarter of the century—one can see falling into place many of the reforms often proposed by critics of Pentagon procurement practices. The tank program was to provide a test of many of these reform proposals.

There would be intense competition, prices would be fixed as soon as practical, performance would be guaranteed, risky technology would be avoided, costs would be ruthlessly controlled, and schedules would be rigidly enforced. The congressional mandate to have two manufacturers build prototypes fitted in with another of the then-popular reforms, known as fly-before-you-buy.

Much of this was the reverse of the way the Army had always done business. In the past its own arsenals had designed tanks, sometimes built and tested prototypes, and then delivered blueprints to industry with the instruction "Build this." Under the new system the successful bidders would be told in broad terms what the Army wanted the tank to do and would then be responsible for the design.

The Army, desperate for a new tank, went along with the reforms. But it was not entirely comfortable with this unfamiliar approach. Hiring two contractors to build prototypes would cost about $150 million, and what if the Army didn't like the result? It was surrendering a good deal of control to try out an untested theory.

There was another problem in going to industry. Unlike the Air Force and the Navy, the Army is not really a part of the military-industrial complex. Both the Navy and the Air Force are served by companies that do all or most of their business with the Pentagon, many of them working primarily with one service. This relationship creates just the opposite of a monopoly, in which one supplier dominates the market. In the military-industrial complex one customer dominates the market. The term the economists use for that kind of relationship is "monopsony."

Companies in the aerospace industry spend all their time trying to please their one customer. Many of them are geared up to produce relatively small numbers of very complex, very expensive machines. Much of their work is done in sterile, laboratorylike conditions, quite unlike a tank factory, where delicate adjustments are made with a twelve-pound sledge.

Many companies showed an interest in the tank program. In fact, ninety-eight were present at the initial bidders' conference. But it was not to Lockheed or McDonnell Douglas or Boeing that the Army looked for a tank maker. Realistically, it seemed to the Army that only the Big Three automakers had the skills to produce a tank. But the main business of Ford, General Motors, and Chrysler is almost the opposite of the typical military-industrial company. Their specialty is mass production and mass marketing, not producing a few complex items for a single demanding and often unpredictable customer. To them, turning out 40 or 50 units an hour in every factory was mass production; turning out 60 or even 150 tanks a month was not. While small groups in each company were eager to build tanks, the attitude at the top corporate levels ranged from moderate interest to indifference.

The greatest interest was shown by Chrysler, which had been the Army's tank maker for more than two decades. While this was a tiny part of the company's business, it was a steady source of income, and the firm wanted to keep it.

Many in the Army looked forward to working with another contractor, especially on a brand-new tank which had lots of room for fresh ideas. Ford, which hadn't been in the tank business since World War II, gave the project serious consideration. General Motors, after its frustrating experience as the contractor on the MBT-70, the XM-803 and an ill-fated truck program, was reluctant but finally agreed to enter the competition.

On May 8, 1973, the bids came in. GM and Chrysler submitted proposals. Ford, which had hoped to use Israeli tank designers on its staff, couldn't get them cleared for security and decided to drop out. On June 28 development contracts were awarded, but the amounts the two companies received were different. Chrysler's bid was for $68.2 million. GM asked for and received an $87 million contract. Each company was to build three prototypes: one to test the gun and fire control system; one to test the propulsion, track, and suspension; and one to be shot at to test the armor. They were given two and a half years to do the work and almost complete freedom.

Freedom was, of course, a relative thing. The developers were to find themselves constantly squeezed between the cost ceiling and the Army's requirements and desirable characteristics. The six mandatory requirements were: Have a weight of 58 tons; have a width of 144 inches to permit passage through tunnels encountered in Europe; remain on schedule; provide significant improvement over the M-60; meet standards of reliability, availability, maintainability, and durability; and stay under the cost ceiling of $507,790 in 1972 dollars. So long as they stayed under the cost ceiling and met all six mandatory requirements, the competitors could make trade-offs among the nineteen characteristics the task force had listed in order of priority, from crew survivability at the top of the list to transportability at the bottom.

The contractors agreed to deliver the prototypes for testing early in 1976, and the Army promised a decision in the summer of that year. Both teams faced a formidable challenge in building the basic vehicle before they reached the point where it would be furnished with guns and electronic devices to make it a fighting machine. They needed a suspension and a track capable of supporting the formidable weight of the special armor. They needed a transmission capable of transferring the power from the engine to the track without coming apart. Most of all, they needed an engine far more powerful than any tank engine then in use.

5

Turbine in the Dust

BY THE TIME Bill Clements hoisted himself out of the driver's compartment of Chrysler's prototype at Aberdeen Proving Ground one day in the spring of 1976 and a muddy, shaken Martin Hoffmann climbed down from the tank commander's position, the Army was convinced it had a friend in the highest places. Chrysler was happy it still had a tank.

William P. Clements, Jr., a self-made Texas millionaire who had built a small drilling supply service into an international operation, was the deputy secretary of defense, the department's number two man. He relished the opportunity to escape the paper work, to get some mud on his boots and some grease on his hands and see for himself how the military's newest machinery was coming along.

When Clements visited Aberdeen, he was invited to drive the Chrysler prototype. Hoffmann, the secretary of the army, climbed up into the tank commander's position in the turret. Clements lay back in the couchlike driver's compartment down in the hull, peering out through his open hatch, the turret swiveling just above his head. Manipulating the control bar—patterned after the controls on a motorcycle—he moved out carefully, feeling his way along, gradually going faster. As he picked up speed, the tracks threw up a shower of mud, liberally coating the occupants.

Suddenly a deer bolted from the woods, and Clements took off in pursuit. The tank handled like a dream. Its suspension smoothed out the rough terrain; the turbine provided instant speed; the responsive controls made it easy to follow the bounding deer. To the horror of company and Army officials watching through binoculars, Clements seemed not to have noticed a large concrete wall, partially hidden by bushes. He was heading straight toward it at about forty miles an hour. Chrysler's prototype was about to be turned into scrap metal, to say nothing of the fate of two of the Pentagon's top officials.

At the last minute Clements swerved and missed the wall by about ten feet. He wheeled the tank back in front of the grandstand, hauled himself up out of the driver's compartment, and climbed down to the ground, grinning with pleasure, like a child with an expensive new toy.

Hoffmann had direct responsibility for choosing the tank builder, handing out the biggest contract in Army history. But Defense Secretary Donald Rumsfeld had delegated Clements to oversee the tank program. Regardless of Hoffmann's decision, the winner would still have to pass muster with Clements, and he obviously liked the Chrysler.

After two and a half years of work Chrysler and General Motors had each delivered a full-scale prototype tank to the Army at Aberdeen on February 3, 1976. Each had also provided a chassis with a nonfunctional turret for automotive testing along with armored models of the hull and turret to be shot at.

Surprisingly, at first glance the two companies' wares seemed almost identical. Both design teams had faced the same basic problem of fitting to the tank the big rectangular boxes housing the special armor, and both had responded in very similar ways. Each tank had a sharply rectangular chassis topped by a large, boxy turret. In each case the front of the chassis and the turret sloped backward to increase the distance a shell would have to travel to penetrate into the crew compartment.

From a short distance away there was only one readily apparent difference between the two: General Motors had six wheels to a side, while Chrysler, concerned that the tank would eventually grow in weight, had provided seven wheels. Even the designers were reduced to counting road wheels.

But as soon as the two prototypes were seen in motion,

differences became apparent. The GM entry looked and sounded the way a tank was supposed to look and sound. As it moved cross-country, a plume of black smoke rose from its exhaust ("Old Smokey" the Chrysler people dubbed it), and the throaty roar of its powerful diesel heralded its coming and going. In comparison, the Chrysler tank had no telltale exhaust smoke, and the high-pitched whine of its turbine engine was barely perceptible from a short distance away.

The difference in the approach taken by the two companies went back to the very beginning, as each of the competitors assembled its team of about three hundred design and management experts in the summer of 1973. The head of the Chrysler team was Dr. Philip W. ("Phil") Lett, a soft-spoken man who seems strangely out of place as a builder of killing machines. He had gone straight to Chrysler after winning his doctorate in mechanical engineering at the University of Michigan in 1950 and had been building tanks ever since. From the beginning he knew that one of his most important and difficult decisions would be the choice of an engine.

Lett looked at three engines. Two were diesels—similar to the engines that power large trucks—and one was a turbine, adapted form the power plant of a helicopter. The Germans had developed a very powerful water-cooled Daimler-Benz diesel for their Leopard 2 tank. An American firm, Teledyne Continental Motors, had developed its own powerful diesel. It had the advantage of being smaller and lighter than the German model, and even more important, it was air-cooled. Ever since World War II the Army had worried about the loss of cooling fluid in combat and had insisted on air-cooled engines for its tanks.

The engine designers faced a daunting problem. The Army demanded an engine at least twice as powerful as those in existing tanks. For the first time each of the twelve cylinders in the diesel would have to turn out more than a hundred horsepower, more power than the entire engine in many autos on the American highways.

The Germans took the brute-force approach. They built a

massive engine capable of the needed power and then added a heavy liquid cooling system to control the engine temperature.

The Americans took a more subtle and difficult approach. They designed a complex system that permitted the compression of the cylinders to change to meet the power demands on the engine. This variable compression diesel, as it was called, was smaller and lighter than the German engine, and it was also air-cooled. But the technology was new and therefore more risky.

Finally, it was politics more than technology that ruled out the German engine. Choice of the Teledyne engine would mean fifteen hundred to two thousand jobs in Muskegon, Michigan. The Pentagon was unlikely to risk the political flak of moving those jobs to West Germany.

The alternative to the diesel was a helicopter engine adapted for use in a tank by Avco Lycoming. Although it would be built in Connecticut rather than Michigan, at least it would provide jobs in the United States, not in Europe. Congressmen from both states lobbied for "their" engine, but their efforts had no apparent influence on the final decision.

Technically the diesel and turbine engines use entirely different methods of producing power. In a diesel, fuel is squirted into each of the cylinders in turn. As the fuel is compressed and then burns, it forces the cylinder to the bottom of its shaft. Each of the cylinders is attached to a crankshaft that runs through the engine compartment. As the cylinders move up and down, they turn the crankshaft and provide power to the transmission.

The turbine is basically a simpler mechanism. Fans suck in air and compress it. Fuel is mixed with the air and burned at a high temperature. The hot gas that results swirls through a large fan, or turbine. The spinning turbine feeds power into the transmission. Both the turbine and the diesel can burn a variety of fuels, from high-octane gasoline to heating oil, but the turbine works efficiently on any flammable liquid while the diesel works best on diesel oil and less well on other fuels.

To Lett, the advantages of the turbine made an impressive list: It was smaller and lighter than a diesel—three tons lighter than the German engine—and this would permit the tank to carry more armor. It was smokeless and far quieter than a diesel. It started instantly in any weather, required no warm-up period, and could go from idle to full power in seconds, giving unprecedented acceleration for a vehicle as big as a tank. The turbine also promised to be more reliable and easier and cheaper to maintain, primarily because it had one-third fewer moving parts than the diesel.

There were some disadvantages to be listed: Even in the best of circumstances, tank tracks throw up a shower of dust or mud. In battle the air is filled with noxious fumes and dirt from exploding shells. Would the turbine, with its insatiable hunger for clean air, survive in this dirty environment? Also, the turbine tank, with an engine far thirstier than the diesel, would have to carry more fuel, which meant more room in the tank and an added strain on the Army's logistics system. Since the Army would continue to have many older diesel tanks, switching to a turbine for the new tank would require separate training, overhaul, and spare parts systems for the two engines.

All the technical pros and cons were overshadowed by two practical questions: Would the Army buy a turbine that cost forty thousand dollars more than a diesel? Would the Army buy a turbine in any case, no matter how good it was? Lett was dealing with a staunchly conservative institution that had seen two tank programs killed because they pushed technology too far and cost too much.

Lett had put together what he considered the world's finest tank design team. He chose a retired colonel—Louis F. ("Lou") Felder—as his key aide, and he set up an advisory group of Chrysler employees who were former soldiers.

He also relied heavily on the advice of sergeants from Fort Knox in designing his tank. Before deciding on the unusual compartment in which the driver lies on his back and manipulates controls on a handlebar suspended in front of him, he had the sergeants experiment with a variety of configurations, from the prone position to one in which the driver sat straight up, as in a normal tank. They liked the couchlike seat—and saved Lett a few inches in the height of the vehicle.

Chrysler gave Lett a broad-based charter: Build the best tank you know how and win the competition. The company brass left Lett and the tank-building division pretty much alone, guided by two unwritten rules: (1) Don't embarrass the company and (2) don't lose any money. Number one was more important.

When the influence of the automaking side of the company was felt, it came in the imposing form of William S. ("Bill") Blakeslee, a senior vice-president. Felder, a former Green Beret and jungle fighter, was not easily awed. But coming wide-eyed into this strange corporate culture, he found Blakeslee something to behold. To Felder, he seemed to be the stereotype of the automotive executive: big, bluff, white-haired, profane, domineering, difficult to work for. But the two men developed a bond, born of the respect each had for the other's contribution to the development of the tank.

Blakeslee's contribution was a sense of style, imposed on the soldiers' "simple tin box." The tank makers later credited him with making all the right decisions—for all the wrong reasons. His insistence on giving the tank a more stylish look, for example, resulted in reducing its height by as much as fourteen inches. He also demanded a full skirt over the tracks at the rear of the tank because it looked better that way. Later that full skirt kept dust from the engine during crucial tests.

Normally Blakeslee met with Lett, Felder, and several of Lett's key aides once a week, on Saturday mornings. This was when decisions had to be made, explained, and justified, and there was always at least a little nervous tension in the air. The pressure on Lett grew as each Saturday morning passed and he delayed for one more week the decision on the engine.

Finally a choice could be avoided no longer. One last time all the arguments were rehearsed. Technically the turbine was ahead on points, but that didn't really answer the question of which engine Chrysler should choose. For a moment there was silence around the table. Then Blakeslee pointed his finger at Lett and demanded: "Which is it going to be?"

Lett looked him in the eye and said: "Let's go with the turbine."

Blakeslee nodded his agreement, and the fateful decision was made.

Lett's counterpart at General Motors was Fred A. Best. Unlike Lett, who had spent his career in the tank business, Best was an electrical engineer and an experienced GM manager whose very first assignment as a tank builder was the M-1 project. Instead of creating a special tank-building division, GM made Best's unit a separate operation under its Detroit Diesel Allison Division, which had extensive experience in building diesel engines and transmissions for track-laying vehicles. Allison engineers also worked independently with both Best and Lett to build the transmissions used in both tanks.

Best pulled together a strong engineering team, including veterans of the MBT-70 effort. He proved to be a more cautious manager than Lett, relying more on his engineers than on the sergeants and sticking with existing, tested technology. There were no crisis judgments like the turbine decision at Chrysler. Instead, decisions were made step by step. If one decision pushed up the weight or the cost, then something else had to give. Best told his team its job was to produce the "optimum tank for the dollar."

If he could have looked in on the Saturday morning meeting at Chrysler, he would have been surprised by the agony over the engine. He had taken a serious look at the turbine but found the American diesel a fairly straightforward choice. It offered lower fuel consumption, seemed to promise superior reliability, and cost forty thousand dollars less than the turbine.

Much of the testing at Aberdeen centered on the performance of the two engines because so much was demanded of the power plant. While the tank weighs about the same as a large tractor-trailer, its engine is five times more powerful, and it must race cross-country as well as speed down a smooth highway.

The proving ground is nestled at the upper end of the Chesapeake Bay, about twenty-five miles north of Baltimore, and the test section covers nearly a hundred square miles of land and water. It provides a vast torture chamber for machines and, incidentally, for men as well. With the mud and the wind and the constant dampness from the bay, it seemed to those involved in the tests in the early months of 1976 that winter would never end.

At the heart of the proving ground is a permanent test center, a kind of open-air laboratory where different vehicles can be subjected to nearly identical stresses and their performance measured precisely. There the tanks ran through a bin filled with slippery clay. They crawled over a frame twister in which alternating bumps compressed one part of the suspension system and then another. They had to demonstrate they could cross an eighteen-foot gap without falling in, climb in and out of a deep ditch, drive along forty-degree side slopes, and dash over a washboard surface with six-inch-high bumps. In one particularly scary test the crews headed straight up a sixty-degree ramp, steeper than the streets of San Francisco, and then stopped to make sure fuel would not leak out and oil would not drain away from the engine and transmission—and to see if the brakes would hold.

As Clements's ride demonstrated, the tanks performed so well while zooming across rough terrain that the difference from all previous tanks was almost unbelievable. Soldiers delighted in demonstrating the tanks' performance for visiting dignitaries by "going airborne": speeding over a rise in the ground so fast that the tracks left the earth and the entire fifty-eight-ton monster flew through the air for a few yards.

For the engineers of both companies, it was a nervous few months, nursing their machines through tests that would mean a multibillion-dollar contract for the winner—and nothing for the loser. There were moments when nothing seemed to go right. On one test of its ability to ford a stream, the seals on the Chrysler tank leaked, and it sent up a cloud of steam that looked like a small Vesuvius. But by the time the tests were finished, the tanks had performed so well that both companies were convinced they deserved to win.

Throughout the test period the results were channeled to rented offices in a shopping center near the tank plant north of Detroit. There a Source Selection Evaluation Board, independent of Baer's project manager's office, sorted through mountains of data to draw up a scorecard on the performance of the two contenders. The board had a staff of more than fifty and called in many more experts from universities and industry.

When the board finished its work, it did not make a choice between the two competitors. That was the responsibility of the secretary of the army. Those who were given a look at the scoreboard could see that the competitors were virtually neck and neck.

The turbine, as expected, gave Chrysler more pickup and agility. The Chrysler tank also did somewhat better in the firing tests. General Motors rated higher in armor protection, and it seemed, in a number of ways, more finely engineered than the Chrysler entry. There was no doubt in the minds of those who sat in on the many briefings presented by the board that if a vote had been taken, GM would have been the winner—largely because of the less expensive and supposedly less risky diesel engine.

The most important result of the tests to Baer was the impressive performance of both tanks. He felt he had two winners. To this point the fly-before-you-buy testing of prototypes seemed a rousing success. Moreover, because the Army had paid for the research, it was free to incorporate all the good points of the loser into the winner.

Baer was even beginning to feel a little better about a decision made by Hoffmann's predecessor following the death of Abrams at the age of fifty-nine on September 4, 1974. He had succumbed of complications following surgery for lung cancer. Howard ("Bo") Callaway, a former congressman serving as secretary of the army, impulsively announced that the new tank—then known as the XM-1 because it was still considered experimental—would be named for Abrams, scrapping the Army's secret plan to name it for General Marshall.

It was an appropriate decision. The tank truly represented Abrams's philosophy of what the Army needed to win in armored warfare. But Baer and others, including Abrams's widow, were distinctly uncomfortable with the decision. They preferred the announcement to have been delayed until the tank had been proved a success. Baer tried to reassure Mrs. Abrams. He told her it would be the Abrams if the tests went well but would become the Baer if it was a lemon.

She was not mollified. But by mid-1976 the program manager himself was optimistic that the Army would have an Abrams, not a Baer, whichever way Hoffmann's decision went. He was convinced that the Army was prepared to move smoothly along with the business of building its next generation of tanks.

One reason for the Army's confidence was the close relationship Baer had established with Clements. For months the program manager had been flying in from Detroit for regular Friday afternoon meetings with Clements in his Pentagon office.

The sessions with Clements, going far over their heads, brought frowns from some of Baer's uniformed superiors. But Baer's relationship with Clements had Hoffmann's strong support. It was part of their strategy to lure the Pentagon's number two man out to drive the tank and fire the gun, to keep him interested and informed.

July 20, 1976, the day of decision, began with an early-morning briefing for Hoffmann. He did not state his choice, but no one in the room doubted it was General Motors.

Army officials were so confident of the forthcoming decision that announcements naming the winner were typed up. Officers waited on Capitol Hill to deliver sealed envelopes to key members of Congress, probably by midafternoon. But the afternoon drew on into evening, and the calls did not come.

By the time the phones should have been ringing, it was obvious to Hoffmann and an entourage of top Army officials who had accompanied him to Clements's office shortly after lunch that the tank program was in serious trouble. When the last slide faded away at the end of the Army's presentation, Clements looked around the room and, as Baer remembers it, pronounced his verdict: "That's an excellent briefing and an excellent study you've made. But you chose the wrong system." He wanted to see a tank with a turbine and room for a bigger 120 mm cannon.

After a stunned silence, the Army officials protested that trying to incorporate the turbine and the bigger gun at this late date would doom the program. Clements insisted it could be done. "I'm going to make you eat the biggest goddamn crow I can find," he told the program manager.

"You didn't read your mail!" Clements exclaimed. "We told you to go out and find newer technology." Baer realized that despite his weekly meetings with the Pentagon's number two man, he had underestimated how hard Clements, with his fascination with machinery, had been trying to push the Army to be more daring.

About 4:30 P.M. the meeting with Clements broke up and the gloomy Army officials trooped next door to Rumsfeld's office. They argued in favor of announcing the winner. Clements held out for a delay of several months. Rumsfeld agreed to postpone his decision until the next day.

Shocked Army officials gathered that night in an all-out effort to stay on schedule. The tank program was in intensive care on life support, and the atmosphere was about as joyful as a deathbed vigil. Baer, single-mindedly focused on keeping his program alive, calculated that a delay not only would take time but could cost nearly a billion dollars. When Rumsfeld heard that figure, he scoffed: "Whoever prepared this is stupid. On the other hand, he was pretty smart. He didn't sign his name."

About 4:00 A.M. the gathering broke up, leaving behind the remnants of a late-night order from a fast-food shop. George Mohrman, one of the officers who had been waiting on the Hill to deliver the envelopes, wondered what more could go wrong as he walked out to his car in the predawn darkness through the lonely expanse of the Pentagon parking lot. He didn't have long to wait to find out. When he turned the ignition key, he realized he had left his lights on when he had parked and hurried to the meeting hours before. If one were inclined to look for omens of the tank program's future, the dead battery was not a good one.

By laboring through the night, the Army worked out three options to present to Rumsfeld. They were: Award the contract to General Motors and then negotiate changes; delay the award about five days to develop better estimates of the cost of the changes; or delay the program by several months and ask for new bids with a choice of engines and gun sizes. The first option was the Army's choice, the second was its fallback position, and the third was what Clements proposed—and the Army wanted desperately to avoid.

When Hoffmann and a small group of Army officials arrived at Rumsfeld's office about eleven o'clock the next morning, they felt they had done everything they could to keep the tank program moving forward. But they were not optimistic.

Clements argued that it made no sense to award a contract and then to negotiate with the winner. He later told a Senate hearing his reasoning: "I was unalterably opposed to making these changes in a sole source environment after the contractor was selected. I wanted to know what those unit costs were, what the delays in the program might be, if any, and have those costs determined competitively between the two contractors. That is the reason we made the decision we did."

The Army officials argued that not only was it unfair to the contractors to change the rules at the last minute, but a formal protest from either contractor could tie things up for as much as a year and a half. Rumsfeld brushed aside the Army's appeal and agreed with Clements: Delay the program four months, pay the contractors ten million dollars apiece, and give them until mid-November to revise their bids. The new proposals would provide for use of either engine and include a turret capable of handling either a 105 or 120 mm gun.

This delay satisfied Clements's desire to push for more advanced technology. It also left open another option of extreme importance to Rumsfeld. A former ambassador to NATO, the defense secretary had long been concerned about the jumble of mismatched weapons fielded by the Western allies. One country's ammunition wouldn't fit in another's guns. Soldiers from one country couldn't talk to neighboring units because their radios were different. The Germans still operated many aging American M-48 tanks. But if both countries built different new tanks, even that common link would be lost.

If some degree of standardization of the allied tanks could not be achieved before the contract was awarded, Rumsfeld feared, there wouldn't be another chance for twenty years or more. He very much wanted a deal with the Germans that would result in a common tank or two tanks with many common parts.

The Army knew of his feelings and had been involved in talks with the Germans over the previous three years. In December 1974 the United States and Germany had even signed an agreement under which the Leopard 2 would be tested in competition with the U.S. prototypes and, if judged best, would be built in America for the U.S. Army. As recently as a few weeks before the contract was to be awarded, Army officials had been in Europe, on Rumsfeld's orders, for more talks with the Germans.

Somehow, through all this, the Army largely succeeded in ignoring the growing political pressure for cooperation with the Germans and its meaning for their tank program. Perhaps it was because the Army couldn't imagine itself going to war in a German tank. Perhaps it was the memory of the wasted years devoted to the ill-fated MBT-70. Undoubtedly there was the human tendency to avoid unpleasant thoughts. Whatever the reason, it was a serious mistake for the Army to fail to take seriously Rumsfeld's deep personal commitment to joint international arms development. The very day after his decision to delay the contract award, he sent a high-ranking delegation to Europe with orders to work out a deal with the Germans.

Baer and another general were instructed to tag along like a couple of lowly horse holders, and they bitterly resented the order. It seemed to them that their role was just to "lend a little military green" to the delegation and to make it appear they favored the decision to delay when they really believed it didn't make any sense. For Baer this was a very difficult period. He had invested four years of his life in the new weapon, and now he felt as if he had been run over by one of his own creations. He was so worried that the disruption would result in the death of the tank that he protested in a letter to the chief of staff of the Army. But by that time even the Army's top uniformed officer had lost control of the Army's most important weapons program.

The Pentagon delegation returned from Europe a few days later with an agreement for sharing tank technology with the Germans. But the details were kept secret. In fact, through this whole period Congress was kept almost totally in the dark.

Baer was deeply worried about the congressional reaction. He feared that Congress would conclude that the Army couldn't make up its mind and that the evidence of indecision would prove fatal. The heart and soul of his approach had been to spell out what he was going to do and then to do it, on schedule and within the budget. If a skeptical Congress cut the funding and slowed down the program, this would inevitably cost more money and spawn more problems. He could see his credibility going up in smoke, with the M-1 added to the scrap heap along with the MBT-70 and the XM-803.

His major concern centered on the House. He had worked hard to build strong support there for keeping the tank program on track, and he did not want that support to slip away.

The reaction was worse than Baer feared. Support didn't

slip away; it was more like an avalanche. The members of Congress who were the best informed about the tank program and who had been most supportive felt betrayed. When they learned what the Pentagon had done behind their backs, they were outraged. Representative Elwood Hillis (Republican-Indiana), a World War II infantryman whose district included a large GM plant, spluttered: "We shouldn't have been informed at the same time the cabdrivers and waitresses were. . . ."

Clements eventually apologized for not keeping Congress informed, but that was one of the few conciliatory moments in a series of sizzling, confrontational hearings conducted by a subcommittee headed by Representative Samuel Stratton (Democrat-New York). He had long had a special interest in tanks because tank guns are made at the Watervliet Arsenal in his upstate New York district.

The subcommittee's outrage was intensified when the hearings jarred loose the text of the agreement with the Germans signed on July 28. It provided for separate German and American tanks using the same fuel, ammunition, track, transmission, night vision device, and gunner's telescope. Differences would be permitted in the suspension, hull, and turret designs and the fire control systems.

At the heart of the agreement was what looked like an even-handed deal: The Americans would use the German 120 mm gun, and in return the Germans would use the American turbine. But those like Stratton who had been following the tank program closely recognized this for what it was: a lopsided agreement, "a phony." He knew that the Leopard 2 was so far along in development that production would be almost finished before the turbine was fully developed and ready to be installed in a tank. There wasn't a chance the Germans would use the American turbine, but it was almost certain, if the agreement held, that the Americans would end up with the German 120 mm gun.

Stratton set out almost single-handedly to upset Rumsfeld's action and get the tank program back on the track originally laid down by the Army. He and Hillis, the other member of the two-man subcommittee investigating the tank program, produced a report on September 23. It was designed to turn Rumsfeld's action topsy-turvy and force the Pentagon to award the contract on the basis of the original proposals.

A decision by the full Armed Services Committee was set for Tuesday, September 28. In the intervening five days Pentagon officials, led by Rumsfeld and Clements, swarmed over the Hill in a lobbying blitz. Stratton condemned the effort as unprecedented and appalling. What angered him most was that it was effective.

On the day of the vote a Pentagon official called Hillis out of his morning shower and convinced him to back a substitute resolution that would undercut Stratton and permit the program to continue on the path set by Rumsfeld. The committee scrapped Stratton's plan and agreed to the motion backed by the Pentagon. It gave the Army until November 17 to choose a contractor on the basis of the new, rather than the original, contract proposals. It also ordered the Army to choose the best engine, regardless of the understanding with the Germans.

If there was anger and confusion on the Hill, there was even more consternation among the design teams. Both contractors were rightly angry and suspicious. Lett concluded that the Army wanted to award the contract to GM on price and then put the turbine, which had made his bid higher, into the GM tank. That, in fact, was the Army proposal that Rumsfeld had rejected. Best and his people, surprised and bitterly disappointed, suspected that the delay was a sneaky way of stealing their victory and giving the contract to Chrysler.

With the information now available, it appears that the two contractors had a roughly equal chance to win the contract. Chrysler had a somewhat easier engineering task, but GM had already won the Army's favor with its original entry. In effect, the score was tied, and the two were like professional ball teams going into extra innings. They reacted to this extension of the competition differently.

Members of the GM tank design team had gotten wind of the tentative decision in their favor and had begun to think of a victory party. When they heard of the delay, morale dropped so low that there was talk of protesting the decision and then dropping out of the competition rather than dragging the members of the team through another futile four months of work.

On August 2 the president of GM wrote an angry letter to Rumsfeld denouncing the reopening of the competition as "improper." But he did not file the kind of formal protest that the Army dreaded, and he ordered the tank team to prepare a new proposal. Once over the initial disappointment, Best rallied his team, and they settled down to try to produce a winner.

Members of the Chrysler team were, at first, equally discouraged and inclined to file a protest. Then they learned they had been underbid and would have lost if the contract had been awarded on schedule. They seized on the delay as a new lease on life. In the next four months they had two big challenges: Redesign the tank to meet the new requirements, and reduce the cost.

Felder took to the road with other top officials. They personally visited all of the company's major contractors and most of its subcontractors, spread over forty-five states, and "leaned on them" to get better prices and delivery schedules.

Lett's designers went back over their drawings, looking for ways to save even a few hundred dollars. One example: The intial design used a six-hundred-dollar reservoir borrowed from the M-60 to hold the overflow hydraulic oil as it heats up and expands when the gun is fired. An engineer preparing to drive to work on a frosty morning checked the windshield washer reservoir on his car and had an idea. As soon as he got to the office, he changed the specifications to substitute a similar transparent plastic container, costing about twenty-five dollars, for the six-hundred-dollar reservoir and gauge.

When the new proposals were opened, it seemed to the Army that GM had done a good job of fitting the turbine and the bigger gun into its tank but had made few other improvements. Chrysler, on the other hand, came in with a markedly better tank and it had succeeded in lowering its price, with the bulk of the savings from redesign of the turret.

To Baer, the turbine-powered Chrysler tank seemed to be the clear winner, and top Army officials agreed. He put in a call to Best and told him the bad news. As soon as Baer hung up, Best called together a few key members of his team and told them: "It's all over. Let's start dismantling."

In Baer's mind, Chrysler had suffered on the first go-around because it had taken a higher-risk approach to the design of the new tank while GM was more conservative. The extra innings gave Chrysler time to refine and improve its design and whittle down the cost.

The bids were: $196 million for Chrysler; $232 million for General Motors. In July Chrysler had been high at $221 million, and GM low at $208 million. On November 12, 1976, Chrysler signed a contract for full-scale engineering development of the Army's new main battle tank.

In many ways the contract was a model of the kinds of reforms that were supposed to cure at least the most glaring of the Pentagon's procurement ills by putting a heavy burden of responsibility on the winning contractor. The contract was for development, not production. But it gave the Army an option of ordering the first 462 tanks—two years' production—at a fixed price. Chrysler also assumed financial responsibility for the performance of its subcontractors. As part of the deal Chrysler also provided a warranty that its tanks would meet Army specifications. The warranty did not cover the test vehicles; but it did cover the tanks turned out in the first two years of production, and the company eventually spent several million dollars correcting problems such as electromagnetic interference in the stabilization system and the tendency of the rubber to fall off the road wheels.

Chrysler was, in effect, signing on for a lengthy period of development and then locking itself into a production phase that would not even begin for five years. Lett considered it a very racy course with an awful lot of risk.

Award of the contract vindicated the position taken by Clements in July. The Army had gained a choice of engines and guns in both competing tanks. Chrysler had lowered its bid and improved its tank. The program had been delayed only four months. On the other hand, the Army was committed to some fairly risky new technology, and Rumsfeld's hopes for a standardized tank had by no means been assured.

Several nagging questions marred Chrysler's victory. Did the company, learning of the lower General Motors bid, artificially drop its price to get the contract, hoping to make up for the lower bid with later changes and price increases? And did the Ford administration knowingly let Chrysler get away with this tactic—familiar in the military-industrial complex as a buy-in—because the company was weaker financially than GM?

Lett says he feared that under pressure to push down the price, he might inadvertently bid too low, so he set up a special audit system to make sure that didn't happen. But something that occurred shortly after the contract award continues to be cited as evidence of a buy-in.

The ink on the contract was still damp when the Army added $41.2 million to the Chrysler contract, bringing the total to $237.2 million—$5.2 million more than the GM bid. The additional money was to pay for more research than Chrysler had planned, especially on the turbine. Pentagon officials explained that such contract adjustments were not unusual and that GM would also have received more money if it had won.

The "buy-in" criticism surfaces from time to time. But there is very little evidence that it is what happened. The money added to the contract was for additional work, not additional pay for work included in the original bid. This would not help Chrysler if it had bid too low on the basic contract. In fact, Chrysler lost money on the early production phase of the program.

As it turned out, Baer was right to put more money into engine development. His error was in adding too little, rather than too much. He badly underestimated the difficulty of adapting a helicopter engine for use in a tank.

Avco Lycoming, which had built helicopter engines and had developed the tank turbine during the old MBT-70 program, was given the engine contract. The company started with some daunting handicaps, not the least of which was the government-owned plant in Stratford, Connecticut, where the Navy's Corsair fighters had been built in World War II.

When the workers arrived to begin setting up shop, they found paint hanging in strips from the ceiling and so many puddles on the floor that visitors had to borrow galoshes to walk through the high-ceilinged hangarlike plant. Up above, birds flew freely in and out the myriad broken windows, and their droppings were a constant annoyance.

In some areas there was no electricity or heat, and bathrooms were often a block or more away. It struck a visitor from the Pentagon as the way a factory might look in a country suddenly at war and under enemy attack. Morale was low, company managers seemed unable to master the basic task of producing quality engines on time, and top corporate officers were slow to recognize the problem and order the kind of shake-up that was needed.

Workable engines were in such short supply when assembly of the first production-line tanks started at the Lima plant in February 1980 that there weren't enough to equip the new tanks. To avoid shutting down the entire operation, the few available engines were used over and over. An engine would be installed in a tank long enough for a whirl around the test track. Then the tank was stored, and the engine switched to propel another tank through the test procedure. At the worst period in early 1983, thirty-five engineless tanks were in storage, and the spectacle of tanks without engines became a symbol of problems with the program. Workers at Lima wondered what the Russians thought when they saw the satellite photos of all those new tanks sitting there immobile.

What happened at Lima was nothing new for the Army. In 1941 two locomotive manufacturers hurrying to produce their first tanks had only one transmission between them. They used it to demonstrate one tank for the secretary of war, then rushed the transmission to the other plant before the secretary arrived so he could see the other tank in action.

Avco's performance was so bad that for a while it was in danger of losing all or part of the contract, worth $340 to $370 million annually in sales, and it had to fight a bitter struggle in Congress to head off a plan by Pentagon civilians to establish a second source for tank engines.

At one point production was lagging by fifty or sixty engines, and, a company official later acknowledged, even the ones produced were "crappy." Under increasing pressure from the Army, Avco finally brought in new management, modernized the plant and equipment, and, belatedly, got a handle on production and quality control problems. After losing money on the M-1 engine for the first three years of production, the company eventually reached the point where it was delivering engines ahead of schedule and began making a profit in 1983.

But the improvement in quality and on-time deliveries was a long time coming, and the engine was, for several years, a matter of deep concern to the Army. Much of the concern about the performance of the turbine stemmed from tests, beginning in 1978, of Chrysler's eleven handmade preproduction models.

Lett had pleaded with Baer for a "honeymoon." He wanted six months and half a dozen prototypes so he could identify problems and fix them before the Army's testing began. Baer smiled understandingly—and said no. He figured prototypes would cost four or five million dollars apiece and any delay in the rigid schedule would cost two million dollars a month. He was determined to stay on schedule and within the cost ceiling.

Baer realized that rushing prototypes directly from the factory to testing without a shakedown period was asking for trouble. He was willing to take the risk, but neither he nor anyone else realized how bad the troubles would be.

Problems began to become apparent within days after the

first of the tanks arrived at Aberdeen in March 1978 for developmental testing, which is one of two kinds of tests done on new equipment. In these tests engineers and other experts use sophisticated instruments to rate the vehicle's performance against rigid standards. The other ordeal to which new equipment is subjected is known as operational testing, in which soldiers try to evaluate how the weapon would perform in combat. If something like the tank commander's position is poorly designed (as it was) or if something is going to break (as the control handle on the tank commander's machine gun did), this is where the Army finds out.

Normally the tests by the soldiers are conducted after problems identified by the engineers have been fixed. But to keep the M-1 on its rigid schedule, developmental and operational testing overlapped. The Aberdeen tests ran from March 1978 to September 1979. The operational tests in the sandy desert at Fort Bliss, Texas, went from May 1978 to February 1979.

At Aberdeen test crews worked two ten-hour shifts, six days a week. During the first six months so many things went wrong it seemed that the Army had a real lemon on its hands. Too often it was impossible to tell whether there was a defect in the new tank or a fault in the old testing equipment.

Despite the growing list of problems at Aberdeen, the rush to get started with operational testing by a specially created Army unit was so great that the first few tanks were actually flown to Fort Bliss. Lett watched anxiously as they were snatched from his hands, leaving him without a single prototype on which to try to duplicate and solve problems reported back from the test sites.

In view of the problems that cropped up, Baer is inclined to agree with Lett that it would have been better to provide more test vehicles. But Lou Felder recognized that given half a chance, engineers will never stop tinkering. He believes Baer's decision not to relax the budget or the time schedule was the right one.

Years before, Lieutenant General Bill Desobry, who headed the tank task force in 1972, looked at the rigid test schedule and the limited number of prototype tanks and exclaimed: "I'd sure hate to be the guy who has to test this tank!" In 1979 he was called back out of retirement as a consultant, and there he was, one of those involved in the testing.

When he got to Bliss, he found a "hybrid" military unit that was supposed to represent a cross section of the Army and avoid the kind of bias that might result if the tank had been given to an elite outfit for testing. But the soldiers had no unit cohesion, no esprit de corps. They didn't even know each other.

"It was a lousy damn outfit. It stunk," Desobry says. "The whole thing was rotten. It was probably the biggest disaster I've ever seen in the Army. I'm not blaming the soldiers or the officers. I'm blaming the setup. It was unbelievably unprofessional. It almost killed the tank. I've never been so low in my life. That was my baby."

Desobry was so concerned that he called the vice chief of staff of the Army in Washington, who had served under him in Germany, to warn him of impending disaster.

Almost everything that could go wrong did go wrong. Because the tank was brand-new and different in almost every way from the M-60, with which the troops were familiar, a whole new set of manuals was required so the soldiers would know how to operate and maintain the tank. Chrysler, in its rush to build the machine itself, neglected this part of its job. The manuals provided to the troops at Fort Bliss were virtually unusable. It took awhile for the company to realize how bad the manuals were and to get the cooperation of the soldiers in a crash effort to rewrite them.

The new tank also required an elaborate set of test equipment to enable maintenance men to find and fix problems. Again, Chrysler had not devoted enough attention to this task, and another major effort was required to design and build workable test devices.

There were a few bright spots, but not many. The torsion bar suspension—lighter, cheaper, and simpler than a hydraulic system—worked surprisingly well. And the soldiers loved the new tank—when it worked.

Back in Detroit, Felder agonized over the bad news flooding

in from Bliss. Some of the problems could be traced back to conditions in the field. A former General Motors engineer was so dismayed when he saw the troops using contaminated hydraulic fluid and failing to keep connections tight that he flew home to Detroit and resigned on the spot.

Solutions were found for many problems as the tests went on. Desobry and a Chrysler tank mechanic who had served in both the Russian and German armies spent a week under an M-1, trying to find how to keep mud and dirt from getting wedged up under the hull and causing the tank to throw its track. It was the same problem the Soviets had encountered with their Josef Stalin tank thirty years before. The solution was a scraper to remove the mud as the track turned. The two men fashioned a scraper copied from that on the Stalin tank and attached it to the M-1.

Two problems simply could not be ignored. One was the destruction of engines by dust. The other was, despite the scraper, the persistent throwing of tracks. No one knew what was causing them.

From the beginning everyone had been concerned about dust getting into the turbine. A turbine is less susceptible to damage from grit than a diesel because it has fewer moving parts and more room between parts. But the volume of air flowing through a turbine is so great that even a small leak in a filter can permit enough dust to enter the engine to cause harm.

When engines at Bliss began to break down because of dust ingestion, the problem was particularly troubling because an early prototype of the turbine-engined tank had operated successfully in the sandy desert near Yuma, Arizona. With the help of the stylish skirt Blakeslee had insisted on, the tank had seemed to be immune to damage from dust. Lett and Felder reluctantly faced up to the fact that if they couldn't find a way to keep the tracks on and prevent the engine from grinding itself to death, the Army didn't have a new tank. It had a sitting duck. They wrung a grudging okay from Blakeslee and asked the Army to suspend the tests for thirty days.

The engine problem required a real feat of detection. This is what had happened: In the middle of one night when the workers were trying to lower the engine and transmission—known as the power pack—into the first test model, they couldn't make it fit. They woke an engineer at home and asked him to hurry down. He told the workers to trim a little metal off the engine air inlet. The same "fix" was made on all eleven pilot models, but the change seemed so minor it was not reported to Chrysler executives.

When the workers sealed the air filter to the engine air inlet, enough metal had been removed from the inlet to leave a tiny gap—an open sesame to engine-killing grit. Unfortunately this built-in flaw was hidden from view at the bottom of the engine inlet. Only later was it found that the reason the engine wouldn't fit was that when the armored bulkhead that separates the crew compartment from the power plant was installed in the handmade tanks, it was out of position by a fraction of an inch.

During their detective work the Chrysler engineers found still another problem that permitted dust to enter the engine. In his effort to cut costs, Felder had decided to have his people make their own air filters rather than buy them from a high-priced vendor.

"We did a lousy job," Felder says. "When the filters were inserted, they did not seal. There was a gap of about a half to three-fourths of an inch on each of the seals. Again, you couldn't see that."

With tracks flying off one tank after another, it didn't take an expert to see that something was wrong. One obvious cause was the exuberance with which the soldiers drove the new vehicle—going faster, turning sharper than they had ever been able to do with older tanks. Baer concluded that both the Army and Chrysler had made a serious mistake in not foreseeing the stresses on the track and suspension system that would be created by a tank that was heavier and twice as fast as its predecessor. But even when the tanks were driven carefully, track throwing persisted, and no one knew why.

Not until months later was a major cause of the track throwing found: The gauge that indicates track tension had been miscalibrated by the manufacturer. As a result, the tracks were fastened on too loosely. Fixing this problem reduced track throwing to a relatively minor nuisance.

As if engine failure and track throwing were not enough reason for concern, reports from Bliss also showed an unexpectedly high rate of failure for the transmission. Since the transmission controls steering and brakes as well as transfers power from the engine to the tracks, a failure can be disastrous. In the early tests at Aberdeen in 1976 the transmission on a Chrysler prototype suffered a partial failure. The monster went careering off through the woods without steering or brakes. The crew managed to halt the vehicle before it suffered serious damage, and after a few such problems in the early shakedown period, the transmission had performed well in the developmental tests at Aberdeen. Why should it work in Maryland but come apart in Texas?

The answer turned out to be a novel "bowtie maneuver" invented by the soldiers at Bliss. Normally a tank hides behind a rise in the earth or in a hole in the ground until a target is spotted. As soon as the commander identifies a target and tells the loader what kind of ammunition to use, he orders: "Driver, move out!" The tank lurches up over the berm which has shielded it from view, and the commander orders: "Driver, stop!" The gunner sets the range with his laser, fires, and, if he has a hit, exclaims: "Target!" The driver quickly pulls back behind the berm.

Even though this whole process has taken less than fifteen seconds and the tank is again hidden from direct view, the muzzle flash and the crack of the gun have exposed its position. The result may be a barrage of artillery shells. Or the tank may be picked off the next time it pops over the berm.

In experimenting with the turbine, the soldiers discovered that their electronic controls permitted them to shift between forward and reverse with a simple twist of the wrist. And so the bowtie maneuver was born. This is the way it works: As the tank moves up over the berm, the driver switches into reverse. By the time the gunner fires, the tank is already beginning to move backward. Because the fire control system is stabilized, the gunner's aim is not disturbed by the abrupt movement. As the tank is still rolling rapidly backward, the driver flicks it into forward gear and moves to a new firing position. The tank is no longer where the enemy saw the muzzle flash. Unfortunately the effect of this maneuver is the same as shifting a moving car from reverse to forward and stepping on the gas. The transmission comes apart.

Chrysler engineers got together with those at Detroit Diesel Allison in Indianapolis, where the transmission is made, and came up with a device that keeps the tank from shifting between reverse and forward until it has come almost to a complete stop. It was a neat engineering solution to a difficult problem—and it made Desobry furious. To an old tanker, the bowtie maneuver was a brilliant innovation that could save lives on the battlefield, but instead of finding a way to permit the soldier to keep using this trick, the engineers found a way to keep him from hurting "their" tank.

By the time the tests at Bliss were completed, the Army knew it had some serious problems to solve and some that it would simply have to live with. It was no surprise that the turbine used more fuel than a diesel, but the tests brought home to the soldiers the fact that they would have to be much more concerned about fuel supplies than they had been since the switch from gasoline to diesel engines two decades earlier. Not only was the turbine twice as powerful as—and therefore much thirstier than—the diesel in the M-60, but it used almost as much fuel when idling as it did when traveling at full speed. It was little comfort to note that the M-1 was more fuel-efficient, pound for pound, than a Volkswagen Beetle.

Of the problems that remained, those closest to the situation were convinced they did not have any "program stoppers." Although the M-1 continued to be plagued for years by reports of engine failure caused by dust ingestion, that problem had been solved before the Bliss tests ended. Solutions also seemed to be at hand for track throwing and transmission failures.

Still, the biggest problems exposed by the tests had concerned the tank's mobility, and a tank that can't move is as good as dead. Persistent and repeated engine failures, it was later concluded, stemmed mostly from poor quality control by the engine maker. But these failures fueled lingering concern that there might be some basic design flaw in the engine or that a turbine really was unsuited for use in a ground combat vehicle.

Teledyne Continental Motors seized on doubts about the turbine for a last-gasp effort to sell its diesel to the Army. It hired a retired colonel who had served as a company commander under Abrams in World War II to provide expertise and launched a concerted lobbying campaign. It picked up support from the General Accounting Office (GAO) and some outside critics and even won a fourteen-million-dollar congressional research appropriation.

But the Army's tank experts were by that time sold on the turbine. If there was any money available, they argued, it should be used to perfect the turbine rather than fritter it away on the diesel. They were right. The diesel, with its complex variable compression cylinders, never did work properly. If the Army had switched to the diesel, it probably would have ended up with an unworkable engine or an expensive rescue operation—or both.

As the time for a production decision neared, however, there were still doubts in the highest levels of the Pentagon. General Bernard Rogers, when he was chief of staff, sometimes awoke at night and wondered if the Army had made the wrong choice of an engine.

Harold Brown, who had become defense secretary in 1977, ordered one more round of tests before he would approve the 352 tanks in the Army's 1980 budget. Three of the preproduction models were hurriedly fitted with all the latest improvements and taken to Fort Knox, where each of them was driven four thousand miles—as far as a tank would normally go in four or five years of duty—between June and October 1979.

These tests focused on mobility—whether the engine and transmission kept working and whether the tracks fell off—rather than how the gun and fire control system worked. The tanks did much better at Knox than they had done at Bliss.

But the tests were not without serious problems. Four engines suffered catastrophic failures. In one case a bolt came loose, wore its way through a screen, and was sucked into the rapidly spinning turbine. There were three catastrophic failures of the transmission. When the tests ended, an Army committee had to sort through these and other problems to determine which should be counted as failures of the engine or transmission (the engine destroyed by the loose bolt was not counted) and give its judgment of the durability of the systems that keep the tank moving.

The result was a test score well above the goal set by Brown for a production go-ahead. But Pentagon officials also studied the opinions of a nine-member panel of engine experts.

At the end of its first study, in April 1979, the panel reported: "The turbine engine was a good choice for the XM-1 program and will, if properly developed, provide significant benefits." But it warned: "The panel was deeply concerned . . . that the demonstrated reliability and durability of the power train was [*sic*] significantly below that projected, and unless positive steps were taken to improve the situation, the engine failure rate would adversely impact the entire XM-1 program. . . ."

When it submitted its second report in February 1980, the panel said: "We are pleased to report that significant progress has been made in the improvement of the reliability and durability of the XM-1 tank. . . . The success has been outstanding." With "aggressive action," it said, the Army could make the engine more reliable and durable than the diesel then in use.

The guarded optimism of the blue-ribbon panel was not

shared by the General Accounting Office. In one report after another, the GAO recommended halting or slowing down production while more work was done to make sure the engine, transmission, and tracks would perform as well as they were supposed to.

The GAO reports reflected a basic difference in philosophy with the Army. The soldiers believed in staying on schedule and going back to fix problems as they were discovered. The GAO believed in stopping the program until problems were fixed. The GAO feared that the Army, in its rush, would deploy junk. The Army feared that if the GAO had its way, nothing would ever be deployed.

The most direct appeal for a slowdown came in a GAO letter to Brown on April 16, 1979. It said: "We are . . . concerned that there is already deployed in Europe a number of systems whose availability for combat has been considerably reduced because of design problems. Had they been identified and corrected during system development, the combat readiness of U.S. forces would be enhanced. To rush the tank into production may run the risk of adding still another critical weapon to this list. . . ."

Brown, a physicist who had served as the Pentagon's chief of research and development in the 1960s, is the most technically competent defense secretary the nation has ever had. He agreed with the Army and, in October 1979, gave the go-ahead for the beginning of production.

But that did not mean that all the development problems had been solved. While much attention had been focused on the tank's mobility—its engine, transmission, and suspension—as much or more attention was being devoted to its main gun and fire control system, the things that made it a fighting machine. And here international politics played at least as big a role as technology.

6

The Five-Billion-Dollar Half Inch

ON A CRISP, clear December morning in 1977, General Sir Hugh Beach, Britain's master general of ordnance, looked over the high-ranking soldiers and civilians from the United States, Germany, and Great Britain gathered at Aberdeen Proving Ground and sized up the situation: "This is the most important battle fought on the Chesapeake Bay since Yorktown."

His comment was hyperbole with a sound base in fact. The Revolutionary War Battle of Yorktown, at the southern end of the bay, had been a great artillery duel, and on its outcome hung the fate of a nation. Another artillery duel was the attraction at Aberdeen on December 8, 1977. The stakes were not as high as they had been two centuries earlier, but they were still very high. Not only would the four-year-long tank gun competition, coming to its climax at Aberdeen, determine the cannon to be carried by the new American tank, but also at stake were billions of dollars, jobs in Düsseldorf and upstate New York, national prestige, and, almost lost sight of in the political infighting, the issue of winning or losing on the battlefield.

Acting as host, Brigadier General Philip A. Bolté, who had represented the United States through all the tests, had set up bleachers and a large tent to shelter the dignitaries.

On the firing line, fastened into heavy naval gun mounts, were three tank guns. One was the 105 mm American gun. Next in line were the German 120 mm gun and a somewhat different British 120 mm entry. Downrange a hundred meters—about a city block—were three targets, each about three feet square, designed by NATO experts to be as difficult to penetrate as a heavy Soviet tank. When the time for the shooting came, the VIPs all huddled behind a concrete wall and watched the test through closed-circuit television.

The Americans went first and penetrated the target. Then the British fired, with impressive results. Then the German round was loaded and clunk . . . reloaded, clunk. Nothing. Reloaded, clunk. Nothing. Even those desperately eager to see their gun prevail were embarrassed for the Germans. An irrepressible British brigadier didn't help by loudly volunteering to fire again.

Experts from all three countries gathered about the German gun. Nothing appeared wrong. They backed off and tried again. On the tenth try, with the same round of ammunition still in the breech, the gun fired. It was the only time during the tests that the weapon had failed to go off, and no one was ever able to explain the failure. By the time the gun fired, the visitors had long since examined the targets and drifted off to their limousines and helicopters. They would have another month to wait before learning which gun would arm the American tank, but those in the know weren't ready to write off the German entry.

To someone who is not a tanker, the intensity of the competition involving the two different-size weapons is puzzling. The physical difference between 105 and 120 mm—the metric measure of the interior diameter of the gun barrel—seems hardly enough to fight about. The 105 is about 4⅛ inches in diameter, the 120 about 4¾ inches—a difference of just a little more than half an inch. The projectile from the 105 leaves the muzzle at 4,850 feet per second, a little under a mile a second. The projectile from the 120 mm gun goes a little faster at 5,500 feet per second, five times the speed of sound. A sharp-eyed observer can catch a fleeting glimpse of the projectile as it leaves the muzzle.

While the press and Congress largely ignored this seemingly tiny difference and focused attention on other matters such as engine reliability, the gun was, for the Army, by far the biggest issue for the better part of a decade, from 1973 to the early 1980s. Top Pentagon civilians, enamored of the goal of common weapons for the NATO alliance and strongly influenced by alliance politics, favored the German gun. But Army officers were committed to the smaller 105 mm gun.

The big cannon not only is the most important weapon carried by the tank but also may be the most important weapon on the battlefield because it is the best tank killer. As such it is the culmination of centuries of development, going back to the ancient stone-hurling catapult. Artillery has always evoked mixed emotions. The first artillery employing gunpowder was condemned as the work of the devil. Later in the Middle Ages sentiment changed, and artillerymen even claimed their own patron, St. Barbara. Still later the church banned artillery as immoral, though the ban was fleeting.

For the people of that unscientific age, artillery was awesome, not only for the destruction it wrought but also because it involved very high technology, all of it a mystery to the populace. The cannon maker had learned to cast molten metal so it would hold up to the pressures and temperatures of repeated firings. Individual cannons were given names—the Great Devil, Basiliske, The Dragon (actually shaped like a dragon), the Great Mortar of Moscow, and Zam-Zammah—and became famous. The gunners had to know enough chemistry to mix their powder so it would provide force to hurl the projectile at the target without bursting the cannon, and they needed enough mathematics to calculate ranges and the trajectory of the projectile.

That all this gave rise to the popular image of the artilleryman as an ally of the devil is not difficult to understand. Gunners found that premixed powder would, more often than not, fail to fire. So they carried the ingredients with them to the battlefield, and there they could be seen, like so many alchemists, concocting their explosives, inserting them into the weapon, and then causing a tremendous blast. At one point the medieval cannon crews gained an undeserved reputation for sanctity when they could be heard reciting the Apostle's Creed after igniting the fuze. Actually the twenty seconds or so that it took to say the prayer was the time it took the fuze to burn.

When the Army set about the lengthy task of choosing a gun for its new tank, the tankers first had to decide what they wanted the weapon to do. In the background a difference of philosophy divided the German and British soldiers from the Americans.

The Europeans are convinced that bigger is better. At some point during World War II the British, Germans, and Russians all had been outgunned, and they didn't relish the experience. The Americans had come away from the war equally determined never to be outgunned. But as their ranks began to fill with systems analysts, they adopted what they considered a more analytic, scientific approach.

Their analyses told the Americans that it was foolhardy to carry the biggest possible gun. Instead, they concluded that the goal should be the smallest gun that can puncture the enemy's armor. With a smaller gun the tank itself can be smaller, it can carry more armor and ammunition, and the shells it carries will be smaller and cheaper.

The bias of American tankers in favor of a smaller gun—if it will do the job—was described by Lieutenant General James F. Hollingsworth in testimony before the House Armed Services Committee in September 1976. Although he was recently retired, members of the committee recognized him as an actor in a familiar drama in which a respected retired officer testifies boldly about things that active-duty officers don't feel free to say. His testimony came in the midst of the battle over gun size between the uniformed Army and top civilians. The outspoken general made a strong case: "I would rather have a 22-caliber tank weapon, myself, so you could carry about 5,000 rounds in there—if you could get a 22-caliber to eat up an enemy tank. . . . The larger the gun, the less consideration you have got for the man that's got to fight it. This is the fellow we have got to think about. The harder it is to load, the fewer rounds you can carry, the greater psychological impact it has on the crew. . . ."

The U.S. Army is a fairly late convert to the smaller-is-better school of thought. A blue-ribbon panel of scientists studied the tank armament issue in 1958 and recommended that "conventional weapon programs, including hypervelocity fin-stabilized penetrators and guns, be sharply curtailed" so money would be available for a big tank-mounted missile capable of knocking out enemy tanks at long ranges. For the next decade this was Army policy.

But the experience with the Shillelagh system, which combined a monstrous 152 mm gun and a missile, was a bitter one. By the time the M-1 came along, the Army had turned completely around, deciding to leave the targets beyond one and a half to two miles to missiles carried by other vehicles and to use the gun to fight tank battles at relatively short ranges of up to about a mile and a half.

A good technical reason supports use of a gun, rather than a missile, on a tank. The tank gun is what is called a direct-fire weapon. Unlike the projectile from conventional artillery, which flies in a long arc high into the sky before falling back down, the projectile from the tank gun speeds almost straight to the target. The tank gun is a sudden-death weapon: If the gunner's aim is accurate, he is virtually assured of a hit a second or two after he fires. A missile, on the other hand, may take fifteen seconds or more to reach its target, giving the enemy tanker time to fire back and duck out of the way.

The Germans favored arming their tank with a gun—not a missile—capable of hitting the enemy as hard as they could, as far away as they could. There would be no more battles like Prokhorovka, the culminating clash at Kursk, where the Russians rushed in close and overcame the advantage of the powerful guns on the new German tanks.

The concept of a shoot-off involving British, American, and German guns, born of that old dream of international weapons systems, came out of a meeting of the three nations' defense ministers late in 1973. They ordered a Tripartite Main Armament Evaluation Program to be completed by September 1975.

The first tests were conducted at two British ranges, one at Shoeburyness, east of London, the other at Kirkcudbright, in Scotland. The ranges served as open-air laboratories for the precise measurement of the performance of the guns. But the tests had a direct relationship to the turmoil of the battlefield. The gunner who can shoot from the farthest distance is likely to win (range). But he must hit his target (accuracy). And if he hits the target, he must kill it (penetration).

Range and accuracy were tested at Shoeburyness, the British equivalent of Aberdeen. Another damp, often chilly test range, it is on the north side of the Thames River, where it runs into the North Sea. There the test rounds were fired rapidly, ten or fifteen shots in a few minutes, at twenty-foot-square white cloth targets each with a black cross in the middle at ranges up to two thousand meters, a little over a mile.

Tests of armor penetration were conducted at Kirkcudbright. Although the British and Americans were well along in development of Chobham, or special, armor, the new armor was still considered so secret that it was not used in the firing tests. Instead, the guns were aimed at several of the standard armor plate targets used by the NATO allies, called by names such as NATO heavy single and NATO heavy triple. The triple target represented the difficulty a projectile would face in penetrating the skirt, road wheel, and hull of a Soviet tank—a tough, complex target.

These tests were fired at only a hundred meters so that even if the guns had problems with accuracy, they would be sure to hit the targets. Varying amounts of powder were removed from the shells so their impact was the same as if they had been fired with a standard charge of powder at longer ranges. Because of the time it takes to set up the targets at the proper angles and then reposition or replace them after each shot, penetration testing is tedious. On some days only one or two projectiles were fired.

The German entry in the contest was a still-experimental 120 mm cannon. The British entered a 110 mm gun for which they had great hopes, although it was only in early development. The U.S. Army entered its version of a 105 mm cannon adopted from the British years before, but with new ammunition.

When the shooting was done, it was not completely clear which gun had won, but it was very clear which had lost. The British 110 was the loser because it combined the disadvantages of being smaller and new. The German entry showed real promise. And surprising everyone, the old American cannon, with its new ammunition, did remarkably well, even at the longer ranges.

The first round of the competition took a year and a half, cost ten million dollars, and resulted in a report almost a foot high. In the early fall of 1975 five senior working group members—two Americans, two Germans, and one British—met at Aberdeen to write the conclusions and recommendations. They still differed on many issues, but they decided on a compromise report that contained something for everyone and skirted the most contentious issues. The report favored continued use of the 105 mm cannon (the American choice) while further tests were conducted on larger guns favored by the Germans and British. This meant both the American M-1 and the German Leopard 2 tanks would be fitted with the 105 mm gun, at least in the early production models. The British weren't at the time preparing to field a new tank.

After review by a group of generals the report went to a sub-cabinet-level group of officials from the United States, Britain, and Germany, with a representative of France sitting in. The others quickly received a dazzling lesson in international politics from Hans Eberhard, the German tank czar. A retired brigadier general with an advanced degree in engineering, Eberhard had risen in the German defense bureaucracy until he was in charge of all land fighting vehicles. In this one imposing person the Germans had combined the authority exercised by a whole platoon of high-ranking Americans. When the meeting convened in London, no one on the American side could match Eberhard's knowledge or his sense of the direction he wanted the group to take.

He brushed aside the recommendations of the test group and submitted a paper written by his staff that said, in effect, that the 120 mm gun was the wave of the future and the allies should adopt it as quickly as possible. This would require further tests. The others in the room bowed to Eberhard's apparently superior knowledge and agreed to his position, although this did not commit their armies to switch to the bigger gun. When the Americans who had been involved in the tests heard what had happened, they felt as though they had been sold down the river.

The British later learned how important "winning" had been to the Germans. It came about this way: The Germans had not yet manufactured very many fuzes, so they were permitted to substitute weights for the fuzes in the accuracy and range tests. Since the firing at Shoeburyness involved inert projectiles, the fuze was not essential.

About a year after the tests, at the time of an unusually low tide, several British officers waded out, retrieved one of the German shells, and sawed it in half, lengthwise, to see how it was made. To their surprise, their little exercise in friendly espionage revealed that the weight had not been put in the base, where it belonged, but in the nose, making the projectile more stable and therefore more accurate.

The British passed on pictures of the bisected shell to their American colleagues and shared a knowing chuckle. But they did not make an issue of possible cheating, perhaps because they didn't care to explain their spying on an ally. Whether or not the Germans had played a fast one in this instance, there is no question that all three nations indulged in a good deal of maneuvering for advantage. In the Aberdeen tests, for example, the American gun, with a dazzling coat of white paint, stood out handsomely alongside the gunmetal-colored British and German guns. The purpose wasn't cosmetic, however. The paint reflected the sunlight, reduced "droop" of the barrel, and slightly improved the gun's accuracy.

For the round of tests set for late 1976 at Aberdeen, Bolté was determined the shooting would involve realistic targets made of the most advanced armor. He felt that the introduction of new armor technology was a critical factor in the selection of the main gun for the M-1 tank. If the 105 mm gun, with its new ammunition, could defeat the new armor, that would be a strong mark in its favor. But if none of the guns could cut through the advanced armor, that meant more work was needed to produce a weapon even more powerful than the 120 mm gun favored by the Germans.

Bolté asked the scientists at the Ballistic Research Laboratories to develop two targets. One, later labeled "BRL-1," would provide a degree of protection comparable with the armor on the M-1 tank, although the armor would be deliberately made so that it would not look like the secret armor on the M-1. The other, BRL-2, would be tougher. Bolté wanted enough difference between the two that some of the rounds fired in the tests would penetrate neither, or one but not the other, and other rounds would penetrate both.

In the process the scientists at BRL, using their computers and their knowledge of Soviet design philosophy and technology, actually designed two hypothetical "Soviet" tanks with different levels of armor protection on the basis of an estimate of what the Soviets might achieve in tanks deployed a decade hence. This enabled the testers to shoot at the armor targets from various angles and see what would have happened if they had hit a real tank.

The hypothetical tanks designed at Aberdeen did not reflect any specific intelligence about tanks on drawing boards in the Soviet Union. For the Americans, with their just-enough-gun philosophy, it was vitally important to know as nearly as possible what they would be shooting at in a future war. But accurate intelligence about Soviet weapons often lags years behind actual developments. The result is that the United States often makes decisions based on faulty information. It sometimes fails to respond to a real threat. That was the case in the early seventies when decisions on tank and antitank weapons were made without knowledge of the new Soviet T-64 tank. Other times it spends needlessly. The classic example of that kind of error occurred in the early 1960s, when the United States embarked on a missile-building campaign to close what later turned out to be a nonexistent "missile gap."

General Starry, now retired, worries about the failure to anticipate Soviet developments. Often the United States has a good idea of early experimental work in the Soviet Union because tests are conducted outdoors, where they can be monitored by spy satellites. But then, when work moves indoors to the production line, it is much harder to find out what is happening. Years later, when a new weapon is issued to troops, the West may be in for a rude shock.

This is exactly what happened with the T-64, described in the hypothetical battle in Chapter 1. There was a flood of confusing information in the mid-sixties, but it was not until a decade later that American intelligence accurately identified this new tank and concluded it was different from another tank that came into use about the same time. In 1983 the Pentagon described the T-64 publicly as the "first truly modern post–World War II tank" and set the time of its introduction into service as the mid-1960s.

Accurate information about the performance of a tank depends, far more than it does with most other weapons, on being able to run it through the test course at Aberdeen, take it apart and put it back together again, fire its guns, analyze the materials in its armor, and, finally, hit it with a variety of ammunition. Spy photos or even smuggled blueprints are no substitute for a good shakedown at Aberdeen. But obtaining the tank of a potential foe is one of the most demanding intelligence tasks. The Yom Kippur War of 1973 produced a rare bonanza in the form of captured T-62 tanks, introduced in the 1960s. But it was not until the mid-eighties that the first T-72 was obtained, even though it had been in service for many years and was the Soviet export model provided to a number of other countries. At this writing, the United States has yet to obtain a T-64, which has been reserved for the use of Soviet troops and has not been exported.

The most glaring indication of the paucity of hard intelligence on Soviet tanks came in 1982 with the publication of the first issue of *Soviet Military Power*, the Pentagon's annual rundown of military developments in the Eastern bloc. It contained an artist's rendering of what was described as the "T-80 tank, now in experimental production." With its angular M-1–like turret, it looked like a tank designed in Detroit.

Nongovernment experts, who had long heard rumors of a secret new supertank, quickly concluded that whatever the drawing showed, it wasn't a T-80. The Pentagon admitted as much when it later published pictures of a quite different-looking vehicle and described it as a T-80. The experts recognized this new "T-80," and it was neither secret nor new. Rather, it was a slightly improved model of the T-72 and had been in service for more than a decade.

To Starry, the lack of information posed by the lag in accurate intelligence poses the danger that the United States in event of war, could be badly surprised by superior Soviet armor. Bolté saw the problem of poor intelligence from the other end. Throughout the battle over the 105 and 120 mm guns, he encountered what seemed to be a constant effort to hype Soviet tank developments to justify the bigger gun. These "dial-a-threat" tactics meant that every time he presented evidence indicating the smaller gun would do the job, the supposed Soviet threat increased.

That there was little real intelligence concerning future Soviet tanks became evident at one high-level meeting at the Pentagon. The room was darkened, and a drawing of a formidable-looking tank was flashed on the screen. Here, the group was told, was what a future Soviet tank might look like. Bolté blinked, looked again, and then grinned in recognition. It wasn't a real tank at all. It was one of the "Soviet tanks" that BRL had conjured out of its computers, at his request, for the second round of the gun competition.

The dispute over Soviet armor provided a kind of discordant background music, not the major theme, during the tests. Even if the West didn't know much about the Soviet tanks it might face on a future battlefield, the targets created by the scientists at BRL would still be useful in testing the guns from the three countries.

By the time the second round of the competition commenced, the British had dropped their 110 mm gun and joined the Germans in the 120 mm world. In a crash program the British had set to work to develop a new weapon and new ammunition. For these trials they used their older 120 mm gun with the new ammunition. From the beginning, however, there had been a major difference, apart from size, between the two countries' guns.

The inside of the British tube is rifled. In other words, it has grooves cut on its inner lining to impart a spin to the projectile, much as a quarterback's fingers cause a football to spin and keep it stable on the way to the receiver. The rifled tube added significantly to accuracy when it was introduced in the last century, and it works fine with conventional high-explosive and solid-shot projectiles.

With shaped charge antitank ammunition developed for tank guns beginning in the late 1950s and the more recent kinetic energy long rod penetrator ammunition, however, the rapid-spinning motion is undesirable. The spin spreads the energy of both types of projectiles when they hit the target. And if the length-to-diameter ratio of the long rod is more than about four-to-one, the spin causes it to become unstable in flight.

The Germans dealt with this problem by using a smoothbore barrel, which is both simpler and less expensive than the rifled tube. To keep the projectile stable in flight, the ammunition for the smoothbore gun is fitted with a fin, like the feathers on an arrow.

Firing the long rod penetrator poses a special problem. The projectile, being as long and thin as possible, is much thinner in diameter than a gun tube. To solve this problem, the projectile is encased in a plastic sheath that fills the full diameter of the inside of the barrel. The sheath is called a sabot, from the French word for a "wooden shoe." As the projectile emerges from the barrel, it kicks off its shoes—discards its sabot—and becomes a simple thin dart with a pointed windshield at one end and a fin at the other.

The British, with their rifled tube, seemed to be at a serious disadvantage in firing the new types of ammunition until the Ballistic Research Laboratories came up with an idea so seemingly simple that one wonders why it had not become obvious long before. Their invention is called a slipping driving band. In effect, it is a ring attached loosely around the projectile and fitted into the grooves of the rifled barrel. When the gun is fired, the ring spins in the grooves and pushes the projectile forward, giving the projectile itself only a slight spin. As it emerges from the muzzle, it sheds its sabot and speeds on its way almost as though it had been fired from a smoothbore.

The British, who had introduced a 120 mm gun on their Chieftain in 1966—nearly fifteen years earlier than any of their allies—knew they couldn't afford to replace all their rifled barrels with smoothbores, and they feared that the alliance might go smoothbore and leave them, the pioneers, out on a limb. With the new U.S. invention, their fears were eased. The slipping driving band also gave a new lease on life to the thousands of rifled bore 105 mm tank guns already in service in the NATO armies and made the American 105 mm gun a credible entry in the contest.

Despite the fact that they had to scramble to be competitive, the British did well in the second round. In fact, the performance of the three guns was so close that a third round of tests became inevitable, more for political than for technical reasons. The politicians kept hoping that the tests would ease their burden of making a decision by producing a clear-cut winner, although the gun experts knew that was unlikely.

The fact that the Americans, with their smaller gun, were able to hang on round after round in this tough competition, getting better and better penetration without changing the gun itself, is largely attributable to the superior performance of advanced kinetic energy ammunition coming out of the Ballistic Research Labs. Earlier kinetic energy rounds were like the old-fashioned cannonball. They hit with great power, but they spread their energy, making it difficult to penetrate the armor. One type wasn't designed to penetrate at all. Instead, it hit so hard that it shook off chunks of metal from the inside of the turret to injure or kill the crew. As the name implies, the long rod penetrator is designed not to shock but to cut through to the inside of the turret. The latest models are more than two feet long and concentrate all their energy in an area of about a square inch. The challenge facing the scientists was to make the rod as long, thin, and heavy as possible. The rod also had to be strong so it would retain its dartlike shape but not be so brittle as to shatter when it hit the target. The improvements achieved by the Americans in making this type of ammunition astonished the experts from the other countries.

Since the tests in the 1970s, in which titanium or tungsten was used to make the projectiles, the United States has developed even newer ammunition using depleted uranium, the same green salt used in the latest armor for the M-1. It is plentiful and relatively cheap, and it has two advantages for the ammunition designer: It is more flexible than tungsten, so a projectile made of it is less likely to break up when it hits enemy armor, and it has a "pyrophoric effect," which means that chips of the material burn at an intense heat, like white phosphorus. Burns caused by DU penetrate quickly to the bone, killing or disabling the crew. It is very nasty stuff.

The Germans were the first to use uranium in ammunition because of a World War II metal shortage. But West Germany and most other nations, worried about adverse political reaction, have shied away from the use of depleted uranium, which is mildly radioactive and can be dangerous to tank crews and the environment. The one known exception is the United States, although there is some inconclusive intelligence indicating that the Soviet Union may also be using this technology. The Americans argue that in wartime the danger to crews and the environment from the use of DU ammunition would be negligible compared with all the other hazards of the battlefield. In peacetime crews cannot practice with DU ammunition in Germany and are permitted to train with it in the United States only on certain ranges that have been approved by the Environmental Protection Agency.

Everyone agreed that regardless of the type of ammunition, the larger size of the 120 mm gun yields better performance than the smaller gun. Because the barrel is bigger around, the 120 mm gun can accept a shaped charge round with a larger diameter, and the bigger the diameter of the shell and the more explosive it contains, the deeper it penetrates. The bigger gun also provides room for a larger shell with more powder for propulsion to make the long rod penetrator go faster and penetrate deeper at longer ranges. At some point, the Americans conceded, something more powerful than their cannon would be needed. But they argued that time had not yet come, and when it did, the 120 mm gun might itself be inadequate. To switch, at that time, to an even more powerful weapon would be difficult, time-consuming, and very expensive.

One reason the American tankers clung so tenaciously to the 105 mm cannon was their suspicion of the Germans. This went well beyond a xenophobic reluctance to mount a foreign gun on their tank. Their underlying worry was that the delay, expense, and confusion of adopting the German cannon would cause Congress to kill the M-1. If that happened, the American Army was likely to end up not only with a foreign gun but with an entire German tank.

On the German side there was a good deal of resentment about the way they were treated by the Americans. They had shared the specifications for the new armor on their tank, but they got nothing in return. In fact, at the beginning of the second round of the gun competition, in which the targets would be made of special armor, the Americans wouldn't even let the Germans examine the targets they were shooting at. There were no such restrictions on the British, who had originally shared the secret of their new armor with the United States. Even after one Bundeswehr officer was singled out and given special permission to go downrange, the Germans still felt they were being treated as second-class allies.

Although the working relationship on the test range was businesslike and correct, if not cordial, the atmosphere was so strained that any little spark could have caused an explosion. The spark was struck one day in January 1977, when Colonel Robert J. Sunell, who was Baer's deputy and later became program manager for the M-1, was sitting on the hull of a Leopard 2, chatting with some other tankers. He idly tapped the hull of the German tank with his knuckles and heard a strange sound, like an empty fifty-five-gallon drum.

What came to be known as the hollow tank was a full-scale prototype of the Leopard, one of three models delivered to Aberdeen from Munich on September 9, 1976, by Krauss Maffei Aktiengesellschaft, the German tank maker, to be subjected to the same grueling tests that had been inflicted on the entries from Detroit. Evaluation of the Leopard was separate from the gun tests. It was coincidence that discovery of the hollow tank occurred at Aberdeen just as the gun evaluation was winding up.

The models shipped to Aberdeen were known as the Leopard 2AV. The "AV" stood for "austere version," but it would be a mistake to take this as an indication of a stripped-down, inferior model. The Leopard then nearing a production decision had been drastically modified to come close to the U.S. Army's requirements, although it ended up heavier and more expensive than the U.S. competition. The Germans realized it would be a miracle for their tank to be judged best, but they had worked hard and spent some twenty-five million dollars to prepare for the tests. In the process they had made a number of improvements. The models at Aberdeen were in many ways better than the prototypes back home.

When Sunell told his colleagues about the hollow sound, their immediate thought was to make a secret midnight X ray of the Leopard to see what was inside the turret where tons of armor—or weights to simulate armor—should have been. But first they decided to confront Colonel Franz E. Kettmann, the gray-haired commander of the sixty-man German team at Aberdeen.

Kettmann surprised everyone. Yes, he acknowledged, the tank was hollow. He even put it in writing in a memo which said: "Due to excessive cost and delay in production schedule, the German government did not design and build PT19 [the designation for the prototype] with any special armor in the hull or turret. . . ."

Officials of the new Carter administration were just moving into the Pentagon. One of their major concerns was working out an agreement with Germany for the purchase of a fleet of airborne warning and control system (AWACS) aircraft for NATO. The last thing the new administration needed was a flap over the weight of a tank. Detection of the hollow tank was a diplomatic fiasco, and Pentagon civilians, with the AWACS deal uppermost in their minds, tried to hush up the whole affair. Baer found his civilian leaders "very antsy." But catching the Germans red-handed with a hollow tank was too good a story to hold. An aide to Baer let a friendly staffer on the House Armed Services Committee in on the secret. Baer was called to the Hill.

He testified that the full-scale Leopard, with the 120 mm

gun and a full load of armor, would have weighted 64 tons, instead of the 59.6 tons certified by the Germans. This means the tests of the power plant and suspension were invalid because the Leopard was 8,800 pounds lighter than the full-scale vehicle with all its armor would have been.

Eberhard could not deny the tank was underweight, especially since Kettmann had admitted it in writing. "If the weight was too low," he says, "it was a mistake on the German side which should not have happened. But all components were tested for higher weights, and they are now carrying higher weights. It was irritating and unnecessary, this whole affair. However, since this is the only case where one could have blamed us with unfairness, we must accept this blame."

Shortly afterward the Germans quietly withdrew their tank as a possible choice by the American Army. Although a very good tank and even superior to the M-1 in some aspects, such as lower fuel consumption and a better sighting system for the tank commander, it was heavier, it cost more, and most important, the tests showed that its armor was inferior. After withdrawal of the Leopard the Americans still worried that it might come back to life contending for a place in the U.S. Army, but the Germans focused all their attention on the outcome of the gun shoot-off.

The competition involved very high commercial stakes for both the Germans and the British. The standard NATO tank weapon had for years been the British-designed 105 mm gun. The United States, West Germany, and a number of other countries either paid the British for the right to use their weapon or actually bought guns and ammunition from them.

The suspicion of many Americans involved in the tank and gun programs was that the German interest in the 120 mm gun was motivated less by military need than by the commercial advantages involved in breaking the British monopoly and replacing it with a German monopoly. Only by introducing a new gun could the Germans hope to do this.

Baer saw the German interest in the 120 mm gun at that

time as primarily "just a desire to make a sale." But he realized it was not only the cannon itself at issue. The country whose gun was established as the NATO standard would sell ammunition as well as guns, and in the arms business the real money is in ammunition. It is not much of an exaggeration to say that a country could afford to give away tanks and guns if it thereby assured a monopoly on sale of ammunition.

Whatever part the commercial benefits of the choice of the German weapon played in shaping Eberhard's position, there is no reason to doubt that he sincerely believed in the 120 mm gun. All the tests and all the intelligence he had seen had convinced him the bigger gun was needed. He never was able to understand why the U.S. Army was so lukewarm when presented with the chance to own a superior weapon. And, he says, if anyone continues to insist that the Germans pushed the big gun for commercial reasons, this is "consciously wrong."

In the third round of tests—the one that concluded with the embarrassing failure of the German gun to fire—all three guns scored well. The German 120, which had been under development longer, did marginally better than the British gun. The older American 105, with less power, came in a strong third.

Precise results of the tests are classified and will probably remain so forever because no one knows how to declassify them. When the tests began, the working group chairmen took it upon themselves to create a trilateral security classification. They had a rubber stamp made and stamped the test documents. The stamp was so impressive that security officials at Aberdeen refused to release copies of the report to the British and Germans. Bolté was forced to sign for the documents himself, cart them off in the beat-up old Gremlin he had borrowed from his son that day, have them inspected at the Army Materiel Command headquarters in northern Virginia, and then get permission from the Army's top security officer to deliver them to the West German and British embassies in Washington. The whole affair was like an episode from a slapstick comedy.

By the time the tests ended, Bolté was in an increasingly

uncomfortable position. While he continued to believe the U.S. Army should stick with the 105 mm gun and spend its money leapfrogging to a more advanced tank weapon, political pressure favored the German 120 mm gun. Officials in the Pentagon's civilian hierarchy didn't care much about tank guns one way or the other, but they saw the Army's adoption of the German gun as a way to assure approval for NATO purchase of the American-made AWACS planes.

In a way the 120 mm gun had ceased to be a question of what was best for the American tank. Instead, it had become, to many of the European allies, a test of the willingness of the Americans to buy weapons in Europe—what was called the two-way street. When, in 1978, Congress moved toward cutting off money for purchase of the German gun, there was a frantic reaction. Congressman Stratton, the House Armed Services Committee's watchdog over the tank program, described it for his colleagues: "The telephones were ringing from the Pentagon and General [Alexander] Haig [supreme allied commander in Europe] was on the phone to me, and he didn't say this is a tremendous gun and we need it in our tank. He said, if you cut this money out, you are going to jeopardize the NATO summit that is meeting in Washington."

Pressure also came directly from the Germans. The Washington lobbying firm of DGA International was hired by Krauss Maffei, the maker of the tank, to push for use of the Leopard 2 or at least German components, including the 120 mm gun, by the U.S. Army. The lobbying campaign was legal, but that didn't make it any more palatable to the Army. Baer saw it as one more dangerous threat to his program. "They spent a pot of money. They were very aggressive," he says.

Carl Damm, a member of the Bundestag, made an unusual appearance before a Senate Armed Services subcommittee on March 31, 1976, to plead for American purchase of five to six hundred Leopard 2 tanks as part of the "armor business of the century." This was before the German tank had been withdrawn from contention. "To speak quite frankly, I personally do not see any possibility for the Federal Republic of Germany to take part in the AWACS program unless the USA spends a corresponding amount on German tanks. This would be a fair deal, a 'two-way street,' " Damm declared.

Within the Army a small group of officers shared Bolté's conviction that the 105 should be retained on the American tank while a much better weapon was developed. A larger group of officers didn't care deeply which gun was used. What they did fear was that a switch to the 120 would delay, and very likely kill, the whole tank program. And they all resented the fact that their tank seemed to be playing second fiddle to an airplane. The tanker, they complained, doesn't see the AWACS in his mess line.

Sunell, Bolté, and a handful of colonels undertook a behind-the-scenes fight to save the 105—and kill the 120. They deliberately kept the generals—Baer and his successor as program manager—out of the fight so as not to jeopardize their chances for promotion to positions where they would be better able to protect the tank program.

While the Army worked officially through its legislative liaison office under rules that barred it from "lobbying," the tankers set up an informal and much more effective arrangement involving a small group of officers and congressional staffers. This link was forged almost by accident one day when Justus ("Judd") White, a new member of the House Armed Services Committee staff, called Bolté for some information. What evolved, says White, was "a tiny cabal of willful people who pushed this program."

White asked tough questions, but when the soldiers convinced him they were right, he provided vital access to key staffers and some members of Congress. Most important, he made sure that the right questions were asked when those involved in the tank program were called to testify before Stratton's Armed Services subcommittee. It was through this process that news of the hollow tank got into the public record.

White was also instrumental in forcing the Army to do some

long-range thinking, which had been badly neglected. In 1972 the Desobry task force had decided the Army should have 3,312 M-1 tanks, an unrealistically low number. Under pressure from the Hill, stimulated by White, the Army raised its goal to 7,058 Abrams tanks, with another 7,000 upgraded versions of the older M-60 to fill out the force.

The informal dealing with White and others bolstered the Army's position on the Hill, but within the Pentagon Bolté felt growing pressure in favor of the 120 mm gun when he prepared to report on the results of the trilateral tests. He was given strict instructions not to sum up his briefings with any conclusions or recommendations. He suspected his civilian masters knew what he would recommend and didn't want to hear it. An independent committee headed by a retired lieutenant general was commissioned to study the gun issue. To the dismay of the civilians, the committee backed Bolté. Even so, by this time he was fearful the Army was going to have the 120 mm gun shoved down its throat, like it or not.

It was not really a surprise, then, when the civilian army secretary called a press conference at the Pentagon to announce his decision on the main armament for the Army's new tank. As soon as possible, he decreed, the M-1 would be equipped with the German smoothbore. His announcement came on January 31, 1978, less than two months after the ignominious failure of the German gun to fire in the shoot-off at Aberdeen. The Army's gun experts didn't oppose the German gun because of that incident. They understood that kind of thing can happen to anyone. But they felt that politics had triumphed over the facts developed in the long series of tests.

Almost to a man, the soldiers involved in the tank program favored the smaller gun. But once the decision had been made, many of them quickly became strong supporters of the bigger weapon. Partly this was due to the Army officer's ingrained tendency to fall into line once a decision has been made. Partly it was due to Baer's leadership. Throughout the five years he headed the program and the additional three years he served in the matériel command, he had one goal in mind: to build the best tank he could and deliver it to the troops as soon as possible. He didn't waste time refighting lost battles.

While the fight over the size of the gun tube was going on, other details that would make the M-1 a formidable fighting machine were falling into place. A gun without a fire control system to find, aim at, and hit the enemy is useless. In the Abrams the fire control system, with its heavy reliance on advanced electronics, is the single most expensive part of the tank, accounting for nearly a quarter of its total cost. Lett and his Chrysler engineers contributed several innovations that were brilliant or daring, or both.

One of their most agonizing decisions—second only to the choice between the turbine and the diesel—was what kind of computer to use to make the calculations for aiming the gun. By the mid-seventies technology had advanced to the point where it was possible to build a computer small enough and rugged enough to be installed in the tank.

This was a challenging task. The first fire control directors—very rudimentary computers—were developed in the early years of this century by the British and American navies and installed in battleships right after World War I. These were huge, complex instruments with motors, vacuum tubes, and specially shaped gears. Until that time each gun was aimed by an individual gun spotter with a telescope. With the director, a single fire control officer could aim and fire all the ship's guns.

Cumbersome as these early computers were, they were effective. An entire salvo of fourteen- or sixteen-inch shells could be dropped within a hundred-yard circle at a distance of twenty miles.

In the design of the M-1, there was no question that a fire control computer was needed. But there was sharp disagreement over whether to use an older analog computer or a more modern digital computer.

The analog computer is basically a mechanical device, like

a clock with hands, a modern version of the old naval fire director. The digital computer is an electronic device in which calculations are made by spurts of electricity, traveling at close to the speed of light. When technological developments, such as a new kind of ammunition, come along, the mechanism of the analog computer must be changed. But the digital computer can be updated easily with a change of software.

Now that digital computers are so commonplace, the choice seems obvious. But engineers at the Army's Frankford Arsenal in Philadelphia, which was responsible for fire control systems, had experimented with a digital computer and were not happy with its performance. They strongly favored the conservative approach of sticking with the familiar, if increasingly old-fashioned, analog system. Lett, whose first assignment at Chrysler had been to develop the fire control for the M-48 tank in the early 1950s, had no doubt the time had come to switch to a digital system, but the Army's experts told him to his face that he was out of his mind. He had good reason to worry that pushing new technology on a reluctant Army might result in the rejection of his tank.

As with the turbine, he made the gutsy choice and went for the digital system. Coupled with a laser device to measure the distance to the target, the computer is one of the stellar features of the Abrams. Though it is only the size of a bread box, less than a cubic foot, it is the soul of the tank. With it the gunner can fire fast and accurately. If he can see the target, he can hit it.

The computer also helps the gunner hit a moving target while bounding across country at speeds up to forty-five miles an hour. This feat requires not only a good computer but a good stabilization system.

The Army may seem laggard for taking so long to find a way to stabilize its tank guns. After all, naval ships have long been able to fire accurately despite the motion of the sea. The Navy had begun using a highly effective system known as continuous aim firing at the turn of the century after studies of the Spanish-American War proved that hardly any of the thousands of shells fired at sea hit anything. But the tank designers faced a different and more difficult problem than the naval architects. The rolling of a battleship is a relatively smooth movement—down, up . . . down, up. Because of its mass and its own inertia, the ship's gun tends to stay in the same plane in relation to the earth as the ship rolls beneath it. With this aid from gravity, it is a relatively simple task for the gun crew to keep the gun aimed at the target.

But the tank, speeding cross-country, doesn't roll like a ship. The motion is abrupt, more like that of a bucking bronco. No gunner, no matter how well coordinated, can keep the gun aimed at the target under such conditions.

Early stabilization systems permitted the gunner to aim on the move. But the tank had to stop while he locked on the target and fired. In the MBT-70 the decision was made to stabilize the relatively lightweight sight rather than the heavy gun. Then the bouncing cannon was rigged so it would fire only when aimed at the target. The Chrysler engineers found they could do this system one better by stabilizing the sight only in the vertical plane. They used sensors to detect the motion of the tank and fed this information into the computer, which was then able to trick the sight into acting as though it were also stabilized horizontally. The system worked almost as well as a fully synchronized system and saved forty thousand dollars.

Lett and his designers are credited with one of the most useful innovations on the M-1. If you look very closely at the tank gun, you will notice a little bulge at the top of the end of the barrel. It is called the muzzle reference system, or MRS. When a tank gun is fired, it gets hot and droops. As it cools, it gradually straightens up again. Wind, rain, and sun have a different effect, causing an unpredictable bending of the barrel. The gunner cannot see these changes, but he sees the result plainly enough when he misses his target. In the past the gunner would correct for this problem by the burst-on-target method—that is, he would shoot, see how far he missed, correct his aim, and shoot again, all the while exposed to enemy fire. Lett's invention is a secret combination of simple mirrors and electronics that permits the gunner to line up his fire control system with the barrel so his first shot will hit the target despite rain, wind, sun, or prolonged firing.

With all these improvements in fire control and stabilization, only one more breakthrough was needed to make the tank even more formidable. That was to enable the crew to see in the dark and through the fog of battle without being seen. Flares had long been used, but they illuminate friend as well as foe. Early night vision devices, which first came into use during the Vietnam War, were a partial solution. They work by gathering every available bit of light, such as that from the stars, and intensifying it. The result is a murky image—better than nothing but far from perfect.

The M-1 uses a quite different system, largely the product of research done by the Night Vision and Electro Optics Laboratory at Fort Belvoir, Virginia. The new thermal imaging system (TIS) needs no light at all. Instead, it relies on a detector made with a rare nonmetallic element known as tellurium to measure the differences in the amount of heat given off by objects within its field of view. The detector is coupled to a cooling system that keeps it at a precise temperature so it can accurately measure even slight differences in heat.

The TIS is hooked up to the gunner's optical sight. When he turns on the TIS, an image of the outside world is presented on a kind of television screen. He can see on dark, starless nights, and he can look right through fog, smoke, and camouflage. Tanks stand out so clearly that the gunner can even count the road wheels. Deer, rabbits, and birds are tracked with startling clarity. The image can be adjusted to display hot objects as black on a white background or white on a black background. The gunner can also adjust the sensitivity so he will not be blinded by the glare of burning tanks or the flash of exploding artillery shells.

The Army was so eager to have this new technology in

service that it jumped almost directly from the laboratory into operational tanks. The result was a shortage of the sights and difficulty in controlling the temperature of the sensors. And when the new tanks were issued to the troops, the system broke down far more than expected. The reason, the Army finally learned, was that the soldiers kept the system running day as well as night. While the scientists had calculated that the TIS would operate a maximum of eight hours a day, soldiers in Germany, where there is often heavy fog, were using it sixteen to eighteen hours a day. The device was modified to take this into account.

As the TIS and other parts of the fire control system were gradually perfected, the effort to adapt the 120 mm gun for use in the Abrams presented its own problems. Even well into the eighties there was a real question whether the German gun could be successfully mated with the M-1. The Germans had claimed their weapon was fully tested and about ready to be put into a production tank. As soon as the Americans saw the test records, they realized the Germans, in their eagerness to sell their cannon, had misrepresented its development. They were astonished, for example, when the Germans were able to supply only fifty-five rounds of ammunition for test firings, far fewer than were needed to assure safety.

Guns have, historically, often been almost as much a threat to friends as to enemies. In 1460, during the siege of Roxburgh Castle, King James II of Scotland stood too close when a monstrous cannon named the Lion was fired. He was killed when it burst. Two hundred years later Mons Meg, a legendary thirteen-foot cannon with a twenty-inch bore, which had been in use for a century, broke from an overcharge and injured, but did not kill, the duke of York.

A cracked barrel was not the only hazard. For centuries the cannon was built with a small hole in the top of the tube through which the fuze carried the flame to the powder. After each shot, one man stood at the muzzle and plunged a bundle of rags attached to a ramrod down the barrel to clean it out. Another crew member was always supposed to block the hole with a piece of leather to prevent sparks from being drawn into the barrel and igniting unburned powder. If he failed in this task, a spear of flame would erupt from the muzzle and engulf his mate.

Such dangers might be marginally acceptable in a siege gun or a field artillery piece, because the crew could take some shelter before the gun was fired, but they are totally out of place in a tank, where the gunner, loader, and tank commander all are confined inside the turret, their heads only a few inches from the breech end of the gun. In the M-1A1 the loader, who sits or stands to the left of the gun, takes a sixty-pound shell from a compartment behind his right shoulder, slams it into the gun, and flicks a lever to close the breech. When the gunner squeezes the trigger on his control handle, a pin in the breech snaps forward to ignite the powder encased within the shell. The next fraction of a second is a blur of sound, motion, and odors. The crew members feel, as much as hear, the explosion as the gun fires and compresses the air in the turret. The gun springs toward the rear of the turret, right between the tank commander and the loader. As the gun recoils, the breech block slides open automatically with a sharp metallic clack. The hot shell is ejected and falls to the floor. In later-model tanks most of the shell is burned up inside the gun, and only a small cartridge stub is ejected. A powerful fan draws off the fumes, but not before the crew members smell the acrid odor of the burning powder.

For the safety of the crew, the gun, recoil mechanism, and breech all must work perfectly time after time. In the narrow confines of the turret there is no room for anything to go wrong. The Army had not had a fatal tank gun accident since the 1950s, when two tankers were killed at Fort Knox in the explosion of a faulty round of ammunition. Continuing that safety record would require years of testing and the firing of thousands of rounds of ammunition. The Army could not, as might be supposed, simply buy the new gun from the Germans, stick it in their tank, and be ready to go in short order. Adapting and testing a new gun and ammunition could be expected to take up to seven years.

In one set of tests the gun is fired time after time to see how long the barrel will last and whether, and at what point, it will fail. Other test rounds are fired at ranges in Alaska, Arizona, and Panama to determine the effects of cold and hot weather and humidity. Ammunition is deliberately left exposed to dirt, grease, and extremes of weather for weeks to see if it will deteriorate. Not only is the breech tested by firing, but in addition, it is filled with oil, and then a special hydraulic pressure device "pulses" it to simulate the effect of repeated firings.

The Americans weren't satisfied with the amount of testing done by the Germans. But even if they had been, further testing would have been required to assure that the gun and ammunition met U.S. Army standards, which are different from those of the Bundeswehr.

For example, an artillery shell is designed not to go off until it has been fired from a cannon, and this is controlled by the fuze. Inside the fuze is a miniature Rube Goldberg contraption of little cogs and weights. The moment the shell begins to move, the weights shift toward the base of the shell to start arming the warhead. Other weights react to the spin of the shell and use the number of rotations to calculate the distance the projectile has traveled before completing the arming process. The Germans are content if the shell is not armed until it leaves the barrel. But the Americans insist that the arming should not be completed until the projectile has passed safely over the heads of friendly troops. This required changes in the German ammunition design and special tests.

When the high-explosive projectile with its shaped charge warhead reaches the target, the fuze has another task: to sense the presence of the target and explode the shell. The shaped charge projectile has a long snout tipped with a piezoelectric crystal wafer, which takes advantage of the fact that certain materials will, when crushed, generate a tiny electrical charge.

When the tip of the shell smashes against the target, it sends an electrical pulse through a wire to the fuze. This split second of early warning permits the fuze to set off the shaped charge just before it hits the target.

Further redesign was needed to meet another American requirement. The German explosive shell will not go off unless it hits the target nearly head-on. If it glances off, it doesn't explode. The Americans decided to put special feelers in the nose of their projectile to increase its "graze sensitivity," so it would sense the impact of a glancing blow and explode, and this required more tests.

All these tests applied to the shaped charge shell. The long rod penetrator is basically a much simpler warhead. Since the projectile relies entirely on its weight and speed to penetrate enemy armor, it carries no explosive and requires no fuze to arm it or set it off.

Even though the U.S. Army is embarrassed by the fact that it has seldom designed its own tank guns, it has become expert at Americanizing foreign guns and at manufacturing the guns themselves. This is done at Watervliet Arsenal, just to the north of Albany, New York. The process begins with a casting roughly shaped like a gun tube. It is machined to near-exact dimensions. Then it is subjected to a process developed by the French and known as autofrettage—literally, "self-hooping," so named because hoops or tightly wrapped wire were once used to add strength to a gun barrel.

The autofrettage process creates strength in the barrel itself by a python-and-pig system in which the gun plays the role of the snake, although in this case it is force-fed. The role of the pig is played by a metal plug slightly larger than the bore of the barrel. It is forced through the tube by a powerful hydraulic ram. As it squeezes through, the plug enlarges the barrel. The exterior expands only slightly, but the size of the bore grows about 6 percent and remains under tension. Paradoxically, even though this process stresses the metal beyond its elastic limit, the result, after proper heat treatment, is to double the resistance of the gun to the pressure to which it will be subjected when it is fired.

In addition to all the work on the gun and ammunition, the Army was forced to redesign the turret of its tank to accept the bigger gun even though the program had been held up for four months in 1976 while Chrysler and General Motors designed "hybrid" turrets capable of taking both sizes of guns. The redesign was needed because although the turret was made big enough to handle either gun, it was optimized for the smaller weapon.

A major purpose of the redesign was to make the turret capable of accepting the German gun, but it didn't really do that because the Americans insisted on a major difference between their system and the Germans'. In the Leopard 2 the recoil mechanism is outside the turret, where it is easier to work on. The Americans put theirs inside, where it takes up room and is more difficult to repair but where it is protected by the tank's heavy frontal armor.

The Leopard 2 and the Abrams use the same tube and breech, but because of all the changes and the difference in tank-building philosophy, the guns are not interchangeable. By the time everything had been Germanized and Americanized, standardization was almost completely out the window, and the goal of providing the NATO allies with interchangeable arms was more remote than ever.

Concern for standardization faded into insignificance, however, when two potential program stoppers suddenly cropped up. One of them is listed cryptically in a chronology of work on the 120 mm gun system: "3 Mar 83 CATASTROPHIC failure of XM256 breech during Oil Soak Test with XM827 at −40 degrees F."

The failure involved a test firing of cartridges which had been soaked in oil and then cooled to forty degrees below zero. Excess pressure in the tube blew the breech block clear off the rear of the cannon, a reminder that the rigid safety rules at Aberdeen are not just paranoia. It took ten months—until January 1984—for the Army to sort out the problems with the gun and breech and give a limited go-ahead for further work on the weapon and its installation in the tank.

At about the same time Sunell, by this time the program manager for the M-1, was struggling with an even more difficult problem. In an effort to hold down the weight and make it possible for one man to load the ammunition for the larger gun, the shell for the 120 mm weapon has a case made of plastic rather than copper. All of the case, except for a small base plug and the stub of a primer, is burned up or vaporized when the gun is fired. Many American tankers have a well-justified fear of such ammunition because the plastic cases can break open, spilling powder inside the tank. This kind of ammunition proved disastrous when it was used in the Sheridan tank in Vietnam. After several crews had been burned to death, tankers were ordered to bail out as soon as their tank was hit or even before a hit if they saw an incoming shell break through the treeline.

In the Abrams a major effort was made to assure the survival of the crew if the ammunition was hit. The shells are stored in a special compartment with heavy steel doors. They open briefly when the loader pushes a trigger with his knee and then slide shut automatically when he extracts a shell and turns toward the gun, releasing pressure on the door switch. The top of the ammunition compartment is weaker than the doors. If the ammo is hit by enemy fire, these blowout panels give way and direct the force of the blast away from the crew. The tankers will be badly shaken and deafened, perhaps permanently, but they will be alive.

The system works fine with the solid-case 105 mm ammunition if the loader doesn't lock the door open, as sometimes happens. But Sunell was appalled when he saw films of a test in which a projectile was fired into an ammo compartment containing the shells for the bigger gun.

An outside camera showed, in slow motion, the round entering the compartment, the explosion, and the blowout panels flying off, just as they should. But an inside camera presented

As a lieutenant colonel, Abrams led the Fourth Division's 37th Tank Battalion in some of the most aggressive American armored operations of World War II. He is shown here in the turret of one of a series of tanks—all named "Thunderbolt"—he wore out in the dash across Europe. (U.S. Army photo courtesy of Patton Museum)

To tankers who knew him only in his later years, Abrams, who died in 1974, is remembered as the tough, hard-charging, cigar-chomping four-star who commanded U.S. forces in Vietnam and later served as Chief of Staff of the Army. Abrams, for whom the M-1 is named, played an important role in its design and made the crucial decision to increase the weight to take full advantage of the new Chobham, or special, armor. (U.S. Army photo)

A T-34/85 model acquired from the Soviet Union in the days immediately after World War II is put through its paces at Fort Knox. Even though the United States was familiar with the Soviet tank, T-34s operated by the North Koreans rolled over American units in the early days of the Korean War in 1950. (U.S. Army photo courtesy of *Armor* magazine)

The MBT-70, a joint development of the United States and West Germany, pushed tank technology to the extreme. Its 152 mm gun was also capable of firing a missile, and its stabilization system gave it true shoot-on-the-move capability. But rising costs and the difficulty of the international effort doomed the tank, which never went into service. Here the MBT-70 is seen in action during tests in the late 1960s. (U.S. Army photo courtesy of *Armor* magazine)

While the United States dallied, the Soviets produced a series of advanced tanks during the 1960s and 1970s. The T-62 came into use in the early 1960s. Although otherwise of conventional design, it shocked the West with its big 115 mm gun. (U.S. Department of Defense photo)

The T-64, shown here in a model introduced in the mid-1970s, was an impressive secret weapon when it was issued to Red Army troops beginning in the late 1960s. With an automatic loader, three-man crew, new engine, and new suspension system, it was the first truly innovative tank to be put into service since World War II. (U.S. Army photo courtesy of *Armor* magazine)

For years, U.S. experts were puzzled by the similar-looking T-64 and T-72, shown here. It is now believed that the T-72, despite the higher number, is a less advanced tank than the T-64. For years, models of the T-72 were exported to other countries while the T-64 was reserved for Soviet troops. (U.S. Army photo courtesy of *Armor* magazine)

The M-60, one of which is shown here crossing the Maas River in the Netherlands in 1983, was described in the early 1970s as the "tired, old, second-rate M-60." Although improved with a new fire control system, the M-60, with its commander's cupola, is one of the highest targets on the battlefield. About half the Army's fourteen thousand tanks will probably still be M-60s at the turn of the century although units that would face the most modern Soviet equipment are being issued late-model M-1 tanks as soon as possible. (U.S. Army photo by SP4 Frederick Sutter)

When engineers from the two competing companies, General Motors and Chrysler, first saw what the other firm had turned out early in 1976, they were amazed at the similarity between the two tanks. From a short distance away even the designers were forced to count road wheels to tell one tank from another. The GM model (top) had six while the Chrysler model had seven—to allow for expected growth in weight. (U.S. Army photos)

Both the Netherlands and Switzerland have purchased the Leopard 2 from Germany. Here a Dutch Leopard 2 is shown covered with camouflage netting during Exercise Spearpoint in September 1984. (U.S. Army photo by SP4 Lenny Waite)

Dr. Philip Lett, head of the Chrysler tank division, talks with Major General Robert Baer, the Army program manager, during early tests at Aberdeen. When Baer ended five years managing the tank project, his staff gave him a scrapbook with balloon captions added to the pictures. This fictional exchange between Lett and Baer captures one of the overriding concerns of everyone involved: cost. (Photo courtesy of Lieutenant General [Ret.] Robert Baer)

Another major concern is capsulized in the balloons above the heads of Colonel Franz Kettmann, who represented the Bundeswehr during tests of the Leopard 2 at Aberdeen in 1976 and 1977, and Baer. The Germans withdrew the Leopard from the tests after an American officer discovered the tank being tested was underweight by several tons. Kettmann owned up to the "hollow tank" in a written statement. (Photo courtesy of Lieutenant General [Ret.] Robert Baer)

The first M-1 tanks reached units in Europe in 1981. Here, one of the early models, with its 105 mm gun, is shown moving from the Grafenwöhr to the Hohenfels training area in February 1982. (U.S. Army photo by R. G. Crossley)

A photograph of a T-80 published in 1987 does appear to be a distinct new class of tank. Western experts noticed two important characteristics. It is still a relatively small tank with the traditional inverted skillet turret, an indication the Soviets have not yet fitted their tanks with armor of the type used by the United States and Britain and, in a different form, by the West Germans. Of special interest were the small boxlike rectangular shapes that can be seen to the left of the main gun. These contain explosives designed to destroy a high-explosive shell before it can reach the tank's armor, a sign that Soviet armor, unlike that on the Abrams, can be penetrated by such shells. (*Soviet Military Power,* 1987)

ON THE OPPOSITE PAGE, TOP TO BOTTOM:

In 1982 the Pentagon published this artist's conception of the Soviet T-80 tank. When actual photos of the T-80 were obtained several years later, it looked nothing like the Pentagon's version, an indication of the difficulty the West has in keeping track of Soviet tank development. (*Soviet Military Power,* 1982)

This photo of what was identified by the Pentagon as a "T-80" was published in 1984. Independent experts decided it was probably an improved model of the older T-72 rather than a new tank. (*Soviety Military Power,* 1984)

A late-model Abrams tank, the M-1A1, is being issued to troops in Europe. It is distinguished by its bigger 120 mm gun and the rack at the rear of the turret where the crewmen store their gear. The crew is also protected from nuclear, biological, and chemical weapons by a system that purifies outside air before it enters the turret. The M-1A1 has thicker armor than earlier versions, and an even further improved armor—incorporating depleted uranium—is installed on tanks built beginning in the latter part of 1988. (General Dynamics Land Systems Division photos)

a frightening picture. The doors buckled, and the crew compartment was suddenly filled with fumes and flame.

The late Major General Duard D. Ball, Sunell's predecessor, favored going ahead with the program, and he had backing from high-level officials who did not want the tank delayed. Even if some crews might die because of faulty ammunition doors, they argued, this otherwise superior tank would help other crews to survive if they had to go to war. Strangely, Congress showed little interest in this issue even after a high-ranking general volunteered during a hearing that he favored fielding the tank with the faulty doors if they couldn't be fixed.

Sunell, horrified by the thought of a crew seared by flame and choking on toxic fumes, recommended stopping work until the problem was solved. If no solution could be found, he was prepared to scrap the effort to install the big gun with its plastic cartridge cases. Lou Felder, the retired colonel on the manufacturer's team, backed him all the way. Felder was so outraged that he threatened to make a public issue of the problem if the Army tried to brush it aside and field the tank anyway.

Eventually the ammo compartment doors were successfully redesigned with special seals built to a tolerance of thirty-thousandths of an inch, and a public controversy was avoided.

Chrysler delivered its first two production-line tanks with the 105 mm gun on February 28, 1980, six years and eight months after the contract had been signed and eight years after the Desobry task force had begun its work. By peacetime standards the development cycle had been remarkably rapid. But it had also been seventeen years since Tom Dolvin had started work on the MBT-70 and even longer since the Army had decided it urgently needed a new tank.

Another five years elapsed before the first M-1A1 tank with the 120 mm gun rolled off the production lines at Detroit on August 28, 1985. Because the new version carried the bigger gun and better armor, plus a turret sealed against nuclear, biological, and chemical attack, the Army hurried to issue the new tank to troops on the potential front line in Germany. But the question lingers: Was the German gun necessary, and was it worth the cost?

Baer and almost all the tankers who were involved in the great tank gun battles now agree it is fortunate the civilians forced the Army—perhaps for the wrong reasons—to adopt the bigger cannon. Their judgment is based on classified calculations involving intelligence about Soviet armor and assumptions about the distances at which tank duels would be fought. It is difficult, if not impossible, for a layperson without access to secret information to challenge them.

Certainly the performance of the M-1A1 tanks with the bigger gun in maneuvers at the National Training Center at Fort Irwin, California, has been impressive. With its ability to kill enemy tanks at ranges of well over a mile and a half, the new gun has forced commanders of the Opposing Force—simulating a Soviet Guards regiment—to scramble to devise new tactics to keep from being wiped out.

Bolté is one of the few who still insist the Army made a bad mistake. To him the real choice was not between the 105 and 120 mm guns but between the 120 and something far better. He is not sure what that something better would be: perhaps rocket-assisted shells; perhaps a liquid propellant; perhaps a new type of hypervelocity gun. But choosing the marginally better German gun, he argues, forced a starvation diet for a research program that might have produced a truly superior gun-ammunition combination.

Scant attention has been paid to the true cost of adopting the bigger gun. In the spring of 1984, in a burst of candor, the Army provided an estimate of the cost over the next twenty years—the life cycle of the tank—to have the larger gun on the twenty-two hundred M-1A1 tanks then planned. The startling answer: $4.7 billion more than the cost of the tanks with the 105 mm gun. If the hundreds of millions already spent on the program are added on, the total soars to $5 billion or more.

The cost is counted not only in dollars but in other ways as well. With its larger gun and ammunition, the new tank is slightly slower and substantially heavier than the first M-1, and it carries forty-four rounds rather than the fifty-five rounds carried by its older brother, the M-1.

All this relates directly, of course, to assumptions about how a tank will be used in combat. Theoretically armies decide how they intend to fight a war and then develop weapons to match the doctrine. In the U.S. Army this process has been turned almost completely around. The decision to produce the M-1 and the rest of the Big Five weapons was made in 1972, and then the Army set about devising a doctrine to govern their use in war. It was a process in which the United States borrowed shamelessly—from the Russians, the Germans, the Israelis, even from Genghis Khan and Hannibal. The result was a revolutionary change from the Army's traditional way of fighting a war.

7

A New Way to Fight

IN 1976 DONN STARRY, by then a lieutenant general and commander of the Army's Fifth Corps in Germany, visited the Israeli command post at Kuneitra, atop the Golan Heights. His experience was almost like a biblical revelation.

His host pointed off toward Damascus, clearly visible in the desert air fifty miles away. He described how, in the Yom Kippur War of 1973, fifteen hundred Syrian tanks had filled the landscape, advancing in Soviet-style echelons, one row behind the other. Suddenly Starry visualized what he had not been able to see in the often foggy mountains and forests of Central Europe. If the Red Army attacked back there in the Fulda Gap, his men would face the same tactics.

He wondered: What if it were possible to stop the Russians' second, third, and fourth echelons from piling on and adding their strength to the assault by the first echelon? Would the defenders be able to win, even though badly outnumbered? That was exactly what the U.S. Army had to be prepared to do in Europe.

At that time, in the mid-seventies, many, perhaps even most, American soldiers believed that in the event of a non-nuclear Soviet attack the Army would quickly lose. Following his first visit back to Europe after service in Vietnam, Starry reported to General Abrams at the Pentagon that he had seen an army that didn't think it could win. Both men were deeply disturbed. Abrams, in his blunt fashion, told Starry to get the Army "off its ass."

About the same time General DePuy, who had just become the first commander of the new Training and Doctrine Command, began his own effort to convert America's soldiers from losers to winners. DuPuy and Starry gradually decided that the best way to make the Army believe it could win was to fashion an entirely new way for it to fight its wars.

Although the Army had never put its philosophy into a written document, it had almost always acted on the assumption that it was likely to lose the first few battles of any war and that it could afford such defeats. After absorbing these early losses, the United States would call on its great reservoir of manpower and productive capacity to overwhelm the enemy with men and machines.

This was not ivory tower theorizing. It was directly related to a deeply felt American attitude toward the military. While Americans rather like a permanent navy, they are distinctly uncomfortable with a standing army. This philosophy is rooted right in the Constitution. While it empowers Congress to "provide and maintain a navy," it limits the power of Congress to "raise and support armies" by providing that "no appropriation of money to that use shall be for a longer term than two years." Today's all-volunteer Army consists of fewer than 800,000 men and women, half the size of the Vietnam War force and a fraction of the 8.3 million on duty in 1945.

In World War II the United States did not begin mobilizing until well after the war had begun, and it did not begin to create an armored force until the devastating power of the blitzkrieg had already been demonstrated in Poland and France.

When American tanks first met the Germans, no great talent was needed to pick the winner. In February 1943, more than a year after Pearl Harbor, the thirty thousand men of the American Second Corps, under General Dwight D. Eisenhower, met Field Marshal Erwin Rommel's Afrika Corps at the Kasserine Pass and received a bloody on-the-job lesson in armored warfare. Although Rommel's army was groggy from a series of bad lickings at the hands of the British, he was sti able to shatter the American force and send it reeling fifty mile back across the desert.

The Germans lost 989 men killed, wounded, and missin or captured. The Americans, who had entered the battle poorl armed, poorly led, and overly cocky, lost nearly 6,300 me plus close to a thousand tanks, artillery pieces, and other vehi cles. Kasserine Pass was not just a defeat. For the Army, espe cially for the new armored force, it was the same kind o incredible, sobering shock the nation had suffered at Pearl Har bor.

But losing an early battle was in the Army's dogged, pile it-on tradition, with the emphasis on wearing the enemy dowr rather than on outwitting him with brilliant tactics and rapid, daring maneuver.

In the Army's long history the occasional flashes of brilliance stand out because they are so rare. George Washington's strategy of outmaneuvering and outthinking the British brought his ragtag Continental Army victory over a stronger force. In the Civil War General Ulysses S. Grant is often seen as the prototypical practitioner of the grinding, bloody style of conflict known as attrition warfare. But he is remembered by the Army for the "most brilliant campaign ever fought on American soil," the attack in which he outmaneuvered the Confederates to take Vicksburg and Jackson, Mississippi. General George S. Patton, Jr., in his blitzkrieglike sweep across France and Germany in World War II, and General Douglas MacArthur, in his Inchon landing during the Korean War, broke from the pattern. But these were the exceptions to the rule.

As DePuy, Starry, and their associates looked around the world at the places where the Army might be called upon to fight, it was obvious that what might be called the sleeping giant doctrine of warfare was simply not good enough. Nowhere could the Army afford to lose the first few battles, or even the first battle, without losing the war. What's worse, the Army would almost certainly be outnumbered almost anywhere in the world it might have to fight.

The situation was most critical in Central Europe, where the East-West border describes an arc, nowhere more than about an hour's drive from Hamburg, Hanover, Frankfurt, Nuremberg, and Munich, the great business and military centers of West Germany. Three obvious ways to deal with a threatened or actual Soviet attack suggest themselves. One is to strike first and try to fight the war east of the border. Another is to fight between the border and the Rhine River, with the river as the main line of defense. The third alternative is for the defenders to plant their feet on the border, with no room for maneuver. The first two alternatives are politically unacceptable, and the third doesn't make sense militarily. Whether, when, and how nuclear, biological, and chemical weapons might be employed present serious military problems and even knottier political questions.

Since the early sixties, when the United States abandoned its policy of massive retaliation with nuclear bombs in favor of a doctrine of flexible response, in which forces ranging from small commando units to nuclear weapons might be used, it had been obvious that battlefield weapons without the threat of an all-out nuclear strike would not be enough to stop a determined Soviet attack. But the new weapons coming along in the seventies might do the trick, if only a way could be found to use them effectively.

The beginning of a serious attempt to figure out how to prepare for war in Central Europe and, at the same time, devise a plan plausible enough to convince the soldiers they had a chance to win can be dated to July 23, 1974. On that date DePuy sent a "pot of French soup" letter to seven other generals enclosing a rough outline of a new war-fighting doctrine.

"In France," he wrote, "in the house of a peasant there is always a pot of soup boiling on the fireplace. From time to time someone throws in a potato, leek, some chicken stock or beef gravy, an occasional carrot or whatever. Over time the soup gets better and better. Everyone can add to it and anyone may partake. I view the attached paper somewhat the same way. . . . I don't care who sees it or how many copies are made. I just want to keep it like that pot of French soup."

It is no coincidence that DePuy's letter, calling for this wide-open reexamination of Army doctrine, was written in the aftermath of the Yom Kippur War. The ferocity of the conflict, the staggering losses of men and machines, and the use of deadly new weapons all shocked military men throughout the world. Looking at reports coming in from Israel, DePuy realized that the U.S. Army's existing plans for fighting a war had, in significant part, ceased to be valid on the modern battlefield. The eighteen-day war, in which U.S. military involvement was limited to that of a weapons supplier, exerted a far more important influence on the Army's thinking about how to fight a war than all its long, frustrating years in Southeast Asia. This brief, bloody conflict is worth a careful look.

Israel had been at war with its Arab neighbors off and on since May 15, 1948, the day after the new nation's declaration of independence. Badly outnumbered and often relying on a motley collection of outmoded weapons, Israel emerged the victor each time fighting broke out: in 1948 and 1956 and again in the Six-Day War of 1967. Each conflict brought a humiliating Arab defeat and an expansion of Israel's borders.

Six years later the Arabs, with shrewd advice and arms from their Soviet friends, seemed to have learned their lesson. Nothing was left to chance.

It was to be a two-front war, with surprise attacks from the east by the Syrians and from the west, across the Suez Canal, by the Egyptians. Even the day for the onslaught was carefully chosen. It was October 6, the tenth day of the Muslim celebration of Ramadan and the anniversary of the day that the Prophet Muhammad began the preparations in 624 for the Battle of Badr, which helped open the way for his entry into Mecca. The attack became Operation Badr, a boost to the morale of the soldiers. The sixth also happened to be Yom Kippur, the holiest day in the Jewish calendar, a day on which the Israeli soldiers were more likely to be in a holiday than a war-fighting mood.

Along both banks of the canal the two sides had erected huge sand barriers—50 or more feet high, 200 feet across, and 100 miles long. Behind the dune on the Egyptian side was stationed an army of 800,000 men, 1,700 to 2,000 tanks, 2,300 artillery pieces, 150 antiaircraft batteries, and 568 aircraft. The Bar Lev Line on the other side of the canal was a gossamer-thin shield of 8,000 men spread over the 100-mile front—enough, the Israelis hoped, to hold out until reserves arrived.

The attack began without warning at two o'clock in the afternoon with the kind of overwhelming artillery barrage typically employed by the Red Army—10,500 rounds in the first minute—followed by 300 sorties by fighters and bombers against Israeli command centers. At a quarter after the hour 8,000 infantrymen crossed the canal in 1,000 rubber boats. They included soldiers with rope ladders who had spent months practicing climbing dunes. Once ladders were in place, the more heavily laden troops scrambled to the top and swarmed down the other side to set up a light antitank barrier a mile or two into the desert. Virtually every man carried an antiaircraft or antitank rocket.

As soon as the first fortress fell at 3:00 P.M., Egyptian engineers wheeled Soviet hydraulic mining equipment into position and trained high-pressure water cannons on the sand barrier. Before dark they had cut through the line in sixty places.

Israel did not begin to mobilize until fighting began. Reserves rushed to the front in private cars, buses, and requisitioned trucks and joined the battle piecemeal. Emboldened by the ease of their 1967 victory, the Israeli armor commanders attacked without waiting for infantry or adequate artillery support. This was a violation of the most basic rules of tank warfare, and they paid for it with blood and burning tanks.

The battle on the western front came to a climax on Sunday, October 14, when the Egyptians carried the attack to a new Israeli defensive line anchored on the passes that dominate the central part of the Sinai desert. What ensued was one of history's great tank battles, the most massive armor confrontation since World War II, with sixteen hundred or more armored vehicles engaged. Tanks fired at virtually point-blank range. A traditional weakness of Soviet tanks quickly became apparent. As the Soviet-supplied Egyptian T-54 and T-55 tanks and the newer T-62s were hit by the intense fire rained down on them from the heights held by the enemy, they exploded and burned. The crack of armor-piercing projectiles striking tanks was followed by the explosion of fuel and ammunition and a cloud of oily black smoke. The Israeli gunners spoke of "lighting bonfires." After the war, when the Americans loaded a captured T-62 with fuel and ammunition and fired a single shot into the turret, the tank burned and crackled with exploding ammunition for the next twelve hours.

The battle also highlighted another basic flaw, the Soviet penchant for building their tanks close to the ground. The low silhouette permits the tank to hide behind slight undulations in the earth, but it limits the amount the tank gun can be raised or lowered. The Egyptians found themselves unable to fire back at the Israelis on the heights above. If they were in a position to fire down, they had to come out into the open to point their cannons downward.

For the first time on the battlefield both sides were equipped with wire-guided missiles. The Egyptians had crossed the canal armed with thousands of Soviet Sagger antitank missiles. Before the war the Israelis had shown little interest in this new weapon. But they learned fast. On October 12, two days before the battle of the Sinai passes, American planes began arriving with loads of the U.S. Army's TOW missiles, which were rushed to the front. By the time the surviving Egyptian tanks turned and fled back toward the safety of their air defenses, the battlefield was festooned with thousands of wires that had been trailed out across the desert as the new missiles were guided toward their targets.

The eastern front saw another great clash of armor, climaxing in what came to be known as the Valley of Tears. There the Israeli Seventh Brigade, the only armor unit brought close to full strength early in the battle, withstood wave after wave of attacking Syrian tanks. The Syrians fought relentlessly around the clock, taking advantage of superior night fighting equipment supplied to them by the Soviets. The Israeli tankers fought so long without sleep that some finally collapsed and slept through murderous artillery barrages.

Standing in their turrets, trying to see the enemy through the smoke of battle, tank commanders were shredded by shrapnel. Even though the Israelis had begun the battle badly outnumbered in tanks, they were able to patch up damaged vehicles and send them back into combat. But the same was not true of crews. As the fighting wore on into the third day, the Israeli forces found themselves with more tanks than fresh crews to man them. One after the other, crews reported running out of ammunition. One commander ran out entirely and loaded his pockets with hand grenades to continue the battle.

Finally, the Seventh Brigade was down to twenty running tanks out of its original hundred, and they were desperately low on ammunition. But while the situation might have seemed nearly hopeless to the defenders, the Syrians had suffered a terrible mauling as they fought through the rugged volcanic rocks of the Golan. As the Israeli commander watched from his post above Kuneitra, he saw the Syrian supply train begin to turn back. He radioed the order to the brigade: "Attack!" The tanks of the Seventh Brigade pursued the retreating Syrians to the tank ditch that had been Israel's first line of defense and then stopped, exhausted and virtually out of ammunition.

Of five divisions committed to the battle by the Syrians, only one remained in fighting order. Other Israeli units, exploiting the time gained by the Seventh Brigade, cut deep into Syrian territory in two broad salients.

On October 24 the superpowers imposed an armistice. For eighteen frightening days the existence of Israel had hung in the balance, but the nation emerged intact.

Brief as the Yom Kippur War was, it has continued to fascinate military analysts. Even though the conflict was limited in both time and area, it was still a full-scale war. The Arabs mustered a force roughly equal to what the North Atlantic Treaty Organization would have been able to put in the field that year. The Egyptians had 1,700 or more tanks, the Syrians about 1,500 and the Israelis about 1,700. Iraq and Jordan committed a total of about 350 tanks so the total on both sides reached more than 5,200. Tank battles in the Sinai desert and at the Golan Heights were the largest since World War II.

The war was a revealing test of rival equipment and tactics. It was, in a much briefer time frame, a showcase for weapons and tactics similar to the involvement of the Soviet Union on one side and Germany and Italy on the other in the Spanish Civil War of the 1930s. The Arabs, for the most part, used Soviet-supplied arms and followed classic Soviet-style tactics. Most of the Israelis' arms came from the United States, Britain, and other Western nations, and the tactics they used were similar to those that would be used by NATO armies. Their aggressive use of armor was clearly, if ironically, patterned on the tactics pioneered by Guderian and Rommel during World War II.

Four main lessons emerged from the war. First, the bitter Israeli experience in the opening days of the conflict had made clear beyond any doubt that while tanks are the most powerful force on the battlefield, they cannot fight alone. They must be supported by infantry, artillery, and, if at all possible, air power. Although the Israeli commanders had forgotten this basic truth, the lesson came as no surprise to Abrams and other American Army experts. In fact, the need for effective use of combined arms had been reconfirmed in maneuvers at Fort Bliss only a short time before the war.

Second, the expenditure of ammunition and other supplies and the loss of equipment reached a startlingly high level. In the eighteen days of battle the two sides used up half the equipment, ammunition, and other supplies they had on hand at the beginning of the fight and were increasingly dependent on new supplies flown in daily by the United States and the Soviet Union. The Israeli loss in tanks alone was equivalent to three years' U.S. production. The war proved to U.S. Army planners that they needed not only substantial stocks of weapons and ammunition but production facilities capable of quickly replacing stocks used up in a war. This led to the decision to establish two production lines for the M-1 tank, rather than only one, with a combined capacity of 150 tanks a month.

The effect of the increased lethality of weapons was also a shock. In World War II a U.S. tank had to fire thirteen rounds to have a fifty-fifty chance of hitting a standing target at fifteen hundred meters. In the mid-seventies, it required only one round. The speed at which a shell leaves the muzzle had doubled since World War II, to nearly a mile a second. Guided missiles had also doubled the range at which a tank might be hit and knocked out.

Many military experts, including U.S. Army leaders, made the mistake of concluding that because weapons had become more powerful, war had become more deadly. Actually casualty rates in the Yom Kippur War were no higher than those of World War II and were much lower than in the battles of antiquity. This is true even when comparing the percentage of troops killed in action, rather than total casualties, and thus avoiding the question of how many lives are saved by better medical care.

When the exaggerations of wartime propaganda had been winnowed out, losses worked out to about 1,270 tanks on the Arab side and 420 on the Israeli side—a total of just under 1,700 tanks destroyed in eighteen days of fighting. This loss rate of about 36 percent for the Arabs and 25 percent for the Israelis is not as severe as losses in the more concentrated twelve-day Battle of El Alamein in World War II. The British entered that battle with 1,100 tanks and lost 400, or about 36 percent. Rommel had 600 tanks at the beginning and lost almost all of them.

What the experts failed to take into account is that as weapons have become more lethal, soldiers have spread out more and more. In ancient times, when men stood toe to toe and hacked at each other with swords, each soldier occupied about 10 square meters on the battlefield, and almost all of them were involved in the fighting. In the 1973 war there was 40,000 square meters for each man, and many of them were far from the fighting. The U.S. Army recognizes this change in the amount of territory for which it holds a brigade commander responsible. In World War I his unit covered 163 acres. In World War II it was 387 acres. Today it is 9,884 acres. This dispersion more than offsets the increased lethality of the weapons.

Where the deadliness of the new weapons did make a difference was when dispersed forces came together to give battle. Several Israeli armor units, rushing into the fight, were virtually destroyed in a matter of minutes. Late in the morning of October 8, almost forty-eight hours into the battle, an Israeli armored battalion, counterattacking in the north, had almost reached the Bar Lev Line—the original Israeli defenses—when hundreds of Egyptian infantrymen suddenly emerged from the dunes, firing antitank rockets. Within minutes the wounded battalion commander was forced to withdraw, leaving twelve burning tanks behind.

A short time later another Israeli tank battalion (later enlarged to a brigade in Egyptian propaganda statements) approached within half a mile of the canal only to be surrounded by thousands of infantrymen firing antitank weapons. Eighteen tanks were set afire and destroyed, and the officer leading the attack was captured.

Planners for any future war had to take into account that companies, battalions, regiments might suddenly disappear from the calculus of forces on the battlefield. Even a large force, caught in a killing zone by a smaller force, could be destroyed in a matter of minutes.

The third lesson was that while wire-guided missiles are an important new element on the battlefield, most tanks are still killed by other tanks. During and immediately after the war a number of Pentagon civilians and some members of Congress concluded that these new weapons had made the tank obsolete. It was some time after the war before the true lesson became clear.

An Army panel went to the Sinai battlefield to inspect some 800 tanks that still lay where they had been knocked out. A special analysis was done on 101 of the tanks to determine what had destroyed them. Missiles make a distinctive hole, so it was easy to see where they had struck. But most tanks knocked out in combat are hit a number of times, often with a variety of weapons. It is hard to tell which shot did the lethal damage. The panel found that six of the tanks had clearly been killed by missiles and that sixteen, with multiple hits, might have been destroyed by a missile. The conclusion was that 90 percent or more of the tanks put out of service in the battle had been knocked out by guns rather than missiles.

The introduction of the wire-guided missile was of special concern to the Red Army. More than two hundred high-ranking officers and military experts were called together in November 1974 for a conference at the Malinovsky Tank Academy to consider the lessons from the Middle East battlefield. If the new guided missiles were overwhelmingly effective, the Soviet Army, whose entire strategy depended on its huge tank force, had a good deal to worry about. Because the war ended with the battlefield in Israeli hands, the Red Army experts did not have the opportunity to make the kind of on-the-scene assessment carried out by the Americans. Uncertainty about the effectiveness of the missiles simply added to Soviet concern. In a second conference two months later A. A. Grechko, then minister of defense, summed up the problem his army faced: ". . . tanks have become more vulnerable, and the use of them on the battlefield more complicated."

The fourth lesson of the war—a welcome one for the Americans—was that an outnumbered force can win, even if it is taken by surprise and even if it loses air superiority.

This lesson was most impressive on the Syrian front. There the attacking forces moved forward under such a formidable air defense that Israeli pilots couldn't get through to strike the follow-on echelons. Even with these reserve forces piling on, the outnumbered Israeli tank troops on the Golan Heights were still able to defeat the attack.

The American strategists went back to the history books, and there they found proof after proof that the commander with the biggest army is not always the winner. In fact, there were so many instances in which the winner began the battle outnumbered that it began to seem that the smaller force had the advantage. Robert E. Lee, whose forces were eventually overcome by the North's strength in manpower and weapons, still managed to win many battles, even when badly outnumbered. He dismissed attempts to determine the outcome of a battle by counting the forces arrayed on each side as "just cypherin'." Moreover, despite the rule of thumb which says the attacker should outnumber the defender by at least three to one, there have been plenty of instances where the attacker entered the battle with a smaller force and still won.

At Arbela, in 331 B.C., Alexander had fewer than fifty thousand troops while Darius had a much larger number, arrayed in a carefully prepared defensive position. Yet the smaller force seized the initiative and won an overwhelming victory.

A little more than a century later, on August 3, 216 B.C., Hannibal's Carthaginian army met the Romans at Cannae in one of history's classic battles. Hannibal, with 50,000 men, took up a defensive position to meet the onslaught of the 85,000-man Roman force. Hannibal's light infantry, in the center of the line, gradually fell back. Then the heavy infantry swung in from both sides while the cavalry hit the Romans from the rear. Even the battle-hardened Carthaginians were awed by the slaughter. The Romans lost 50,000 dead and another 3,000 captured, while Hannibal's losses were 6,000 killed and wounded. Despite his battlefield victories, Hannibal never did conquer Rome. Eventually he withdrew to Carthage, where a

Roman army defeated him in 202 B.C.

On the other hand, another commander who almost always fought outnumbered—Genghis Khan—established in the thirteenth century the largest contiguous empire the world has ever known, extending from Mongolia into eastern Europe. His army was a model of efficiency that has never been equaled. Each of his soldiers had several sturdy little horses, capable of living off the land. Almost all of them were mares, and mare's milk was the staple of the soldiers' diet. Their horses were, at once, a means of transportation and a mobile food supply.

In battle, individual Mongolians often withdrew to the rear, only to hurry back on fresh horses. The Europeans concluded that fresh troops were constantly being fed into the battle and assumed themselves outnumbered by the "Mongolian hordes." The opposite was almost always the case.

Genghis knew how to fight outnumbered and win. He was also a master of speed, deception, and surprise. All these were to play an important part in the emerging U.S. Army doctrine. Genghis may also have been the first to use in a systematic way what the Germans call *Auftragstaktik*, literally, "assignment tactics." This concept, copied directly from German doctrine by the Americans, means that subordinate commanders are given wide latitude in determining how they will fight their part of the battle so long as it conforms to the overall plan. There is no sitting around waiting for new orders. In an army with skilled subordinate commanders and a clear-cut mission plan, this concept, which the Americans call mission orders, permits high-speed operations and great flexibility in taking advantage of an unexpected opportunity or recovering from a setback.

Of all the peoples overrun by the Mongols, the Russians, whose territory was occupied for nearly a century, learned the most about the military thinking of their conquerors. As late as the first part of the present century Russian cavalry tactics still showed a strong Mongol influence. Yet as Western strategists looked at Soviet war-fighting plans, the most important missing element seemed to be the flexibility that had made the Mongols such an effective fighting force.

Perhaps the solution to the dilemma of how to fight a war in Central Europe could be found in this apparent weakness. If the Americans could think faster and move faster than their foe, then it might be possible to fight outnumbered and win, even though they were taken by surprise.

The Army's first attempt to set forth a new war-fighting doctrine dealing with the realities of the situation in Central Europe was published in 1976 in a green-jacketed paperback booklet called *Field Manual 100-5 Operations*. This document, known in the Army as *one-hundred-dash-five*, was the first revision of the basic how-to-fight manual since 1968 and it was the direct result of DePuy's "pot of French soup" letter. It reflected the lessons of the Yom Kippur War, the Army's renewed focus on a possible conventional conflict with the Soviets in Europe, and the availability of the Big Five and the other modern arms soon to come into the arsenal. It summed up the situation faced by the Army this way:

> We cannot know when or where the U.S. Army will again be ordered into battle, but we must assume the enemy we face will possess weapons generally as effective as our own. And we must calculate that he will have them in greater numbers than we will be able to deploy. . . .
>
> Because the lethality of modern weapons continues to increase sharply, we can expect very high losses in short periods of time. Entire forces could be destroyed quickly if they are improperly employed.
>
> Therefore the first battle of our next war could well be its last battle. . . . The United States could find itself in a short, intense war—the outcome of which may be dictated by the results of initial combat. This circumstance is unprecedented: We are an Army historically unprepared for its first battle. We are accustomed to victory wrought with the weight of materiel and population brought to bear after the onset of hostilities. Today the U.S. Army must, above all else, prepare to win the first battle of the next war.

The plan called for an "active defense," using the high mobility soon to be provided by the Abrams and the new Bradley fighting vehicle. They would be able to move quickly into position to blunt the enemy's attack. Largely because of this emphasis on defense, *one-hundred-dash-five* quickly became one of the most controversial documents the Army had ever published. To many critics, it looked like a warmed-over version of the old plan to stand fast in defense of the East-West border—a formula for losing.

Its most serious flaw was that it failed to deal with the problem posed by the Soviet tactic of spreading out forces, with one echelon behind the other. Winning the first battle was essential, but that was not good enough. If succeeding echelons were permitted to pile on, the weakened defenders would eventually be defeated in the second or third or fourth battle.

Starry, as commander of the Armor Center at Fort Knox, had worked closely with DePuy in developing the new doctrine. But he soon realized its shortcomings. He was sent to Europe in February 1976 to command the Fifth Corps. Soon after his visit to the battlefields of the Yom Kippur War, he set planners at his corps headquarters to work trying to understand the "vision" he had experienced on the Golan Heights. He wanted to know more about the Soviet echelon formations and how they might be attacked.

The Red Army's echelon concept of feeding troops into battle in successive waves was a clever and perhaps the only realistic answer to one of the most difficult questions of the nuclear age: How can an army mass sufficiently to defeat the enemy without risking destruction of the entire force by battlefield nuclear weapons?

In the Soviet plan only the first echelon—the one directly in contact with the enemy—will be so tightly grouped as to present a suitable target for nuclear attack. But the hope is that it will be so close to the other side's troops as to rule out such an attack. The follow-on echelons will be spread out so widely as to make a poor target for a nuclear strike—so spread out, in fact, that the enemy will have trouble identifying individual military units. But they also have to be able to mass quickly when it becomes their turn to join the battle.

Clearly it was an offensive-oriented doctrine. Whether or not it indicated an intention to attack the West, American planners had to assume the worst case: that fighting would begin with a surprise attack, that they would be outnumbered, and that one echelon after another would keep up the pressure on the front lines.

In searching for a way to deal with this problem, Starry and his staff came up with an intriguing concept. They decided to try to create a "calculus" of the battlefield that would tell commanders what to do under almost any circumstances. They began by analyzing 150 possible battle situations and then feeding into their computer information about past tank battles and intelligence gleaned from Soviet maneuvers. The likely size of enemy units and the terrain over which they would attack were known, so the advance rate could be calculated. Information about probable weather conditions was also taken into account so commanders would know how far gunners might be able to see. This is the way an Army publication described the goal of this ambitious effort: "In the battle calculus, measurable quantities were computed and analyzed in terms of minutes into the battle. Analytical categories included ratios of opposing forces by troop strength and weapon type, rate of enemy advance, intervisibilities across terrain, best ranges of fire, number and opportunities to fire, number of commander decisions, and time lengths to call for and receive attack helicopter support and Air Force close air support."

When Starry returned from Europe in July 1977 to succeed DePuy as commander of the Training and Doctrine Command at Fort Monroe, Virginia, he immediately put his staff to work to expand the battle calculus work done in Germany and create what he called a battlefield technology plan. Clearly another major revision of the Army's basic war-fighting doctrine was in the works. Even though DePuy was the principal force behind the 1976 manual, he later acknowledged that it had, in a number of ways, "missed the boat," and he became one of the most enthusiastic supporters of the effort to improve the doctrine.

Early in work on the new manual, the precise minute-by-minute formulas of the battle calculus fell by the wayside. The calculus was a far too mechanical portrayal of what the battlefield would really be like, and it left out such imponderables as the courage and cowardice of soldiers and the brilliance and stupidity of commanders. But the effort to analyze the battlefield did yield one exciting insight into the problem of dealing with oncoming echelons.

The dilemma faced by the Army was that any attempt to attack the second and succeeding echelons to keep them from piling on would require an outnumbered commander, already fighting a desperate battle with the first echelon, to use some of his scarce troops and weapons to seek out and strike the enemy units headed toward the front lines. It seemed like a "heads, you win; tails, I lose" situation.

Researchers at the Army's Field Artillery School set up in their computers a battle situation involving several divisions, and then they fought the same battle over and over. Each time they varied the amount of artillery and air support "borrowed" from the immediate confrontation with the first echelon. If they made no attempt to block the follow-on echelons, the enemy's frontline strength remained at about the same level and the defenders eventually lost, no matter how well they fought. But if they "borrowed" firepower from the defenders, they were able to produce abrupt dips in the enemy's frontline strength at predictable times.

The conclusion was that carefully planned and timed interdiction of the follow-on forces could have a dramatic impact on the battlefield by creating opportunities for counterattack. The studies showed that the defender could deliberately open these "windows of opportunity" and then have as much as four days to prepare a killing zone. He could shape the battle situation to his liking and muster his forces to fight at a time and place of his choosing where he would have the initiative and might well outnumber the enemy.

This analysis also helped the Army understand how responsibility for fighting a war should be divided. Commanders up to division level would focus on the immediate battle area: enemy troops within about seventy kilometers, capable of entering the fighting within about twenty-four hours. The corps commander, responsible for three or more divisions and some fifty thousand men, assumed a key role in thwarting the enemy's follow-on echelons. He would try to look out beyond the immediate fighting, as far as ninety-six hours in time or three hundred kilometers into enemy territory. He would have control of his own corps artillery; he would coordinate attacks by the Air Force; and he would plan and direct strikes with nuclear artillery shells, rockets, and bombs if approval for their use came from higher authorities.

By the early eighties the technology that could make this all feasible was becoming available, and this was an area in which the United States had a distinct edge. Satellites, side-looking radar, and other ways of gathering intelligence would give an accurate, timely picture of where the enemy forces were. Computers would enable the commander to analyze the situation quickly and help him to make the correct decisions. New electronic communications would permit him to move his forces quickly and precisely. And the key to making this all work was the tank—the "primary offensive weapon." Armored units equipped with the Abrams, with its cross-country mobility and its heavy armor, would be able to respond with unprecedented speed to the commander's order and go where no other forces could survive.

When the new field manual was published in 1982, it incorporated all this new thinking. And it quickly became even more controversial than the 1976 edition, though for quite different reasons. While the earlier version had been criticized for being too defense-minded, the new *one-hundred-dash-five* went even further in the opposite direction, shocking the United States' NATO allies. It was a boldly offense-oriented document. In effect, the U.S. Army's plans for reacting to a Soviet attack were far more violent and aggressive than NATO's.

While NATO would use air power against follow-on forces, it ruled out moving ground troops across the East-West border. NATO's goal was to end the war with the border unchanged. The new Army doctrine assumed, on the other hand, that once war had started, the border would cease to exist. As much as possible the war would be fought in the other side's backfield, with deep penetration not only by bombers but by armored forces, paratroops, and helicopter-borne infantry.

"Commanders," the new doctrine said, "need to use the entire depth of the battlefield to strike the enemy and to prevent him from concentrating his firepower or maneuvering his forces to a point of his choice. Commanders also need adequate space for disposition of their forces, for maneuver, and for dispersion."

As far as the future border was concerned, Starry described the Army's new policy this way: "Once political authorities commit military forces in pursuit of political aims, military forces must win something—else there will be no basis from which political authorities can bargain to win politically. Therefore, the purpose of military operations cannot be simply to avert defeat—but rather it must be to win." In other words, move the border eastward. The Red Army could no longer plan an attack and assume that, at worst, it would end up back on the existing border.

The new doctrine was also controversial for the open way in which it considered the possibility, even the likelihood, that both nuclear and chemical weapons would be used in a European war. Not for two decades or more had an Army document dealt so forthrightly with this sensitive issue. Starry, explaining the new doctrine, said that "it would be advantageous to use tactical nuclear and chemical weapons at an early stage and in enemy territory." Soldiers were advised to be prepared, from the first moment, for the use of such weapons by either side.

"By extending the battlefield and integrating conventional, nuclear, chemical and electronic means, forces can exploit enemy vulnerabilities anywhere," the manual advised. "The battle extends from the point of close combat to the forces approaching from deep in the enemy rear. Fighting this way, the U.S. Army can quickly begin offensive action by air and land forces to conclude the battle on its terms."

Chemical weapons cannot, under U.S. policy, be used unless an enemy has used them first. Battlefield nuclear weapons can be used first but not before there has been a release by top political officials of the NATO nations. The new doctrine, by requiring commanders to focus their attention well into the future, provided time to request and obtain authority to use nuclear weapons and to use them far enough in the enemy's rear so they would not endanger friendly troops.

Surprisingly this aspect of the new doctrine, which made first use of nuclear weapons by U.S. forces seem more plausible, did not arouse the kind of public debate that swirled around the so-called neutron bomb and plans to install nuclear-tipped intermediate-range missiles in Europe. Instead, opposition came from NATO leaders, including General Bernard Rogers, commander of NATO forces and former chief of staff of the U.S. Army. They objected strenuously to the Army's plans for crossing the border with tanks and other ground forces in the event of war. To the critics, the doctrine seemed inconsistent with NATO doctrine, too enthusiastic about offensive, cross-border operations, and insensitive in its consideration of the use of nuclear and chemical munitions.

The Army tried to explain that the doctrine was intended as a guide for fighting anyplace in the world. In Europe, it insisted, the Army would, of course, follow NATO policy. This explanation was totally unconvincing since the whole impetus for writing a new doctrine had come from the Army's concern with the riddle of how to fight a war in Central Europe.

The doctrine writers were sent back, once more, to their computerized war games and word processors.

The result was the publication, in 1986, of yet another revision of *one-hundred-dash-five*. This time the Army stressed that its operations would be in accordance with NATO doctrine and that the decision on whether or not to cross the border would be made by the politicians. The more offense-minded language was toned down, and the subject of chemical and nuclear weapons was treated far more delicately.

References to the possible use of nuclear weapons were especially cautious: "U.S. nuclear weapons may of course only be used following specific directives by the National Command Authorities after appropriate consultation with allies. Even were such authority granted, however, the employment of nuclear weapons would be guided more by political and strategic objectives than by the tactical effect a particular authorized employment might produce."

The 1976 and 1982 versions of the manual represented significant advances in the Army's thinking about how it should fight a war. While the 1986 version offered some refinements, especially in its treatment of the role of the corps commander in attacking the follow-on echelons, it was primarily an effort to make Army doctrine more palatable politically.

The new version retained a good deal of the offensive orientation of the 1982 edition, especially its emphasis on disorienting the enemy commander by making things happen so fast he can't keep up. Soldiers were admonished to "move fast, strike hard and finish rapidly," and they were told: "Engagements must be violent to shock, paralyze and overwhelm the enemy force quickly. They must be terminated rapidly to allow the force to disperse and avoid effective enemy counterstrikes."

Great emphasis was put on speed:

Agility—the ability of friendly forces to act faster than the enemy—is the first prerequisite for seizing and holding the initiative. Such greater quickness permits the rapid concentration of friendly strength against enemy vulnerabilities. This must be done repeatedly so that by the time the enemy reacts to one action, another has already taken place, disrupting his plans and leading to late, uncoordinated and piecemeal enemy responses. It is this process of successive concentration against locally weaker or unprepared enemy forces which enables smaller forces to disorient, fragment, and eventually defeat much larger opposing formations.

The goal, in other words, was to create a military force with a central nervous system of a higher order than that of the enemy. The Army's thinking centered on large-scale armored warfare, but the same rules apply to small-scale guerrilla warfare, as the Vietcong demonstrated in Southeast Asia.

It took the Army the better part of a decade to work out its new doctrine. DePuy's "pot of French soup" was a particularly apt metaphor for the process: No useful idea was too "foreign" to be included. The comments of outside critics who had condemned the 1976 version and questioned the 1982 edition were welcomed. Some of the concepts that found their way into the doctrine can be traced far back into history. But there are four major twentieth-century sources that heavily influenced the Army's thinkers, the British, Germans, Americans, and Russians.

The British Influence: The emphasis on hard-hitting, fast-moving offensive action is based directly on the theories of Major General J. F. C. Fuller, the most important military thinker of the century. He devised the tactics for the first use of tanks in World War I, and he was the first to see clearly how the mobility, firepower, and armor protection of the tank would revolutionize warfare. Even the most hidebound skeptics became believers after they saw Fuller's theories brought to the battlefield in the German blitzkrieg.

Fuller was the first, during World War I, to set down in writing the "principles of war." These nine rules were adopted by the U.S. Army in 1921. But somehow, over the years, they were almost forgotten. The 1976 edition of *one-hundred-dash-five* contained no reference to these fundamental concepts. After older officers complained, the principles were spelled out in an appendix to the later editions, and their presence can be sensed on almost every page. They provide a simple, succinct guide to success on the battlefield:

OBJECTIVE: Direct every military operation towards a clearly defined, decisive, and attainable objective.

OFFENSIVE: Seize, retain and exploit the initiative.

MASS: Concentrate combat power at the decisive place and time.

ECONOMY OF FORCE: Allocate minimum essential combat power to secondary efforts.

MANEUVER: Place the enemy in a position of disadvantage through the flexible application of combat power.

UNITY OF COMMAND: For every objective, ensure unity of effort under one responsible commander.

SECURITY: Never permit the enemy to acquire an unexpected advantage.

SURPRISE: Strike the enemy at a time or place, or in a manner, for which he is unprepared.

SIMPLICITY: Prepare clear, uncomplicated plans and clear, concise orders to ensure thorough understanding.

The German Influence: It was long after the war that Creighton Abrams acknowledged that the U.S. Army had much to learn from his old enemy the Germans. After all, he had helped beat the hell out of them. But in the early seventies, after a friendly meeting with the chief of staff of the Bundeswehr, he assigned DePuy to work with a high-ranking German officer to coordinate the war-fighting plans of the two nations.

During Starry's tour of duty as a corps commander in Germany, he was much impressed by the German doctrinal manual, Army Service Regulation HDv 100-100, *Command and Control in Battle*. As a result of DePuy's work and Starry's interest in the German manual, some of the key concepts in the U.S. Army's doctrine, such as *Auftragstaktik*, or "mission orders," and *Schwerpunkt*, or "point of main effort of attack," were lifted almost verbatim from the German.

The American Influence: The Army has long had a corps of officers who believed strongly in the tactics preached by Fuller and practiced by the Germans in their blitzkrieg. But often they have had little influence. In the years immediately prior to the U.S. entry into World War II, at least two of the officers who later performed brilliantly in combat were severly reprimanded for using fast-moving tactics. Senior officers, whose minds were still in the trenches, were furious at these young mavericks for winning fast and ending their carefully planned maneuvers ahead of time.

Both these officers—Major General John S. Wood, who later commanded the Fourth Armored Division in World War II, and General Bruce Clarke, who blunted the German offensive in the Battle of the Bulge—were mentors to Abrams, and their hell-for-leather offensive tactics were reflected, through him, in the thinking of those who devised the new doctrine.

Wood, Clarke, and Abrams all served under Patton, who strongly believed that carefully planned, violently aggressive tactics were the secret for winning battles and saving American lives. While other commanders would slug it out with the enemy mile after mile, priding themselves that heavy casualties demonstrated their aggressiveness, Patton looked for the breakthrough.

A marvelously profane man with a disappointingly high, squeaky voice, Patton used to exhort his officers: "Cut through and end up in the rear. Then do something, goddam it, do something! Throw a fit! Burn a town! Goddam it, do something! You're back there with the finance corps and the quartermaster. Those people are not used to cordite."

Through Abrams and those he influenced, such as DePuy and Starry, this aggressive spirit, with its reliance on a tank-heavy armored force, became the key component of the doctrine that eventually emerged.

The Russian Influence: Although the U.S. Army didn't consciously set out to borrow from Soviet doctrine, as it did from British and German thinking and its own traditions, those who wrote the doctrine spent a good deal of time studying the Red Army's war-fighting plans, and the influence came through.

During the years when the United States relied primarily on the threat of the use of nuclear weapons to make war unthinkable, Soviet strategists continued to think about how a war, whether waged with conventional or nuclear weapons, could be fought and won. In a significant change the U.S. Army, in its new doctrine, has come around to the Soviet way of considering war thinkable and perhaps even winnable. One important result of this change may be to make war less likely by making U.S. plans more understandable to the Russians—and thus more believable.

Doctrine, of course, is just words on paper. A more revealing guide to how the Army would fight—and how well it would do—is provided by a look at maneuvers in the California desert and at units deployed along the East-West border in Germany. To carry out its new doctrine, the Army relies heavily on its new tank. But even as the Abrams was being deployed in the field, serious questions were raised about its performance. One outspoken critic even called it a "very bad tank."

8

"Whispering Death"

It was not unusual for the Army to run into problems with a new weapon, and it was normal for the brass to be grilled by Congress and the press. But the generals faced an entirely new experience when a young woman named Dina Rasor appeared on the scene in the spring of 1981.

No one in the Army had even heard of her before she showed up one day as a witness before a Senate committee. Not only was the Abrams too expensive and too complex, she charged, but it was so unreliable as to be a danger to its own crews.

Who is this woman, the perplexed generals asked, and where did she come from? A 1978 graduate in political science and journalism from the University of California at Berkeley, Rasor had come to Washington straight form college, hoping to leapfrog a tedious journalistic internship in Podunk and begin covering national politics. With encouragement from a veteran Pentagon whistle-blower and financial aid from a foundation, she set up the Project on Military Procurement in a small rented office on Capitol Hill. Her ambitious goal was to expose waste, fraud, and fat in the military budget and to "reform the military procurement system toward an effective and reliable defense."

The first target in her big-game hunt was the M-1: the biggest of the Army's Big Five, rapidly turning into a twenty-billion-dollar procurement. As she later told a Senate hearing, "the bureaucracy would sit up and take notice if you cracked down on one weapon system as an example and . . . the M-1 would be a good place to start."

Although there had been a few critical reports about the M-

1 in the press up to that time, the deluge came after Rasor began issuing press releases about the tank and putting reporters in touch with an anonymous "underground" of experts. For about two years, until the press shifted its interest elsewhere, there was one news article and television program after another about the tank, most of them critical.

At the invitation of a senator she visited Fort Hood in July 1981. Then-Major General Richard Lawrence, who had been on the Desobry task force nearly a decade before, was commander of the First Cavalry Division, doing the final troop testing of the M-1 before full-scale deployment. When nervous superiors in Washington called, Lawrence told them he was going to put her in both the M-60 and the M-1 and let her see for herself.

Rasor, looking younger than her twenty-five years, found the bizarre situation just as awkward as the Army did. She had never been in a tank and had never fired a gun, and she felt like a freak in a sideshow, an intruder into a male bastion. But she was looking forward to the experience.

By the time she collapsed on her bed in the cool darkness of her motel room that afternoon, she had driven both the M-60 and the M-1 and fired her first shots—four bull's-eyes with a 105 mm cannon. She was bruised from being tossed around inside the tank, her toe was bleeding where a shell had dropped on it, and she was thankful she would never have to go to war.

Lawrence felt that the ability of a woman with no previous experience to operate the tank and hit her targets demonstrated the quality of the M-1. But Rasor ended her visit more convinced than ever that a callous Army bureaucracy was about to field a weapon that not only was overly expensive but would cause the deaths of American soldiers.

Rasor's opinions on the relative merits of tanks were not formed in her brief visit to Fort Hood and did not originate with her. To a large extent they reflected the thinking of Pierre Sprey, a brilliant former Pentagon analyst and one of the leading exponents of the argument that the military is better off with a larger number of relatively inexpensive weapons than with a small number of expensive, technologically complex weapons. The Air Force accepted Sprey's logic in its decision to buy the relatively inexpensive F-16 fighter-bomber. Turning his attention to Army weapons, he focused on the M-1, arguing that the Army should buy M-60 tanks—three times as many—for the same money it planned to spend on the new tank.

Few would take issue with the argument that numbers do make a difference on the battlefield. Even inferior weapons, in sufficient numbers, can prevail over smaller numbers of superior weapons. But Sprey's argument failed to account for the fact that the size of the Army is fixed by law at 780,000 men—and that allows for only about a hundred armored battalions. The Army might be able to buy more M-60 tanks, but it couldn't pay the soldiers to operate them. If, as the Army's new doctrine assumed, its next conflict would be a come-as-you-are affair in which the peacetime force suddenly goes to war, an inferior tank and small numbers would be a fatal combination.

The preference for the cheaper M-60 might still make sense if the Abrams was, as Rasor put it, a "very bad tank." Sprey put the same charge in more technical terms: If account is taken of the crippling effects of high fuel consumption and the breakdown rate in the early tests, "the M-1's effective force size may be less than one-tenth that of the M-60."

These charges demand serious consideration, if only because they are based largely on results of tests conducted by the Army over the previous three years and on the Army's own unclassified internal documents. The question to be asked is whether those concerns remain valid now that the Abrams has been in service for a number of years. Has the M-1 turned out to be a bad tank?

One of the most serious continuing technical problems is the lightweight track—part of the price paid to load the tank with as much armor as possible. One difficulty is that on ice the tank becomes a sixty-ton hockey puck unless its crews have been able to install special cleats. Another difficulty is that the rubber shoes wear out after roughly a year of use—eight hundred to twelve hundred miles—and the tank needs a new track. Replacing tracks is the single biggest maintenance cost associated with the Abrams, averaging out to about fourteen dollars a mile. But this is largely a peacetime budget problem. In wartime the tanks could keep rolling on their metal tracks, although this would tear up roads used by other vehicles.

In February 1988 the Army finally faced up to this problem when it awarded a $140 million five-year contract to FMC to provide a new track guaranteed to last at least twenty-one hundred miles. As older tracks wear out, they will be replaced with the new version, which is also being installed on new tanks.

Another problem highlighted by Rasor first became apparent in the Yom Kippur War of 1973. Whenever an enemy shell penetrated the armor of an American-made M-60 tank and cut hydraulic lines, the reddish hydraulic fluid, nicknamed cherry juice, vaporized and burned, creating a fireball inside the turret. Many Israeli tankers suffered severe burns. The U.S. Army quickly changed to a new type of fluid for both the M-60 and the M-1 and assured anxious congressmen the problem was under control. It wasn't. The new fluid has a flash point of 450 degrees Fahrenheit, higher than the 230 degrees of the liquid it replaced but still much below the temperature of shell fragments. The threat of a flash fire may even be more severe in the M-1 than in the M-60—if the turret is penetrated—because the designers of the Abrams made lavish use of hydraulic power for many heavy-duty tasks such as operating the ammunition doors.

The Army has decided to live with this problem. The decision was based on three considerations: First, the M-1 has an automatic fire extinguisher system that can sense a flame and smother it with halon gas in a fraction of a second, before it has had time to inflict burns. Second, the Abrams, with its agility and armor, is far less likely to be penetrated by an enemy shell than is the M-60. And third, if a shell cuts through the armor, it poses a more severe threat to the crew than any fire it might ignite. Future tanks will either use a new, safer fluid now under development or, more likely, rely on electrical rather than hydraulic power.

Another problem singled out by Rasor and Sprey, and readily acknowledged by the Army, is the difficulty of providing enough diesel fuel for the M-1, with its thirsty turbine consuming nearly 500 gallons in a day of combat. The American experience in World War II illustrates the problem. In August 1944, as Patton pursued the Germans across France, his Third Army burned 350,000 gallons of gasoline a day. To provide fuel and other supplies for the advancing army, the Allies stripped three divisions of their trucks, leaving them immobile, and organized the Red Ball Express, running night and day across France. The six thousand supply trucks themselves used up some 300,000 gallons of gas a day. Despite this effort, Patton's army ran out of fuel and was forced to halt.

The sobering fact facing Army logistics experts is that a single M-1 division will, in one day in combat, consume 600,000 gallons of fuel. That's nearly twice as much as Patton's entire army used, and he ran out of gas.

This extraordinary thirst is a major reason that Hans Eberhard, the German tank czar, rejected the turbine, despite its many advantages, and equipped the Leopard 2 with a heavier and less speedy diesel.

American tankers are so pleased with the turbine's performance that they wouldn't trade it for Eberhard's diesel. But they acknowledge they have a problem. To deal with it, the Army is equipping its armored units with large tank trucks designed to provide fuel in sufficient quantity to keep the tanks moving. But the fuel trucks are not armored. Destroying one or two trucks can be easier than, but almost as disruptive as, destroying several platoons of tanks. The Americans, who have almost always enjoyed air superiority, tend to worry less about this problem than they should. For the Germans, whose army suffered so much from air attack during World War II, concern with operating when the enemy controls the air is close to an obsession.

The turbine runs well on almost any flammable liquid, so crews cut off from normal supplies will try to scrounge fuel someplace—from the underground storage of a gasoline station or from abandoned vehicles. But if they can't, they will be stranded.

The second big concern in keeping the tanks moving is an adequate supply of spare parts. Unlike earlier tanks, on which a good deal of maintenance could be done by the tank crew itself, most of the innards of the Abrams are off limits. If something goes wrong, the crew is supposed to radio for a highly trained maintenance team and then wait. The mechanics bring with them test equipment packed in ten suitcases weighing sixty pounds each, accompanied by fourteen instruction manuals—an awkward bundle to carry into an area under enemy fire.

When the problem with the tank is found, usually the next step is to replace the faulty part rather than try to fix it. Even out in the field the complete power pack—the engine and transmission system—can be removed and replaced in less than half an hour. But this switch of parts can take place only if a replacement is on hand.

The Army seems to have built up an adequate supply of parts. Even though training battalions in the United States have to wait longer for parts than units in Germany, they routinely keep 90 percent or more of their tanks operating. When the General Accounting Office examined records of the Seventh Army in Germany in 1984, it did not find a parts shortage, as might have been expected with a new tank. Instead, the GAO complained that the Army had stockpiled half a million dollars' worth of parts that hardly ever required replacement.

The prediction of such critics as Rasor and Sprey that the M-1 would prove so unreliable as to be almost useless has fortunately not come true. The engine, transmission, and fire control systems, after early problems, have proved highly reliable. Still, the Abrams is a complex piece of machinery and requires meticulous attention by battalion commanders and their maintenance crews. One of the major criticisms of the Army in the aftermath of the Vietnam War was that it had made its officers into managers rather than leaders. Experience has repeatedly demonstrated, however, that a battalion commander must first be a good manager. If he doesn't pay close attention to the maintenance of his machines, his supplies of fuel and spare parts, and the welfare of his troops, he will soon find himself with nothing to lead.

For a long time there was a good deal of worry that the new tank was so complex that the average soldier would not be able to operate it. This is a myth that has been a long time dying despite a growing mass of evidence to the contrary.

Both experience in the field and carefully controlled tests show crews perform better in the Abrams than in older, less sophisticated equipment. The soldier may not know the scientific principle behind his thermal sight or understand how the tank's stabilization system works, but he has no difficulty understanding that with them, he can see in the dark and shoot accurately on the move.

In many ways the computers and electronic devices in the tank do much of the most technically demanding work for the soldier. The gunner relies on his computer to take into account the movement of his tank and the target, the ballistic characteristics of his ammunition, the amount his gun barrel has drooped, the air temperature, the wind speed and direction, and even the number of times his gun has been fired. To start the tank, the driver does little more than push a button and rely on the computer to make sure the engine is not damaged during the starting process.

In 1984 the Army ran a test to see if there was scientific evidence that the Abrams was as user-friendly as it seemed. Detailed records were kept of the performance of 1,131 M-60 and M-1 crews as they went through the individual crew qualification course on the firing range at Grafenwöhr, West Germany, firing at targets that suddenly popped up or darted across the landscape on tracks.

Data on the crews included their mental categories—from Category 1, the brightest, to Category 4, the lowest level accepted by the Army. As might be expected, the bright soldiers did better than those in the lower mental categories. The researchers were startled, however, by the impact that the type of tank had on the performance of the crew. On average, the M-1 crews did 46.7 percent better than those in the M-60. The performance of the brightest crews was 25 percent better while that of the Category 4 crews was a phenomenal 85 percent better.

Rasor's contention that the M-1 is a "very bad tank" has not been borne out by the experience of troops operating it in Europe and the United States since the early 1980s. Even officials of the General Accounting Office, who were so concerned about reliability that they tried to delay a production decision, now reject Rasor's fear that the tank is so faulty that it is a danger to its crews.

Her campaign against the M-1 turned out to be largely a media event, without any real effect on the tank program, although she did give the Army brass some anxious moments. If she had come on the scene a couple of years earlier, the outcome might have been different. But by 1981 the Army had solutions for most of the early problems, the tank was already popular with troops, and the program had strong support within the Pentagon and on Capitol Hill. There was never any serious question of scrapping the M-1 and buying more and cheaper M-60's.

The period of intense public criticism of the Abrams in the early 1980s has, however, left a popular image that the M-1 program was badly managed and that it was typical of the mishandling of big weapons by the Army and the Pentagon generally. The truth is close to the opposite. With all the problems occasioned by a tight budget and a strict timetable, the Abrams program ranks as one of the Army's best managed. In this case the Army did many things right: It put the early development in the hands of tankers; it avoided gold-plating; it used competition effectively; and it produced a new tank in what, by peacetime standards, was a remarkably short time. Of course, it had some blind luck. If the joint program with the Germans in the 1960s had not stumbled so badly and the Army had been able to build the thousands of tanks it wanted, it almost certainly would have been like the British, unable to afford to take advantage of the breakthrough in armor technology.

Unfortunately the Abrams program is far from typical. Development of too many other weapons is hampered by a chronic inability to agree on what is needed and by crippling restrictions on the freedom of program managers. Baer, who was in charge during the critical early years of the Abrams, says he had much more latitude in running his program than today's weapons developers. The result, often, is soaring costs and long delays in getting new weapons into the hands of the troops.

In the case of the M-1 the Army did remarkably well in keeping costs under control. In 1988, a decade and a half after the rather artificial design-to-unit-cost goal was set at $507,790, the Army claimed that the individual tank, including the bigger gun and other improvements, was coming in at just a little over that price—in 1972 dollars. Of course, the rise in inflation over that period, plus research and other costs not included in the figure set in 1972, had pushed up the price tag to $2.8 million per tank by 1988. And a doubling of the number of tanks to be produced, with inflation added in, had brought the total cost of the entire tank production program to just under $20 billion.

During the research and development phase the Army also met its goal of staying on schedule. In the production phase it has not done so well. Schedules slipped in the early eighties because of a shortage of engines and thermal sights. There was another even more serious slippage in mid-decade as work was beginning on the M-1A1. In 1982 Chrysler, teetering on the edge of bankruptcy, sold its tank division—the only profitable part of its operation—to General Dynamics for $336.1 million.

Since the government owned the two plants and most of the equipment, what the aerospace giant bought was a contract, betting that it could produce tanks efficiently enough to earn back its investment and make money on future production.

The transition was rocky—more rocky than the Army acknowledged to Congress. It took General Dynamics executives awhile to adjust to the differences between a plane, flown by a commissioned officer, and a tank, driven by a private first class. The most vexing problem was the company's stormy relationship with its unionized blue-collar work force. The workers had made concessions to help Chrysler in its time of troubles, and they felt, when their profitable division was sold, that they should receive raises to make up for the concessions. When General Dynamics refused their demands, they struck in the fall of 1985, just as the company was preparing for the switchover to the M-1A1 tank.

Management produced a few tanks during the strike but nothing like the 840 tanks a year it was supposed to turn out. Deliveries lagged by 300 tanks, and the company, which gets paid on delivery, lost tens of millions of dollars. By late 1986, with the strike behind it, General Dynamics had pushed monthly production up to 100 tanks a month, but catching up on the backlog was a lengthy process, especially with a still-sullen work force, its mood reflected by this bit of graffiti chalked on a tank at Lima: "Remember the GD corporate motto: Screw someone today."

By 1989, the company and its unions had worked out most of their grievances and the relationship with General Dynamics is proving to be a beneficial one for the Army. The company has put more money into research than Chrysler did, and it has spent its own money to buy new machinery that has resulted in a significant improvement in the quality of the tanks. Quality was a problem in 1984 and 1985, but by the fall of 1986 it was not unusual for inspectors in Germany to check new tanks arriving from the factory and find no defects at all.

While much attention is focused on such issues as quality,

costs, and schedules, the most important question to be asked about the M-1 is how well it performs as a fighting machine. One way to answer this question is to compare it with what is known about the latest Soviet tanks. Despite the difficulty of gathering accurate intelligence about the Red Army's tanks, there seems little doubt that on a tank-for-tank basis, an American crew in its Abrams has the advantage over the Soviets in their T-80. The Americans are better trained; their computers, electronics, and night vision systems all are superior; and they have greater speed and acceleration. The main guns of the two tanks are roughly comparable, but the American ammunition is superior. The T-80 is smaller and has a lower silhouette, so it is harder to see and hit. But its turret is cramped, and the crew members have no protection against a hit that ignites their own ammunition.

The Americans enjoy one overwhelming advantage, and that is the quality of their armor. It would be impossible to overestimate the importance of the British armor breakthrough in the mid-sixties, the belated American adoption of the new armor, and the later American improvements. The very first M-1s were immune to hits anywhere in the front of the tank by the dreaded shaped charge shells. With the latest improvement in armor, tanks produced after mid-1988 are immune to frontal attack with kinetic energy ammunition—long rod penetrators—as well.

Even the late-model Soviet T-80, on the other hand, appears to be vulnerable to both types of ammunition. The evidence for this is recent intelligence pictures. They show the Red Army is layering the vital front sections of both T-64 and T-80 tanks with reactive armor. This type of armor consists of panels containing explosives. The panels are hung outside a tank's normal armor. When the point of a projectile hits the panel, the explosive goes off and destroys the projectile. The Israelis first used this type of armor in their invasion of Lebanon in 1982, but the Soviets were already at work on the new technology and began applying it to their tanks in about 1984.

They seem to be trying, by hanging layers of armor on the outside of their tanks, to do what the United States has already done with the special armor that is an integral part of its M-1. When the first photos came in showing reactive armor on Soviet tanks, the reaction in Western military circles was one of alarm because this new armor had the potential to defeat the antitank rockets and shaped charge shells then in the Western arsenals. For the West, it meant the difficult and expensive task of developing new rockets and shells capable of cutting through reactive armor and providing it to the troops as quickly as possible.

Viewed from the Soviet perspective, however, the addition of reactive armor to first-line tanks can only be seen as, at best, a partial and unsatisfactory solution to the very serious problem that has worried Moscow since at least as long ago as the Yom Kippur War. New shaped charge ammunition capable of defeating reactive armor has already been developed and is replacing older projectiles on hand in Europe, making the Soviet tanks once again vulnerable to attack by shaped charge shells and rockets. Their problem is compounded by the fact that reactive armor provides little or no protection against the long rod penetrators fired by Western tank guns.

The United States is beginning to use reactive armor, too, but it is being applied to older M-60 tanks deployed in Korea, not to its first-line M-1 tanks. The decision to use this armor was taken with reluctance because it has some serious deficiencies. It obviously adds to the weight of the tank. When it explodes, it is a serious threat to infantry accompanying the tank. And as soon as it explodes, that portion of the tank is again vulnerable to attack.

It is hard to avoid the conclusion that the Soviet Union, as the result of a colossal failure to understand and take full advantage of the latest technology, has equipped its troops with thousands of dangerously defective tanks and that the use of reactive armor is part of a frantic, but largely futile, effort to make up for this mistake.

The reason for this failure is puzzling. The Soviets are good at metallurgy, they have used composite materials in their armor, and they have certainly learned a good deal, through their spy network, about the breakthrough in Western armor. The likeliest reason their tanks are not protected by the best possible armor is that they remained so wedded to the concept of a relatively small tank that they could not bring themselves to the same bold decision made by General Abrams in 1972, when he decreed that the Army would pay the price in added weight and size to take full advantage of the new armor.

American analysts expect the next generation of Soviet tanks—what they call the future Soviet tank, or FST—coming into service in the mid-nineties to have much better frontal armor than existing tanks. But they also expect the armor on other parts of the tank to be thinner and the barely tolerable turret to be even more cramped in an effort to meet the traditional demand of the Red Army for tanks that are relatively small and light while carrying a gun of 135 mm.

The difference in the degree of armor protection enjoyed by American and Soviet tank crews is vital. But it is still only one of the factors that would influence the outcome of a battlefield confrontation. All those factors come into focus in frequent battles at the most realistic training area the Army has ever had—the National Training Center (NTC) at Fort Irwin, spread over a thousand square miles of the high desert near Barstow, California.

Going through this course is as close as troops can come to actual combat without suffering casualties. From a mountain peak, television cameras and other monitors record every movement on the battlefield. Even in the dark the activities of scout and reconnaissance teams are recorded. All this goes onto videocassettes so the visiting battalion can review the battle after it has returned home.

The rocky, treeless terrain at Fort Irwin is a far cry from the wooded hills and valleys of central Germany. Yet many of the problems the soldiers face in the desert—from smoke screens and simulated chemical attacks to carefully planned killing zones and the confusion of battle—are much the same as those they would confront in a real-life war along the East-West border in Europe. With some imagination, one can see the similarities between an attack through the training center's Bowling Alley into the Valley of Death and an attack over Outpost Alpha into the Fulda Gap. What happens in the maneuvers tells much about the way the Abrams tank and the Army's new war-fighting doctrine would measure up in a real-life war.

This is how one such battle unfolded on a pleasantly warm, sunny day in the fall of 1986. On one side was Lieutenant Colonel Peter F. ("Pete") Manza, commander of the Thirty-second Guards Motorized Rifle Regiment, a handpicked team of fifteen hundred veteran soldiers drilled in Red Army tactics and riding in 170 tanks, personnel carriers, and helicopters modified to look and perform like Soviet models. He was cast as the attacker, assigned an objective on the far side of the ominously named Valley of Death. On the defense was Lieutenant Colonel Paul E. Lenze, carrying the scars of wounds suffered when he was ambushed in South Vietnam. He commanded a battalion from the Second Armored Division at Fort Hood, Texas, and, in keeping with the Army's doctrine that its forces must be prepared to fight outnumbered and win, he was outnumbered more than three to one by the guards regiment.

A briefing the night before gave Manza a difficult choice. He could take the long route, swinging south of a rugged mountain ridge into a broad valley, where he would have room to maneuver, and then fight his way back up to his objective. Or he could concentrate everything he had on an attempt to break through the defense line in the narrow Valley of Death to the north of the mountain ridge.

Scout reports and intercepted radio chatter told Manza that Lenze had placed the bulk of his force—two of his four companies, with twenty-eight tanks—in the broad valley to the south of the ridge, with another company positioned to move north or south. In the Valley of Death, bulldozers had been seen digging a deep ditch and holes to hide Abrams tanks along the hillsides above the valley.

Both sides were busy during the night. Lenze took advantage of his superior night vision equipment to sneak three Bradley fighting vehicles onto a ridge overlooking the route Manza would have to take, no matter which choice he made. When the attackers sent a powerful reconnaissance unit to feel out the defenses, the Bradleys destroyed it.

Manza hesitated until the last minute. Finally, at a predawn briefing in a dimly lit tent, he told his staff he was going to the north, into the Valley of Death. He would have more room to maneuver in the broader valley to the south, but the concentration of firepower there scared him off—just as Lenze hoped it would. True, if he went to the south, he would still outnumber the defenders. But the speed of the Abrams tanks and their ability to shoot on the move would take away at least some of that advantage. From previous experience Manza knew that even a couple of well-positioned tanks could bring him to his knees. In another phase of the maneuvers just the night before, a single M-1 had knocked out fourteen of his simulated Soviet T-72 tanks.

But Manza also understood the danger he faced if Lenze managed to reinforce his troops in the north. In an effort to prevent that from happening, he ordered his artillery to fire poison gas shells behind the enemy lines. The guards regiment is permitted to simulate the use of gas, but the Americans are not.

Lenze, in his M-1 tank, took up a position on a promontory where he could see both the broader valley to the south and the narrower Valley of Death and control the movement of his forces down to the basic fighting level—the four-tank platoon. As soon as it was clear Manza was heading north, Lenze moved the company that had been straddling the two valleys into the north and ordered one of his two companies from the south to swing around behind the mountain ridge that divided the battlefield to join the defense in the Valley of Death. Even though his early-model tanks did not have special protection against poison gas, the crews were able to move safely through the contaminated area by closing their hatches and donning gas masks.

Traveling cross-country at speeds up to twenty-five miles an hour (a speed limit imposed by the Army for safety reasons), the tanks covered the seven miles in fewer than fifteen minutes and swept onto the battlefield prepared to destroy any enemy forces that breached the tank barrier. Using their thermal sights, the gunners were able to see through the smoke and fire on the move.

By shifting the balance of his forces swiftly into the Valley of Death, Lenze constructed an awesome defense in depth, with the combined firepower of nine of his twelve platoons spread over an area about 2.5 miles wide and 12 miles deep. Almost everything he had—individual soldiers with Dragon rockets; artillery; forty-four Abrams tanks, many of them dug in along the sides of the valley; mines; TOW missiles; Bradley fighting vehicles; helicopter gunships; A-10 antitank aircraft; and even occasional flights of F-16 fighter-bombers—was devoted to making the Valley of Death a killing zone.

Manza, riding in a Sheridan modified to look like a Soviet armored personnel carrier, took a position in the midst of his long column of armored vehicles to avoid calling attention to himself. He and his command group climbed through the pass called the Bowling Alley toward the battlefield. Suddenly they were confronted by a yellow flare indicating the rough dirt road had been blocked by a barrage of artillery-delivered mines. As the column turned off the road to find a way around the mines, it came under fire from the automatic cannon of one of the Bradley scout vehicles hidden on the hillside above the night before. Instead of bullets, the gun fired a laser beam that triggered flashing yellow beacons on the vehicles it hit.

There was a moment of panic as the soldiers scanned the hillside in an unsuccessful effort to see and shoot back at their attacker. But it was all over in less than a minute. Manza's vehicle and sixteen others were knocked out. In that brief time the guards regiment had lost its commander, its deputy commander, and 10 percent of its fighting force, unable to fire a single shot in response. Although Lenze didn't know it until later, the attacking force had been decapitated early in the battle.

While Manza sat on a rocky outcropping, cursing in frustration, the remainder of his force, commanded by the senior surviving officer, a captain, rumbled on toward the enemy line, hidden by a cloud of smoke four miles away.

By the time the regiment snaked through the mountain pass, deployed as well as it could, and moved up to the ditch, more than half its 170 armored vehicles had been destroyed, their yellow beacon lights blinking eerily through the smoke of battle. Almost all the rest died in Lenze's killing zone. Only three tanks and three personnel carriers succeeded in fighting their way to the other side of the barrier, and they all were picked off well short of the objective. The clash in the Valley of Death didn't begin until about 10:00 A.M., and it was all over before noon.

The exercise was a vivid demonstration of the speed with which large military forces can be obliterated when they give up the protection provided by wide dispersal and mass together to fight. Even veteran officers were shocked by the experience. At a briefing afterward one of Manza's staff, still shaken by the suddenness and the totality of the calamity they had suffered, exclaimed: "It was a real Armageddon out there!" The defeat was a bitter one for Manza. With daily experience fighting over the same terrain, he usually wins. "This was not a good day," he muttered.

Although Lenze's victory was a triumph of the skillful use of combined arms—from the weapons of the individual soldiers to the long-range missiles—the key to his success was the speed of his Abrams tanks. With the older, slower M-60s, he wouldn't have dared leave the northern side of his line so lightly defended in order to invite Manza into his killing zone. With his speedy new tanks, he was able to rearrange the battlefield to his own liking.

The theory is that the experience at the NTC substitutes for the first few days of fighting so that soldiers who have been through the course will, in a sense, be "combat" veterans. A real war will, nevertheless, prove a very strict schoolmaster. The Abrams crews will be fighting outnumbered. They will have to learn fast and well, or they may not survive long enough to apply their lessons. These mock battles give an indication of how M-1–equipped troops would perform in a real war; but they are only a pale approximation of the horror and confusion of the battlefield, and they raise some intriguing questions to which there are no certain answers.

A major uncertainty is how well soldiers would fight in the first few days of a war. Troops on both sides would go through a highly traumatic learning period as they suddenly found themselves plunged into the maelstrom of a modern high-intensity war. The armies on both sides, from privates up to commanding generals, all would be too young to have personal experience of such fighting.

In the crucial first few days the professional soldiers of the all-volunteer U.S. Army would almost certainly have an advantage. Not only are they trained in the field, but the Army is also using simulators in which computers present battlefield situations and then score the crews' reactions. The result is superior performance on the firing range. When soldiers who had practiced in the simulator underwent a special test at the Grafenwöhr Training Center in Germany, the average crew was able to identify a target as it popped up and get off its first shot in an average of 4.7 seconds, with a 77 percent chance of hitting with that shot. Defectors who have served in the Red Army say that is two or three times as fast as the best Soviet crews.

But good as the Abrams tankers are, they are unlikely to perform as well in the early days of a real war as they do on the firing range. The closest approximation of actual war is the live-fire range at the National Training Center, where crews not only shoot real shells but have to worry about the targets shooting back with laser beams. There, in something approximating the confusion and stress of battle, gunners sometimes fail to fire. When they fire, they often miss but don't realize they've missed. Platoon leaders become tongue-tied and forget to talk to each other. Units are caught by surprise. Some battalions do well, but too many do poorly. Even when they win, the number of flashing yellow lights indicates they have paid an unacceptably high price for the victory.

One of the most vexing challenges for soldiers on both sides will be to find the enemy. Despite their size, tanks are hard to see and identify. The United States is compounding this problem for its foes by fielding decoy tanks made of big balloons that can be moved around easily and blown up in a matter of minutes. They even have a small heater to deceive infrared detectors. M-1 tanks are also coated with a special sixty-dollar-a-gallon paint that not only provides camouflage to fool the eye but also masks the heat given off by the machine. To add to the confusion, both sides will fill the airwaves with static to blank out the others' communications.

Even crews who have done well at the training center will be shocked by their first exposure to the violence of real war. Almost everything each side has will be aimed at the other side's tanks: artillery, wire-guided missiles, bombs and missiles from airplanes and helicopters, and even more sophisticated missiles designed to detect a tank by the shadow it makes in the earth's natural radiation of microwaves.

Artillery barrages will be especially unnerving to the crews. Nothing in their training prepares the men for this experience, in which they will be surrounded by the sounds of sudden death, their tanks rocking and bucking from the impact of near misses. With the air filled with pieces of hot metal, crews will quickly give up the peacetime luxury of fighting with open hatches. As soon as a tank's hatches are bolted down, the men find themselves sealed in a tiny claustrophobic capsule, their view of the outside world abruptly limited to what can be seen through periscopes and gunsights. Even inside the tank, the roar of exploding shells will be almost deafening, but not so loud that they will be unable to hear the distinctive loud CHUNK! that means another tank has been hit.

As enemy tanks are struck or hit mines, they explode and burst into flames. There is none of the chivalry of warfare at sea. As the crews clamber to escape from the fire, they are hosed down by machine guns—a reminder to the Abrams crews of their own fate if they are forced to leave the safety of their armor.

All this will be the ultimate test of the quality of arms and the skill and training of the soldiers and a stern measure of that elusive quality known as courage. There is good reason to believe the Abrams crews will measure up well because of the contribution their tank makes to their bravery.

This is the one vital factor that is most difficult to deal with in calculations of which side will win a war. War games and computer-simulated battles can be useful, but the answers they provide are often incomplete and may even be misleading. Such games often match two forces and then have them fight until one is annihilated. But soldiers don't fight that way if they have any choice. Sometimes a unit becomes trapped in a killing zone and is wiped out, and that may happen more often as increasingly lethal weapons come into use. But in most real-life battles the fighting breaks off short of the point where either side is annihilated; the soldiers make their own judgments about when it makes sense to continue fighting and when it makes sense to stop.

This is where the relation between the crew and its tank makes a difference. Soldiers may well fight bravely even if they think they are going to lose. But if they think they are going to die, they are apt to run away or, more likely, simply hide until the shooting is over. That old question of the antiwar activists—"What if they gave a war and no one came?"—is something commanders have to worry about.

A tanker who is outgunned and thinks he is going to be killed may well use his engine and tracks to remove himself from harm's way rather than use his guns to fight. If he is in what seems to be a relatively safe place, he has a powerful incentive to stay there and not give away his position by firing his weapons. It requires an act of courage simply to risk the uncertain dangers of moving.

The Army's latest how-to-fight manual deals with the question of bravery this way: "Commanders and their staffs must understand the effects of battle on soldiers, units and leaders because war is fundamentally a contest of wills, fought by men, not machines. Ardant DePiq [*sic*], a 19th century soldier and student of men in battle, reminded us that 'you can reach into the well of courage only so many times before the well runs dry.' Even before that, Marshall De Saxe [*sic*], writing in the 18th century, pointed out that 'a soldier's courage must be reborn daily.' "

By surrounding the crew of the M-1 with special armor and by protecting them in the event their own ammunition is hit, the tank designers did much to assure that Abrams crews will fight bravely. When the new tank was introduced, the troops were shown a motion picture taken at Aberdeen Proving Ground in which a tank was hit time after time by antitank rockets and shells. Some of the hits caused fuel and ammunition fires. There were no men in the tank, but instruments inside the turret and chassis verified that the crew, although probably deafened, would have survived hits that would have destroyed an M-60 and killed its crew. After each hit a crew is shown climbing into the tank and driving off. Short of actual battlefield experience, the film went a long way toward convincing armor crewmen that their new tank would not only get them onto the battlefield but get them back off again alive.

One of those who saw the film when it was first shown to Abrams crews was John Baer, then a captain stationed at Fort Knox. Baer had followed his father, the first program manager for the M-1, into armor because "I like to fire those big bullets."

Even though he was already more familiar with the Abrams than most soldiers, he found that filmed demonstration of its survivability a real eye-opener—more impressive than anything else about the new tank. Later, as a lieutenant colonel, Baer was assigned to the Eleventh Armored Cavalry Regiment as commander of an Abrams-equipped squadron responsible for patrolling the area near Outpost Alpha in the Fulda Gap.

The confidence M-1 crew members have in their machine is also enhanced by its quick acceleration, its high speed, and its ability to shoot on the move. It is easier to work up the courage to move around on the battlefield if you know the odds are good that you can dash from one hiding place to another before an enemy gunner can get you in his sights and if he knows you can shoot at him while you're moving.

But the capacity of a tank to boost the courage of its crew is a two-edged sword. It is not only a plus but also a serious problem for the Army. The problem is that the Pentagon plans a tank force made up half of modern M-1 tanks and half of older M-60 tanks, roughly seven thousand of each. To complicate matters, there will be at least four versions of the M-1, each better than the ones before.

With the M-1 the Army deliberately embarked on a practice that it had followed only in a haphazard and reluctant fashion in the past. It decided to build the Abrams tanks in a series of models. Each model would consist of several thousand tanks, and each new model would incorporate improvements over the previous ones. First came the basic M-1, produced from 1980 to 1984. The second group, produced from 1984 to 1986, was called the Improved Performance M-1, and it had better armor. The third, called the M-1A1 and produced in the 1986-1988 period, added the bigger gun, still better armor, and protection from chemical, biological, and nuclear attack.

The fourth model, first deployed to Europe in October 1988, contains depleted uranium in its armor and is called the M-1A1-Heavy Armor. Scheduled for production in 1992 is the M-1A2. It will incorporate some improvements that might have been included in the first model a decade earlier if it hadn't been for the rigid ceiling on the cost of the individual tank. For example, it will have the hunter-killer sighting system that permits the tank commander to aim at a second target while the gunner is shooting at the first. It also will have an automatic communications system to permit the tank commander to call up orders, maps, and other data on an eight-by-ten-inch display panel and to flash reports and sketches of the battlefield situation back to headquarters. A built-in system to locate malfunctions will do away with the cumbersome six hundred pounds of special test equipment used with the earlier models.

Ideally the tanks with the thinnest armor would have the largest, most powerful gun. This would permit the crew to remain as far back from the enemy as possible while still being able to hit the tanks on the other side. But the M-60 has both thinner armor and a smaller gun than the later model M-1. And the early M-1s, while far superior to the M-60s, have less armor protection and a smaller gun than the later M-1s.

This means the commander of a division or a corps cannot think of his tank battalions as interchangeable. He will always have to take into account the type of tank each battalion has and how that fact will influence the bravery of the crews and their ability and willingness to fight.

The Army's partial solution to this problem is to provide the newest tanks to the troops who are most likely to meet the best Soviet tanks in the event of war. But this means that troops in Korea, who might face somewhat older Soviet-type tanks, will continue to be equipped with M-60s, as will many units in the United States that would be sent into battle as reserves.

In Europe the prospect for American tankers is far different from and more encouraging than it was in 1972, when the Soviets had a secret new tank and when the American soldiers, with their old equipment, didn't think they could win. On paper, NATO and the Warsaw Pact are about even in manpower, with 2.4 million active-duty ground forces in the West and 2.3 million in the East. The most crucial discrepancy between the two forces is in tanks.

NATO is credited with a total of 22,200 main battle tanks, and the Warsaw Pact with 52,200. But only about a third of those are the T-64, T-72, and T-80 models built in the last twenty years. The remainder are of 1950s vintage, no match, on a one-for-one basis, for the more modern tanks—the German Leopard 2, the British Challenger, and the American Abrams—that constitute a growing part of the NATO arsenal. The Soviet advantage is also eroded by the fact that because of the time it takes to bring reserve divisions up to full fighting strength, the Red Army would be able to deploy only about 14,000 tanks at the beginning of a war in Central Europe, compared with some 10,000 on the NATO side.

Still, those tank figures are worrisome. As the World War II experience demonstrated, the technical superiority of the German armor force could not overcome the more numerous American tanks. Largely because of the Soviet bloc's advantage in tanks and in artillery weapons, the military balance tilts to the Warsaw Pact side, especially in a conflict in which the choice of where and when to fight would be made by the Soviet commanders. American planners assume that their troops could find themselves outnumbered by three or even five tanks for each of their own. But unlike 1972, there is a new confidence among American soldiers that they could make an attack on the West a terribly costly affair for the Red Army. As Donn Starry, one of the architects of the new American doctrine, says, "We will have to kill a hell of a lot of them to get their attention."

The Army's plans for defense of the Fulda Gap illustrate the change that has taken place since the early seventies. It would be natural to assume that the elite Eleventh Armored Cavalry Regiment (ACR), garrisoned almost on the border and in the middle of the gap, would absorb the first shock and then fall back. But, thanks to the high speed of the Abrams and Bradley, that is not the way it would be.

This is the likely scenario for a defense of the Fulda Gap: At the first solid warning of an impending attack, two divisions based farther back move up to man planned defensive positions near the border. The Eleventh ACR is ordered to a rendezvous point well back from the border. The divisions shifting forward to replace the cavalry regiment deploy a screening force, like a boxer's probing left fist, to delay the attack, feel out the enemy's strength, and try to discern his intentions.

The battle is some hours old, and the enemy has made a significant penetration into friendly territory before the five-thousand-man cavalry regiment is called into action. In keeping with the Army's new doctrine of trying to influence the front-line battle by striking the follow-on forces, the corps commander has waited until the moment when the enemy's second echelon, battered by air attack and artillery, is approaching the battle line. During this critical window of opportunity the cavalry regiment, with its Abrams tanks and Bradley fighting vehicles, bypasses the immediate battle and swings around for a flank attack on a division in the second echelon.

If the movement goes as planned, the regiment will make its high-speed run undetected, traveling thirty to sixty miles in fewer than two hours, mostly on paved two-lane roads, to descend on the enemy's flank with a withering surprise attack. If the battle situation permits, the attack will come at night, when the Americans' night vision equipment gives them the advantage. The goal of this lightning assault is not only to permit a smaller force to destroy a larger one, but, more important, to confuse and disorient the enemy commander—in effect, to use the destruction of a division as a means of disrupting the operations of an entire corps or army. Success of the maneuver hinges on good intelligence, timing, stealth, and, especially, high speed.

Even with all those, no one denies that this is a risky maneuver. If the enemy division, which outnumbers the American regiment by more than two to one, has time to prepare defensive positions, the smaller American cavalry unit is likely to be badly mauled. Even worse, it could stumble into one of the Red Army's two new operational maneuver groups (OMG). These are hard-hitting multidivision units, much more powerful than the forces normally found in the second echelon, and their mission is to smash through the enemy's defenses and penetrate deep into his rear area. For the American cavalry regiment, encountering an OMG would be like sticking its nose in a hornets' nest.

Despite the risks, the ability of the fast-moving Abrams-equipped units to hit the enemy from unexpected directions has been demonstrated so often in peacetime maneuvers that many armor officers are confident the tactic would also work in wartime. It was initially used in 1982 by one of the first M-1 units deployed in Europe. In NATO maneuvers the high speed of the Abrams and the quietness of its engines and tracks enabled the Americans to go rampaging through the enemy's rear areas and catch a Canadian unit, representing a hostile task force, totally by surprise. The Canadians neither saw nor heard the Americans until their amber lights began to blink. Shocked, they called the new tank Whispering Death.

The armored cavalry's first clash with the enemy would take place west of the border. But the entire border area would quickly become part of the battlefield. There would be no fixed front line. Instead, the situation would be dominated by fluid, high-speed maneuvers and great volumes of bullets, artillery shells, rockets, and bombs. In those circumstances, how seriously would the Army regard the prewar border?

Top Army commanders in Europe have insisted they were bound by NATO's rules against border crossing by ground troops. But those who would be on the firing line have a more realistic view of what it would be like when the fighting started.

General Crosbie E. ("Butch") Saint, a former leader of the Eleventh ACR, was promoted to commander in chief of the U.S. Army Europe in June 1988. Earlier, when he led the Third Corps at Fort Hood, Saint put it this way: "For the guy in the pit, the boundary has no meaning. The requirement is to maneuver around so you'll have an advantageous position. So you would go backwards and forwards across the boundary, depending on the enemy and the terrain. I don't think the question of the boundary is relevant when you're down in the pit with the knife.

"If you get a small enough scale map and use a fat grease pencil, it doesn't make a hoot. The question is, Do I want to be in the middle of the woods here or would I rather be in that great position two hundred meters in front of me where I can have great visibility and bring fire on the enemy? I don't give a rat's ass if it's twenty feet on the other side of the boundary, which is a mythical thing drawn by men who didn't know what the hell they were doing in the first place."

In the melee of battle Army troops might penetrate as much as thirty miles into enemy territory. Saint says: "I'm not going to fight from a poor piece of terrain to satisfy a politician. That doesn't mean I'm going to Moscow. Doesn't even mean I'm necessarily going to Dresden. But I'm not going to fight on this side of the creek if it's going to cause some of my troops to get killed if I can move a hundred meters and do a better job. Anybody who wants to come down and keep track of me, be my guest. Come on down here in the pit, and we'll show you."

There is always the possibility, when combat has begun, that NATO political leaders would permit the kind of deep penetration called for in Army doctrine. The chance that this might happen vastly complicates the chore of Red Army war planners. To contemplate an attack concentrated at the weakest point in the NATO line while the American Army is kept busy at the border by a relatively small force is one thing. To worry about the Americans crossing the border in strength on the Red Army's flank is quite another thing—a major concern added to worries about antitank weapons and the Abrams and the other superior tanks in the Western arsenal.

The Army plans to build 7,467 Abrams tanks, with production scheduled to average 720 tanks a year through fiscal 1992. There will be 2,374 of the basic M-1s; 894 of the IPM-1s;

and 4,199 of the M-1A1 and M-1A2 models. The U.S. Marine Corps has also agreed to buy the tank and several foreign countries are interested in adding M-1s to their arsenals.

The Army has begun looking beyond the M-1 to an entire new family of vehicles, all of them using many of the same basic components. At Fort Eustis, Virginia, where study of the new generation tanks and other vehicles has been centered, the twenty-first-century tank is emerging as a quite different-looking machine.

Instead of a chassis and turret, it could have a low-slung chassis-crew compartment. The gun might be perched on a mast extending above the chassis, and in most circumstances the tip of the mast, including the gun plus periscopes and other sensing devices, will be the only thing visible to the enemy.

The gun may be of a revolutionary new type, hurling a long rod penetrator much faster than the mile-a-second rate of existing guns. One proposal is to do away with the powder now used in tank guns and substitute two liquids that would become explosive only after they had been piped into the breech of the gun. This would virtually eliminate the danger of an explosion caused by a shell hitting stored ammunition. The gun would, of course, require a complex automatic loader to carry projectiles from a storage compartment in the chassis up the mast to the gun.

The engine of the new tank will probably be a diesel—not an admission that the turbine in the Abrams was a mistake but a recognition of impressive advances in diesel technology.

Instead of relying on two-foot-thick armor, as in the Abrams, the twenty-first-century tank may surround itself with an electronic shield to detect incoming shells and rockets. The projectiles will be destroyed before they reach their target, either electronically or by explosives hurled out from the exterior of the vehicle.

Down in the crew compartment there are likely to be only two men, sharing the work now done by the Abrams's four-man crew. But there will also be another two-man crew assigned to the tank. The two crews will take turns inside the tank, permitting virtual round-the-clock operations. All four men will be available for such heavy work as loading ammunition and maintenance.

With the crew deep in the chassis, protected by their electronic shield and with the danger of an ammunition explosion virtually eliminated, the new design will provide a major advance in crew survivability. American tankers familiar with the studies like the concept.

In West Germany, however, the armor community has given strict instructions to its tank designers. At this early stage, at least, the Bundeswehr wants nothing to do with a tank whose crew cannot get at the gun to fix it in case of malfunction. They want to be where the gun is: that means the traditional turret. Unless there are some changes in thinking as work progresses and the soldiers have a chance to try out various designs, two of the major NATO allies could enter the new century with tanks even more different from each other than the incompatible tanks with which they are now equipped.

What seems more likely, considering the movement toward arms reductions in Europe, is that the Army will stick with the M-1 for the foreseeable future, with continuing improvements in technology and perhaps the addition of an even larger gun than the 120mm model.

Whatever shape the future tanks take, the Abrams will remain the mainstay of the American armor force well into the early years of the next century, thirty years or more after the basic outlines of the tank were laid down at Fort Knox in 1972. Armor officers are convinced that the Abrams and its crews will acquit themselves well if they are called upon to fight. But there are so many uncertainties that no one can be sure how a war in Central Europe would turn out. For NATO, whose purpose is not to win a war but to prevent one from happening, that element of uncertainty may be just enough to deter an attack and avoid war. If the Abrams never fires a shot in anger—never has to prove itself king of the killing zone—it will represent twenty billion dollars well spent.

MAIN BATTLE TANK PROGRAM MANAGERS

Lieutenant General (Retired) Welborn G. Dolvin.
(MBT-70.) August 1963–October 1966

Major General Edwin H. Burba. (Deceased.)
(MBT-70.) November 1966–June 1968

Brigadier General (Retired) Bernard R. Luczak.
(MBT-70 and XM-803.) July 1968–June 1972

Lieutenant General (Retired) Robert J. Baer.
(M-1.) July 1972–July 1977

Lieutenant General (Retired) Donald M. Babers.
(M-1.) July 1977–June 1980

Major General Duard D. Ball. (Deceased.)
(M-1.) July 1980–May 1983

Major General (Retired) Robert J. Sunell.
(M-1.) June 1983–July 1984

Colonel William R. Rittenhouse.
(M-1.) July 1984–February 1987

Colonel Joseph Raffiani, Jr.
(M-1A1.) September 1983–June 1987

Colonel John E. Longhouser.
(M-1 and M-1A1.) June 1987–present.

A Note on Sources

King of the Killing Zone is a work of journalism, written by a journalist, not a historian, but it falls on the borderline between journalism and history.

I had the advantage not only of the voluminous written record generated by the Army's largest and most important weapons program of the last third of the century but also of tape-recorded interviews with all of the program managers, except for the two who were no longer living, and with many others involved in the effort to provide the Army with a new tank, from designers in Detroit to soldiers in the field in the United States and Germany.

1. IN THE FOOTSTEPS OF THE DINOSAUR

The account in this chapter of the development of the MBT-70 relies heavily on an interview with General Welborn G. Dolvin, conducted as we sat in his pickup truck at his Christmas tree plantation in Virginia. His memory of his experience as program manager for the MBT-70 was supplemented by a detailed account of his stewardship published in 1966 by the U.S. Army Management Engineering Training Agency at Rock Island, Illinois: *Lessons Learned: Joint International Program Management for the U.S./FRG Main Battle Tank*.

A similar, although less detailed, report was issued in June 1972 by Brigadier General Bernard R. Luczak, program manager for both the MBT-70 and the XM-803 from July 1968 to June 1972. His "Lessons Learned—from Program Manager Viewpoint," was the most candid report written by any of the program managers. General Luczak added to his written report in a tape-recorded response to questions sent to his home in San Diego.

The MBT-70 program also spawned a number of very useful independent studies. They include: Philip L. Bolté, "MBT-70: A Case Study in Research and Development," U.S. Army War College, March 6, 1970; Thomas L. McNaugher, *Collaborative Development of Main Battle Tanks: Lessons from the U.S. German Experience, 1963–1978*, a Rand Note published in August 1981 by the Defense Technical Information Center of the Defense Logistics Agency;

and Jack Edmund Peckett, "The Main Battle Tank Program, 1963–1978: America's Military-Industrial Complex in Action," a Ph.D. dissertation submitted to New York University in 1979.

Much of the material in Chapters 1 and 2 on Soviet tank development is drawn from a series of articles by Lieutenant Colonel F. M. von Senger und Etterlin on "The Evolution of the Soviet Battle Tank." They appeared in the January–February and March–April 1968 issues of *Armor* magazine.

The description of the Soviet T-64 comes largely from a number of articles on Soviet tank technology appearing in *Armor*. The most valuable was "T-80: The Soviet Solution," by Captain James M. Warford in the January–February 1987 issue. In that article he dismisses the contention of some experts that the T-64 was a failure and classes it as the direct predecessor of the late-model T-80.

General James Polk told me of his World War II experiences and his frustration at the Army's failure to field a new tank during an interview at his Washington home.

At Fort Knox, Mark Falkovich, who has spent a long career in tank development, shared his thoughts on the Abrams tank and lent me his personal copy (he thinks it may be the only one remaining) of the 1958 "Report of the Ad Hoc Group on Armament for Future Tanks or Similar Combat Vehicles," headed by E. A. Kamp. This was the report that committed the Army to its ill-fated effort to equip its tanks with a big missile.

2. FROM CHARIOT TO LAND IRONCLAD

The account in this chapter of the evolution of armored warfare is drawn from a number of military histories.

Major General J. F. C. Fuller, historian as well as the century's leading military theorist, covers the subject from the earliest times to the Battle of Leyte Gulf in his three-volume *A Military History of the Western World* (New York: Funk & Wagnalls, 1954).

A more selective look at the history of warfare is offered in Lieutenant Colonel Joseph B. Mitchell, *Twenty Decisive Battles of the World* (New York: Macmillan, 1964). In this volume Mitchell updated and, to some extent, rewrote Sir Edward Creasy's classic *Fifteen Decisive Battles of the World*.

A more recent and quite readable history is John Keegan and Richard Holmes, *Soldiers: A History of Men in Battle* (New York: Viking, 1986), written to supplement a television series.

Also useful were: Karel Toman, *A Book of Military Uniforms and Weapons* (London: Westbook House, 1964), and Arther Ferrill, *The Origins of War: From the Stone Age to Alexander the Great* (New York and London: Thames & Hudson, 1985).

Especially helpful in developing the history of tanks and armored warfare were the bountifully illustrated Ian Hogg, *Fighting Tanks* (New York: Grosset & Dunlap, 1977); Kenneth Macksey, *Tank Warfare: A History of Tanks in Battle* (New York: Stein & Day, 1972), and Steven J. Zaloga and Lieutenant Colonel James W. Loop, *Modern American Armor* (London-Melbourne-Harrisburg: Arms & Armour Press, 1982).

Much of the information on the development of American armor came, again, from *Armor* magazine. A four-part series in 1969 by Timothy K. Nenninger covered the period from 1917 to the beginning of World War II. In the November–December 1968 issue, Konrad F. Schreier, Jr., "The American Six-Ton Tank," described the very rapid effort to develop and build a tank during World War I. A broad overview of the development of tanks was presented by *Armor* in a series—"Tank Development: Ours and Theirs"—by Major General Donn A. Starry, then commander of the Armor Center at Fort Knox, in the September–October 1975 through March–April 1976 issues.

A fascinating account of the frustrating period between the wars was offered in "The Ten Lean Years," a four-part series based on the diaries of the late Major General Robert W. Grow, printed by *Armor* in 1987.

Surprisingly little has been written about J. Walter Christie. He was the subject of "Not Without Honor," a two-part series by Arthur Lee Homan and Keith Marvin in the June and July 1965 issues of *Antique Automobile*. The articles covered not only his pioneering work on tanks but his designs for racing cars and fire engines as well. His career as a tank designer was summarized in an article, "America's Forgotten Tanker," by Captain John E. Ciccarelli in the July–August 1965 issue of *Armor*. Another article on Christie appeared in the February 1975 issue of *Military Affairs*. Written by George F. Hofman, it was titled "A Yankee Inventor and the Military Establishment: The Christie Tank Controversy."

For all its importance, the Battle of Kursk has received scant attention in the West. Some of the most vivid and detailed accounts of the epic battle come from Soviet sources, such as Marshal Georgi K. Zhukov, "The Battle of Kursk," *Military Review* (August 1969). On the thirtieth anniversary of the battle, the *Soviet Military Review* devoted its entire June 1973 issue to "A Clash of 1,500 Tanks," repeating, in English, accounts written by Red Army combat correspondents on the scene. Probably the best Western account of the battle is Geoffrey Jukes, *Kursk: The Clash of Armor* (New York: Ballantine Books, 1968).

My account of the American armor experience in Vietnam draws on articles in *Armor* during the conflict and on General Bruce Palmer, Jr., *The 25-Year War. America's Military Role in Vietnam*, (Lexington, Ky: University Press of Kentucky, 1984). This book was also the source of some of the anecdotal material about General Creighton W. Abrams that appears in later pages.

3. "A SIMPLE TIN BOX"

Most of the material in this chapter came from interviews with those involved in the events of 1972.

In an interview in a hideaway office he continued to use at the Pentagon long after his retirement, General William DePuy told me of the evolution of the Big Five weapons and his role in development of the M-1.

Lieutenant General William B. Desobry provided a wealth of material for this and subsequent chapters during a lengthy interview at his retirement home on the outskirts of San Antonio. The two colonels who served as his key aides on the tank task force are now retired generals. I found Major General Charles Heiden at his home in Louisville, Kentucky, and met with Lieutenant General Richard Lawrence at his home and office in the Washington area.

Colonel James Logan, who was also on the Desobry task force in 1972, provided me with a copy of the letter from General Bruce Clarke, General Jacob L. Devers, and three other World War II tank commanders setting out their suggestions for the new tank.

Major General John B. Willis, whom I interviewed in London, gave me, in his description of the tank as a "simple tin box," a feeling for the technical challenges involved in designing and building a tank.

4. WHAT PRICE ARMOR?

The account of how the Americans almost built their tank without the revolutionary new armor developed by the British was pieced together from a variety of sources, an effort made more difficult by the extreme secrecy that still surrounds armor technology.

Generals Desobry, Heiden, and Lawrence gave me their accounts of how they began their work in ignorance of the new armor and then learned of it by chance.

In London Major General Jonathan Dent, a retired British officer, told me of his efforts to get the Americans to take the invention seriously.

Several accounts published when the British briefly lifted the veil of secrecy helped fill out my nontechnical account of how the new armor works. Three articles were especially helpful: "The Next Generation of Battle Tanks," by R. M. Ogorkiewicz, and "Improved Chieftain for Iran," both included in a special issue on battle tanks published by *International Defense Review* in 1976, and E. J. Grove, "Shape of Tanks to Come," in the February–March 1977 issue of NATO's *15 Nations*.

Donald Creuzinger, who, disillusioned by the impact of politics on the tank program, retired as a colonel in 1976 and is now president of the XMCO Corporation in Reston, Virginia, told me of his key role in writing the report that caused the Pentagon to continue to dismiss the British armor well after it had won begrudging interest from American armor experts.

For my account of the Pentagon meeting at which the weight of the tank was set at fifty-eight tons by General Abrams, I am indebted to Larry E. Willner. As a lieutenant colonel he attended that meeting and made notes as rapidly as he could as the drama unfolded. He shared his memories with me in an interview. He also used his notes in a study of the M-1 program: *XM-1: The Birth of a Main Battle Tank: The First Two Years. A Case Study*, published by the Industrial College of the Armed Forces in March 1975.

This chapter and subsequent ones could not have been written without the cooperation of Lieutenant General Robert Baer, program manager during the key early years of the M-1 program, who patiently answered my questions in a series of interviews.

5. TURBINE IN THE DUST

This account of the choice of the turbine engine and problems encountered as it was put into service is based on interviews with Baer; his successor, Lieutenant General Donald Babers; Brigadier General Peter F. McVey, program executive for the Abrams and the Army's other close-combat vehicles; Dr. Philip Lett, the Chrysler program manager and later vice-president of General Dynamics's Land Systems Division; Joseph J. ("Joe") Yeats, a retired West Pointer who, at Chrysler, played a key role in design of the M-1; Lieutenant General Howard Cooksey, former head of Army research; Eddie Meadows, chief of the tracked vehicle division at Aberdeen Proving Ground; Donald Robinson, manager of the Washington office of General Motors' Detroit Diesel Allison Division; Colonel James H. Leach, a company commander under Abrams in World War II and key adviser to Continental Teledyne in its effort to sell its diesel engine to replace the turbine; and Justus White, who played a key role as a member of the staff of the House Armed Services Committee.

Louis E. ("Lou") Felder, a retired colonel who was Lett's key aide, answered my questions in a lengthy tape recording and gave me a sage bit of advice: "Talk to the generals, talk to the contractors, but listen to the troops."

Fred A. Best, the General Motors program manager, responded to my questions in a detailed letter.

The written record includes two reports by the blue-ribbon panel on the tank power train and a series of reports from the General Accounting Office containing a wealth of detail. Hyman Baras, who headed the GAO's investigations of the tank program, spoke with me at his office in Washington.

Also helpful was Steven J. Zaloga, *The M-1 Abrams Battle Tank* (London: Osprey Publishing, 1985).

6. THE FIVE-BILLION-DOLLAR HALF INCH

Transcripts of the congressional hearings, especially those conducted by a series of subcommittees of the House Armed Services Committee headed by Representative Samuel Stratton (Democrat-New York), provided valuable background throughout my research. They were most helpful in piecing together the long dispute over the type of gun to be installed in the new tank.

Brigadier General Philip L. Bolté, who headed the American team in the international gun competition, reviewed that period with me in a series of interviews. I also spoke, in London, with Major General John Hamilton-Jones, who represented the British, and, in Bonn, with Colonel Albert Klenke, a key member of the Bundeswehr team in the competition. Peter Buch, whom I met at his office at the sprawling Rheinmetall plant north of Düsseldorf, gave me a concentrated course in tank guns and ammunition. I received a similar briefing at the Pentagon from Colonel Dale K. Brudvig, who was long involved in both the tank and tank gun issues. Carl M. Zilian, a retired colonel, interviewed at his office at Hughes Aircraft in Ingleside, California, helped me understand how the M-1's thermal sight works.

Major General Robert Sunell told me of his accidental discovery that the Leopard 2 being tested at Aberdeen was a hollow tank and also described his concern over the danger to M-1 crews posed by the ammunition for the 120 mm gun.

Dr. Hans Eberhard, who headed the German tank effort, answered my questions in writing from his home in Bonn, and Peter Eigen, my neighbor in Washington, translated his letter for me. Field Marshal Sir John Stanier, retired commander in chief of United Kingdom Land Forces and chief of staff of the Royal Army's general staff, wrote to me from his home in Hampshire about his long experience with armor and with international cooperation—and lack of it. Colonel David A. ("Dave") Appling, who served as Bolté's deputy and was later in charge of adapting the German 120 mm gun for use in the American tank, helped me with both tape-recorded and written comments mailed from his office in San Jose, California.

Technical background on tank guns and ammunition came from *Brassey's Artillery of the World*, 2d ed. (Oxford: Brassey's Publishers Ltd., 1981); *Introduction to Battlefield Weapons Systems and Technology* (Oxford: Brassey's, 1981); J. W. Ryan, *Guns, Mortars & Rockets* (Oxford: Brassey's; 1982); and Major Theodore C. Ohart, *Elements of Ammunition* (New York: John Wiley & Sons, 1946). Especially helpful was a series of articles on armor and armor penetration written by Joseph E. Backofen, Jr., and published in *Armor* during 1980.

7. A NEW WAY TO FIGHT

The background for this chapter was provided by an Army publication: John L. Romjue, *From Active Defense to AirLand Battle: The Development of Army Doctrine 1973–1982*, published by the historical office of the Army Training and Doctrine Command at Fort Monroe, Virginia in June 1984. Other key sources were the versions of *Army Field Manual 100-5 Operations*, issued in 1976, 1982, and 1986. There were also a number of articles, in *Armor* and other publications, as the doctrine evolved in the late 1970s and early 1980s. One of the most comprehensive was Major General John W. Woodmansee, Jr., "Blitzkrieg and the AirLand Battle," *Military Review* (August 1984).

Interviews with Generals DePuy and Starry, who were instrumental in evolution of the new doctrine, and General Bruce Clarke, who told of the frustrations of pre–World War II tankers, were important contributions to this chapter. General Bernard Rogers, former Army chief of staff and then supreme allied commander in Europe, told me, in an interview in Washington, of his discomfort with the 1982 version of the doctrine. General Glenn Otis, commander of U.S. Army forces in Europe, in an interview at his headquarters in Heidelberg, explained the Army's effort to adapt its aggressive doctrine to the more cautious policies of the NATO alliance.

It would be difficult to overestimate the impact of the Yom Kippur War of October 1973 on Army thinking. It was the subject of the keynote addresses of the annual Armor Conferences by Lieutenant General John R. Deane, Jr., in 1974 and by Starry in 1975. Both addresses were printed in subsequent issues of *Armor* magazine.

The war also spawned a number of articles in military journals and several books. Among the most useful were Major General Chaim Herzog, *The War of Atonement* (Boston: Little, Brown, 1975), and London Sunday Times Insight Team, *The Yom Kippur War* (New York: Doubleday, 1974).

My account of the Army's humiliating introduction to modern armored warfare in World War II is based on Martin Blumenson, *Kasserine Pass* (Boston: Houghton Mifflin, 1967), and Henry E. Gardner, "Kasserine Pass," *Armor* (September–October 1979).

The fascinating feat of Obersturmführer Michael Wittman in wiping out an entire British unit is described in First Lieutenant Charles E. White, "One Tiger," *Armor* (July–August 1978).

An important contribution to this chapter was the analysis of battlefield casualty rates in Colonel Trevor N. DePuy, *The Evolution of Weapons and Warfare* (Indianapolis-New York: Bobbs-Merrill Co., 1980). His analysis contrasts with the conclusions of John Keegan in his classic *The Face of Battle: A Study of Agincourt, Waterloo & the Somme* (New York: Vintage Books, 1977). Keegan was so awed by the lethality of modern weapons that he ended his book with the suspicion that "battle has already abolished itself." DePuy, however, demonstrates convincingly that, despite more powerful weapons, the battlefield has, overall, become less deadly because soldiers are spread out over much larger areas.

8. "WHISPERING DEATH"

Dina Rasor, founder of the Project on Military Procurement, spoke with me at her offices on Capitol Hill and made available from her files a substantial amount of congressional testimony and unclassified Army reports on the M-1. Her experiences as a Pentagon procurement gadfly are described in her *Pentagon Underground* (New York: Times Books, 1985).

I met briefly with Pierre Sprey, who had a strong influence on Rasor's thinking, but I was unwilling to agree to his insistence that we speak on a not-for-attribution basis. However, he told me that his views had been set out accurately in a symposium at West Point that resulted in Asa A. Clark, ed., *The Defense Reform Debate* (Baltimore: Johns Hopkins Press, 1984).

My conclusions on the performance of the Abrams tank were reached after extensive interviews at the Lima and Detroit Army tank plants and the Army Tank-Automotive Command in Warren, Michigan and with Robert Truxell, president of General Dynamics's Land Systems Division, and other General Dynamics officials. I also visited with tank crews, officers and maintenance men at Fort Knox, Kentucky, Fort Hood, Texas, Fort Irwin, California, the Third Armored Division at Hanau and Gelnhausen, West Germany, the Eleventh Armored Cavalry Regiment at Fulda, and the Combined Arms Training Center at Vilseck, West Germany. One of those who helped me understand the importance of careful maintenance was Captain Charles Heiden, whose father served on the Desobry task force in 1972. A career officer, he has served in both M-60 and M-1 units and was a member of the Soviet-style guards regiment at the National Training Center when we spoke.

A useful analysis of the entire program is contained in *Lessons Learned: M-1 Abrams Tank System*, published by the Department of Research and Information of the Defense Systems Management College, Fort Belvoir, Virginia, July 1983.

During a visit to the Bundeswehr's Gneisenau Kaserne at Koblenz, Major Jobst Schulze Büttger, executive officer of Tank Battalion 344, arranged for me to ride in a Leopard 2 so I could compare it with the Abrams.

General John R. ("Jack") Guthrie, who long headed the matériel command, shared with me his thoughts on the Army's process for designing and building new weapons—and his frustration with the Army's seeming inability to design a tank gun or to move weapons quickly through development and get them out to the troops in a timely way.

Information on the opposing forces in Central Europe is from the basic sources used by most analysts: the annual reports to Congress of the U.S. secretary of defense and the Joint Chiefs of Staff; *Soviet Military Power*, issued each year by the Pentagon; and *The Military Balance*, compiled annually by the International Institute for Strategic Studies in London. A useful analysis of these figures—"Beyond the Bean Count"—was released in January 1988 by Senator Carl Levin (Democrat-Michigan), chairman of the Senate Armed Services subcommittee on Conventional Forces and Alliance Defense. A detailed and surprisingly optimistic appraisal of the military situation in Europe was provided in a twenty-two-page special section of *The Economist*, by James Meacham, in the August 30–September 5, 1986, issue.

The close relationship between the quality of a weapon and a soldier's bravery came up in a number of interviews. General James Polk; Joseph Ameel, a retired colonel who had been a key aide to Baer; and Dr. Friedhart Sellschopp, a German tank designer in Bonn, all stressed this vital linkage.

Comparisons between the Abrams and the latest Soviet tanks are drawn from interviews and a number of articles. They include: James M. Warford, "T-80: The Soviet Solution" *Armor* (January–February 1967); Captain Warford, "Reactive Armor: New Life for Soviet Tanks" *Armor* (January–February 1988); "The T-80 Tank Unveiled," *Jane's Defense Weekly* (May 3, 1966); Steven J. Zaloga, "Soviet Reactive Armor Update," *Jane's Defense Weekly* (May 23, 1987); and Lieutenant Colonel (IDF retired) David Eshel, "Soviet Tanks: An Israeli View," *Armor* (May to June 1988).

To try to determine how well the Abrams would perform in combat, I talked in Fulda with Major Harry Lesser, intelligence officer of the Eleventh Armored Cavalry Regiment and other officers and men of the regiment, including Major John Baer, eldest son of the M-1's longtime program manager. I also participated in mock battles at the National Training Center at Fort Irwin, California, and Fort Hood, Texas, in which Abrams-equipped units played a key role. During my visit to Fort Hood, Lieutenant General Crosbie Saint, commander of the Third Corps, gave me his candid appraisal of how a war in Central Europe would be fought.

A disturbing report about the performance of Army crews on the live-fire range at the National Training Center is contained in Lieutenant Colonel Douglas B. Campbell, "Combat Gunnery: Observations from the NTC" *Armor* (September–October 1987). The article sums up Campbell's conclusions after nearly three years as chief of live fire at the range.

The preview of what the successor to the Abrams might look like came from Sunell, at the time heading the Army's effort to define its new family of armored vehicles.

Index